The Last of the Belles

and Other Stories

F. Scott Fitzgerald

D1328687

ALMA CLASSICS LTD
London House
243-253 Lower Mortlake Road
Richmond
Surrey TW9 2LL
United Kingdom
www.almaclassics.com

This collection first published by Alma Classics Ltd in 2015

Extra Material © Richard Parker

Printed and bound by CPI Group (UK) Ltd, Croydon, CR0 4YY

ISBN: 978-1-84749-405-4

Contents

Other books by F. SCOTT FITZGERALD
published by Alma Classics

All the Sad Young Men

Babylon Revisited and Other Stories

Basil and Josephine

The Beautiful and Damned

Flappers and Philosophers

The Great Gatsby

The Last Tycoon

The Pat Hobby Stories

Tales of the Jazz Age

Tender Is the Night

This Side of Paradise

F. Scott Fitzgerald (1896–1940)

Edward Fitzgerald,
Fitzgerald's father

Mary McQuillan Fitzgerald,
Fitzgerald's mother

Ginevra King

Zelda Fitzgerald

The Fitzgeralds' house in Montgomery, Alabama

The Fitzgeralds' grave in Rockville, Maryland,
inscribed with the closing line from *The Great Gatsby*

The cover of the 1935 collection *Tap at Reveille*, in which
Fitzgerald included 'A Short Trip Home', 'The Last of
the Belles', 'Majesty' and 'Two Wrongs'

The Last of the Belles
and Other Stories

Jacob's Ladder

1

IT WAS A PARTICULARLY SORDID and degraded murder trial, and Jacob Booth, writhing quietly on a spectators' bench, felt that he had childishly gobbled something without being hungry, simply because it was there. The newspapers had humanized the case, made a cheap, neat problem play out of an affair of the jungle, so passes that actually admitted one to the courtroom were hard to get. Such a pass had been tendered him the evening before.

Jacob looked around at the doors, where a hundred people, inhaling and exhaling with difficulty, generated excitement by their eagerness, their breathless escape from their own private lives. The day was hot and there was sweat upon the crowd – obvious sweat in large dewy beads that would shake off on Jacob if he fought his way through to the doors. Someone behind him guessed that the jury wouldn't be out half an hour.

With the inevitability of a compass needle, his head swung towards the prisoner's table and he stared once more at the murderess's huge blank face garnished with red button eyes. She was Mrs Choynski, née Delehanty, and fate had ordained that she should one day seize a meat axe and divide her sailor lover. The puffy hands that had swung the weapon turned an ink bottle about endlessly; several times she glanced at the crowd with a nervous smile.

Jacob frowned and looked around quickly; he had found a pretty face and lost it again. The face had edged sideways into his consciousness when he was absorbed in a mental picture of Mrs Choynski in

3

action; now it was faded back into the anonymity of the crowd. It was the face of a dark saint with tender, luminous eyes and a skin pale and fair. Twice he searched the room, then he forgot and sat stiffly and uncomfortably, waiting.

The jury brought in a verdict of murder in the first degree; Mrs Choynski squeaked, "Oh, my God!" The sentence was postponed until next day. With a slow rhythmic roll, the crowd pushed out into the August afternoon.

Jacob saw the face again, realizing why he hadn't seen it before. It belonged to a young girl beside the prisoner's table and it had been hidden by the full moon of Mrs Choynski's head. Now the clear, luminous eyes were bright with tears, and an impatient young man with a squashed nose was trying to attract the attention of the shoulder.

"Oh, get out!" said the girl, shaking the hand off impatiently. "Le' me alone, will you? Le' me alone. Geeze!"

The man sighed profoundly and stepped back. The girl embraced the dazed Mrs Choynski, and another lingerer remarked to Jacob that they were sisters. Then Mrs Choynski was taken off the scene – her expression absurdly implied an important appointment – and the girl sat down at the desk and began to powder her face. Jacob waited; so did the young man with the squashed nose. The sergeant came up brusquely and Jacob gave him five dollars.

"Geeze!" cried the girl to the young man. "Can't you le' me alone?" She stood up. Her presence, the obscure vibrations of her impatience, filled the courtroom. "Every day itsa same!"

Jacob moved nearer. The other man spoke to her rapidly:

"Miss Delehanty, we've been more than liberal with you and your sister and I'm only asking you to carry out your share of the contract. Our paper goes to press at—"

Miss Delehanty turned despairingly to Jacob. "Can you beat it?" she demanded. "Now he wants a pitcher of my sister when she was a baby, and it's got my mother in it too."

"We'll take your mother out."

"I want my mother though. It's the only one I got of her."

"I'll promise to give you the picture back tomorrow."

"Oh, I'm sicka the whole thing." Again she was speaking to Jacob, but without seeing him except as some element of the vague, omnipresent public. "It gives me a pain in the eye." She made a clicking sound in her teeth that comprised the essence of all human scorn.

"I have a car outside, Miss Delehanty," said Jacob suddenly. "Don't you want me to run you home?"

"All right," she answered indifferently.

The newspaperman assumed a previous acquaintance between them; he began to argue in a low voice as the three moved towards the door.

"Every day it's like this," said Miss Delehanty bitterly. "These newspaper guys!" Outside, Jacob signalled for his car and, as it drove up, large, open and bright, and the chauffeur jumped out and opened the door, the reporter, on the verge of tears, saw the picture slipping away and launched into a peroration of pleading.

"Go jump in the river!" said Miss Delehanty, sitting in Jacob's car. "Go – jump – in – the – river!"

The extraordinary force of her advice was such that Jacob regretted the limitations of her vocabulary. Not only did it evoke an image of the unhappy journalist hurling himself into the Hudson, but it convinced Jacob that it was the only fitting and adequate way of disposing of the man. Leaving him to face his watery destiny, the car moved off down the street.

"You dealt with him pretty well," Jacob said.

"Sure," she admitted. "I get sore after a while and then I can deal with anybody no matter who. How old would you think I was?"

"How old are you?"

"Sixteen."

She looked at him gravely, inviting him to wonder. Her face, the face of a saint, an intense little Madonna, was lifted fragilely out of the mortal dust of the afternoon. On the pure parting of her lips no breath hovered; he had never seen a texture pale and immaculate as her skin, lustrous and garish as her eyes. His own well-ordered person seemed for the first time in his life gross and well worn to him as he knelt suddenly at the heart of freshness.

"Where do you live?" he asked. The Bronx, perhaps Yonkers, Albany – Baffin's Bay. They could curve over the top of the world, drive on for ever.

Then she spoke, and as the toad words vibrated with life in her voice, the moment passed: "Eas' Hun'erd Thuyty-thuyd. Stayin' with a girl friend there."

They were waiting for a traffic light to change and she exchanged a haughty glance with a flushed man peering from a flanking taxi. The man took off his hat hilariously. "Somebody's stenog," he cried. "And oh, what a stenog!"

An arm and hand appeared in the taxi window and pulled him back into the darkness of the cab.

Miss Delehanty turned to Jacob, a frown, the shadow of a hair in breadth, appearing between her eyes. "A lot of 'em know me," she said. "We got a lot of publicity and pictures in the paper."

"I'm sorry it turned out badly."

She remembered the event of the afternoon, apparently for the first time in half an hour. "She had it comin' to her, mister. She never had a chance. But they'll never send no woman to the chair in New York State."

"No, that's sure."

"She'll get life." Surely it was not she who had spoken. The tranquillity of her face made her words separate themselves from her as soon as they were uttered and take on a corporate existence of their own.

"Did you use to live with her?"

"Me? Say, read the papers! I didn't even know she was my sister till they come and told me. I hadn't seen her since I was a baby." She pointed suddenly at one of the world's largest department stores. "There's where I work. Back to the old pick and shovel day after tomorrow."

"It's going to be a hot night," said Jacob. "Why don't we ride out into the country and have dinner?"

She looked at him. His eyes were polite and kind. "All right," she said.

Jacob was thirty-three. Once he had possessed a tenor voice with destiny in it, but laryngitis had despoiled him of it in one feverish week ten years before. In despair that concealed not a little relief, he bought a plantation in Florida and spent five years turning it into a golf course. When the land boom came in 1924, he sold his real estate for eight hundred thousand dollars.

Like so many Americans, he valued things rather than cared about them. His apathy was neither fear of life nor was it an affectation; it was the racial violence grown tired. It was a humorous apathy. With no need for money, he had tried – tried hard – for a year and a half to marry one of the richest women in America. If he had loved her, or pretended to, he could have had her; but he had never been able to work himself up to more than the formal lie.

In person, he was short, trim and handsome. Except when he was overcome by a desperate attack of apathy, he was unusually charming; he went with a crowd of men who were sure that they were the best of New York and had by far the best time. During a desperate attack of apathy he was like a gruff white bird, ruffled and annoyed, and disliking mankind with all his heart.

He liked mankind that night under the summer moonshine of the Borghese Gardens. The moon was a radiant egg, smooth and bright as Jenny Delehanty's face across the table; a salt wind blew in over the big estates collecting flower scents from their gardens and bearing them to the roadhouse lawn. The waiters hopped here and there like pixies through the hot night, their black backs disappearing into the gloom, their white shirt fronts gleaming startlingly out of an unfamiliar patch of darkness.

They drank a bottle of champagne and he told Jenny Delehanty a story. "You are the most beautiful thing I have ever seen," he said, "but as it happens you are not my type and I have no designs on you at all. Nevertheless, you can't go back to that store. Tomorrow I'm going to arrange a meeting between you and Billy Farrelly, who's directing a picture on Long Island. Whether he'll see how beautiful you are I don't know, because I've never introduced anybody to him before."

There was no shadow, no ripple of a change in her expression, but there was irony in her eyes. Things like that had been said to her before, but the movie director was never available next day. Or else she had been tactful enough not to remind men of what they had promised last night.

"Not only are you beautiful," continued Jacob, "but you are somehow on the grand scale. Everything you do – yes, like reaching for that glass, or pretending to be self-conscious, or pretending to despair of me – gets across. If somebody's smart enough to see it, you might be something of an actress."

"I like Norma Shearer* the best. Do you?"

Driving homeward through the soft night, she put up her face quietly to be kissed. Holding her in the hollow of his arm, Jacob rubbed his cheek against her cheek's softness and then looked down at her for a long moment.

"Such a lovely child," he said gravely.

She smiled back at him; her hands played conventionally with the lapels of his coat. "I had a wonderful time," she whispered. "Geeze! I hope I never have to go to court again."

"I hope you don't."

"Aren't you going to kiss me goodnight?"

"This is Great Neck," he said, "that we're passing through. A lot of moving-picture stars live here."

"You're a card, handsome."

"Why?"

She shook her head from side to side and smiled. "You're a card."

She saw then that he was a type with which she was not acquainted. He was surprised, not flattered, that she thought him droll. She saw that, whatever his eventual purpose, he wanted nothing of her now. Jenny Delehanty learnt quickly; she let herself become grave and sweet and quiet as the night, and as they rolled over Queensboro Bridge into the city she was half asleep against his shoulder.

2

H E CALLED UP BILLY FARRELLY next day. "I want to see you," he said. "I found a girl I wish you'd take a look at."

"My gosh!" said Farrelly. "You're the third today."

"Not the third of this kind."

"All right. If she's white, she can have the lead in a picture I'm starting Friday."

"Joking aside, will you give her a test?"

"I'm not joking. She can have the lead, I tell you. I'm sick of these lousy actresses. I'm going out to the Coast next month. I'd rather be Constance Talmadge's* water boy than own most of these young..." His voice was bitter with Irish disgust. "Sure, bring her over, Jake. I'll take a look at her."

Four days later, when Mrs Choynski, accompanied by two deputy sheriffs, had gone to Auburn to pass the remainder of her life, Jacob drove Jenny over the bridge to Astoria, Long Island.

"You've got to have a new name," he said – "and remember, you never had a sister."

"I thought of that," she answered. "I thought of a name too – Tootsie Defoe."

"That's rotten," he laughed, "just rotten."

"Well, you think of one if you're so smart."

"How about Jenny... Jenny... oh, anything... Jenny Prince?"

"All right, handsome."

Jenny Prince walked up the steps of the motion-picture studio, and Billy Farrelly, in a bitter Irish humour, in contempt for himself and his profession, engaged her for one of the three leads in his picture.

"They're all the same," he said to Jacob. "Shucks! Pick 'em up out of the gutter today and they want gold plates tomorrow. I'd rather be Constance Talmadge's water boy than own a harem full of them."

"Do you like this girl?"

"She's all right. She's got a good side face. But they're all the same." Jacob bought Jenny Prince an evening dress for a hundred and eighty dollars and took her to the Lido that night. He was pleased with himself, and excited. They both laughed a lot and were happy.

"Can you believe you're in the movies?" he demanded.

"They'll probably kick me out tomorrow. It was too easy."

"No, it wasn't. It was very good – psychologically. Billy Farrelly was in just the one mood—"

"I liked him."

"He's fine," agreed Jacob. But he was reminded that already another man was helping to open doors for her success. "He's a wild Irishman, look out for him."

"I know. You can tell when a guy wants to make you."

"What?"

"I don't mean he wanted to make me, handsome. But he's got that look about him, if you know what I mean." She distorted her lovely face with a wise smile. "He likes 'em; you could tell that this afternoon."

They drank a bottle of charged and very alcoholic grape juice.

Presently the head waiter came over to their table.

"This is Miss Jenny Prince," said Jacob. "You'll see a lot of her, Lorenzo, because she's just signed a big contract with the pictures. Always treat her with the greatest possible respect."

When Lorenzo had withdrawn, Jenny said, "You got the nicest eyes I ever seen." It was her effort, the best she could do. Her face was serious and sad. "Honest," she repeated herself, "the nicest eyes I ever seen. Any girl would be glad to have eyes like yours."

He laughed, but he was touched. His hand covered her arm lightly. "Be good," he said. "Work hard and I'll be so proud of you – and we'll have some good times together."

"I always have a good time with you." Her eyes were full on his, in his, held there like hands. Her voice was clear and dry. "Honest, I'm not kidding about your eyes. You always think I'm kidding. I want to thank you for all you've done for me."

"I haven't done anything, you lunatic. I saw your face and I was… I was beholden to it – everybody ought to be beholden to it."

Entertainers appeared and her eyes wandered hungrily away from him.

She was so young – Jacob had never been so conscious of youth before. He had always considered himself on the young side until tonight.

Afterward, in the dark cave of the taxicab, fragrant with the perfume he had bought for her that day, Jenny came close to him, clung to him. He kissed her, without enjoying it. There was no shadow of passion in her eyes or on her mouth; there was a faint spray of champagne on her breath. She clung nearer, desperately. He took her hands and put them in her lap.

She leant away from him resentfully.

"What's the matter? Don't you like me?"

"I shouldn't have let you have so much champagne."

"Why not? I've had a drink before. I was tight once."

"Well, you ought to be ashamed of yourself. And if I hear of your taking any more drinks, you'll hear from me. "

"You sure have got your nerve, haven't you?"

"What do you do? Let all the corner soda jerkers maul you around whenever they want?"

"Oh, shut up!"

For a moment they rode in silence. Then her hand crept across to his. "I like you better than any guy I ever met, and I can't help that, can I?"

"Dear little Jenny." He put his arm around her again.

Hesitating tentatively, he kissed her and again he was chilled by the innocence of her kiss, the eyes that at the moment of contact looked beyond him out into the darkness of the night, the darkness of the world. She did not know yet that splendour was something in the heart; at the moment when she should realize that and melt into the passion of the universe he could take her without question or regret.

"I like you enormously," he said, "better than almost anyone I know. I mean that about drinking though. You mustn't drink."

"I'll do anything you want," she said, and she repeated, looking at him directly, "Anything."

The car drew up in front of her flat and he kissed her goodnight.

He rode away in a mood of exultation, living more deeply in her youth and future than he had lived in himself for years. Thus, leaning forward a little on his cane, rich, young and happy, he was borne along dark streets and light towards a future of his own which he could not foretell.

3

A MONTH LATER, CLIMBING into a taxicab with Farrelly one night, he gave the latter's address to the driver. "So you're in love with this baby," said Farrelly pleasantly. "Very well, I'll get out of your way."

Jacob experienced a vast displeasure. "I'm not in love with her," he said slowly. "Billy, I want you to leave her alone."

"Sure! I'll leave her alone," agreed Farrelly readily. "I didn't know you were interested – she told me she couldn't make you."

"The point is you're not interested either," said Jacob. "If I thought that you two really cared about each other, do you think I'd be fool enough to try to stand in the way? But you don't give a darn about her, and she's impressed and a little fascinated."

"Sure," agreed Farrelly, bored. "I wouldn't touch her for anything." Jacob laughed. "Yes, you would. Just for something to do. That's what I object to... anything... anything casual happening to her."

"I see what you mean. I'll let her alone."

Jacob was forced to be content with that. He had no faith in Billy Farrelly, but he guessed that Farrelly liked him and wouldn't offend him unless stronger feelings were involved. But the holding hands under the table tonight had annoyed him. Jenny lied about it when he reproached her; she offered to let him take her home immediately, offered not to speak to Farrelly again all evening. Then he had seemed silly and pointless to himself. It would have been easier, when Farrelly said "So you're in love with this baby", to have been able to answer simply, "I am."

But he wasn't. He valued her now more than he had ever thought possible. He watched in her the awakening of a sharply individual temperament. She liked quiet and simple things. She was developing the capacity to discriminate and shut the trivial and the unessential out of her life. He tried giving her books; then wisely he gave up that and brought her into contact with a variety of men. He made situations and then explained them to her, and he was pleased, as appreciation and politeness began to blossom before his eyes. He valued, too, her utter trust in him and the fact that she used him as a standard for judgements on other men.

Before the Farrelly picture was released, she was offered a two-year contract on the strength of her work in it – four hundred a week for six months and an increase on a sliding scale. But she would have to go to the Coast.

"Wouldn't you rather have me wait?" she said, as they drove in from the country one afternoon. "Wouldn't you rather have me stay here in New York – near you?"

"You've got to go where your work takes you. You ought to be able to look out for yourself. You're seventeen."

Seventeen – she was as old as he; she was ageless. Her dark eyes under a yellow straw hat were as full of destiny as though she had not just offered to toss destiny away.

"I wonder if you hadn't come along, someone else would of," she said – "to make me do things, I mean."

"You'd have done them yourself. Get it out of your head that you're dependent on me."

"I am. Everything is, thanks to you."

"It isn't, though," he said emphatically, but he brought no reasons; he liked her to think that.

"I don't know what I'll do without you. You're my only friend" – and she added – "that I care about. You see? You understand what I mean?"

He laughed at her, enjoying the birth of her egotism implied in her right to be understood. She was lovelier that afternoon than he had ever seen her, delicate, resonant and, for him, undesirable. But sometimes he wondered if that sexlessness wasn't for him alone, wasn't a side that, perhaps purposely, she turned towards him. She was happiest of all with younger men, though she pretended to despise them. Billy Farrelly, obligingly and somewhat to her mild chagrin, had left her alone.

"When will you come out to Hollywood?"

"Soon," he promised. "And you'll be coming back to New York."

She began to cry. "Oh, I'll miss you so much! I'll miss you so much!" Large tears of distress ran down her warm ivory cheeks. "Oh, geeze!" she cried softly. "You been good to me! Where's your hand? Where's your hand? You been the best friend anybody ever had. Where am I ever going to find a friend like you?"

She was acting now, but a lump arose in his throat, and for a moment a wild idea ran back and forth in his mind, like a blind man, knocking over its solid furniture – to marry her. He had only to make the suggestion, he knew, and she would become close to him and know no one else, because he would understand her for ever.

Next day, in the station, she was pleased with her flowers, her compartment, with the prospect of a longer trip than she had ever taken before. When she kissed him goodbye her deep eyes came close to his again and she pressed against him as if in protest against the separation.

Again she cried, but he knew that behind her tears lay the happiness of adventure in new fields. As he walked out of the station, New York was curiously empty. Through her eyes he had seen old colours once more; now they had faded back into the grey tapestry of the past. The next day he went to an office high in a building on Park Avenue and talked to a famous specialist he had not visited for a decade.

"I want you to examine the larynx again," he said. "There's not much hope, but something might have changed the situation."

He swallowed a complicated system of mirrors. He breathed in and out, made high and low sounds, coughed at a word of command. The specialist fussed and touched. Then he sat back and took out his eyeglass. "There's no change," he said. "The cords are not diseased – they're simply worn out. It isn't anything that can be treated."

"I thought so," said Jacob, humbly, as if he had been guilty of an impertinence. "That's practically what you told me before. I wasn't sure how permanent it was."

He had lost something when he came out of the building on Park Avenue – a half-hope, the love child of a wish, that some day...

"New York desolate," he wired her. "The nightclubs all closed. Black wreaths on the Statue of Civic Virtue. Please work hard and be remarkably happy."

"Dear Jacob," she wired back, "miss you so. You are the nicest man that ever lived and I mean it, dear. Please don't forget me. Love from Jenny."

Winter came. The picture Jenny had made in the East was released, together with preliminary interviews and articles in the fan magazines. Jacob sat in his apartment, playing the Kreutzer Sonata over and over on his new phonograph, and read her meagre and stilted but affectionate letters and the articles which said she was a discovery of Billy Farrelly's. In February he became engaged to an old friend, now a widow.

They went to Florida and were suddenly snarling at each other in hotel corridors and over bridge games, so they decided not to go through with it after all. In the spring he took a stateroom on the *Paris*, but three days before sailing he disposed of it and went to California.

4

J ENNY MET HIM AT THE STATION, kissed him and clung to his arm in the car all the way to the Ambassador Hotel. "Well, the man came," she cried. "I never thought I'd get him to come. I never did."

Her accent betrayed an effort at control. The emphatic "Geeze!" with all the wonder, horror, disgust or admiration she could put in it was gone, but there was no mild substitute, no "swell" or "grand". If her mood required expletives outside her repertoire, she kept silent.

But at seventeen, months are years, and Jacob perceived a change in her; in no sense was she a child any longer. There were fixed things in her mind – not distractions, for she was instinctively too polite for that, but simply things there. No longer was the studio a lark and a wonder and a divine accident; no longer "for a nickel I wouldn't turn up tomorrow". It was part of her life. Circumstances were stiffening into a career which went on independently of her casual hours.

"If this picture is as good as the other – I mean if I make a personal hit again, Hecksher'll break the contract. Everybody that's seen the rushes says it's the first one I've had sex appeal in."

"What are the rushes?"

"When they run off what they took the day before. They say it's the first time I've had sex appeal."

"I don't notice it," he teased her.

"You wouldn't. But I have."

"I know you have," he said and, moved by an ill-considered impulse, he took her hand.

She glanced quickly at him. He smiled – half a second too late. Then she smiled and her glowing warmth veiled his mistake.

"Jake," she cried, "I could bawl, I'm so glad you're here! I got you a room at the Ambassador. They were full, but they kicked out somebody because I said I had to have a room. I'll send my car back for you in half an hour. It's good you came on Sunday, because I got all day free."

They had luncheon in the furnished apartment she had leased for the winter. It was 1920 Moorish, taken over complete from a favourite of yesterday. Someone had told her it was horrible, for she joked about it; but when he pursued the matter he found that she didn't know why.

"I wish they had more nice men out here," she said once during luncheon. "Of course there's a lot of nice ones, but I mean… Oh, you know, like in New York – men that know even more than a girl does, like you."

After luncheon he learnt that they were going to tea. "Not today," he objected. "I want to see you alone."

"All right," she agreed doubtfully. "I suppose I could telephone. I thought… It's a lady that writes for a lot of newspapers and I've never been asked there before. Still, if you don't want to…"

Her face had fallen a little and Jacob assured her that he couldn't be more willing. Gradually he found that they were going not to one party but to three.

"In my position, it's sort of the thing to do," she explained. "Otherwise you don't see anybody except the people on your own lot, and that's narrow." He smiled. "Well, anyhow," she finished – "anyhow, you smart alec, that's what everybody does on Sunday afternoon."

At the first tea, Jacob noticed that there was an enormous preponderance of women over men, and of supernumeraries – lady journalists, cameramen's daughters, cutters' wives – over people of importance. A young Latin named Raffino appeared for a brief moment, spoke to Jenny and departed; several stars passed through, asking about children's health with a domesticity that was somewhat overpowering. Another group of celebrities posed immobile, statue-like, in a corner. There was a somewhat inebriated and very much excited author apparently trying to make engagements with one girl after another. As the afternoon waned, more people were suddenly a little tight; the communal voice was higher in pitch and greater in volume as Jacob and Jenny went out the door.

At the second tea, young Raffino – he was an actor, one of innumerable hopeful Valentinos – appeared again for a minute, talked to Jenny a little longer, a little more attentively this time, and went out. Jacob gathered that this party was not considered to have quite the swagger of the other. There was a bigger crowd around the cocktail table. There was more sitting down.

Jenny, he saw, drank only lemonade. He was surprised and pleased at her distinction and good manners. She talked to one person, never to everyone within hearing; then she listened, without finding it necessary to shift her eyes about. Deliberate or not on her part, he noticed that at both teas she was sooner or later talking to the guest of most consequence. Her seriousness, her air of saying "This is my opportunity of learning something", beckoned their egotism imperatively near.

When they left to drive to the last party, a buffet supper, it was dark and the electric legends of hopeful real-estate brokers were gleaming to some vague purpose on Beverly Hills. Outside Grauman's Theater a crowd was already gathered in the thin, warm rain.

"Look! Look!" she cried. It was the picture she had finished a month before.

They slid out of the thin Rialto of Hollywood Boulevard and into the deep gloom of a side street; he put his arm about her and kissed her.

"Dear Jake." She smiled up at him.

"Jenny, you're so lovely; I didn't know you were so lovely."

She looked straight ahead, her face mild and quiet. A wave of annoyance passed over him and he pulled her towards him urgently, just as the car stopped at a lighted door.

They went into a bungalow crowded with people and smoke. The impetus of the formality which had begun the afternoon was long exhausted; everything had become at once vague and strident.

"This is Hollywood," explained an alert, talkative lady who had been in his vicinity all day. "No airs on Sunday afternoon." She indicated the hostess. "Just a plain, simple, sweet girl." She raised her voice: "Isn't that so, darling – just a plain, simple, sweet girl?"

The hostess said, "Yeah. Who is?" And Jacob's informant lowered her voice again: "But that little girl of yours is the wisest one of the lot."

The totality of the cocktails Jacob had swallowed was affecting him pleasantly, but try as he might, the plot of the party – the key on which he could find ease and tranquillity – eluded him. There was something tense in the air – something competitive and insecure. Conversations with the men had a way of becoming empty and over-jovial or else melting off into a sort of suspicion. The women were nicer. At eleven o'clock, in the pantry, he suddenly realized that he hadn't seen Jenny for an hour. Returning to the living room, he saw her come in, evidently from outside, for she tossed a raincoat from her shoulders. She was with Raffino. When she came up, Jacob saw that she was out of breath and her eyes were very bright. Raffino smiled at Jacob pleasantly and negligently; a few moments later, as he turned to go, he bent and whispered in Jenny's ear and she looked at him without smiling as she said goodnight.

"I got to be on the lot at eight o'clock," she told Jacob presently. "I'll look like an old umbrella unless I go home. Do you mind, dear?"

"Heavens, no!"

Their car drove over one of the interminable distances of the thin, stretched city.

"Jenny," he said, "you've never looked like you were tonight. Put your head on my shoulder."

"I'd like to. I'm tired."

"I can't tell you how radiant you've got to be."

"I'm just the same."

"No, you're not." His voice suddenly became a whisper, trembling with emotion. "Jenny, I'm in love with you."

"Jacob, don't be silly."

"I'm in love with you. Isn't it strange, Jenny? It happened just like that."

"You're not in love with me."

"You mean the fact doesn't interest you." He was conscious of a faint twinge of fear.

She sat up out of the circle of his arm. "Of course it interests me – you know I care more about you than anything in the world."

"More than about Mr Raffino?"

"Oh – my – gosh!" she protested scornfully. "Raffino's nothing but a baby."

"I love you, Jenny."

"No, you don't."

He tightened his arm. Was it his imagination or was there a small instinctive resistance in her body? But she came close to him and he kissed her.

"You know that's crazy about Raffino."

"I suppose I'm jealous." Feeling insistent and unattractive, he released her. But the twinge of fear had become an ache. Though he knew that she was tired and that she felt strange at this new mood in him, he was unable to let the matter alone. "I didn't realize how much a part of my life you were. I didn't know what it was I missed – but I know now. I wanted you near."

"Well, here I am."

He took her words as an invitation, but this time she relaxed wearily in his arms. He held her thus for the rest of the way, her eyes closed, her short hair falling straight back, like a girl drowned.

"The car'll take you to the hotel," she said when they reached the apartment. "Remember, you're having lunch with me at the studio tomorrow."

Suddenly they were in a discussion that was almost an argument, as to whether it was too late for him to come in. Neither could yet appreciate the change that his declaration had made in the other. Abruptly they had become like different people, as Jacob tried desperately to turn back the clock to that night in New York six months before, and Jenny watched this mood, which was more than jealousy and less than love, snow under, one by one, the qualities of consideration and understanding which she knew in him and with which she felt at home.

"But I don't love you like that," she cried. "How can you come to me all at once and ask me to love you like that?"

"You love Raffino like that!"

"I swear I don't! I never even kissed him – not really!"

"H'm!" He was a gruff white bird now. He could scarcely credit his own unpleasantness, but something illogical as love itself urged him on. "An actor!"

"Oh, Jake," she cried, "please lemme go. I never felt so terrible and mixed up in my life."

"I'll go," he said suddenly. "I don't know what's the matter, except that I'm so mad about you that I don't know what I'm saying. I love you and you don't love me. Once you did, or thought you did, but that's evidently over."

"But I do love you." She thought for a moment; the red-and-green glow of a filling station on the corner lit up the struggle in her face. "If you love me that much, I'll marry you tomorrow."

"Marry me!" he exclaimed. She was so absorbed in what she had just said that she did not notice.

"I'll marry you tomorrow," she repeated. "I like you better than anybody in the world and I guess I'll get to love you the way you want me to." She uttered a single, half-broken sob. "But... I didn't know this was going to happen. Please let me alone tonight."

Jacob didn't sleep. There was music from the Ambassador grill till late and a fringe of working girls hung about the carriage entrance waiting for their favourites to come out. Then a long-protracted quarrel between a man and a woman began in the hall outside, moved into the next room and continued as a low two-toned mumble through the intervening door. He went to the window sometime towards three o'clock and stared out into the clear splendour of the California night. Her beauty rested outside on the grass, on the damp, gleaming roofs of the bungalows, all around him, borne up like music on the night. It was in the room, on the white pillow, it rustled ghostlike in the curtains. His desire recreated her until she lost all vestiges of the old Jenny, even of the girl who had met him at the train that morning. Silently, as the night hours went by, he moulded her over into an image of love – an image that would endure as long as love itself, or even longer – not to perish till he could say, "I never really loved her." Slowly he created it with this and that illusion from his youth, this and that sad old yearning, until she stood before him identical with her old self only by name.

Later, when he drifted off into a few hours' sleep, the image he had made stood near him, lingering in the room, joined in mystic marriage to his heart.

5

"I WON'T MARRY YOU unless you love me," he said, driving back from the studio. She waited, her hands folded tranquilly in her lap. "Do you think I'd want you if you were unhappy and unresponsive, Jenny – knowing all the time you didn't love me?"

"I do love you. But not that way."

"What's 'that way'?"

She hesitated, her eyes were far off. "You don't… thrill me, Jake. I don't know – there have been some men that sort of thrilled me when they touched me, dancing or anything. I know it's crazy, but—"

"Does Raffino thrill you?"

"Sort of, but not so much."

"And I don't at all?"

"I just feel comfortable and happy with you."

He should have urged her that that was best, but he couldn't say it, whether it was an old truth or an old lie.

"Anyhow, I told you I'll marry you; perhaps you might thrill me later."

He laughed, stopped suddenly. "If I didn't thrill you, as you call it, why did you seem to care so much last summer?"

"I don't know. I guess I was young. You never know how you once felt, do you?"

She had become elusive to him, with that elusiveness that gives a hidden significance to the least significant remarks. And with the clumsy tools of jealousy and desire, he was trying to create the spell that is ethereal and delicate as the dust on a moth's wing.

"Listen, Jake," she said suddenly. "That lawyer my sister had – that Scharnhorst – called up the studio this afternoon."

"Your sister's all right," he said absently, and he added: "So a lot of men thrill you."

"Well, if I've felt it with a lot of men, it couldn't have anything to do with real love, could it?" she said hopefully.

"But your theory is that love couldn't come without it."

"I haven't got any theories or anything. I just told you how I felt. You know more than me."

"I don't know anything at all."

There was a man waiting in the lower hall of the apartment house. Jenny went up and spoke to him; then, turning back to Jake, said in a low voice: "It's Scharnhorst. Would you mind waiting downstairs while he talks to me? He says it won't take half an hour."

He waited, smoking innumerable cigarettes. Ten minutes passed. Then the telephone operator beckoned him.

"Quick!" she said. "Miss Prince wants you on the telephone."

Jenny's voice was tense and frightened. "Don't let Scharnhorst get out," she said. "He's on the stairs, maybe in the elevator. Make him come back here."

Jacob put down the receiver just as the elevator clicked. He stood in front of the elevator door, barring the man inside. "Mr Scharnhorst?"

"Yeah." The face was keen and suspicious.

"Will you come up to Miss Prince's apartment again? There's something she forgot to say. "

"I can see her later." He attempted to push past Jacob. Seizing him by the shoulders, Jacob shoved him back into the cage, slammed the door and pressed the button for the eighth floor.

"I'll have you arrested for this!" Scharnhorst remarked. "Put into jail for assault!"

Jacob held him firmly by the arms. Upstairs, Jenny, with panic in her eyes, was holding open her door. After a slight struggle, the lawyer went inside.

"What is it?" demanded Jacob.

"Tell him, you," she said. "Oh, Jake, he wants twenty thousand dollars!"

"What for?"

"To get my sister a new trial."

"But she hasn't a chance!" exclaimed Jacob. He turned to Scharnhorst. "You ought to know she hasn't a chance."

"There are some technicalities," said the lawyer uneasily – "things that nobody but an attorney would understand. She's very unhappy there, and her sister so rich and successful. Mrs Choynski thought she ought to get another chance."

"You've been up there working on her, heh?"

"She sent for me."

"But the blackmail idea was your own. I suppose if Miss Prince doesn't feel like supplying twenty thousand to retain your firm, it'll come out that she's the sister of the notorious murderess."

Jenny nodded. "That's what he said."

"Just a minute!" Jacob walked to the phone. "Western Union, please. Western Union? Please take a telegram." He gave the name and address of a man high in the political world of New York. "Here's the message:

> "The convict Choynski threatening her sister, who is a picture actress, with exposure of relationship stop Can you arrange it with warden that she be cut off from visitors until I can get East and explain the situation stop Also wire me if two witnesses to an attempted blackmailing scene are enough to disbar a lawyer in New York if charges proceed from such a quarter as Read, Van Tyne, Biggs & Company, or my uncle the surrogate stop Answer Ambassador Hotel, Los Angeles.
>
> "Jacob C.K. Booth."

He waited until the clerk had repeated the message. "Now, Mr Scharnhorst," he said, "the pursuit of art should not be interrupted by such alarms and excursions. Miss Prince, as you see, is considerably upset. It will show in her work tomorrow and a million people will be just a little disappointed. So we won't ask her for any decisions. In fact you and I will leave Los Angeles on the same train tonight."

6

THE SUMMER PASSED. Jacob went about his useless life, sustained by the knowledge that Jenny was coming East in the fall. By fall there would have been many Raffinos, he supposed, and she would find that the thrill of their hands and eyes – and lips – was much the same. They were the equivalent, in a different world, of the affairs at a college house party, the undergraduates of a casual summer. And if it was still true that her feeling for him was less than romantic, then he would take her anyway, letting romance come after marriage as – so he had always heard – it had come to many wives before.

Her letters fascinated and baffled him. Through the ineptitude of expression he caught gleams of emotion – an ever-present gratitude, a longing to talk to him and a quick, almost frightened reaction towards him, from – he could only imagine – some other man. In August she went on location; there were only postcards from some lost desert in Arizona, then for a while nothing at all. He was glad of the break. He had thought over all the things that might have repelled her – of his portentousness, his jealousy, his manifest misery. This time it would be different. He would keep control of the situation. She would at least admire him again, see in him the incomparably dignified and well-adjusted life.

Two nights before her arrival, Jacob went to see her latest picture in a huge night-bound vault on Broadway. It was a college story. She walked into it with her hair knotted on the crown of her head – a familiar symbol for dowdiness – inspired the hero to a feat of athletic success and faded out of it, always subsidiary to him, in the shadow of the cheering stands. But there was something new in her performance: for the first time the arresting quality he had noticed in her voice a year before had begun to get over on the screen. Every move she made, every gesture, was poignant and important. Others in the audience saw it too. He fancied he could tell this by some change in the quality of their breathing, by a reflection of her clear, precise expression in their casual and indifferent faces. Reviewers, too, were aware of it, though most of them were incapable of any precise definition of a personality.

But his first real consciousness of her public existence came from the attitude of her fellow passengers disembarking from the train. Busy as they were with friends or baggage, they found time to stare at her, to call their friends' attention, to repeat her name.

She was radiant. A communicative joy flowed from her and around her, as though her perfumer had managed to imprison ecstasy in a bottle. Once again there was a mystical transfusion, and blood began to course again through the hard veins of New York – there was the pleasure of Jacob's chauffeur when she remembered him, the respectful frisking of the bell boys at the Plaza, the nervous collapse of the head waiter at the restaurant where they dined. As for Jacob, he had control of himself now. He was gentle, considerate and polite, as it was natural for him to be – but as, in this case, he had found it necessary to plan. His manner promised and outlined an ability to take care of her, a will to be leant on.

After dinner, their corner of the restaurant cleared gradually of the theatre crowd, and the sense of being alone settled over them. Their faces became grave, their voices very quiet.

"It's been five months since I saw you." He looked down at his hands thoughtfully. "Nothing has changed with me, Jenny. I love you with all my heart. I love your face and your faults and your mind and everything about you. The one thing I want in this world is to make you happy."

"I know," she whispered. "Gosh, I know!"

"Whether there's still only affection in your feeling towards me, I don't know. If you'll marry me, I think you'll find that the other things will come, will be there before you know it – and what you called a thrill will seem a joke to you, because life isn't for boys and girls, Jenny, but for men and women."

"Jacob," she whispered, "you don't have to tell me. I know."

He raised his eyes for the first time. "What do you mean – you know?"

"I get what you mean. Oh, this is terrible! Jacob, listen! I want to tell you. Listen, dear, don't say anything. Don't look at me. Listen, Jacob, I fell in love with a man."

"What?" he asked blankly.

"I fell in love with somebody. That's what I mean about understanding about a silly thrill."

"You mean you're in love with me?"

"No."

The appalling monosyllable floated between them, danced and vibrated over the table: "No – no – no – no – no!"

"Oh, this is awful!" she cried. "I fell in love with a man I met on location this summer. I didn't mean to – I tried not to – but first thing

I knew there I was in love and all the wishing in the world couldn't help it. I wrote you and asked you to come, but I didn't send the letter, and there I was, crazy about this man and not daring to speak to him, and bawling myself to sleep every night."

"An actor?" he heard himself saying in a dead voice. "Raffino?"

"Oh, no, no, no! Wait a minute, let me tell you. It went on for three weeks, and I honestly wanted to kill myself, Jake. Life wasn't worthwhile unless I could have him. And one night we got in a car by accident alone and he just caught me and made me tell him I loved him. He knew – he couldn't help knowing."

"It just… swept over you," said Jacob steadily. "I see."

"Oh, I knew you'd understand, Jake! You understand everything. You're the best person in the world, Jake, and don't I know it?"

"You're going to marry him?"

Slowly she nodded her head. "I said I'd have to come East first and see you." As her fear lessened, the extent of his grief became more apparent to her and her eyes filled with tears. "It only comes once, Jake, like that. That's what kept in my mind all those weeks I didn't hardly speak to him – if you lose it once, it'll never come like that again, and then what do you want to live for? He was directing the picture – he was the same about me."

"I see."

As once before, her eyes held his like hands. "Oh, Ja-a-ake!" In that sudden croon of compassion, all-comprehending and deep as a song, the first force of the shock passed off. Jacob's teeth came together again and he struggled to conceal his misery. Mustering his features into an expression of irony, he called for the check. It seemed an hour later they were in a taxi going towards the Plaza Hotel.

She clung to him. "Oh, Jake, say it's all right! Say you understand! Darling Jake, my best friend, my only friend, say you understand!"

"Of course I do, Jenny." His hand patted her back automatically.

"Oh-h-h, Jake, you feel just awful, don't you?"

"I'll survive."

"Oh-h-h, Jake!"

They reached the hotel. Before they got out Jenny glanced at her face in her vanity mirror and turned up the collar of her fur cape. In the lobby, Jacob ran into several people and said, "Oh, I'm so sorry," in a strained, unconvincing voice. The elevator waited. Jenny, her face distraught and tearful, stepped in and held out her hand towards him with the fist clenched helplessly.

"Jake," she said once more.

"Goodnight, Jenny."

She turned her face to the wire wall of the cage. The gate clanged.

"Hold on!" he almost said. "Do you realize what you're doing, starting that car like that?"

He turned and went out the door blindly. "I've lost her," he whispered to himself, awed and frightened. "I've lost her!"

He walked over Fifty-Ninth Street to Columbus Circle and then down Broadway. There were no cigarettes in his pocket – he had left them at the restaurant – so he went into a tobacco store. There was some confusion about the change and someone in the store laughed.

When he came out he stood for a moment puzzled. Then the heavy tide of realization swept over him and beyond him, leaving him stunned and exhausted. It swept back upon him and over him again. As one rereads a tragic story with the defiant hope that it will end differently, so he went back to the morning, to the beginning, to the previous year. But the tide came thundering back with the certainty that she was cut off from him for ever in a high room at the Plaza Hotel.

He walked down Broadway. In great block letters over the porte cochère of the Capitol Theater five words glittered out into the night: "Carl Barbour and Jenny Prince".

The name startled him, as if a passer-by had spoken it. He stopped and stared. Other eyes rose to that sign, people hurried by him and turned in.

Jenny Prince.

Now that she no longer belonged to him, the name assumed a significance entirely its own.

It hung there, cool and impervious, in the night, a challenge, a defiance.

Jenny Prince.

"Come and rest upon my loveliness," it said. "Fulfil your secret dreams in wedding me for an hour."

Jenny Prince.

It was untrue – she was back at the Plaza Hotel, in love with somebody. But the name, with its bright insistence, rode high upon the night.

"I love my dear public. They are all so sweet to me."

The wave appeared far off, sent up whitecaps, rolled towards him with the might of pain, washed over him. "Never any more. Never any more." The wave beat upon him, drove him down, pounding with hammers of agony on his ears. Proud and impervious, the name on high challenged the night.

Jenny Prince.

She was there! All of her, the best of her – the effort, the power, the triumph, the beauty.

Jacob moved forward with a group and bought a ticket at the window.

Confused, he stared around the great lobby. Then he saw an entrance and, walking in, found himself a place in the fast-throbbing darkness.

A Short Trip Home

1

I WAS NEAR HER, for I had lingered behind in order to get the short walk with her from the living room to the front door. That was a lot, for she had flowered suddenly and I, being a man and only a year older, hadn't flowered at all, had scarcely dared to come near her in the week we'd been home. Nor was I going to say anything in that walk of ten feet, or touch her; but I had a vague hope she'd do something, give a gay little performance of some sort, personal only in so far as we were alone together.

She had bewitchment suddenly in the twinkle of short hairs on her neck, in the sure, clear confidence that at about eighteen begins to deepen and sing in attractive American girls. The lamplight shopped in the yellow strands of her hair.

Already she was sliding into another world – the world of Joe Jelke and Jim Cathcart waiting for us now in the car. In another year she would pass beyond me for ever.

As I waited, feeling the others outside in the snowy night, feeling the excitement of Christmas week and the excitement of Ellen here, blooming away, filling the room with "sex appeal" – a wretched phrase to express a quality that isn't like that at all – a maid came in from the dining room, spoke to Ellen quietly and handed her a note. Ellen read it and her eyes faded down, as when the current grows weak on rural circuits, and smouldered off into space. Then she gave me an odd look – in which I probably didn't show – and without a word, followed the maid into the dining room and beyond. I sat turning over the pages of a magazine for a quarter of an hour.

Joe Jelke came in, red-faced from the cold, his white silk muffler gleaming at the neck of his fur coat. He was a senior at New Haven, I was a sophomore. He was prominent, a member of Scroll and Keys and, in my eyes, very distinguished and handsome.

"Isn't Ellen coming?"

"I don't know," I answered discreetly. "She was all ready."

"Ellen!" he called. "Ellen!"

He had left the front door open behind him and a great cloud of frosty air rolled in from outside. He went halfway up the stairs – he was a familiar in the house – and called again, till Mrs Baker came to the banister and said that Ellen was below. Then the maid, a little excited, appeared in the dining-room door.

"Mr Jelke," she called in a low voice.

"Joe's face fell as he turned towards her, sensing bad news.

"Miss Ellen says for you to go to the party. She'll come later."

"What's the matter?"

"She can't come now. She'll come later."

He hesitated, confused. It was the last big dance of vacation, and he was mad about Ellen. He had tried to give her a ring for Christmas, and failing that, got her to accept a gold mesh bag that must have cost two hundred dollars. He wasn't the only one – there were three or four in the same wild condition, and all in the ten days she'd been home – but his chance came first, for he was rich and gracious and at that moment the "desirable" boy of St Paul. To me it seemed impossible that she could prefer another, but the rumour was she'd described Joe as much too perfect. I suppose he lacked mystery for her, and when a man is up against that with a young girl who isn't thinking of the practical side of marriage yet – well...

"No, she's not." The maid was defiant and a little scared.

"She is."

"She went out the back way, Mr Jelke."

"I'm going to see."

I followed him. The Swedish servants washing dishes looked up sideways at our approach, and an interested crashing of pans marked our passage through. The storm door, unbolted, was flapping in the wind, and as we walked out into the snowy yard we saw the tail light of a car turn the corner at the end of the back alley.

"I'm going after her," Joe said slowly. "I don't understand this at all."

I was too awed by the calamity to argue. We hurried to his car and drove in a fruitless, despairing zigzag all over the residence section, peering into every machine on the streets. It was half an hour before the futility of the affair began to dawn upon him – St Paul is a city of almost three hundred thousand people – and Jim Cathcart reminded him that we had another girl to stop for. Like a wounded animal he sank into a melancholy mass of fur in the corner, from which position he jerked upright every few minutes and waved himself backward and forward a little in protest and despair.

Jim's girl was ready and impatient, but after what had happened her impatience didn't seem important. She looked lovely though. That's one thing about Christmas vacation – the excitement of growth and change and adventure in foreign parts transforming the people you've known all your life. Joe Jelke was polite to her in a daze – he indulged in one burst of short, loud, harsh laughter by way of conversation – and we drove to the hotel.

The chauffeur approached it on the wrong side – the side on which the line of cars was not putting forth guests – and because of that we came suddenly upon Ellen Baker just getting out of a small coupé. Even before we came to a stop, Joe Jelke had jumped excitedly from the car.

Ellen turned towards us, a faintly distracted look – perhaps of surprise, but certainly not of alarm – in her face; in fact, she didn't seem very aware of us. Joe approached her with a stern, dignified, injured and, I thought, just exactly correct reproof in his expression. I followed.

Seated in the coupé – he had not dismounted to help Ellen out – was a hard, thin-faced man of about thirty-five with an air of being scarred, and a slight but sinister smile. His eyes were a sort of taunt to the whole human family – they were the eyes of an animal, sleepy and quiescent in the presence of another species. They were helpless yet brutal, uphopeful yet confident. It was as if they felt themselves powerless to originate activity, but infinitely capable of profiting by a single gesture of weakness in another.

Vaguely I placed him as one of the sort of men whom I had been conscious of from my earliest youth as "hanging around" – leaning with one elbow on the counters of tobacco stores, watching, through Heaven knows what small chink of the mind, the people who hurried in and out. Intimate to garages, where he had vague business conducted in undertones, to barber shops and to the lobbies of theatres – in such places, anyhow, I placed the type, if type it was, that he reminded me of. Sometimes his face bobbed up in one of Tad's more savage cartoons,* and I had always from earliest boyhood thrown a nervous glance towards the dim borderland where he stood, and seen him watching me and despising me. Once, in a dream, he had taken a few steps towards me, jerking his head back and muttering "Say, kid" in what was intended to be a reassuring voice, and I had broken for the door in terror. This was that sort of man.

Joe and Ellen faced each other silently; she seemed, as I have said, to be in a daze. It was cold, but she didn't notice that her coat had blown open; Joe reached out and pulled it together, and automatically she clutched it with her hand.

Suddenly the man in the coupé, who had been watching them silently, laughed. It was a bare laugh, done with the breath – just a noisy jerk of the head – but it was an insult if I had ever heard one; definite and not to be passed over. I wasn't surprised when Joe, who was quick tempered, turned to him angrily and said:

"What's your trouble?"

The man waited a moment, his eyes shifting and yet staring, and always seeing. Then he laughed again in the same way. Ellen stirred uneasily.

"Who is this… this…" Joe's voice trembled with annoyance.

"Look out now," said the man slowly.

Joe turned to me.

"Eddie, take Ellen and Catherine in, will you?" he said quickly… "Ellen, go with Eddie."

"Look out now," the man repeated.

Ellen made a little sound with her tongue and teeth, but she didn't resist when I took her arm and moved her towards the side door of the hotel. It struck me as odd that she should be so helpless, even to the point of acquiescing by her silence in this imminent trouble.

"Let it go, Joe!" I called back over my shoulder. "Come inside!"

Ellen, pulling against my arm, hurried us on. As we were caught up into the swinging doors I had the impression that the man was getting out of his coupé.

Ten minutes later, as I waited for the girls outside the women's dressing room, Joe Jelke and Jim Cathcart stepped out of the elevator. Joe was very white, his eyes were heavy and glazed, there was a trickle of dark blood on his forehead and on his white muffler. Jim had both their hats in his hand.

"He hit Joe with brass knuckles," Jim said in a low voice. "Joe was out cold for a minute or so. I wish you'd send a bell boy for some witch hazel and court plaster."

It was late and the hall was deserted; brassy fragments of the dance below reached us as if heavy curtains were being blown aside and dropping back into place. When Ellen came out I took her directly downstairs. We avoided the receiving line and went into a dim room set with scraggly hotel palms where couples sometimes sat out during the dance; there I told her what had happened.

"It was Joe's own fault," she said, surprisingly. "I told him not to interfere."

This wasn't true. She had said nothing, only uttered one curious little click of impatience.

"You ran out the back door and disappeared for almost an hour," I protested. "Then you turned up with a hard-looking customer who laughed in Joe's face."

"A hard-looking customer," she repeated, as if tasting the sound of the words.

"Well, wasn't he? Where on earth did you get hold of him, Ellen?"

"On the train," she answered. Immediately she seemed to regret this admission. "You'd better stay out of things that aren't your business, Eddie. You see what happened to Joe."

Literally I gasped. To watch her, seated beside me, immaculately glowing, her body giving off wave after wave of freshness and delicacy – and to hear her talk like that.

"But that man's a thug!" I cried. "No girl could be safe with him. He used brass knuckles on Joe – brass knuckles!"

"Is that pretty bad?"

She asked this as she might have asked such a question a few years ago. She looked at me at last and really wanted an answer; for a moment it was as if she were trying to recapture an attitude that had almost departed; then she hardened again. I say "hardened", for I began to notice that when she was concerned with this man her eyelids fell a little, shutting other things – everything else – out of view.

That was a moment I might have said something, I suppose, but in spite of everything, I couldn't light into her. I was too much under the spell of her beauty and its success. I even began to find excuses for her – perhaps that man wasn't what he appeared to be; or perhaps – more romantically – she was involved with him against her will to shield someone else. At this point people began to drift into the room and come up to speak to us. We couldn't talk any more, so we went in and bowed to the chaperones. Then I gave her up to the bright restless sea of the dance, where she moved in an eddy of her own among the pleasant islands of coloured favours set out on tables and the south winds from the brasses moaning across the hall. After a while I aw Joe Jelke

36

sitting in a corner with a strip of court plaster on his forehead, watching Ellen as if she herself had struck him down, but I didn't go up to him. I felt queer myself – like I feel when I wake up after sleeping through an afternoon, strange and portentous, as if something had gone on in the interval that changed the values of everything and that I didn't see.

The night slipped on through successive phases of cardboard horns, amateur tableaux and flashlights for the morning papers. Then was the grand march and supper, and about two o'clock some of the committee dressed up as revenue agents pinched the party, and a facetious newspaper was distributed, burlesquing the events of the evening. And all the time out of the corner of my eye I watched the shining orchid on Ellen's shoulder as it moved like Stuart's plume* about the room. I watched it with a definite foreboding until the last sleepy groups had crowded into the elevators, and then, bundled to the eyes in great shapeless fur coats, drifted out into the clear, dry Minnesota night.

2

THERE IS A SLOPING MID-SECTION of our city which lies between the residence quarter on the hill and the business district on the level of the river. It is a vague part of town, broken by its climb into triangles and odd shapes – there are names like Seven Corners – and I don't believe a dozen people could draw an accurate map of it, though everyone traversed it by trolley, auto or shoe leather twice a day. And though it was a busy section, it would be hard for me to name the business that comprised its activity. There were always long lines of trolley cars waiting to start somewhere; there was a big movie theatre and many small ones with posters of Hoot Gibson and Wonder Dogs and Wonder Horses outside; there were small stores with *Old King Brady* and *The Liberty Boys of '76** in the windows, and marbles, cigarettes and candy inside; and – one definite place at least – a fancy costumer whom we all visited at least once a year. Some time during boyhood I became aware that on one side of a certain obscure street there were bawdy houses, and all through the district were pawnshops, cheap jewellers, small athletic clubs and gymnasiums and somewhat too blatantly run-down saloons.

The morning after the Cotillion Club party, I woke up late and lazy, with the happy feeling that for a day or two more there was no chapel, no classes – nothing to do but wait for another party tonight. It was crisp and bright – one of those days when you forget how cold it is until your cheek freezes – and the events of the evening before seemed dim and far away. After luncheon I started downtown on foot through a light, pleasant snow of small flakes that would probably fall all afternoon, and I was about half through that halfway section of town – so far as I know, there's no inclusive name for it – when suddenly whatever idle thought was in my hand blew away like a hat and I began thinking hard of Ellen Baker. I began worrying about her as I'd never worried about anything outside myself before. I began to loiter, with an instinct to go upon the hill again and find her and talk to her; then I remembered that she was at a tea, and I went on again, but still thinking of her, and harder than ever. Right then the affair opened up again.

It was snowing, I said, and it was four o'clock on a December afternoon, when there is a promise of darkness in the air and the street lamps are just going on. I passed a combination pool parlour and restaurant, with a stove loaded with hot dogs in the window, and a few loungers hanging around the door. The lights were on inside – not bright lights but just a few pale yellow high up on the ceiling – and the glow they threw out into the frosty dusk wasn't bright enough to tempt you to stare inside. As I went past, thinking hard of Ellen all this time, I took in the quartet of loafers out of the corner of my eye. I hadn't gone half a dozen steps down the street when one of them called to me, not by name but in a way clearly intended for my ear. I thought it was a tribute to my raccoon coat and paid no attention, but a moment later whoever it was called to me again in a peremptory voice. I was annoyed and turned around. There, standing in the group not ten feet away and looking at me with the half-sneer on his face with which he'd looked at Joe Jelke, was the scarred, thin-faced man of the night before.

He had on a black fancy-cut coat, buttoned up to his neck as if he were cold. His hands were deep in his pockets and he wore a derby and high-button shoes. I was startled, and for a moment I hesitated, but I was most of all angry and, knowing that I was quicker with my hands than Joe Jelke, I took a tentative step back towards him. The other men weren't looking at me – I don't think they saw me at all – but I knew that this one recognized me; there was nothing casual about his look, no mistake.

"Here I am. What are you going to do about it?" his eyes seemed to say.

I took another step towards him and he laughed soundlessly, but with active contempt, and drew back into the group. I followed. I was going to speak to him – I wasn't sure what I was going to say – but when I came up he had either changed his mind and backed off, or else he wanted me to follow him inside, for he had slipped off and the three men watched my intent approach without curiosity. They were the same kind – sporty but, unlike him, smooth rather than truculent; I didn't find any personal malice in their collective glance.

"Did he go inside?" I asked.

They looked at one another in that cagey way; a wink passed between them and, after a perceptible pause, one said:

"Who go inside?"

"I don't know his name."

There was another wink. Annoyed and determined, I walked past them and into the pool room. There were a few people at a lunch counter along one side and a few more playing billiards, but he was not among them.

Again I hesitated. If his idea was to lead me into any blind part of the establishment – there were some half-open doors farther back – I wanted more support. I went up to the man at the desk. "What became of the fellow who just walked in here?"

Was he on his guard immediately, or was that my imagination?

"What fellow?"

"Thin face – derby hat."

"How long ago?"

"Oh – a minute."

He shook his head again. "Didn't see him," he said.

I waited. The three men from outside had come in and were lined up beside me at the counter. I felt that all of them were looking at me in a peculiar way. Feeling helpless and increasingly uneasy, I turned suddenly and went out. A little way down the street I turned again and took a good look at the place, so I'd know it and could find it again. On the next corner I broke impulsively into a run, found a taxicab in front of the hotel and drove back up the hill.

Ellen wasn't home. Mrs Baker came downstairs and talked to me. She seemed entirely cheerful and proud of Ellen's beauty, and ignorant of anything being amiss or of anything unusual having taken place the night before. She was glad that vacation was almost over – it was a strain and Ellen wasn't very strong. Then she said something that relieved my mind enormously. She was glad that I had come in, for of course Ellen would want to see me, and the time was so short. She was going back at half-past eight tonight.

"Tonight!" I exclaimed. "I thought it was the day after tomorrow."

"She's going to visit the Brokaws in Chicago," Mrs Baker said. "They want her for some party. We just decided it today. She's leaving with the Ingersoll girls tonight."

I was so glad I could barely restrain myself from shaking her hand. Ellen was safe. It had been nothing all along but a moment of the most casual adventure. I felt like an idiot, but I realized how much I cared about Ellen and how little I could endure anything terrible happening to her.

"She'll be in soon?"

"Any minute now. She just phoned from the University Club."

I said I'd be over later – I lived almost next door and I wanted to be alone. Outside I remembered I didn't have a key, so I started up the Bakers' driveway to take the old cut we used in childhood through the intervening yard. It was still snowing, but the flakes were bigger now against the darkness, and trying to locate the buried walk I noticed that the Bakers' back door was ajar.

I scarcely know why I turned and walked into that kitchen. There was a time when I would have known the Bakers' servants by name. That wasn't true now, but they knew me, and I was aware of a sudden suspension as I came in – not only a suspension of talk but of some mood or expectation that had filled them. They began to go to work too quickly; they made unnecessary movements and clamour – those three. The parlourmaid looked at me in a frightened way and I suddenly guessed she was waiting to deliver another message. I beckoned her into the pantry.

"I know all about this," I said. "It's a very serious business. Shall I go to Mrs Baker now, or will you shut and lock that back door?"

"Don't tell Mrs Baker, Mr Stinson!"

"Then I don't want Miss Ellen disturbed. If she is – and if she is I'll know of it…" I delivered some outrageous threat about going to all the employment agencies and seeing she never got another job in the city. She was thoroughly intimidated when I went out; it wasn't a minute before the back door was locked and bolted behind me.

Simultaneously I heard a big car drive up in front, chains crunching on the soft snow; it was bringing Ellen home, and I went in to say goodbye.

Joe Jelke and two other boys were along, and none of the three could manage to take their eyes off her, even to say hello to me. She had one of those exquisite rose skins frequent in our part of the country, and beautiful until the little veins begin to break at about forty; now, flushed with the cold, it was a riot of lovely delicate pinks like many carnations. She and Joe had reached some sort of reconciliation, or at least he was too far gone in love to remember last night; but I saw that though she laughed a lot she wasn't really paying any attention to him or any of them. She wanted them to go, so that there'd be a message from the kitchen, but I knew that the message wasn't coming – that she was safe. There was talk of the Pump and Slipper dance at New Haven and of the Princeton Prom, and then, in various moods, we four left and separated quickly outside. I walked home with a certain depression of spirit and lay for an hour in a hot bath thinking that vacation was all over for me now that she was gone; feeling, even more deeply than I had yesterday, that she was out of my life.

And something eluded me, some one more thing to do, something that I had lost amid the events of the afternoon, promising myself to go back and pick it up, only to find that it had escaped me. I associated it vaguely with Mrs Baker, and now I seemed to recall that it had poked up its head somewhere in the stream of conversation with her. In my relief about Ellen I had forgotten to ask her a question regarding something she had said.

The Brokaws – that was it – where Ellen was to visit. I knew Bill Brokaw well; he was in my class at Yale. Then I remembered and sat bolt upright in the tub – the Brokaws weren't in Chicago this Christmas: they were at Palm Beach!

Dripping, I sprang out of the tub, threw an insufficient union suit around my shoulders and sprang for the phone in my room. I got the connection quick, but Miss Ellen had already started for the train.

Luckily our car was in, and while I squirmed, still damp, into my clothes, the chauffeur brought it around to the door. The night was cold and dry, and we make good time to the station through the hard, crusty snow. I felt queer and insecure starting out this way, but somehow more confident as the station loomed up bright and new against the dark, cold air. For fifty years my family had owned the land on which it was built, and that made my temerity seem all right somehow. There was always a possibility that I was rushing in where angels feared to tread, but that sense of having a solid foothold in the past made me willing to make a fool of myself. This business was all wrong – terribly wrong. Any idea I had entertained that it was harmless dropped away now; between Ellen and some vague overwhelming catastrophe there stood me, or else the police and a scandal. I'm no moralist – there was another element here, dark and frightening, and I didn't want Ellen to go through it alone.

There are three competing trains from St Paul to Chicago that all leave within a few minutes of half-past eight. Hers was the Burlington, and as I ran across the station I saw the grating being pulled over and the light above it go out. I knew, though, that she had a drawing room with the Ingersoll girls, because her mother had mentioned buying the ticket, so she was, literally speaking, tucked in until tomorrow.

The C., M. & St P. gate was down at the other end and I raced for it and made it. I had forgotten one thing, though, and that was enough to keep me awake and worried half the night. This train got into Chicago ten minutes after the other. Ellen had that much time to disappear into one of the largest cities in the world.

I gave the porter a wire to my family to send from Milwaukee, and at eight o'clock next morning I pushed violently by a whole line of passengers, clamouring over their bags parked in the vestibule, and shot out of the door with a sort of scramble over the porter's back. For a moment the confusion of a great station, the voluminous sounds and echoes and cross-currents of bells and smoke struck me helpless. Then I dashed for the exit and towards the only chance I knew of finding her.

I had guessed right. She was standing at the telegraph counter, sending off Heaven knows what black lie to her mother, and her expression when she saw me had a sort of terror mixed up with its surprise. There was cunning in it too. She was thinking quickly – she would have liked to walk away from me as if I weren't there, and go about her own business, but she couldn't. I was too matter-of-fact a thing in her life. So we stood silently watching each other and each thinking hard.

"The Brokaws are in Florida," I said after a minute.

"It was nice of you to take such a long trip to tell me that."

"Since you've found it out, don't you think you'd better go on to school?"

"Please let me alone, Eddie," she said.

"I'll go as far as New York with you. I've decided to go back early myself."

"You'd better let me alone." Her lovely eyes narrowed and her face took on a look of dumb-animal-like resistance. She made a visible effort, the cunning flickered back into it, then both were gone, and in their stead was a cheerful reassuring smile that all but convinced me.

"Eddie, you silly child, don't you think I'm old enough to take care of myself?" I didn't answer. "I'm going to meet a man, you understand. I just want to see him today. I've got my ticket East on the five-o'clock train. If you don't believe it, here it is in my bag."

"I believe you."

"The man isn't anybody that you know and – frankly, I think you're being awfully fresh and impossible."

"I know who the man is."

Again she lost control of her face. That terrible expression came back into it and she spoke with almost a snarl:

"You'd better let me alone."

I took the blank out of her hand and wrote out an explanatory telegram to her mother. Then I turned to Ellen and said a little roughly:

"We'll take the five-o'clock train east together. Meanwhile you're going to spend the day with me."

The mere sound of my own voice saying this so emphatically encouraged me, and I think it impressed her too; at any rate, she submitted – at least temporarily – and came along without protest while I bought my ticket.

When I start to piece together the fragments of that day a sort of confusion begins, as if my memory didn't want to yield up any of it, or my consciousness let any of it pass through. There was a bright, fierce morning during which we rode about in a taxicab and went to a department store where Ellen said she wanted to buy something and then tried to slip away from me by a back way. I had the feeling, for an hour, that someone was following us along Lake Shore Drive in a taxicab, and I would try to catch them by turning quickly or looking suddenly into the chauffeur's mirror; but I could find no one, and when I turned back I could see that Ellen's face was contorted with mirthless, unnatural laughter.

All morning there was a raw, bleak wind off the lake, but when we went to the Blackstone for lunch a light snow came down past the windows and we talked almost naturally about our friends, and about casual things. Suddenly her tone changed; she grew serious and looked me in the eye, straight and sincere.

"Eddie, you're the oldest friend I have," she said, "and you oughtn't to find it too hard to trust me. If I promise you faithfully on my word of honour to catch that five-o'clock train, will you let me alone a few hours this afternoon?"

"Why?"

"Well" – she hesitated and hung her head a little – "I guess everybody has a right to say… goodbye."

"You want to say goodbye to that—"

"Yes, yes," she said hastily. "Just a few hours, Eddie, and I promise faithfully that I'll be on that train."

"Well, I suppose no great harm could be done in two hours. If you really want to say goodbye…"

I looked up suddenly, and surprised a look of such tense cunning in her face that I winced before it. Her lip was curled up and her eyes were slits again; there wasn't the faintest touch of fairness and sincerity in her whole face.

We argued. The argument was vague on her part and somewhat hard and reticent on mine. I wasn't going to be cajoled again into any weakness or be infected with any – and there was a contagion of evil

45

in the air. She kept trying to imply, without any convincing evidence to bring forward, that everything was all right. Yet she was too full of the thing itself – whatever it was – to build up a real story, and she wanted to catch at any credulous and acquiescent train of thought that might start in my head, and work that for all it was worth. After every reassuring suggestion she threw out, she stared at me eagerly, as if she hoped I'd launch into a comfortable moral lecture with the customary sweet at the end – which in this case would be her liberty. But I was wearing her away a little. Two or three times it needed just a touch of pressure to bring her to the point of tears – which, of course, was what I wanted – but I couldn't seem to manage it. Almost I had her – almost possessed her interior attention – then she would slip away.

I bullied her remorselessly into a taxi about four o'clock and started for the station. The wind was raw again, with a sting of snow in it, and the people in the streets, waiting for buses and streetcars too small to take them all in, looked cold and disturbed and unhappy. I tried to think how lucky we were to be comfortably off and taken care of, but all the warm, respectable world I had been part of yesterday had dropped away from me. There was something we carried with us now that was the enemy and the opposite of all that; it was in the cabs beside us, the streets we passed through. With a touch of panic, I wondered if I wasn't slipping almost imperceptibly into Ellen's attitude of mind. The column of passengers waiting to go aboard the train were as remote from me as people from another world, but it was I that was drifting away and leaving them behind.

My lower was in the same car with her compartment. It was an old-fashioned car, its lights somewhat dim, its carpets and upholstery full of the dust of another generation. There were half a dozen other travellers, but they made no special impression on me, except that they shared the unreality that I was beginning to feel everywhere around me. We went into Ellen's compartment, shut the door and sat down.

Suddenly I put my arms around her and drew her over to me, just as tenderly as I knew how – as if she were a little girl – as she was. She resisted a little, but after a moment she submitted and lay tense and rigid in my arms.

"Ellen," I said helplessly, "you asked me to trust you. You have much more reason to trust me. Wouldn't it help to get rid of all this, if you told me a little?"

"I can't," she said, very low – "I mean, there's nothing to tell."

"You met this man on the train coming home and you fell in love with him, isn't that true?"

"I don't know."

"Tell me, Ellen. You fell in love with him?"

"I don't know. Please let me alone."

"Call it anything you want," I went on, "he has some sort of hold over you. He's trying to use you; he's trying to get something from you. He's not in love with you."

"What does that matter?" she said in a weak voice.

"It does matter. Instead of trying to fight this… this thing… you're trying to fight me. And I love you, Ellen. Do you hear? I'm telling you all of a sudden, but it isn't new with me. I love you."

She looked at me with a sneer on her gentle face; it was an expression I had seen on men who were tight and didn't want to be taken home. But it was human. I was reaching her, faintly and from far away, but more than before.

"Ellen, I want you to answer me one question. Is he going to be on this train?"

She hesitated; then, an instant too late, she shook her head.

"Be careful, Ellen. Now I'm going to ask you one thing more, and I wish you'd try very hard to answer. Coming west, when did this man get on the train?"

"I don't know," she said with an effort.

Just at that moment I became aware, with the unquestionable knowledge reserved for facts, that he was just outside the door. She knew it too;

the blood left her face and that expression of low-animal perspicacity came creeping back. I lowered my face into my hands and tried to think.

We must have sat there, with scarcely a word, for well over an hour. I was conscious that the lights of Chicago, then of Englewood and of endless suburbs, were moving by, and then there were no more lights and we were out on the dark flatness of Illinois. The train seemed to draw in upon itself; it took on the air of being alone. The porter knocked at the door and asked if he could make up the berth, but I said no and he went away.

After a while I convinced myself that the struggle inevitably coming wasn't beyond what remained of my sanity, my faith in the essential all-rightness of things and people. That this person's purpose was what we call "criminal" I took for granted, but there was no need of ascribing to him an intelligence that belonged to a higher plane of human, or inhuman, endeavour. It was still as a man that I considered him, and tried to get at his essence, his self-interest – what took the place in him of a comprehensible heart – but I suppose I more than half knew what I would find when I opened the door.

When I stood up Ellen didn't seem to see me at all. She was hunched into the corner staring straight ahead with a sort of film over her eyes, as if she were in a state of suspended animation of body and mind. I lifted her and put two pillows under her head and threw my fur coat over her knees. Then I knelt beside her and kissed her two hands, opened the door and went out into the hall.

I closed the door behind me and stood with my back against it for a minute. The car was dark save for the corridor lights at each end. There was no sound except the groaning of the couplers, the even click-a-click of the rails and someone's loud sleeping breath farther down the car. I became aware after a moment that the figure of a man was standing by the water cooler just outside the men's smoking room, his derby hat on his head, his coat collar turned up around his neck as if he were cold, his hands in his coat pockets. When I saw him, he turned and went into the smoking room, and I followed. He was sitting in the far corner of the long leather bench; I took the single armchair beside the door.

As I went in I nodded to him and he acknowledged my presence with one of those terrible soundless laughs of his. But this time it was prolonged, it seemed to go on for ever and, mostly to cut it short, I asked: "Where are you from?" in a voice I tried to make casual.

He stopped laughing and looked at me narrowly, wondering what my game was. When he decided to answer, his voice was muffled as though he were speaking through a silk scarf, and it seemed to come from a long way off.

"I'm from St Paul, Jack."

"Been making a trip home?"

He nodded. Then he took a long breath and spoke in a hard, menacing voice:

"You better get off at Fort Wayne, Jack."

He was dead. He was dead as hell – he had been dead all along, but what force had flowed through him, like blood in his veins, out to St Paul and back, was leaving him now. A new outline – the outline of him dead – was coming through the palpable figure that had knocked down Joe Jelke.

He spoke again, with a sort of jerking effort:

"You get off at Fort Wayne, Jack, or I'm going to wipe you out." He moved his hand in his coat pocket and showed me the outline of a revolver.

I shook my head. "You can't touch me," I answered. "You see, I know." His terrible eyes shifted over me quickly, trying to determine whether or not I did know. Then he gave a snarl and made as though he were going to jump to his feet.

"You climb off here or else I'm going to get you, Jack!" he cried hoarsely. The train was slowing up for Fort Wayne and his voice rang loud in the comparative quiet, but he didn't move from his chair – he was too weak, I think – and we sat staring at each other while workmen passed up and down outside the window banging the brakes and wheels, and the engine gave out loud mournful pants up ahead. No one got into our car. After a while the porter closed the vestibule door and passed back along the corridor, and we slid out of the murky yellow station light and into the long darkness.

What I remember next must have extended over a space of five or six hours, though it comes back to me as something without any existence in time – something that might have taken five minutes or a year. There began a slow, calculated assault on me, wordless and terrible. I felt what I can only call a strangeness stealing over me – akin to the strangeness I had felt all afternoon, but deeper and more intensified. It was like nothing so much as the sensation of drifting away, and I gripped the arms of the chair convulsively, as if to hang on to a piece in the living world. Sometimes I felt myself going out with a rush. There would be almost a warm relief about it, a sense of not caring; then, with a violent wrench of the will, I'd pull myself back into the room.

Suddenly I realized that from a while back I had stopped hating him, stopped feeling violently alien to him, and with the realization I went cold and sweat broke out all over my head. He was getting around my abhorrence, as he had got around Ellen coming west on the train; and it was just that strength he drew from preying on people that had brought him up to the point of concrete violence in St Paul, and that, fading and flickering out, still kept him fighting now.

He must have seen that faltering in my heart, for he spoke at once, in a low, even, almost gentle voice: "You better go now."

"Oh, I'm not going," I forced myself to say.

"Suit yourself, Jack."

He was my friend, he implied. He knew how it was with me and he wanted to help. He pitied me. I'd better go away before it was too late. The rhythm of his attack was soothing as a song: I'd better go away – *and let him get at Ellen*. With a little cry I sat bolt upright.

"What do you want of this girl?" I said, my voice shaking. "To make a sort of walking hell of her."

His glance held a quality of dumb surprise, as if I were punishing an animal for a fault of which he was not conscious. For an instant I faltered; then I went on blindly:

"You've lost her; she's put her trust in me."

His countenance went suddenly black with evil, and he cried: "You're a liar!" in a voice that was like cold hands.

"She trusts me," I said. "You can't touch her. She's safe!"

He controlled himself. His face grew bland, and I felt that curious weakness and indifference begin again inside me. What was the use of all this? What was the use?

"You haven't got much time left," I forced myself to say, and then, in a flash of intuition, I jumped at the truth. "You died, or you were killed, not far from here!" Then I saw what I had not seen before – that his forehead was drilled with a small round hole like a larger picture nail leaves when it's pulled from a plaster wall. "And now you're sinking. You've only got a few hours. The trip home is over!"

His face contorted, lost all semblance of humanity, living or dead. Simultaneously the room was full of cold air, and with a noise that was something between a paroxysm of coughing and a burst of horrible laughter, he was on his feet, reeking of shame and blasphemy.

"Come and look!" he cried. "I'll show you..."

He took a step towards me, then another, and it was exactly as if a door stood open behind him, a door yawning out to an inconceivable abyss of darkness and corruption. There was a scream of mortal agony, from him or from somewhere behind, and abruptly the strength went out of him in a long husky sigh and he wilted to the floor...

How long I sat there, dazed with terror and exhaustion, I don't know. The next thing I remember is the sleepy porter shining shoes across the room from me, and outside the window the steel fires of Pittsburgh breaking the flat perspective of the night. There was something extended on the bench also – something too faint for a man, too heavy for a shadow. Even as I perceived it it faded off and away.

Some minutes later I opened the door of Ellen's compartment. She was asleep where I had left her. Her lovely cheeks were white and wan, but she lay naturally – her hands relaxed and her breathing regular and clear. What had possessed her had gone out of her, leaving her exhausted but her own dear self again.

I made her a little more comfortable, tucked a blanket around her, extinguished the light and went out.

3

WHEN I CAME HOME for Easter vacation, almost my first act was to go down to the billiard parlour near Seven Corners. The man at the cash register quite naturally didn't remember my hurried visit of three months before.

"I'm trying to locate a certain party who, I think, came here a lot some time ago."

I described the man rather accurately, and when I had finished, the cashier called to a little jockey-like fellow who was sitting near with an air of having something very important to do that he couldn't quite remember.

"Hey, Shorty, talk to this guy, will you? I think he's looking for Joe Varland."

The little man gave me a tribal look of suspicion. I went and sat near him.

"Joe Varland's dead, fella," he said grudgingly. "He died last winter."

I described him again – his overcoat, his laugh, the habitual expression of his eyes.

"That's Joe Varland you're looking for all right, but he's dead."

"I want to find out something about him."

"What you want to find out?"

"What did he do, for instance?"

"How should I know?"

"Look here! I'm not a policeman. I just want some kind of information about his habits. He's dead now and it can't hurt him. And it won't go beyond me."

"Well" – he hesitated, looking me over – "he was a great one for travelling. He got in a row in the station in Pittsburgh and a dick got him."

I nodded. Broken pieces of the puzzle began to assemble in my head.

"Why was he a lot on trains?"

"How should I know, fella?"

"If you can use ten dollars, I'd like to know anything you may have heard on the subject."

"Well," said Shorty reluctantly, "all I know is they used to say he worked the trains."

"Worked the trains?"

"He had some racket of his own he'd never loosen up about. He used to work the girls travelling alone on the trains. Nobody ever knew much about it – he was a pretty smooth guy – but sometimes he'd turn up here with a lot of dough and he let 'em know it was the janes he got it off of."

I thanked him and gave him the ten dollars and went out, very thoughtful, without mentioning that part of Joe Varland had made a last trip home.

Ellen wasn't West for Easter, and even if she had been I wouldn't have gone to her with the information, either – at least I've seen her almost every day this summer and we've managed to talk about everything else. Sometimes, though, she gets silent about nothing and wants to be very close to me, and I know what's in her mind.

Of course she's coming out this fall, and I have two more years at New Haven; still, things don't look so impossible as they did a few months ago. She belongs to me in a way – even if I lose her she belongs to me. Who knows? Anyhow, I'll always be there.

The Bowl

1

THERE WAS A MAN IN MY CLASS at Princeton who never went to football games. He spent his Saturday afternoons delving for minutiae about Greek athletics and the somewhat fixed battles between Christians and wild beasts under the Antonines.* Lately – several years out of college – he has discovered football players and is making etchings of them in the manner of the late George Bellows.* But he was once unresponsive to the very spectacle at his door, and I suspect the originality of his judgements on what is beautiful, what is remarkable and what is fun.

I revelled in football, as audience, amateur statistician and foiled participant – for I had played in prep school, and once there was a headline in the school newspaper: "Deering and Mullins Star Against Taft in Stiff Game Saturday". When I came in to lunch after the battle the school stood up and clapped and the visiting coach shook hands with me and prophesied – incorrectly – that I was going to be heard from. The episode is laid away in the most pleasant lavender of my past. That year I grew very tall and thin, and when at Princeton the following fall I looked anxiously over the freshman candidates and saw the polite disregard with which they looked back at me, I realized that that particular dream was over. Keene said he might make me into a very fair pole vaulter – and he did – but it was a poor substitute; and my terrible disappointment that I wasn't going to be a great football player was probably the foundation of my friendship with Dolly Harlan. I want to begin

54

this story about Dolly with a little rehashing of the Yale game up at New Haven, sophomore year.

Dolly was started at halfback; this was his first big game. I roomed with him and I had scented something peculiar about his state of mind, so I didn't let him out of the corner of my eye during the whole first half. With field glasses I could see the expression on his face; it was strained and incredulous, as it had been the day of his father's death, and it remained so, long after any nervousness had had time to wear off. I thought he was sick and wondered why Keene didn't see and take him out; it wasn't until later that I learnt what was the matter.

It was the Yale Bowl. The size of it or the enclosed shape of it or the height of the sides had begun to get on Dolly's nerves when the team practised there the day before. In that practice he dropped one or two punts, for almost the first time in his life, and he began thinking it was because of the Bowl.

There is a new disease called agoraphobia – afraid of crowds – and another called siderodromophobia – afraid of railroad travelling – and my friend Doctor Glock, the psychoanalyst, would probably account easily for Dolly's state of mind. But here's what Dolly told me afterwards:

"Yale would punt and I'd look up. The minute I looked up, the sides of that damn pan would seem to go shooting up too. Then when the ball started to come down, the sides began leaning forward and bending over me until I could see all the people on the top seats screaming at me and shaking their fists. At the last minute I couldn't see the ball at all, but only the Bowl; every time it was just luck that I was under it and every time I juggled it in my hands."

To go back to the game. I was in the cheering section with a good seat on the forty-yard line – good, that is, except when a very vague graduate, who had lost his friends and his hat, stood up in front of me at intervals and faltered, "Stob Ted Coy!" under the impression that we were watching a game played a dozen years before. When he realized finally that he was funny he began performing for the gallery and aroused a chorus of whistles and boos until he was dragged unwillingly under the stand.

It was a good game – what is known in college publications as a historic game. A picture of the team that played it now hangs in every barber shop in Princeton, with Captain Gottlieb in the middle wearing a white sweater, to show that they won a championship. Yale had had a poor season, but they had the breaks in the first quarter, which ended 3 to o in their favour.

Between quarters I watched Dolly. He walked around panting and sucking a water bottle and still wearing that strained stunned expression. Afterwards he told me he was saying over and over to himself: "I'll speak to Roper. I'll tell him between halves. I'll tell him I can't go through this any more." Several times already he had felt an almost irresistible impulse to shrug his shoulders and trot off the field, for it was not only this unexpected complex about the Bowl; the truth was that Dolly fiercely and bitterly hated the game.

He hated the long, dull period of training, the element of personal conflict, the demand on his time, the monotony of the routine and the nervous apprehension of disaster just before the end. Sometimes he imagined that all the others detested it as much as he did, and fought down their aversion as he did and carried it around inside them like a cancer that they were afraid to recognize. Sometimes he imagined that a man here and there was about to tear off the mask and say, "Dolly, do you hate this lousy business as much as I do?"

His feeling had begun back at St Regis's School and he had come up to Princeton with the idea that he was through with football for ever. But upperclassmen from St Regis kept stopping him on the campus and asking him how much he weighed, and he was nominated for vice president of our class on the strength of his athletic reputation – and it was autumn, with achievement in the air. He wandered down to freshman practice one afternoon, feeling oddly lost and dissatisfied, and smelt the turf and smelt the thrilling season. In half an hour he was lacing on a pair of borrowed shoes and two weeks later he was captain of the freshman team.

Once committed, he saw that he had made a mistake; he even considered leaving college. For, with his decision to play, Dolly assumed a moral responsibility, personal to him, besides. To lose or to let down, or to be let down, was simply intolerable to him. It offended his Scotch sense of waste. Why sweat blood for an hour with only defeat at the end?

Perhaps the worst of it was that he wasn't really a star player. No team in the country could have spared using him, but he could do no spectacular thing superlatively well, neither run, pass nor kick. He was five feet eleven and weighed a little more than a hundred and sixty; he was a first-rate defensive man, sure in interference, a fair line plunger and a fair punter. He never fumbled and he was never inadequate; his presence, his constant cold sure aggression, had a strong effect on other men. Morally, he captained any team he played on and that was why Roper had spent so much time trying to get length in his kicks all season – he wanted him in the game.

In the second quarter Yale began to crack. It was a mediocre team composed of flashy material, but uncoordinated because of injuries and impending changes in the Yale coaching system. The quarterback, Josh Logan, had been a wonder at Exeter – I could testify to that – where games can be won by the sheer confidence and spirit of a single man. But college teams are too highly organized to respond so simply and boyishly, and they recover less easily from fumbles and errors of judgement behind the line.

So, with nothing to spare, with much grunting and straining, Princeton moved steadily down the field. On the Yale twenty-yard line things suddenly happened. A Princeton pass was intercepted; the Yale man, excited by his own opportunity, dropped the ball, and it bobbed leisurely in the general direction of the Yale goal. Jack Devlin and Dolly Harlan of Princeton and somebody – I forget who – from Yale were all about the same distance from it. What Dolly did in that split second was all instinct; it presented no problem to him. He was a natural athlete and in a crisis his nervous system thought for him. He might have raced the two others for the ball; instead, he took out the Yale man with savage precision while Devlin scooped up the ball and ran ten yards for a touchdown.

This was when the sports writers still saw games through the eyes of Ralph Henry Barbour.* The press box was right behind me, and as Princeton lined up to kick goal I heard the radio man ask:

"Who's Number 22?"

"Harlan."

"Harlan is going to kick goal. Devlin, who made the touchdown, comes from Lawrenceville School. He is twenty years old. The ball went true between the bars."

Between the halves, as Dolly sat shaking with fatigue in the locker room, Little, the back-field coach, came and sat beside him.

"When the ends are right on you, don't be afraid to make a fair catch," Little said. "That big Havemeyer is liable to jar the ball right out of your hands."

Now was the time to say it: "I wish you'd tell Bill…" But the words twisted themselves into a trivial question about the wind. His feeling would have to be explained, gone into, and there wasn't time. His own self seemed less important in this room, redolent with the tired breath, the ultimate effort, the exhaustion of ten other men. He was shamed by a harsh sudden quarrel that broke out between an end and tackle; he resented the former players in the room – especially the graduate captain of two years before, who was a little tight and over-vehement about the referee's favouritism. It seemed terrible to add one more jot to all this strain and annoyance. But he might have come out with it all the same if Little hadn't kept saying in a low voice: "What a takeout, Dolly! What a beautiful takeout!" and if Little's hand hadn't rested there, patting his shoulder.

2

I N THE THIRD QUARTER Joe Dougherty kicked an easy field goal from the twenty-yard line and we felt safe, until towards twilight a series of desperate forward passes brought Yale close to a score. But Josh Logan had exhausted his personality in sheer bravado, and he was outguessed by the defence at the last. As the substitutes came running in, Princeton began a last march down the field. Then abruptly it was over and the crowd poured from the stands, and Gottlieb, grabbing the ball, leapt up in the air. For a while everything was confused and crazy and happy; I saw some freshmen try to carry Dolly, but they were shy and he got away.

We all felt a great personal elation. We hadn't beaten Yale for three years and now everything was going to be all right. It meant a good winter at college, something pleasant and slick to think back upon in the damp cold days after Christmas, when a bleak futility settles over a university town. Down on the field, an improvised and uproarious team ran through plays with a derby, until the snake dance rolled over them and blotted them out. Outside the Bowl, I saw two abysmally gloomy and disgusted Yale men get into a waiting taxi and in a tone of final abnegation tell the driver, "New York." You couldn't find Yale men; in the manner of the vanquished, they had absolutely melted away.

I begin Dolly's story with my memories of this game because that evening the girl walked into it. She was a friend of Josephine Pickman's, and the four of us were going to drive up to the Midnight Frolic in New York. When I suggested to him that he'd be too tired he laughed drily – he'd have gone anywhere that night to get the feel and rhythm of football out of his head. He walked into the hall of Josephine's house at half-past six, looking as if he'd spent the day in the barber shop save for a small and fetching strip of court plaster over one eye. He was one of the handsomest men I ever knew, anyhow; he appeared tall and slender in street clothes, his hair was dark, his eyes big and sensitive and dark, his nose aquiline and, like all his features, some-how romantic. It didn't occur to me then, but I suppose he was pretty vain – not conceited, but vain – for he always dressed in brown or soft light grey, with black ties, and people don't match themselves so suc-cessfully by accident.

He was smiling a little to himself as he came in. He shook my hand buoyantly and said, "Why, what a surprise to meet you here, Mr Deering," in a kidding way. Then he saw the two girls through the long hall, one dark and shining, like himself, and one with gold hair that was foaming and frothing in the firelight, and said in the happiest voice I've ever heard, "Which one is mine?"

"Either you want, I guess."

"Seriously, which is Pickman?"

"She's light."

"Then the other one belongs to me. Isn't that the idea?"

"I think I'd better warn them about the state you're in."

Miss Thorne, small, flushed and lovely, stood beside the fire. Dolly went right up to her.

"You're mine," he said. "You belong to me."

She looked at him coolly, making up her mind; suddenly she liked him and smiled. But Dolly wasn't satisfied. He wanted to do something incredibly silly or startling to express his untold jubilation that he was free.

"I love you," he said. He took her hand, his brown velvet eyes regard-ing her tenderly, unseeingly, convincingly. "I love you."

For a moment the corners of her lips fell as if in dismay that she had met someone stronger, more confident, more challenging than herself. Then, as she drew herself together visibly, he dropped her hand and the little scene in which he had expended the tension of the afternoon was over.

It was a bright cold November night and the rush of air past the open car brought a vague excitement, a sense that we were hurrying at top speed towards a brilliant destiny. The roads were packed with cars that came to long inexplicable halts while police, blinded by the lights, walked up and down the line giving obscure commands. Before we had been gone an hour New York began to be a distant hazy glow against the sky.

Miss Thorne, Josephine told me, was from Washington, and had just come down from a visit in Boston.

"For the game?" I said.

"No, she didn't go to the game."

"That's too bad. If you'd let me know I could have picked up a seat—"

"She wouldn't have gone. Vienna never goes to games."

I remembered now that she hadn't even murmured the conventional congratulations to Dolly.

"She hates football. Her brother was killed in a prep-school game last year. I wouldn't have brought her tonight, but when we got home from the game I saw she'd been sitting there holding a book open at the same page all afternoon. You see, he was this wonderful kid and her family saw it happen and naturally never got over it."

"But does she mind being with Dolly?"

"Of course not. She just ignores football. If anyone mentions it she simply changes the subject."

I was glad that it was Dolly and not, say, Jack Devlin who was sitting back there with her. And I felt rather sorry for Dolly. However strongly he felt about the game, he must have waited for some acknowledgement that his effort had existed.

He was probably giving her credit for a subtle consideration, yet, as the images of the afternoon flashed into his mind he might have welcomed a compliment to which he could respond "What nonsense!" Neglected entirely, the images would become insistent and obtrusive.

I turned around and was somewhat startled to find that Miss Thorne was in Dolly's arms; I turned quickly back and decided to let them take care of themselves.

As we waited for a traffic light on upper Broadway, I saw a sporting extra headlined with the score of the game. The green sheet was more real than the afternoon itself – succinct, condensed and clear:

PRINCETON CONQUERS YALE 10–3
SEVENTY THOUSAND WATCH TIGER TRIM BULLDOG

DEVLIN SCORES ON YALE FUMBLE

There it was – not like the afternoon, muddled, uncertain, patchy and scrappy to the end, but nicely mounted now in the setting of the past:

PRINCETON, 10; YALE, 3

Achievement was a curious thing, I thought. Dolly was largely responsible for that. I wondered if all things that screamed in the headlines were simply arbitrary accents. As if people should ask, "What does it look like?"

"It looks most like a cat."

"Well, then, let's call it a cat."

My mind, brightened by the lights and the cheerful tumult, suddenly grasped the fact that all achievement was a placing of emphasis – a moulding of the confusion of life into form.

Josephine stopped in front of the New Amsterdam Theater, where her chauffeur met us and took the car. We were early, but a small buzz of excitement went up from the undergraduates waiting in the lobby – "There's Dolly Harlan" – and as we moved towards the elevator several acquaintances came up to shake his hand. Apparently oblivious to these ceremonies, Miss Thorne caught my eye and smiled. I looked at her with curiosity; Josephine had imparted the rather surprising information that she was just sixteen years old. I suppose my return smile was rather patronizing, but instantly I realized that the fact could not be imposed on. In spite of all the warmth and delicacy of her face, the figure that somehow reminded me of an exquisite, romanticized little ballerina, there was a quality in her that was as hard as steel. She had been brought up in Rome, Vienna and Madrid, with flashes of Washington; her father was one of those charming American diplomats who, with fine obstinacy, try to recreate the Old World in their children by making their education rather more royal than that of princes. Miss Thorne was sophisticated. In spite of all the abandon of American young people, sophistication is still a Continental monopoly.

We walked in upon a number in which a dozen chorus girls in orange and black were racing wooden horses against another dozen dressed in Yale blue. When the lights went on, Dolly was recognized and some Princeton students set up a clatter of approval with the little wooden hammers given out for applause; he moved his chair unostentatiously into a shadow.

Almost immediately a flushed and very miserable young man appeared beside our table. In better form he would have been extremely prepossessing; indeed, he flashed a charming and dazzling smile at Dolly, as if requesting his permission to speak to Miss Thorne.

Then he said, "I thought you weren't coming to New York tonight."

"Hello, Carl." She looked up at him coolly.

"Hello, Vienna. That's just it: 'Hello Vienna – Hello Carl.' But why? I thought you weren't coming to New York tonight."

Miss Thorne made no move to introduce the man, but we were conscious of his somewhat raised voice.

"I thought you promised me you weren't coming."

"I didn't expect to, child. I just left Boston this morning."

"And who did you meet in Boston – the fascinating Tunti?" he demanded.

"I didn't meet anyone, child."

"Oh, yes, you did! You met the fascinating Tunti and you discussed living on the Riviera." She didn't answer. "Why are you so dishonest, Vienna?" he went on. "Why did you tell me on the phone—"

"I am not going to be lectured," she said, her tone changing suddenly. "I told you if you took another drink I was through with you. I'm a person of my word and I'd be enormously happy if you went away."

"Vienna!" he cried in a sinking, trembling voice.

At this point I got up and danced with Josephine. When we came back there were people at the table – the men to whom we were to hand over Josephine and Miss Thorne, for I had allowed for Dolly being tired, and several others. One of them was Al Ratoni, the composer, who, it appeared, had been entertained at the embassy in Madrid. Dolly Harlan had drawn his chair aside and was watching the dancers. Just as the lights went down for a new number a man came up out of the darkness and, leaning over Miss Thorne, whispered in her ear. She started and made a motion to rise, but he put his hand on her shoulder and forced her down. They began to talk together in low excited voices.

The tables were packed close at the old Frolic. There was a man rejoining the party next to us and I couldn't help hearing what he said:

"A young fellow just tried to kill himself down in the washroom. He shot himself through the shoulder, but they got the pistol away before..." A minute later his voice again: "Carl Sanderson, they said."

When the number was over I looked around. Vienna Thorne was staring very rigidly at Miss Lillian Lorraine, who was rising towards the ceiling as an enormous telephone doll. The man who had leant over Vienna was gone and the others were obliviously unaware that anything had happened. I turned to Dolly and suggested that he and I had better go, and after a glance at Vienna, in which reluctance, weariness and then resignation were mingled, he consented. On the way to the hotel I told Dolly what had happened.

"Just some souse," he remarked after a moment's fatigued consideration. "He probably tried to miss himself and get a little sympathy. I suppose those are the sort of things a really attractive girl is up against all the time."

This wasn't my attitude. I could see that mussed white shirt front with very young blood pumping over it, but I didn't argue, and after a while Dolly said, "I suppose that sounds brutal, but it seems a little soft and weak, doesn't it? Perhaps that's just the way I feel tonight."

When Dolly undressed I saw that he was a mass of bruises, but he assured me that none of them would keep him awake. Then I told him why Miss Thorne hadn't mentioned the game and he woke up suddenly; the familiar glitter came back into his eyes.

"So that was it! I wondered. I thought maybe you'd told her not to say anything about it."

Later, when the lights had been out half an hour, he suddenly said "I see" in a loud clear voice. I don't know whether he was awake or asleep.

3

I've put down as well as I can everything I can remember about the first meeting between Dolly and Miss Vienna Thorne. Reading it over, it sounds casual and insignificant, but the evening lay in the shadow of the game and all that happened seemed like that. Vienna went back to Europe almost immediately and for fifteen months passed out of Dolly's life.

It was a good year – it still rings true in my memory as a good year. Sophomore year is the most dramatic at Princeton, just as junior year is at Yale. It's not only the elections to the upper-class clubs but also everyone's destiny begins to work itself out. You can tell pretty well who's going to come through, not only by their immediate success but by the way they survive failure. Life was very full for me. I made the board of the *Princetonian*, and our house burned down out in Dayton, and I had a silly half-hour fist fight in the gymnasium with a man who later became one of my closest friends, and in March Dolly and I joined the upper-class club we'd always wanted to be in. I fell in love too, but it would be an irrelevancy to tell about that here.

April came and the first real Princeton weather, the lazy green-and-gold afternoons and the bright thrilling nights haunted with the hour of senior singing. I was happy, and Dolly would have been happy except for the approach of another football season. He was playing baseball, which excused him from spring practice, but the bands were beginning to play faintly in the distance. They rose to concert pitch during the summer, when he had to answer the question "Are you going back early for football?" a dozen times a day. On the fifteenth of September he was down in the dust and heat of late-summer Princeton, crawling over the ground on all fours, trotting through the old routine and turning himself into just the sort of specimen that I'd have given ten years of my life to be.

From first to last, he hated it, and never let down for a minute. He went into the Yale game that fall weighing a hundred and fifty-three pounds, though that wasn't the weight printed in the paper, and he and Joe McDonald were the only men who played all through that disastrous game. He could have been captain by lifting his finger – but that involves some stuff that I know confidentially and can't tell. His only horror was that by some chance he'd have to accept it. Two seasons! He didn't even talk about it now. He left the room or the club when the conversation veered around to football. He stopped announcing to me that he "wasn't going through that business any more". This time it took the Christmas holidays to drive that unhappy look from his eyes.

Then at the New Year Miss Vienna Thorne came home from Madrid and in February a man named Case brought her down to the Senior Prom.

4

S HE WAS EVEN PRETTIER than she had been before, softer, externally at least, and a tremendous success. People passing her on the street jerked their heads quickly to look at her – a frightened look, as if they realized that they had almost missed something. She was temporarily tired of European men, she told me, letting me gather that there had been some sort of unfortunate love affair. She was coming out in Washington next fall.

Vienna and Dolly. She disappeared with him for two hours the night of the club dances, and Harold Case was in despair. When they walked in again at midnight I thought they were the handsomest pair I saw. They were both shining with that peculiar luminosity that dark people sometimes have. Harold Case took one look at them and went proudly home.

Vienna came back a week later, solely to see Dolly. Late that evening I had occasion to go up to the deserted club for a book and they called me from the rear terrace, which opens out to the ghostly stadium and to an unpeopled sweep of night. It was an hour of thaw, with spring voices in the warm wind, and wherever there was light enough you could see drops glistening and falling. You could feel the cold melting out of the stars and the bare trees and shrubbery towards Stony Brook turning lush in the darkness.

They were sitting together on a wicker bench, full of themselves and romantic and happy.

"We had to tell someone about it," they said.

"Now can I go?"

"No, Jeff," they insisted, "stay here and envy us. We're in the stage where we want someone to envy us. Do you think we're a good match?"

What could I say?

"Dolly's going to finish at Princeton next year," Vienna went on, "but we're going to announce it after the season in Washington in the autumn."

I was vaguely relieved to find that it was going to be a long engagement.

"I approve of you, Jeff," Vienna said.

"I want Dolly to have more friends like you. You're stimulating for him – you have ideas. I told Dolly he could probably find others like you if he looked around his class."

Dolly and I both felt a little uncomfortable.

"She doesn't want me to be a Babbitt,"* he said lightly.

"Dolly's perfect," asserted Vienna. "He's the most beautiful thing that ever lived, and you'll find I'm very good for him, Jeff. Already I've helped him make up his mind about one important thing." I guessed what was coming. "He's going to speak a little piece if they bother him about playing football next autumn, aren't you, child?"

"Oh, they won't bother me," said Dolly uncomfortably. "It isn't like that…"

"Well, they'll try to bully you into it, morally."

"Oh, no," he objected. "It isn't like that. Don't let's talk about it now, Vienna. It's such a swell night."

Such a swell night! When I think of my own love passages at Princeton, I always summon up that night of Dolly's, as if it had been I and not he who sat there with youth and hope and beauty in his arms.

Dolly's mother took a place on Ram's Point, Long Island, for the summer, and late in August I went East to visit him. Vienna had been there a week when I arrived, and my impressions were: first, that he was very much in love; and, second, that it was Vienna's party. All sorts of curious people used to drop in to see Vienna. I wouldn't mind them now – I'm more sophisticated – but then they seemed rather a blot on the summer. They were all slightly famous in one way or another, and it was up to you to find out how. There was a lot of talk, and especially there was much discussion of Vienna's personality. Whenever I was alone with any of the other guests we discussed Vienna's sparkling personality. They thought I was dull, and most of them thought Dolly was dull. He was better in his line than any of them were in theirs, but his was the only specialty that wasn't mentioned. Still, I felt vaguely that I was being improved and I boasted about knowing most of those people in the ensuing year, and was annoyed when people failed to recognize their names.

The day before I left, Dolly turned his ankle playing tennis, and afterwards he joked about it to me rather sombrely.

"If I'd only broken it things would be so much easier. Just a quarter of an inch more bend and one of the bones would have snapped. By the way, look here."

He tossed me a letter. It was a request that he report at Princeton for practice on September fifteenth and that meanwhile he begin getting himself in good condition.

"You're not going to play this fall?"

He shook his head.

"No. I'm not a child any more. I've played for two years and I want this year free. If I went through it again it'd be a piece of moral cowardice."

"I'm not arguing, but… would you have taken this stand if it hadn't been for Vienna?"

"Of course I would. If I let myself be bullied into it I'd never be able to look myself in the face again."

Two weeks later I got the following letter:

DEAR JEFF:

When you read this you'll be somewhat surprised. I have, actually, this time, broken my ankle playing tennis. I can't even walk with crutches at present; it's on a chair in front of me swollen up and wrapped up as big as a house as I write. No one, not even Vienna, knows about our conversation on the same subject last summer and so let us both absolutely forget it. One thing, though – an ankle is a darn hard thing to break, though I never knew it before.

I feel happier than I have for years – no early-season practice, no sweat and suffer, a little discomfort and inconvenience, but free. I feel as if I've outwitted a whole lot of people, and it's nobody's business but that of your

Machiavellian (sic) friend,

DOLLY

PS: You might as well tear up this letter.

It didn't sound like Dolly at all.

5

ONCE DOWN AT PRINCETON I asked Frank Kane – who sells sporting goods on Nassau Street and can tell you offhand the name of the scrub quarterback in 1901 – what was the matter with Bob Tatnall's team senior year.

"Injuries and tough luck," he said. "They wouldn't sweat after the hard games. Take Joe McDonald, for instance, All-American tackle the year before; he was slow and stale, and he knew it and didn't care. It's a wonder Bill got that outfit through the season at all."

I sat in the stands with Dolly and watched them beat Lehigh 3-0 and tie Bucknell by a fluke. The next week we were trimmed 14-0 by Notre Dame. On the day of the Notre Dame game Dolly was in Washington with Vienna, but he was awfully curious about it when he came back next day. He had all the sporting pages of all the papers and he sat reading them and shaking his head. Then he stuffed them suddenly into the waste-paper basket.

"This college is football-crazy," he announced. "Do you know that English teams don't even train for sports?"

I didn't enjoy Dolly so much in those days. It was curious to see him with nothing to do. For the first time in his life he hung around – around the room, around the club, around casual groups – he who had always been going somewhere with dynamic indolence. His passage along a walk had once created groups – groups of classmates who wanted to walk with him, of underclassmen who followed with their eyes a moving shrine. He became democratic, he mixed around, and it was somehow not appropriate. He explained that he wanted to know more men in his class.

But people want their idols a little above them, and Dolly had been a sort of private and special idol. He began to hate to be alone, and that, of course, was most apparent to me. If I got up to go out and he didn't happen to be writing a letter to Vienna, he'd ask "Where are you going?" in a rather alarmed way and make an excuse to limp along with me.

"Are you glad you did it, Dolly?" I asked him suddenly one day.

He looked at me with reproach behind the defiance in his eyes.

"Of course I'm glad."

"I wish you were in that back field, all the same."

"It wouldn't matter a bit. This year's game's in the Bowl. I'd probably be dropping kicks for them."

The week of the Navy game he suddenly began going to all the practices. He worried; that terrible sense of responsibility was at work. Once he had hated the mention of football; now he thought and talked of nothing else. The night before the Navy game I woke up several times to find the lights burning brightly in his room.

We lost 7 to 3 on Navy's last-minute forward pass over Devlin's head. After the first half Dolly left the stands and sat down with the players on the field. When he joined me afterwards his face was smudgy and dirty as if he had been crying.

The game was in Baltimore that year. Dolly and I were going to spend the night in Washington with Vienna, who was giving a dance. We rode over there in an atmosphere of sullen gloom and it was all I could do to keep him from snapping out at two naval officers who were holding an exultant post-mortem in the seat behind.

The dance was what Vienna called her second coming-out party. She was having only the people she liked this time, and these turned out to be chiefly importations from New York. The musicians, the playwrights, the vague supernumeraries of the arts, who had dropped in at Dolly's house on Ram's Point, were here in force. But Dolly, relieved of his obligations as host, made no clumsy attempt to talk their language that night. He stood moodily against the wall with some of that old air of superiority that had first made me want to know him. Afterwards, on my way to bed, I passed Vienna's sitting room and she called me to come in. She and Dolly, both a little white, were sitting across the room from each other and there was tensity in the air.

"Sit down, Jeff," said Vienna wearily. "I want you to witness the collapse of a man into a schoolboy." I sat down reluctantly. "Dolly's changed his mind," she said. "He prefers football to me."

"That's not it," said Dolly stubbornly.

"I don't see the point," I objected. "Dolly can't possibly play."

"But he thinks he can. Jeff, just in case you imagine I'm being pig-headed about it, I want to tell you a story. Three years ago, when we first came back to the United States, Father put my young brother in school. One afternoon we all went out to see him play football. Just after the game started he was hurt, but Father said, 'It's all right. He'll be up in a minute. It happens all the time.' But, Jeff, he never got up. He lay there, and finally they carried him off the field and put a blanket over him. Just as we got to him he died."

She looked from one to the other of us and began to sob convulsively. Dolly went over, frowning, and put his arm around her shoulder.

"Oh, Dolly," she cried, "won't you do this for me – just this one little thing for me?"

He shook his head miserably. "I tried, but I can't," he said.

"It's my stuff, don't you understand, Vienna? People have got to do their stuff."

Vienna had risen and was powdering her tears at a mirror; now she flashed around angrily.

"Then I've been labouring under a misapprehension when I supposed you felt about it much as I did."

"Let's not go over all that. I'm tired of talking, Vienna; I'm tired of my own voice. It seems to me that no one I know does anything but talk any more."

"Thanks. I suppose that's meant for me."

"It seems to me your friends talk a great deal. I've never heard so much jabber as I've listened to tonight. Is the idea of actually doing anything repulsive to you, Vienna?"

"It depends upon whether it's worth doing."

"Well, this is worth doing – to me."

"I know your trouble, Dolly," she said bitterly. "You're weak and you want to be admired. This year you haven't had a lot of little boys following you around as if you were Jack Dempsey, and it almost breaks your heart. You want to get out in front of them all and make a show of yourself and hear the applause."

He laughed shortly. "If that's your idea of how a football player feels—"

"Have you made up your mind to play?" she interrupted.

"If I'm any use to them – yes."

"Then I think we're both wasting our time."

Her expression was ruthless, but Dolly refused to see that she was in earnest. When I got away he was still trying to make her "be rational", and next day on the train he said that Vienna had been "a little nervous". He was deeply in love with her, and he didn't dare think of losing her; but he was still in the grip of the sudden emotion that had decided him to play, and his confusion and exhaustion of mind made him believe vainly that everything was going to be all right. But I had seen that look on Vienna's face the night she talked with Mr Carl Sanderson at the Frolic two years before.

Dolly didn't get off the train at Princeton Junction, but continued on to New York. He went to two orthopaedic specialists and one of them arranged a bandage braced with a whole little fence of whalebones that he was to wear day and night. The probabilities were that it would snap at the first brisk encounter, but he could run on it and stand on it when he kicked. He was out on University Field in uniform the following afternoon.

His appearance was a small sensation. I was sitting in the stands watching practice with Harold Case and young Daisy Cary. She was just beginning to be famous then, and I don't know whether she or Dolly attracted the most attention. In those times it was still rather daring to bring down a moving-picture actress; if that same young lady went to Princeton today she would probably be met at the station with a band.

Dolly limped around and everyone said, "He's limping!" He got under a punt and everyone said, "He did that pretty well!" The first team were laid off after the hard Navy game and everyone watched Dolly all afternoon. After practice I caught his eye and he came over and shook hands. Daisy asked him if he'd like to be in a football picture she was going to make. It was only conversation, but he looked at me with a dry smile.

When he came back to the room his ankle was swollen up as big as a stovepipe, and next day he and Keene fixed up an arrangement by which the bandage would be loosened and tightened to fit its varying size. We called it the balloon. The bone was nearly healed, but the little bruised sinews were stretched out of place again every day. He watched the Swarthmore game from the sidelines and the following Monday he was in scrimmage with the second team against the scrubs.

In the afternoons sometimes he wrote to Vienna. His theory was that they were still engaged, but he tried not to worry about it, and I think the very pain that kept him awake at night was good for that. When the season was over he would go and see.

We played Harvard and lost 7 to 3. Jack Devlin's collarbone was broken and he was out for the season, which made it almost sure that Dolly would play. Amid the rumours and fears of mid-November the news aroused a spark of hope in an otherwise morbid undergraduate body – hope all out of proportion to Dolly's condition. He came back to the room the Thursday before the game with his face drawn and tired.

"They're going to start me," he said, "and I'm going to be back for punts. If they only knew—"

"Couldn't you tell Bill how you feel about that?"

He shook his head and I had a sudden suspicion that he was punishing himself for his "accident" last August. He lay silently on the couch while I packed his suitcase for the team train.

The actual day of the game was, as usual, like a dream – unreal with its crowds of friends and relatives and the inessential trappings of a gigantic show. The eleven little men who ran out on the field at last were like bewitched figures in another world, strange and infinitely romantic, blurred by a throbbing mist of people and sound. One aches with them intolerably, trembles with their excitement, but they have no traffic with us now, they are beyond help, consecrated and unreachable – vaguely holy.

The field is rich and green, the preliminaries are over and the teams trickle out into position. Head guards are put on; each man claps his hands and breaks into a lonely little dance. People are still talking around you, arranging themselves, but you have fallen silent and your eye wanders from man to man. There's Jack Whitehead, a senior, at end; Joe McDonald, large and reassuring, at tackle; Toole, a sophomore, at guard; Red Hopman, centre; someone you can't identify at the other guard – Bunker probably – he turns and you see his number – Bunker; Bean Gile, looking unnaturally dignified and significant at the other tackle; Poore, another sophomore at end. Back of them is Wash Sampson at quarter – imagine how he feels! But he runs here and there on light feet, speaking to this man and that, trying to communicate his alertness and his confidence of success. Dolly Harlan stands motionless, his hands on his hips, watching the Yale kicker tee up the ball; near him is Captain Bob Tatnall…

There's the whistle! The line of the Yale team sways ponderously forward from its balance and a split second afterwards comes the sound of the ball. The field streams with running figures and the whole Bowl strains forward as if thrown by the current of an electric chair.

Suppose we fumbled right away.

Tatnall catches it, goes back ten yards, is surrounded and blotted out of sight. Spears goes through centre for three. A short pass, Sampson to Tatnall, is completed, but for no gain. Harlan punts to Devereaux, who is downed in his tracks on the Yale forty-yard line.

Now we'll see what they've got.

It developed immediately that they had a great deal. Using an effective crisscross and a short pass over centre, they carried the ball fifty-four yards to the Princeton six-yard line, where they lost it on a fumble, recovered by Red Hopman. After a trade of punts, they began another push, this time to the fifteen-yard line, where, after four hair-raising forward passes, two of them batted down by Dolly, we got the ball on downs. But Yale was still fresh and strong, and with a third onslaught the weaker Princeton line began to give way. Just after the second quarter began Devereaux took the ball over for a touchdown and the half ended with Yale in possession of the ball on our ten-yard line. Score: Yale, 7; Princeton, 0.

We hadn't a chance. The team was playing above itself, better than it had played all year, but it wasn't enough. Save that it was the Yale game, when anything could happen, anything *had* happened, the atmosphere of gloom would have been deeper than it was, and in the cheering section you could cut it with a knife.

Early in the game Dolly Harlan had fumbled Devereaux's high punt, but recovered without gain; towards the end of the half another kick slipped through his fingers, but he scooped it up, and slipping past the end, went back twelve yards. Between halves he told Roper he couldn't seem to get under the ball, but they kept him there. His own kicks were carrying well and he was essential in the only backfield combination that could hope to score.

After the first play of the game he limped slightly, moving around as little as possible to conceal the fact. But I knew enough about football to see that he was in every play, starting at that rather slow pace of his and finishing with a quick side lunge that almost always took out his man. Not a single Yale forward pass was finished in his territory, but towards the end of the third quarter he dropped another kick – backed around in a confused little circle under it, lost it and recovered on the five-yard line just in time to avert a certain score. That made the third time, and I saw Ed Kimball throw off his blanket and begin to warm up on the sidelines.

Just at that point our luck began to change. From a kick formation, with Dolly set to punt from behind our goal, Howard Bement, who had gone in for Wash Sampson at quarter, took the ball through the centre of the line, got by the secondary defence and ran twenty-six yards before he was pulled down. Captain Tasker, of Yale, had gone out with a twisted knee, and Princeton began to pile plays through his substitute, between Bean Gile and Hopman, with George Spears and sometimes Bob Tatnall carrying the ball. We went up to the Yale forty-yard line, lost the ball on a fumble and recovered it on another as the third quarter ended. A wild ripple of enthusiasm ran through the Princeton stands. For the first time we had the ball in their territory with first down and the possibility of tying the score. You could hear the tenseness growing all around you in the intermission; it was reflected in the excited movements of the cheerleaders and the uncontrollable patches of sound that leapt out of the crowd, catching up voices here and there and swelling to an undisciplined roar.

I saw Kimball dash out on the field and report to the referee and I thought Dolly was through at last, and was glad, but it was Bob Tatnall who came out, sobbing, and brought the Princeton side cheering to its feet.

With the first play pandemonium broke loose and continued to the end of the game. At intervals it would swoon away to a plaintive humming; then it would rise to the intensity of wind and rain and thunder, and beat across the twilight from one side of the Bowl to the other like the agony of lost souls swinging across a gap in space.

The teams lined up on Yale's forty-one-yard line and Spears immediately dashed off tackle for six yards. Again he carried the ball – he was a wild unpopular Southerner with inspired moments – going through the same hole for five more and a first down. Dolly made two on a cross buck and Spears was held at centre. It was third down, with the ball on Yale's twenty-nine-yard line and eight to go.

There was some confusion immediately behind me, some pushing and some voices; a man was sick or had fainted – I never discovered which. Then my view was blocked out for a minute by rising bodies and then everything went definitely crazy. Substitutes were jumping around down on the field, waving their blankets, the air was full of hats, cushions, coats and a deafening roar. Dolly Harlan, who had scarcely carried the ball a dozen times in his Princeton career, had picked a long pass from Kimball out of the air and, dragging a tackler, struggled five yards to the Yale goal.

6

SOME TIME LATER the game was over. There was a bad moment when Yale began another attack, but there was no scoring and Bob Tatnall's eleven had redeemed a mediocre season by tying a better Yale team. For us there was the feel of victory about it, the exaltation if not the jubilance, and the Yale faces issuing from out the Bowl wore the look of defeat. It would be a good year, after all – a good fight at the last, a tradition for next year's team. Our class – those of us who cared – would go out from Princeton without the taste of final defeat. The symbol stood – such as it was; the banners blew proudly in the wind. All that is childish? Find us something to fill the niche of victory.

I waited for Dolly outside the dressing rooms until almost everyone had come out; then, as he still lingered, I went in. Someone had given him a little brandy and, since he never drank much, it was swimming in his head.

"Have a chair, Jeff." He smiled, broadly and happily. "Rubber! Tony! Get the distinguished guest a chair. He's an intellectual and he wants to interview one of the bone-headed athletes. Tony, this is Mr Deering. They've got everything in this funny Bowl but armchairs. I love this Bowl. I'm going to build here."

He fell silent, thinking about all things happily. He was content. I persuaded him to dress – there were people waiting for us. Then he insisted on walking out upon the field, dark now, and feeling the crumbled turf with his shoe.

He picked up a divot from a cleat and let it drop, laughed, looked distracted for a minute, and turned away.

With Tad Davis, Daisy Cary and another girl, we drove to New York. He sat beside Daisy and was silly, charming and attractive. For the first time since I'd known him he talked about the game naturally, even with a touch of vanity.

"For two years I was pretty good and I was always mentioned at the bottom of the column as being among those who played. This year I dropped three punts and slowed up every play till Bob Tatnall kept yelling at me, 'I don't see why they won't take you out!' But a pass not even aimed at me fell in my arms and I'll be in the headlines tomorrow."

He laughed. Somebody touched his foot; he winced and turned white.

"How did you hurt it?" Daisy asked. "In football?"

"I hurt it last summer," he said shortly.

"It must have been terrible to play on it."

"It was."

"I suppose you had to."

"That's the way sometimes."

They understood each other. They were both workers; sick or well, there were things that Daisy also had to do. She spoke of how, with a vile cold, she had had to fall into an open-air lagoon out in Hollywood the winter before.

"Six times – with a fever of a hundred and two. But the production was costing ten thousand dollars a day."

"Couldn't they use a double?"

"They did whenever they could – I only fell in when it had to be done."

She was eighteen and I compared her background of courage and independence and achievement, of politeness based upon the realities of cooperation, with that of most society girls I had known. There was no way in which she wasn't inestimably their superior – if she had looked for a moment my way – but it was Dolly's shining velvet eyes that signalled to her own.

"Can't you go out with me tonight?" I heard her ask him.

He was sorry, but he had to refuse. Vienna was in New York; she was going to see him. I didn't know, and Dolly didn't know, whether there was to be a reconciliation or a goodbye.

When she dropped Dolly and me at the Ritz there was real regret, that lingering form of it, in both their eyes.

"There's a marvellous girl," Dolly said. I agreed. "I'm going up to see Vienna. Will you get a room for us at the Madison?"

So I left him. What happened between him and Vienna I don't know; he has never spoken about it to this day. But what happened later in the evening was brought to my attention by several surprised and even indignant witnesses to the event.

Dolly walked into the Ambassador Hotel about ten o'clock and went to the desk to ask for Miss Cary's room. There was a crowd around the desk, among them some Yale or Princeton undergraduates from the game. Several of them had been celebrating and evidently one of them knew Daisy and had tried to get her room by phone. Dolly was abstracted and he must have made his way through them in a somewhat brusque way and asked to be connected with Miss Cary.

One young man stepped back, looked at him unpleasantly and said, "You seem to be in an awful hurry. Just who are you?"

There was one of those slight silent pauses and the people near the desk all turned to look. Something happened inside Dolly; he felt as if life had arranged his role to make possible this particular question – a question that now he had no choice but to answer. Still, there was silence. The small crowd waited.

"Why, I'm Dolly Harlan," he said deliberately. "What do you think of that?"

It was quite outrageous. There was a pause and then a sudden little flurry and chorus: "Dolly Harlan! What? What did he say?"

The clerk had heard the name; he gave it as the phone was answered from Miss Cary's room.

"Mr Harlan's to go right up, please."

Dolly turned away, alone with his achievement, taking it for once to his breast. He found suddenly that he would not have it long so intimately; the memory would outlive the triumph and even the triumph would outlive the glow in his heart that was best of all. Tall and straight, an image of victory and pride, he moved across the lobby, oblivious alike to the fate ahead of him or the small chatter behind.

The Last of the Belles

1

AFTER ATLANTA'S ELABORATE and theatrical rendition of Southern charm, we all underestimated Tarleton. It was a little hotter than anywhere we'd been – a dozen rookies collapsed the first day in that Georgia sun – and when you saw herds of cows drifting through the business streets, hi-yaed by coloured drovers, a trance stole down over you out of the hot light; you wanted to move a hand or foot to be sure you were alive.

So I stayed out at camp and let Lieutenant Warren tell me about the girls. This was fifteen years ago, and I've forgotten how I felt, except that the days went along, one after another, better than they do now, and I was empty-hearted, because up North she whose legend I had loved for three years was getting married. I saw the clippings and newspaper photographs. It was "a romantic wartime wedding", all very rich and sad. I felt vividly the dark radiance of the sky under which it took place and, as a young snob, was more envious than sorry.

A day came when I went into Tarleton for a haircut and ran into a nice fellow named Bill Knowles, who was in my time at Harvard. He'd been in the National Guard division that preceded us in camp; at the last moment he had transferred to aviation and been left behind.

"I'm glad I met you, Andy," he said with undue seriousness. "I'll hand you on all my information before I start for Texas. You see, there're really only three girls here…"

I was interested; there was something mystical about there being three girls.

"…and here's one of them now."

We were in front of a drugstore and he marched me in and introduced me to a lady I promptly detested.

"The other two are Ailie Calhoun and Sally Carrol Happer."

I guessed from the way he pronounced her name that he was interested in Ailie Calhoun. It was on his mind what she would be doing while he was gone; he wanted her to have a quiet, uninteresting time.

At my age I don't even hesitate to confess that entirely unchivalrous images of Ailie Calhoun – that lovely name – rushed into my mind. At twenty-three there is no such thing as a pre-empted beauty; though, had Bill asked me, I would doubtless have sworn in all sincerity to care for her like a sister. He didn't; he was just fretting out loud at having to go. Three days later he telephoned me that he was leaving next morning and he'd take me to her house that night.

We met at the hotel and walked uptown through the flowery, hot twilight. The four white pillars of the Calhoun house faced the street, and behind them the veranda was dark as a cave with hanging, weaving, climbing vines.

When we came up the walk a girl in a white dress tumbled out of the front door, crying, "I'm so sorry I'm late!" and, seeing us, added: "Why, I thought I heard you come ten minutes…"

She broke off as a chair creaked and another man, an aviator from Camp Harry Lee, emerged from the obscurity of the veranda.

"Why, Canby!" she cried. "How are you?"

He and Bill Knowles waited with the tenseness of open litigants.

"Canby, I want to whisper to you, honey," she said, after just a second. "You'll excuse us, Bill."

They went aside. Presently Lieutenant Canby, immensely displeased, said in a grim voice, "Then we'll make it Thursday, but that means sure." Scarcely nodding to us, he went down the walk, the spurs with which he presumably urged on his aeroplane gleaming in the lamplight.

"Come in – I don't just know your name…"

There she was – the Southern type in all its purity. I would have recognized Ailie Calhoun if I'd never heard Ruth Draper or read 'Marse Chan'.* She had the adroitness sugar-coated with sweet, voluble simplicity, the suggested background of devoted fathers, brothers and admirers stretching back into the South's heroic age, the unfailing coolness acquired in the endless struggle with the heat. There were notes in her voice that order slaves around, that withered up Yankee captains, and then soft, wheedling notes that mingled in unfamiliar loveliness with the night.

I could scarcely see her in the darkness, but when I rose to go – it was plain that I was not to linger – she stood in the orange light from the doorway. She was small and very blonde; there was too much fever-coloured rouge on her face, accentuated by a nose dabbed clownish white, but she shone through that like a star.

"After Bill goes I'll be sitting here all alone night after night. Maybe you'll take me to the country-club dances." The pathetic prophecy brought a laugh from Bill. "Wait a minute," Ailie murmured. "Your guns are all crooked."

She straightened my collar pin, looking up at me for a second with something more than curiosity. It was a seeking look, as if she asked, "Could it be you?" Like Lieutenant Canby, I marched off unwillingly into the suddenly insufficient night.

Two weeks later I sat with her on the same veranda, or rather she half-lay in my arms and yet scarcely touched me – how she managed that I don't remember. I was trying unsuccessfully to kiss her, and had been trying for the best part of an hour. We had a sort of joke about my not being sincere. My theory was that if she'd let me kiss her I'd fall in love with her. Her argument was that I was obviously insincere.

In a lull between two of these struggles she told me about her brother who had died in his senior year at Yale. She showed me his picture – it was a handsome, earnest face with a Leyendecker* forelock – and told me that when she met someone who measured up to him she'd marry.

I found this family idealism discouraging: even my brash confidence couldn't compete with the dead.

The evening and other evenings passed like that, and ended with my going back to camp with the remembered smell of magnolia flowers and a mood of vague dissatisfaction. I never kissed her. We went to the vaudeville and to the country club on Saturday nights, where she seldom took ten consecutive steps with one man, and she took me to barbecues and rowdy watermelon parties, and never thought it was worthwhile to change what I felt for her into love. I see now that it wouldn't have been hard, but she was a wise nineteen and she must have seen that we were emotionally incompatible. So I became her confidant instead.

We talked about Bill Knowles. She was considering Bill; for though she wouldn't admit it, a winter at school in New York and a prom at Yale had turned her eyes North. She said she didn't think she'd marry a Southern man. And by degrees I saw that she was consciously and voluntarily different from these other girls who sang nigger songs and shot craps in the country-club bar. That's why Bill and I and others were drawn to her. We recognized her.

June and July, while the rumours reached us faintly, ineffectually, of battle and terror overseas, Ailie's eyes roved here and there about the country-club floor, seeking for something among the tall young officers. She attached several, choosing them with unfailing perspicacity – save in the case of Lieutenant Canby, whom she claimed to despise but, nevertheless, gave dates to "because he was so sincere" – and we apportioned her evenings among us all summer.

One day she broke all her dates – Bill Knowles had leave and was coming. We talked of the event with scientific impersonality – would he move her to a decision? Lieutenant Canby, on the contrary, wasn't impersonal at all, made a nuisance of himself. He told her that if she married Knowles he was going to climb up six thousand feet in his aeroplane, shut off the motor and let go. He frightened her – I had to yield him my last date before Bill came.

On Saturday night she and Bill Knowles came to the country club. They were very handsome together and once more I felt envious and sad. As they danced out on the floor, the three-piece orchestra was playing 'After You've Gone',* in a poignant, incomplete way that I can hear yet, as if each bar were trickling off a precious minute of that time. I knew then that I had grown to love Tarleton, and I glanced about half in panic to see if some face wouldn't come in for me out of that warm, singing, outer darkness that yielded up couple after couple in organdie and olive drab. It was a time of youth and war, and there was never so much love around.

When I danced with Ailie she suddenly suggested that we go outside to a car. She wanted to know why didn't people cut in on her tonight? Did they think she was already married?

"Are you going to be?"

"I don't know, Andy. Sometimes, when he treats me as if I were sacred, it thrills me." Her voice was hushed and far away. "And then…"

She laughed. Her body, so frail and tender, was touching mine, her face was turned up to me, and there, suddenly, with Bill Knowles ten yards off, I could have kissed her at last. Our lips just touched experimentally; then an aviation officer turned a corner of the veranda near us, peered into our darkness and hesitated.

"Ailie."

"Yes."

"You heard about this afternoon?"

"What?" She leant forward, tenseness already in her voice.

"Horace Canby crashed. He was instantly killed."

She got up slowly and stepped out of the car.

"You mean he was killed?" she said.

"Yes. They don't know what the trouble was. His motor—"

"Oh-h-h!" Her rasping whisper came through the hands suddenly covering her face. We watched her helplessly as she put her head on the side of the car, gagging dry tears. After a minute I went for Bill, who was standing in the stag line, searching anxiously about for her, and told him she wanted to go home.

I sat on the steps outside. I had disliked Canby, but his terrible, pointless death was more real to me then than the day's toll of thousands in France. In a few minutes Ailie and Bill came out. Ailie was whimpering a little, but when she saw me her eyes flexed and she came over swiftly.

"Andy" – she spoke in a quick, low voice – "of course you must never tell anybody what I told you about Canby yesterday. What he said, I mean."

"Of course not."

She looked at me a second longer as if to be quite sure. Finally she was sure. Then she sighed in such a quaint little way that I could hardly believe my ears, and her brow went up in what can only be described as mock despair.

"An-dy!"

I looked uncomfortably at the ground, aware that she was calling my attention to her involuntarily disastrous effect on men.

"Goodnight, Andy!" called Bill as they got into a taxi.

"Goodnight," I said, and almost added: "You poor fool."

2

OF COURSE I SHOULD HAVE MADE one of those fine moral decisions that people make in books, and despised her. On the contrary, I don't doubt that she could still have had me by raising her hand.

A few days later she made it all right by saying wistfully, "I know you think it was terrible of me to think of myself at a time like that, but it was such a shocking coincidence."

At twenty-three I was entirely unconvinced about anything, except that some people were strong and attractive and could do what they wanted, and others were caught and disgraced. I hoped I was of the former. I was sure Ailie was.

I had to revise other ideas about her. In the course of a long discussion with some girl about kissing – in those days people still talked about kissing more than they kissed – I mentioned the fact that Ailie had only kissed two or three men, and only when she thought she was in love. To my considerable disconcertion the girl figuratively just lay on the floor and howled.

"But it's true," I assured her, suddenly knowing it wasn't. "She told me herself."

"Ailie Calhoun! Oh, my Heavens! Why, last year at the Tech spring house party…"

This was in September. We were going overseas any week now, and to bring us up to full strength a last batch of officers from the fourth training camp arrived. The fourth camp wasn't like the first three – the candidates were from the ranks; even from the drafted divisions. They had queer names without vowels in them, and save for a few young militiamen, you couldn't take it for granted that they came out of any background at all. The addition to our company was Lieutenant Earl Schoen from New Bedford, Massachusetts – as fine a physical specimen as I have ever seen. He was six foot three, with black hair, high colour and glossy dark-brown eyes. He wasn't very smart and he was definitely illiterate, yet he was a good officer, high-tempered and commanding, and with that becoming touch of vanity that sits well on the military. I had an idea that New Bedford was a country town, and set down his bumptious qualities to that.

We were doubled up in living quarters and he came into my hut. Inside of a week there was a cabinet photograph of some Tarleton girl nailed brutally to the shack wall.

"She's no jane or anything like that. She's a society girl – goes with all the best people here."

The following Sunday afternoon I met the lady at a semi-private swimming pool in the country. When Ailie and I arrived, there was Schoen's muscular body rippling out of a bathing suit at the far end of the pool.

"Hey, lieutenant!"

When I waved back at him he grinned and winked, jerking his head towards the girl at his side. Then, digging her in the ribs, he jerked his head at me. It was a form of introduction.

"Who's that with Kitty Preston?" Ailie asked, and when I told her she said he looked like a streetcar conductor, and pretended to look for her transfer.

A moment later he crawled powerfully and gracefully down the pool and pulled himself up at our side. I introduced him to Ailie.

"How do you like my girl, lieutenant?" he demanded. "I told you she was all right, didn't I?" He jerked his head towards Ailie; this time to indicate that his girl and Ailie moved in the same circles. "How about us all having dinner together down at the hotel some night?"

I left them in a moment, amused as I saw Ailie visibly making up her mind that here, anyhow, was not the ideal. But Lieutenant Earl Schoen was not to be dismissed so lightly. He ran his eyes cheerfully and inoffensively over her cute, slight figure, and decided that she would do even better than the other. Then minutes later I saw them in the water together, Ailie swimming away with a grim little stroke she had, and Schoen wallowing riotously around her and ahead of her, sometimes pausing and staring at her, fascinated, as a boy might look at a nautical doll.

While the afternoon passed he remained at her side. Finally Ailie came over to me and whispered, with a laugh: "He's following me around. He thinks I haven't paid my carfare."

She turned quickly. Miss Kitty Preston, her face curiously flustered, stood facing us.

"Ailie Calhoun, I didn't think it of you to go out and delib'ately try to take a man away from another girl." An expression of distress at the impending scene flitted over Ailie's face. "I thought you considered yourself above anything like that."

Miss Preston's voice was low, but it held that tensity that can be felt farther than it can be heard, and I saw Ailie's clear lovely eyes glance about in panic. Luckily, Earl himself was ambling cheerfully and innocently towards us.

"If you care for him you certainly oughtn't to belittle yourself in front of him," said Ailie in a flash, her head high.

It was her acquaintance with the traditional way of behaving against Kitty Preston's naive and fierce possessiveness or, if you prefer it, Ailie's "breeding" against the other's "commonness". She turned away.

"Wait a minute, kid!" cried Earl Schoen. "How about your address? Maybe I'd like to give you a ring on the phone."

She looked at him in a way that should have indicated to Kitty her entire lack of interest.

"I'm very busy at the Red Cross this month," she said, her voice as cool as her slicked-back blond hair. "Goodbye."

On the way home she laughed. Her air of having been unwittingly involved in a contemptible business vanished.

"She'll never hold that young man," she said. "He wants somebody new."

"Apparently he wants Ailie Calhoun."

The idea amused her.

"He could give me his ticket punch to wear, like a fraternity pin. What fun! If mother ever saw anybody like that come in the house, she'd just lie down and die."

And to give Ailie credit, it was fully a fortnight before he did come in her house, although he rushed her until she pretended to be annoyed at the next country-club dance.

"He's the biggest tough, Andy," she whispered to me. "But he's so sincere."

She used the word "tough" without the conviction it would have carried had he been a Southern boy. She only knew it with her mind; her ear couldn't distinguish between one Yankee voice and another. And somehow Mrs Calhoun didn't expire at his appearance on the threshold. The supposedly ineradicable prejudices of Ailie's parents were a convenient phenomenon that disappeared at her wish. It was her friends who were astonished. Ailie, always a little above Tarleton, whose beaux had been very carefully the "nicest" men of the camp – Ailie and Lieutenant Schoen! I grew tired of assuring people that she was merely distracting herself – and indeed every week or so there was someone new – an ensign from Pensacola, an old friend from New Orleans – but always, in between times, there was Earl Schoen.

Orders arrived for an advance party of officers and sergeants to proceed to the port of embarkation and take ship to France. My name was on the list. I had been on the range for a week and when I got back to camp, Earl Schoen buttonholed me immediately.

"We're giving a little farewell party in the mess. Just you and I and Captain Craker and three girls."

Earl and I were to call for the girls. We picked up Sally Carrol Happer and Nancy Lamar, and went on to Ailie's house – to be met at the door by the butler with the announcement that she wasn't home.

"Isn't home?" Earl repeated blankly. "Where is she?"

"Didn't leave no information about that; just said she wasn't home."

"But this is a darn funny thing!" he exclaimed. He walked around the familiar dusky veranda while the butler waited at the door. Something occurred to him. "Say," he informed me – "say, I think she's sore."

I waited. He said sternly to the butler, "You tell her I've got to speak to her a minute."

"How'm I goin' tell her that when she ain't home?"

Again Earl walked musingly around the porch. Then he nodded several times and said:

"She's sore at something that happened downtown."

In a few words he sketched out the matter to me.

"Look here; you wait in the car," I said. "Maybe I can fix this." And when he reluctantly retreated: "Oliver, you tell Miss Ailie I want to see her alone."

After some argument he bore this message and in a moment returned with a reply:

"Miss Ailie say she don't want to see that other gentleman about nothing never. She say come in if you like."

She was in the library. I had expected to see a picture of cool, outraged dignity, but her face was distraught, tumultuous, despairing. Her eyes were red-rimmed, as though she had been crying slowly and painfully, for hours.

"Oh, hello, Andy," she said brokenly. "I haven't seen you for so long. Has he gone?"

"Now, Ailie—"

"Now, Ailie!" she cried. "Now, Ailie! He spoke to me, you see. He lifted his hat. He stood there ten feet from me with that horrible... that horrible woman – holding her arm and talking to her, and then when he saw me he raised his hat. Andy, I didn't know what to do. I had to go in the drugstore and ask for a glass of water, and I was so afraid he'd follow in after me that I asked Mr Rich to let me go out the back way. I never want to see him or hear of him again."

I talked. I said what one says in such cases. I said it for half an hour. I could not move her. Several times she answered by murmuring something about his not being "sincere", and for the fourth time I wondered what the word meant to her. Certainly not constancy; it was, I half-suspected, some special way she wanted to be regarded.

I got up to go. And then, unbelievably, the automobile horn sounded three times impatiently outside. It was stupefying. It said as plainly as if Earl were in the room, "All right; go to the Devil then! I'm not going to wait here all night."

Ailie looked at me aghast. And suddenly a peculiar look came into her face, spread, flickered, broke into a teary, hysterical smile.

"Isn't he awful?" she cried in helpless despair. "Isn't he terrible?"

"Hurry up," I said quickly. "Get your cape. This is our last night."

And I can still feel that last night vividly, the candlelight that flickered over the rough boards of the mess shack, over the frayed paper decorations left from the supply company's party, the sad mandolin down a company street that kept picking 'My Indiana Home'* out of the universal nostalgia of the departing summer. The three girls lost in this mysterious men's city felt something too – a bewitched impermanence as though they were on a magic carpet that had lighted on the Southern countryside, and any moment the wind would lift it and waft it away. We toasted ourselves and the South. Then we left our napkins and empty glasses and a little of the past on the table, and hand in hand went out into the moonlight itself. Taps had been played; there was no sound but the faraway whinny of a horse, and a loud persistent snore at which we laughed, and the leathery snap of a sentry coming to port over by the guardhouse. Craker was on duty; we others got into a waiting car, motored into Tarleton and left Craker's girl.

Then Ailie and Earl, Sally and I, two and two in the wide back seat, each couple turned from the other, absorbed and whispering, drove away into the wide, flat darkness.

We drove through pine woods heavy with lichen and Spanish moss, and between the fallow cotton fields along a road white as the rim of the world. We parked under the broken shadow of a mill where there was the sound of running water and restive squawky birds and over everything a brightness that tried to filter in anywhere – into the lost nigger cabins, the automobile, the fastnesses of the heart. The South sang to us – I wonder if they remember. I remember – the cool pale faces, the somnolent amorous eyes and the voices:

"Are you comfortable?"

"Yes – are you?"

"Are you sure you are?"

"Yes."

Suddenly we knew it was late and there was nothing more. We turned home.

Our detachment started for Camp Mills next day, but I didn't go to France after all. We passed a cold month on Long Island, marched aboard a transport with steel helmets slung at our sides and then marched off again. There wasn't any more war. I had missed the war. When I came back to Tarleton I tried to get out of the Army, but I had a regular commission and it took most of the winter. But Earl Schoen was one of the first to be demobilized. He wanted to find a good job "while the picking was good". Ailie was noncommittal, but there was an understanding between them that he'd be back.

By January the camps, which for two years had dominated the little city, were already fading. There was only the persistent incinerator smell to remind one of all that activity and bustle. What life remained centred bitterly about divisional headquarters building, with the disgruntled regular officers who had also missed the war.

And now the young men of Tarleton began drifting back from the ends of the earth – some with Canadian uniforms, some with crutches or empty sleeves. A returned battalion of the National Guard paraded through the streets with open ranks for their dead, and then stepped down out of romance for ever and sold you things over the counters of local stores. Only a few uniforms mingled with the dinner coats at the country-club dance.

Just before Christmas, Bill Knowles arrived unexpectedly one day and left the next – either he gave Ailie an ultimatum or she had made up her mind at last. I saw her sometimes when she wasn't busy with returned heroes from Savannah and Augusta, but I felt like an outmoded survival – and I was. She was waiting for Earl Schoen with such a vast uncertainty that she didn't like to talk about it. Three days before I got my final discharge he came.

I first happened upon them walking down Market Street together, and I don't think I've ever been so sorry for a couple in my life; though I suppose the same situation was repeating itself in every city where there had been camps. Exteriorly Earl had about everything wrong with him that could be imagined. His hat was green, with a radical feather; his suit was slashed and braided in a grotesque fashion that national advertising and the movies have put an end to. Evidently he had been to his old barber, for his hair bloused neatly on his pink, shaved neck. It wasn't as though he had been shiny and poor, but the background of mill-town dance halls and outing clubs flamed out at you – or rather flamed out at Ailie. For she had never quite imagined the reality; in these clothes even the natural grace of that magnificent body had departed. At first he boasted of his fine job; it would get them along all right until he could "see some easy money". But from the moment he came back into her world on its own terms he must have known it was hopeless. I don't know what Ailie said or how much her grief weighed against her stupefaction. She acted quickly – three days after his arrival, Earl and I went North together on the train.

"Well, that's the end of that," he said moodily. "She's a wonderful girl, but too much of a highbrow for me. I guess she's got to marry some rich guy that'll give her a great social position. I can't see that stuck-up sort of thing." And then, later: "She said to come back and see her in a year, but I'll never go back. This aristocat stuff is all right if you got the money for it, but…"

"But it wasn't real," he meant to finish. The provincial society in which he had moved with so much satisfaction for six months already appeared to him as affected, "dudish" and artificial.

"Say, did you see what I saw getting on the train?" he asked me after a while. "Two wonderful janes, all alone. What do you say we mosey into the next car and ask them to lunch? I'll take the one in blue." Halfway down the car he turned around suddenly. "Say, Andy," he demanded, frowning, "one thing – how do you suppose she knew I used to command a streetcar? I never told her that."

"Search me."

3

THIS NARRATIVE ARRIVES now at one of the big gaps that stared me in the face when I began. For six years, while I finished at Harvard Law and built commercial aeroplanes and backed a pavement block that went gritty under trucks, Ailie Calhoun was scarcely more than a name on a Christmas card; something that blew a little in my mind on warm nights when I remembered the magnolia flowers. Occasionally an acquaintance of army days would ask me, "What became of that blonde girl who was so popular?" but I didn't know. I ran into Nancy Lamar at the Montmartre in New York one evening and learnt that Ailie had become engaged to a man in Cincinnati, had gone North to visit his family and then broken it off. She was lovely as ever and there was always a heavy beau or two. But neither Bill Knowles nor Earl Schoen had ever come back.

And somewhere about that time I heard that Bill Knowles had married a girl he met on a boat. There you are – not much of a patch to mend six years with.

Oddly enough, a girl seen at twilight in a small Indiana station started me thinking about going South. The girl, in stiff pink organdie, threw her arms about a man who got off our train and hurried him to a waiting car, and I felt a sort of pang. It seemed to me that she was bearing him off into the lost midsummer world of my early twenties, where time had stood still and charming girls, dimly seen like the past itself, still loitered along the dusky streets. I suppose that poetry is a Northern man's dream of the South. But it was months later that I sent off a wire to Ailie, and immediately followed it to Tarleton.

It was July. The Jefferson Hotel seemed strangely shabby and stuffy – a boosters' club burst into intermittent song in the dining room that my memory had long dedicated to officers and girls. I recognized the taxi driver who took me up to Ailie's house, but his "Sure, I do, lieutenant" was unconvincing. I was only one of twenty thousand.

It was a curious three days. I suppose some of Ailie's first young lustre must have gone the way of such mortal shining, but I can't bear witness to it. She was still so physically appealing that you wanted to touch the personality that trembled on her lips. No – the change was more profound than that.

At once I saw she had a different line. The modulations of pride, the vocal hints that she knew the secrets of a brighter, finer antebellum day, were gone from her voice; there was no time for them now as it rambled on in the half-laughing, half-desperate banter of the newer South. And everything was swept into this banter in order to make it go on and leave no time for thinking – the present, the future, herself, me. We went to a rowdy party at the house of some young married people, and she was the nervous, glowing centre of it. After all, she wasn't eighteen, and she was as attractive in her role of reckless clown as she had ever been in her life.

"Have you heard anything from Earl Schoen?" I asked her the second night, on our way to the country-club dance.

"No." She was serious for a moment. "I often think of him. He was the…" She hesitated.

"Go on."

"I was going to say the man I loved most, but that wouldn't be true. I never exactly loved him, or I'd have married him any old how, wouldn't I?" She looked at me questioningly. "At least I wouldn't have treated him like that."

"It was impossible."

"Of course," she agreed uncertainly. Her mood changed; she became flippant: "How the Yankees did deceive us poor little Southern girls. Ah, me!"

When we reached the country club she melted like a chameleon into the – to me – unfamiliar crowd. There was a new generation upon the floor, with less dignity than the ones I had known, but none of them were more a part of its lazy, feverish essence than Ailie. Possibly she had perceived that in her initial longing to escape from Tarleton's provincialism she had been walking alone, following a generation which was doomed to have no successors. Just where she lost the battle, waged behind the white pillars of her veranda, I don't know. But she had guessed wrong, missed out somewhere. Her wild animation, which even now called enough men around her to rival the entourage of the youngest and freshest, was an admission of defeat.

I left her house, as I had so often left it that vanished June, in a mood of vague dissatisfaction. It was hours later, tossing about my bed in the hotel, that I realized what was the matter, what had always been the matter – I was deeply and incurably in love with her. In spite of every incompatibility, she was still, she would always be to me, the most attractive girl I had ever known. I told her so next afternoon. It was one of those hot days I knew so well, and Ailie sat beside me on a couch in the darkened library.

"Oh, no, I couldn't marry you," she said, almost frightened. "I don't love you that way at all... I never did. And you don't love me. I didn't mean to tell you now, but next month I'm going to marry another man. We're not even announcing it, because I've done that twice before." Suddenly it occurred to her that I might be hurt: "Andy, you just had a silly idea, didn't you? You know I couldn't ever marry a Northern man."

"Who is he?" I demanded.

"A man from Savannah."

"Are you in love with him?"

"Of course I am." We both smiled. "Of course I am! What are you trying to make me say?"

There were no doubts, as there had been with other men. She couldn't afford to let herself have doubts. I knew this because she had long ago stopped making any pretensions with me. This very naturalness, I realized, was because she didn't consider me as a suitor. Beneath her mask of an instinctive thoroughbred she had always been on to herself, and she couldn't believe that anyone not taken in to the point of uncritical worship could really love her. That was what she called being "sincere"; she felt most security with men like Canby and Earl Schoen, who were incapable of passing judgements on the ostensibly aristocratic heart.

"All right," I said, as if she had asked my permission to marry. "Now, would you do something for me?"

"Anything."

"Ride out to camp."

"But there's nothing left there, honey."

"I don't care."

We walked downtown. The taxi driver in front of the hotel repeated her objection: "Nothing there now, cap."

"Never mind. Go there anyhow."

Twenty minutes later he stopped on a wide unfamiliar plain powdered with new cotton fields and marked with isolated clumps of pine.

"Like to drive over yonder where you see the smoke?" asked the driver. "That's the new state prison."

"No. Just drive along this road. I want to find where I used to live."

An old racecourse, inconspicuous in the camp's day of glory, had reared its dilapidated grandstand in the desolation. I tried in vain to orient myself.

"Go along this road past that clump of trees, and then turn right – no, turn left."

He obeyed, with professional disgust.

"You won't find a single thing, darling," said Ailie. "The contractors took it all down."

We rode slowly along the margin of the fields. It might have been here...

"All right. I want to get out," I said suddenly.

I left Ailie sitting in the car, looking very beautiful with the warm breeze stirring her long, curly bob.

It might have been here. That would make the company streets down there and the mess shack, where we dined that night, just over the way.

The taxi driver regarded me indulgently while I stumbled here and there in the knee-deep underbrush, looking for my youth in a clapboard or a strip of roofing or a rusty tomato can. I tried to sight on a vaguely familiar clump of trees, but it was growing darker now and I couldn't be quite sure they were the right trees.

"They're going to fix up the old racecourse," Ailie called from the car. "Tarleton's getting quite doggy in its old age."

No. Upon consideration they didn't look like the right trees. All I could be sure of was this place that had once been so full of life and effort was gone, as if it had never existed, and that in another month Ailie would be gone, and the South would be empty for me for ever.

Majesty

1

THE EXTRAORDINARY THING is not that people in a lifetime turn out worse or better than we had prophesied; particularly in America that is to be expected. The extraordinary thing is how people keep their levels, fulfil their promises, seem actually buoyed up by an inevitable destiny.

One of my conceits is that no one has ever disappointed me since I turned eighteen and could tell a real quality from a gift for sleight of hand, and even many of the merely showy people in my past seem to go on being blatantly and successfully showy to the end.

Emily Castleton was born in Harrisburg in a medium-sized house, moved to New York at sixteen to a big house, went to the Brearley School, moved to an enormous house, moved to a mansion at Tuxedo Park, moved abroad, where she did various fashionable things and was in all the papers. Back in her debutante year one of those French artists who are so dogmatic about American beauties included her, with eleven other public and semi-public celebrities, as one of America's perfect types. At the time numerous men agreed with him.

She was just faintly tall, with fine, rather large features, eyes with such an expanse of blue in them that you were really aware of it whenever you looked at her, and a good deal of thick blond hair – arresting and bright. Her mother and father did not know very much about the new world they had commandeered, so Emily had to learn everything for herself, and she became involved in various situations and some of the first bloom wore off. However, there was bloom to spare. There were engagements and semi-engagements, short passionate attractions, and then a big affair at twenty-two that embittered her and sent her wandering the continents looking for happiness. She became "artistic" as most wealthy unmarried girls do at that age, because artistic people seem to have some secret, some inner refuge, some escape. But most of her friends were married now, and her life was a great disappointment to her father; so, at twenty-four, with marriage in her head if not in her heart, Emily came home.

This was a low point in her career and Emily was aware of it. She had not done well. She was one of the most popular, most beautiful girls of her generation, with charm, money and a sort of fame, but her generation was moving into new fields. At the first note of condescension from a former schoolmate, now a young "matron", she went to Newport and was won by William Brevoort Blair. Immediately she was again the incomparable Emily Castleton. The ghost of the French artist walked once more in the newspapers; the most talked-of leisure-class event of October was her wedding day.

Splendour to mark society nuptials... Harold Castleton sets out a series of five-thousand-dollar pavilions arranged like the interconnecting tents of a circus, in which the reception, the wedding supper and the ball will be held... Nearly a thousand guests, many of them leaders in business, will mingle with those who dominate the social world... The wedding gifts are estimated to be worth a quarter of a million dollars.

An hour before the ceremony, which was to be solemnized at St Bartholomew's, Emily sat before a dressing table and gazed at her face in the glass. She was a little tired of her face at that moment, and the depressing thought suddenly assailed her that it would require more and more looking after in the next fifty years.

"I ought to be happy," she said aloud, "but every thought that comes into my head is sad."

Her cousin, Olive Mercy, sitting on the side of the bed, nodded. "All brides are sad."

"It's such a waste," Emily said.

Olive frowned impatiently.

"Waste of what? Women are incomplete unless they're married and have children."

For a moment Emily didn't answer. Then she said slowly, "Yes, but whose children?"

For the first time in her life, Olive, who worshipped Emily, almost hated her. Not a girl in the wedding party but would have been glad of Brevoort Blair – Olive among the others.

"You're lucky," she said. 'You're so lucky you don't even know it. You ought to be paddled for talking like that."

"I shall learn to love him," announced Emily facetiously. "Love will come with marriage. Now, isn't that a hell of a prospect?"

"Why so deliberately unromantic?"

"On the contrary, I'm the most romantic person I've ever met in my life. Do you know what I think when he puts his arms around me? I think that if I look up I'll see Garland Kane's eyes."

"But why, then—"

"Getting into his plane the other day I could only remember Captain Marchbanks and the little two-seater we flew over the Channel in, just breaking our hearts for each other and never saying a word about it because of his wife. I don't regret those men; I just regret the part of me that went into caring. There's only the sweepings to hand to Brevoort in a pink wastebasket. There should have been something more; I thought even when I was most carried away that I was saving something for the one. But apparently I wasn't." She broke off and then added: "And yet I wonder."

The situation was no less provoking to Olive for being comprehensible, and save for her position as a poor relation, she would have spoken her mind. Emily was well spoilt – eight years of men had assured her they were not good enough for her and she had accepted the fact as probably true.

"You're nervous." Olive tried to keep the annoyance out of her voice. "Why not lie down for an hour?"

"Yes," answered Emily absently.

Olive went out and downstairs. In the lower hall she ran into Brevoort Blair, attired in a nuptial cutaway even to the white carnation, and in a state of considerable agitation.

"Oh, excuse me," he blurted out. "I wanted to see Emily. It's about the rings – which ring, you know. I've got four rings and she never decided, and I can't just hold them out in the church and have her take her pick."

"I happen to know she wants the plain platinum band. If you want to see her anyhow…"

"Oh, thanks very much. I don't want to disturb her."

They were standing close together, and even at this moment when he was gone, definitely pre-empted, Olive couldn't help thinking how alike she and Brevoort were. Hair, colouring, features – they might have been brother and sister – and they shared the same shy serious temperaments, the same simple straightforwardness. All this flashed through her mind in an instant, with the added thought that the blond, tempestuous Emily, with her vitality and amplitude of scale, was, after all, better for him in every way; and then, beyond this, a perfect wave of tenderness, of pure physical pity and yearning, swept over her, and it seemed that she must step forward only half a foot to find his arms wide to receive her.

She stepped backward instead, relinquishing him as though she still touched him with the tip of her fingers and then drew the tips away. Perhaps some vibration of her emotion fought its way into his consciousness, for he said suddenly:

"We're going to be good friends, aren't we? Please don't think I'm taking Emily away. I know I can't own her – nobody could – and I don't want to."

Silently, as he talked, she said goodbye to him, the only man she had ever wanted in her life.

She loved the absorbed hesitancy with which he found his coat and hat and felt hopefully for the knob on the wrong side of the door.

When he had gone, she went into the drawing room, gorgeous and portentous; with its painted bacchanals and massive chandeliers and the eighteenth-century portraits that might have been Emily's ancestors, but weren't, and by that very fact belonged the more to her. There she rested, as always, in Emily's shadow.

Through the door that led out to the small, priceless patch of grass on Sixtieth Street now enclosed by the pavilions, came her uncle, Mr Harold Castleton. He had been sampling his own champagne.

"Olive so sweet and fair," he cried emotionally. "Olive, baby, she's done it. She was all right inside, like I knew all the time. The good ones come through, don't they – the real thoroughbreds? I began to think that the Lord and me, between us, had given her too much, that she'd never be satisfied, but now she's come down to earth just like a" – he searched unsuccessfully for a metaphor – "like a thoroughbred, and she'll find it not such a bad place after all." He came closer. "You've been crying, little Olive."

"Not much."

"It doesn't matter," he said magnanimously. "If I wasn't so happy I'd cry too."

Later, as she embarked with two other bridesmaids for the church, the solemn throbbing of a big wedding seemed to begin with the vibration of the car. At the door the organ took it up, and later it would palpitate in the cellos and bass viols of the dance, to fade off finally with the sound of the car that bore bride and groom away.

The crowd was thick around the church, and ten feet out of it the air was heavy with perfume and faint clean humanity and the fabric smell of new clean clothes. Beyond the massed hats in the van of the church the two families sat in front rows on either side. The Blairs – they were assured a family resemblance by their expression of faint condescension, shared by their in-laws as well as by true Blairs – were represented by the

Gardiner Blairs, senior and junior; Lady Mary Bowes Howard, née Blair; Mrs Potter Blair; Mrs Princess Potowki Parr Blair, née Inchbit; Miss Gloria Blair, Master Gardiner Blair III and the kindred branches, rich and poor, of Smythe, Bickle, Diffendorfer and Hamn. Across the aisle the Castletons made a less impressive showing – Mr Harold Castleton, Mr and Mrs Theodore Castleton and children, Harold Castleton Junior and, from Harrisburg, Mr Carl Mercy, and two little old aunts named O'Keefe hidden off in a corner. Somewhat to their surprise the two aunts had been bundled off in a limousine and dressed from head to foot by a fashionable couturière that morning.

In the vestry, where the bridesmaids fluttered about like birds in their big floppy hats, there was a last lip-rouging and adjustment of pins before Emily should arrive. They represented several stages of Emily's life – a schoolmate at Brearley, a last unmarried friend of debutante year, a travelling companion of Europe and the girl she had visited in Newport when she met Brevoort Blair.

"They've got Wakeman," this last one said, standing by the door listening to the music. "He played for my sister, but I shall never have Wakeman."

"Why not?"

"Why, he's playing the same thing over and over – 'At Dawning'.* He's played it half a dozen times."

At this moment another door opened, and the solicitous head of a young man appeared around it. "Almost ready?" he demanded of the nearest bridesmaid. "Brevoort's having a quiet little fit. He just stands there wilting collar after collar—"

"Be calm," answered the young lady. "The bride is always a few minutes late."

"A few minutes!" protested the best man. "I don't call it a few minutes. They're beginning to rustle and wriggle like a circuit crowd out there, and the organist has been playing the same tune for half an hour. I'm going to get him to fill in with a little jazz."

"What time is it?" Olive demanded.

"Quarter of five – ten minutes of five."

"Maybe there's been a traffic tie-up." Olive paused as Mr Harold Castleton, followed by an anxious curate, shouldered his way in, demanding a phone.

And now there began a curious dribbling back from the front of the church, one by one, then two by two, until the vestry was crowded with relatives and confusion.

"What's happened?"

"What on earth's the matter?"

A chauffeur came in and reported excitedly. Harold Castleton swore and, his face blazing, fought his way roughly towards the door. There was an attempt to clear the vestry, and then, as if to balance the dribbling, a ripple of conversation commenced at the rear of the church and began to drift up towards the altar, growing louder and faster and more excited, mounting always, bringing people to their feet, rising to a sort of subdued roar. The announcement from the altar that the marriage had been postponed was scarcely heard, for by that time everyone knew that they were participating in a front-page scandal, that Brevoort Blair had been left waiting at the altar and Emily Castleton had run away.

2

THERE WERE A DOZEN REPORTERS outside the Castleton house on Sixteenth Street when Olive arrived, but in her absorption she failed even to hear their questions; she wanted desperately to go and comfort a certain man whom she must not approach, and as a sort of substitute she sought her Uncle Harold. She entered through the interconnecting five-thousand-dollar pavilions, where caterers and servants still stood about in a respectful funereal half-light, waiting for something to happen, amid trays of caviar and turkey's breast and pyramided wedding cake. Upstairs, Olive found her uncle sitting on a stool before Emily's dressing table. The articles of make-up spread before him, the repertoire of feminine preparation in evidence about, made his singularly inappropriate presence a symbol of the mad catastrophe.

"Oh, it's you." His voice was listless; he had aged in two hours. Olive put her arm about his bowed shoulder.

"I'm so terribly sorry, Uncle Harold."

Suddenly a stream of profanity broke from him, died away, and a single large tear welled slowly from one eye.

"I want to get my massage man," he said. "Tell McGregor to get him." He drew a long broken sigh, like a child's breath after crying, and Olive saw that his sleeves were covered with a dust of powder from the dressing table, as if he had been leaning forward on it, weeping, in the reaction from his proud champagne.

"There was a telegram," he muttered.

"It's somewhere."

And he added slowly,

"From now on *you*'re my daughter."

"Oh, no, you mustn't say that!"

Unrolling the telegram, she read:

I can't make the grade I would feel like a fool either way but this will be over sooner so damn sorry for you

EMILY

When Olive had summoned the masseur and posted a servant outside her uncle's door, she went to the library, where a confused secretary was trying to say nothing over an inquisitive and persistent telephone.

"I'm so upset, Miss Mercy," he cried in a despairing treble. "I do declare I'm so upset I have a frightful headache. I've thought for half an hour I heard dance music from down below."

Then it occurred to Olive that she too was becoming hysterical; in the breaks of the street traffic a melody was drifting up, distinct and clear:

"...Is she fair?
Is she sweet?
I don't care – cause
I can't compete –
Who's the..."

She ran quickly downstairs and through the drawing room, the tune growing louder in her ears. At the entrance of the first pavilion she stopped in stupefaction.

To the music of a small but undoubtedly professional orchestra, a dozen young couples were+ moving about the canvas floor. At the bar in the corner stood additional young men, and half a dozen of the caterer's assistants were busily shaking cocktails and opening champagne.

"Harold!" she called imperatively to one of the dancers. "Harold!"

A tall young man of eighteen handed his partner to another and came towards her.

"Hello, Olive. How did Father take it?"

"Harold, what in the name of—"

"Emily's crazy," he said consolingly. "I always told you Emily was crazy. Crazy as a loon. Always was."

"What's the idea of this?"

"This?" He looked around innocently. "Oh, these are just some fellows that came down from Cambridge with me."

"*But – dancing!*"

"Well, nobody's dead, are they? I thought we might as well use up some of this—"

"Tell them to go home," said Olive.

"Why? What on earth's the harm? These fellows came all the way down from Cambridge—"

"It simply isn't dignified."

"But they don't care, Olive. One fellow's sister did the same thing – only she did it the day after instead of the day before. Lots of people do it nowadays."

"Send the music home, Harold," said Olive firmly, "or I'll go to your father."

Obviously he felt that no family could be disgraced by an episode on such a magnificent scale, but he reluctantly yielded. The abysmally depressed butler saw to the removal of the champagne, and the young people, somewhat insulted, moved nonchalantly out into the more tolerant night. Alone with the shadow – Emily's shadow – that hung over the house, Olive sat down in the drawing room to think. Simultaneously the butler appeared in the doorway.

"It's Mr Blair, Miss Olive."

She jumped tensely to her feet.

"Who does he want to see?"

"He didn't say. He just walked in."

"Tell him I'm in here."

He entered with an air of abstraction rather than depression, nodded to Olive and sat down on a piano stool. She wanted to say, "Come here. Lay your head here, poor man. Never mind." But she wanted to cry, too, and so she said nothing.

"In three hours," he remarked quietly, "we'll be able to get the morning papers. There's a shop on Fifty-Ninth Street."

"That's foolish—" she began.

"I am not a superficial man" – he interrupted her – "nevertheless, my chief feeling now is for the morning papers. Later there will be a politely silent gauntlet of relatives, friends and business acquaintances. About the actual affair I surprise myself by not caring at all."

"I shouldn't care about any of it."

"I'm rather grateful that she did it in time."

"Why don't you go away?" Olive leant forward earnestly. "Go to Europe until it all blows over."

"Blows over." He laughed. "Things like this don't ever blow over. A little snicker is going to follow me around the rest of my life." He groaned. "Uncle Hamilton started right for Park Row to make the rounds of the newspaper offices. He's a Virginian and he was unwise enough to use the old-fashioned word 'horsewhip' to one editor. I can hardly wait to see *that* paper." He broke off. "How is Mr Castleton?"

"He'll appreciate your coming to enquire."

"I didn't come about that." He hesitated. "I came to ask you a question. I want to know if you'll marry me in Greenwich tomorrow morning."

For a minute Olive fell precipitately through space; she made a strange little sound; her mouth dropped ajar.

"I know you like me," he went on quickly. "In fact, I once imagined you loved me a little bit, if you'll excuse the presumption. Anyhow, you're very like a girl that once did love me, so maybe you would..." His face was pink with embarrassment, but he struggled grimly on: "Anyhow, I like you enormously, and whatever feeling I may have had for Emily has, I might say, flown."

The clangour and alarm inside her was so loud that it seemed he must hear it.

"The favour you'll be doing me will be very great," he continued. "My Heavens, I know it sounds a little crazy, but what could be crazier than the whole afternoon? You see, if you married me the papers would carry quite a different story; they'd think that Emily went off to get out of our way, and the joke would be on her after all."

Tears of indignation came to Olive's eyes.

"I suppose I ought to allow for your wounded egotism, but do you realize you're making me an insulting proposition?"

His face fell.

"I'm sorry," he said after a moment. "I guess I was an awful fool even to think of it, but a man hates to lose the whole dignity of his life for a girl's whim. I see it would be impossible. I'm sorry."

He got up and picked up his cane.

Now he was moving towards the door, and Olive's heart came into her throat and a great, irresistible wave of self-preservation swept over her – swept over all her scruples and her pride. His steps sounded in the hall.

"Brevoort!" she called. She jumped to her feet and ran to the door. He turned. "Brevoort, what was the name of that paper – the one your uncle went to?"

"Why?"

"Because it's not too late for them to change their story if I telephone now! I'll say we were married tonight!"

3

THERE IS A SOCIETY IN PARIS which is merely a heterogeneous prolongation of American society. People moving in are connected by a hundred threads to the motherland, and their entertainments, eccentricities and ups and downs are an open book to friends and relatives at Southampton, Lake Forest or Back Bay. So, during her previous European sojourn, Emily's whereabouts, as she followed the shifting Continental season, were publicly advertised; but from the day, one month after the unsolemnized wedding, when she sailed from New York, she dropped completely from sight. There was an occasional letter from her father, an occasional rumour that she was in Cairo, Constantinople or the less frequented Riviera – that was all.

Once, after a year, Mr Castleton saw her in Paris, but, as he told Olive, the meeting only served to make him uncomfortable.

"There was something about her," he said vaguely, "as if... well, as if she had a lot of things in the back of her mind I couldn't reach. She was nice enough, but it was all automatic and formal. She asked about you."

Despite her solid background of a three-month-old baby and a beautiful apartment on Park Avenue, Olive felt her heart falter uncertainly.

"What did she say?"

"She was delighted about you and Brevoort." And he added to himself, with a disappointment he could not conceal: "Even though you picked up the best match in New York when she threw it away..."

...It was more than a year after this that his secretary's voice on the telephone asked Olive if Mr Castleton could see them that night. They found the old man walking his library in a state of agitation.

"Well, it's come," he declared vehemently. "People won't stand still; nobody stands still. You go up or down in this world. Emily chose to go down. She seems to be somewhere near the bottom. Did you ever hear of a man described to me as a" – he referred to a letter in his hand – "dissipated ne'er-do-well named Petrocobesco? He calls himself Prince Gabriel Petrocobesco, apparently from... from nowhere. This letter is from Hallam, my European man, and it encloses a clipping from the Paris *Matin*. It seems that this gentleman was invited by the police to leave Paris, and among the small entourage who left with him was an American girl, Miss Castleton, 'rumoured to be the daughter of a millionaire'. The party was escorted to the station by gendarmes." He handed clipping and letter to Brevoort Blair with trembling fingers. "What do you make of it? Emily come to that!"

"It's not so good," said Brevoort, frowning.

"It's the end. I though her drafts were big recently, but I never suspected that she was supporting—"

"It may be a mistake," Olive suggested. "Perhaps it's another Miss Castleton."

"It's Emily all right. Hallam looked up the matter. It's Emily, who was afraid ever to dive into the nice clean stream of life and ends up now by swimming around in the sewers."

Shocked, Olive had a sudden sharp taste of fate in its ultimate diversity. She with a mansion building in Westbury Hills, and Emily was mixed up with a deported adventurer in disgraceful scandal.

"I've got no right to ask you this," continued Mr Castleton. "Certainly no right to ask Brevoort anything in connection with Emily. But I'm seventy-two and Fraser says if I put off the cure another fortnight he won't be responsible, and then Emily will be alone for good. I want you to set your trip abroad forward by two months and go over and bring her back."

"But do you think we'd have the necessary influence?" Brevoort asked. "I've no reason for thinking that she'd listen to me."

"There's no one else. If you can't go I'll have to."

"Oh, no," said Brevoort quickly. "We'll do what we can, won't we, Olive?"

"Of course."

"Bring her back – it doesn't matter how – but bring her back. Go before a court if necessary and swear she's crazy."

"Very well. We'll do what we can."

Just ten days after this interview the Brevoort Blairs called on Mr Castleton's agent in Paris to glean what details were available. They were plentiful but unsatisfactory. Hallam had seen Petrocobesco in various restaurants – a fat little fellow with an attractive leer and a quench- less thirst. He was of some obscure nationality and had been moved around Europe for several years, living Heaven knew how – probably on Americans, though Hallam understood that of late even the most outlying circles of international society were closed to him. About Emily, Hallam knew very little. They had been reported last week in Berlin and yesterday in Budapest. It was probable that such an undesirable as Petrocobesco was required to register with the police everywhere, and this was the line he recommended the Blairs to follow.

Forty-eight hours later, accompanied by the American vice consul, they called upon the prefect of police in Budapest. The officer talked in rapid Hungarian to the vice consul, who presently announced the gist of his remarks – the Blairs were too late.

"Where have they gone?"

"He doesn't know. He received orders to move them on and they left last night."

Suddenly the prefect wrote something on a piece of paper and handed it, with a terse remark, to the vice consul.

"He says try there."

Brevoort looked at the paper.

"Sturmdorp – where's that?"

Another rapid conversation in Hungarian.

"Five hours from here on a local train that leaves Tuesdays and Fridays. This is Saturday."

"We'll get a car at the hotel," said Brevoort.

They set out after dinner. It was a rough journey through the night across the still Hungarian plain. Olive awoke once from a worried doze to find Brevoort and the chauffeur changing a tyre; then again as they stopped at a muddy little river, beyond which glowed the scattered lights of a town. Two soldiers in an unfamiliar uniform glanced into the car; they crossed a bridge and followed a narrow, warped main street to Sturmdorp's single inn; the roosters were already crowing as they tumbled down on the mean beds.

Olive awoke with a sudden sure feeling that they had caught up with Emily, and with it came that old sense of helplessness in the face of Emily's moods; for a moment the long past, and Emily dominant in it, swept back over her, and it seemed almost a presumption to be here. But Brevoort's singleness of purpose reassured her and confidence had returned when they went downstairs, to find a landlord who spoke fluent American, acquired in Chicago before the war.

"You are not in Hungary now," he explained. "You have crossed the border into Czjeck-Hansa. But it is only a little country with two towns, this one and the capital. We don't ask the visa from Americans."

"That's probably why they came here," Olive thought.

"Perhaps you could give us some information about strangers?" asked Brevoort. "We're looking for an American lady…" He described Emily, without mentioning her probable companion; as he proceeded a curious change came over the innkeeper's face.

"Let me see your passports," he said; then: "And why you want to see her?"

"This lady is her cousin."

The innkeeper hesitated momentarily.

"I think perhaps I be able to find her for you," he said.

He called the porter; there were rapid instructions in an unintelligible patois. Then:

"Follow this boy – he take you there."

They were conducted through filthy streets to a tumbledown house on the edge of town. A man with a hunting rifle, lounging outside, straightened up and spoke sharply to the porter, but after an exchange of phrases they passed, mounted the stairs and knocked at a door. When it opened a head peered around the corner; the porter spoke again and they went in.

They were in a large, dirty room which might have belonged to a poor boarding house in any quarter of the Western world – faded walls, split upholstery, a shapeless bed and an air, despite its bareness, of being overcrowded by the ghostly furniture, indicated by dust rings and worn spots, of the last decade. In the middle of the room stood a small stout man with hammock eyes and a peering nose over a sweet, spoilt little mouth, who stared intently at them as they opened the door, and then with a single disgusted "*Chut!*" turned impatiently away. There were several other people in the room, but Brevoort and Olive saw only Emily, who reclined in a chaise longue with half-closed eyes.

At the sight of them the eyes opened in mild astonishment; she made a move as though to jump up, but instead held out her hand, smiled and spoke their names in a clear, polite voice, less as a greeting than as a sort of explanation to the others of their presence here. At their names a grudging amenity replaced the sullenness on the little man's face.

The girls kissed.

"Tutu!" said Emily, as if calling him to attention – "Prince Petrocobesco, let me present my cousin, Mrs Blair, and Mr Blair."

"*Plaisir*," said Petrocobesco. He and Emily exchanged a quick glance, whereupon he said, "Won't you sit down?" and immediately seated himself in the only available chair, as if they were playing Going to Jerusalem.

"*Plaisir*," he repeated. Olive sat down on the foot of Emily's chaise longue and Brevoort took a stool from against the wall, meanwhile noting the other occupants of the room. There was a very fierce young man in a cape who stood, with arms folded and teeth gleaming, by the door, and two ragged, bearded men, one holding a revolver, the other with his head sunk dejectedly on his chest, who sat side by side in the corner.

"You come here long?" the prince asked.

"Just arrived this morning."

For a moment Olive could not resist comparing the two – the tall, fair-featured American and the unprepossessing South European, scarcely a likely candidate for Ellis Island.* Then she looked at Emily – the same thick bright hair with sunshine in it, the eyes with the hint of vivid seas. Her face was faintly drawn, there were slight new lines around her mouth, but she was the Emily of old – dominant, shining, large of scale. It seemed shameful for all that beauty and personality to have arrived in a cheap boarding house at the world's end.

The man in the cape answered a knock at the door and handed a note to Petrocobesco, who read it, cried "*Chut!*" and passed it to Emily.

"You see, there are no carriages," he said tragically in French. "The carriages were destroyed – all except one, which is in a museum. Anyhow, I prefer a horse."

"No," said Emily.

"Yes, yes, yes!" he cried. "Whose business is it how I go?"

"Don't let's have a scene, Tutu."

"Scene!" He fumed. "Scene!"

Emily turned to Olive: "You came by automobile?"

"Yes."

"A big deluxe car? With a back that opens?"

"Yes."

"There," said Emily to the prince. "We can have the arms painted on the side of that."

"Hold on," said Brevoort. "This car belongs to a hotel in Budapest."

Apparently Emily didn't hear.

"Janierka could do it," she continued thoughtfully.

At this point there was another interruption. The dejected man in the corner suddenly sprang to his feet and made as though to run to the door, whereupon the other man raised his revolver and brought the butt down on his head. The man faltered and would have collapsed had not his assailant hauled him back to the chair, where he sat comatose, a slow stream of blood trickling over his forehead.

"Dirty townsman! Filthy, dirty spy!" shouted Petrocobesco between clenched teeth.

"Now that's just the kind of remark you're not to make!" said Emily sharply.

"Then why we don't hear?" he cried. "Are we going to sit here in this pigsty for ever?"

Disregarding him, Emily turned to Olive and began to question her conventionally about New York. Was Prohibition any more successful? What were the new plays? Olive tried to answer and simultaneously to catch Brevoort's eye. The sooner their purpose was broached, the sooner they could get Emily away.

"Can we see you alone, Emily?" demanded Brevoort abruptly.

"Why, for the moment we haven't got another room."

Petrocobesco had engaged the man with the cape in agitated conversation and, taking advantage of this, Brevoort spoke hurriedly to Emily in a lowered voice:

"Emily, your father's getting old; he needs you at home. He wants you to give up this crazy life and come back to America. He sent us because he couldn't come himself and no one else knew you well enough…"

She laughed. "You mean, knew the enormities I was capable of."

"No," put in Olive quickly. "Cared for you as we do. I can't tell you how awful it is to see you wandering over the face of the earth."

"But we're not wandering now," explained Emily. "This is Tutu's native country."

"Where's your pride, Emily?" said Olive impatiently. "Do you know that affair in Paris was in the papers? What do you suppose people think back home?"

"That affair in Paris was an outrage." Emily's blue eyes flashed around her. "Someone will pay for that affair in Paris."

"It'll be the same everywhere. Just sinking lower and lower, dragged in the mire and one day deserted—"

"Stop, please!" Emily's voice was cold as ice. "I don't think you quite understand…"

Emily broke off as Petrocobesco came back, threw himself into his chair and buried his face in his hands.

"I can't stand it," he whispered. "Would you mind taking my pulse? I think it's bad. Have you got the thermometer in your purse?"

She held his wrist in silence for a moment.

"It's all right, Tutu." Her voice was soft now, almost crooning. "Sit up. Be a man."

"All right."

He crossed his legs as if nothing had happened and turned abruptly to Brevoort:

"How are financial conditions in New York?" he demanded.

But Brevoort was in no humour to prolong the absurd scene. The memory of a certain terrible hour three years before swept over him. He was no man to be made a fool of twice, and his jaw set as he rose to his feet.

"Emily, get your things together," he said tersely. "We're going home."

Emily did not move; an expression of astonishment, melting to amusement, spread over her face. Olive put her arm around her shoulder.

"Come, dear. Let's get out of this nightmare." Then:

"We're waiting," Brevoort said.

Petrocobesco spoke suddenly to the man in the cape, who approached and seized Brevoort's arm. Brevoort shook him off angrily, whereupon the man stepped back, his hand searching his belt.

"No!" cried Emily imperatively.

Once again there was an interruption. The door opened without a knock and two stout men in frock coats and silk hats rushed in and up to Petrocobesco. They grinned and patted him on the back, chattering in a strange language, and presently he grinned and patted them on the back and they kissed all around; then, turning to Emily, Petrocobesco spoke to her in French.

"It's all right," he said excitedly. "They did not even argue the matter. I am to have the title of king."

With a long sigh Emily sank back in her chair and her lips parted in a relaxed, tranquil smile.

"Very well, Tutu. We'll get married."

"Oh, Heavens, how happy!" He clasped his hands and gazed up ecstatically at the faded ceiling. "How extremely happy!" He fell on his knees beside her and kissed her inside arm.

"What's all this about kings?" Brevoort demanded. "Is this… is he a king?"

"He's a king. Aren't you, Tutu?" Emily's hand gently stroked his oiled hair and Olive saw that her eyes were unusually bright.

"I am your husband," cried Tutu weepily. "The most happy man alive."

"His uncle was Prince of Czjeck-Hansa before the war," explained Emily, her voice singing her content. "Since then there's been a republic, but the peasant party wanted a change and Tutu was next in line. Only I wouldn't marry him unless he insisted on being king instead of prince."

Brevoort passed his hand over his wet forehead.

"Do you mean that this is actually a fact?"

Emily nodded. "The assembly voted it this morning. And if you'll lend us this deluxe limousine of yours we'll make our official entrance into the capital this afternoon."

4

OVER TWO YEARS LATER, Mr and Mrs Brevoort Blair and their two children stood upon a balcony of the Carlton Hotel in London, a situation recommended by the management for watching royal processions pass. This one began with a fanfare of trumpets down by the Strand, and presently a scarlet line of Horse Guards came into sight.

"But, Mummy," the little boy demanded, "is Aunt Emily Queen of England?"

"No, dear: she's queen of a little tiny country, but when she visits here she rides in the queen's carriage."

"Oh."

"Thanks to the magnesium deposits," said Brevoort drily.

"Was she a princess before she got to be queen?" the little girl asked.

"No, dear: she was an American girl and then she got to be a queen."

"Why?"

"Because nothing else was good enough for her," said her father. "Just think, one time she could have married me. Which would you rather do, baby – marry me or be a queen?"

The little girl hesitated.

"Marry you," she said politely, but without conviction.

"That'll do, Brevoort," said her mother. "Here they come."

"I see them!" the little boy cried.

The cavalcade swept down the crowded street. There were more Horse Guards, a company of dragoons, outriders, then Olive found herself holding her breath and squeezing the balcony rail, as between a double line of beefeaters a pair of great gilt-and-crimson coaches rolled past. In the first were the royal sovereigns, their uniforms gleaming with ribbons, crosses and stars, and in the second their two royal consorts, one old, the other young. There was about the scene the glamour shed always by the old empire of half the world, by her ships and ceremonies, her pomps and symbols; and the crowd felt it, and a slow murmur rolled along before the carriage, rising to a strong steady cheer. The two ladies bowed to left and right, and though few knew who the second queen was, she was cheered too. In a moment the gorgeous panoply had rolled below the balcony and on out of sight.

When Olive turned away from the window there were tears in her eyes.

"I wonder if she likes it, Brevoort. I wonder if she's really happy with that terrible little man."

"Well, she got what she wanted, didn't she? And that's something."

Olive drew a long breath.

"Oh, she's so wonderful," she cried – "so wonderful! She could always move me like that, even when I was angriest at her."

"It's all so silly," Brevoort said.

"I suppose so," answered Olive's lips. But her heart, winged with helpless adoration, was following her cousin through the palace gates half a mile away.

At Your Age

1

TOM SQUIRES CAME INTO THE DRUGSTORE to buy a toothbrush, a can of talcum, a gargle, Castile soap, Epsom salts and a box of cigars. Having lived alone for many years, he was methodical, and while waiting to be served he held the list in his hand. It was Christmas week and Minneapolis was under two feet of exhilarating, constantly refreshed snow; with his cane Tom knocked two clean crusts of it from his overshoes. Then, looking up, he saw the blonde girl.

She was a rare blonde, even in that Promised Land of Scandinavians, where pretty blondes are not rare. There was warm colour in her cheeks, lips and pink little hands that folded powders into papers; her hair, in long braids twisted about her head, was shining and alive. She seemed to Tom suddenly the cleanest person he knew of, and he caught his breath as he stepped forward and looked into her grey eyes.

"A can of talcum."

"What kind?"

"Any kind… That's fine."

She looked back at him apparently without self-consciousness, and, as the list melted away, his heart raced with it wildly.

"I am not old," he wanted to say. "At fifty I'm younger than most men of forty. Don't I interest you at all?"

But she only said, "What kind of gargle?"

And he answered, "What can you recommend?… That's fine."

Almost painfully he took his eyes from her, went out and got into his coupé.

"If that young idiot only knew what an old imbecile like me could do for her," he thought humorously – "what worlds I could open out to her!"

As he drove away into the winter twilight he followed this train of thought to a totally unprecedented conclusion. Perhaps the time of day was the responsible stimulant, for the shop windows glowing into the cold, the tinkling bells of a delivery sleigh, the white gloss left by shovels on the sidewalks, the enormous distance of the stars brought back the feel of other nights thirty years ago. For an instant the girls he had known then slipped like phantoms out of their dull matronly selves of today and fluttered past him with frosty, seductive laughter, until a pleasant shiver crawled up his spine.

"Youth! Youth! Youth!" he apostrophized with conscious lack of originality, and, as a somewhat ruthless and domineering man of no morals whatsoever, he considered going back to the drugstore to seek the blonde girl's address. It was not his sort of thing, so the half-formed intention passed; the idea remained.

"Youth, by heaven – youth!" he repeated under his breath. "I want it near me, all around me, just once more before I'm too old to care."

He was tall, lean and handsome, with the ruddy, bronzed face of a sportsman and a just faintly greying moustache. Once he had been among the city's best beaus, organizer of cotillions and charity balls, popular with men and women, and with several generations of them. After the war he had suddenly felt poor, gone into business, and in ten years accumulated nearly a million dollars. Tom Squires was not introspective, but he perceived now that the wheel of his life had revolved again, bringing up forgotten yet familiar dreams and yearnings. Entering his house, he turned suddenly to a pile of disregarded invitations to see whether or not he had been bidden to a dance tonight.

Throughout his dinner, which he ate alone at the Downtown Club, his eyes were half closed and on his face was a faint smile. He was practising so that he would be able to laugh at himself painlessly, if necessary.

"I don't even know what they talk about," he admitted. "They pet – prominent broker goes to petting party with debutante. What is a petting party? Do they serve refreshments? Will I have to learn to play a saxophone?"

These matters, lately as remote as China in a newsreel, came alive to him. They were serious questions. At ten o'clock he walked up the steps of the College Club to a private dance with the same sense of entering a new world as when he had gone into a training camp back in '17. He spoke to a hostess of his generation and to her daughter, overwhelmingly of another, and sat down in a corner to acclimate himself.

He was not alone long. A silly young man named Leland Jaques, who lived across the street from Tom, remarked him kindly and came over to brighten his life. He was such an exceedingly fatuous young man that, for a moment, Tom was annoyed, but he perceived craftily that he might be of service.

"Hello, Mr Squires. How are you, sir?"

"Fine, thanks, Leland. Quite a dance."

As one man of the world with another, Mr Jaques sat, or lay, down on the couch and lit – or so it seemed to Tom – three or four cigarettes at once.

"You should of been here last night, Mr Squires. Oh, boy, that was a party and a half! The Caulkins. Hap-past five!"

"Who's that girl who changes partners every minute?" Tom asked… "No, the one in white passing the door."

"That's Annie Lorry."

"Arthur Lorry's daughter?"

"Yes."

"She seems popular."

"About the most popular girl in town – anyway, at a dance."

"Not popular except at dances?"

"Oh, sure, but she hangs around with Randy Cambell all the time."

"What Cambell?"

"D.B."

There were new names in town in the last decade.

"It's a boy-and-girl affair." Pleased with this phrase, Jaques tried to repeat it: "One of those boy-and-girls affair... boys-and-girl affairs..." He gave it up and lit several more cigarettes, crushing out the first series on Tom's lap.

"Does she drink?"

"Not especially. At least I never saw her passed out... That's Randy Cambell just cut in on her now."

They were a nice couple. Her beauty sparkled bright against his strong, tall form, and they floated hoveringly, delicately, like two people in a nice, amusing dream. They came near and Tom admired the faint dust of powder over her freshness, the guarded sweetness of her smile, the fragility of her body calculated by Nature to a millimetre to suggest a bud, yet guarantee a flower. Her innocent, passionate eyes were brown, perhaps – but almost violet in the silver light.

"Is she out this year?"

"Who?"

"Miss Lorry."

"Yes."

Although the girl's loveliness interested Tom, he was unable to picture himself as one of the attentive, grateful queue that pursued her around the room. Better meet her when the holidays were over and most of these young men were back in college "where they belonged". Tom Squires was old enough to wait.

He waited a fortnight while the city sank into the endless northern midwinter, where grey skies were friendlier than metallic blue skies, and dusk, whose lights were a reassuring glimpse into the continuity of human cheer, was warmer than the afternoons of bloodless sunshine. The coat of snow lost its press and became soiled and shabby, and ruts froze in the street; some of the big houses on Crest Avenue began to close as their occupants went South. In those cold days Tom asked Annie and her parents to go as his guests to the last Bachelors' Ball.

The Lorrys were an old family in Minneapolis, grown a little harassed and poor since the war. Mrs Lorry, a contemporary of Tom's, was not surprised that he should send mother and daughter orchids and dine them luxuriously in his apartment on fresh caviar, quail and champagne. Annie saw him only dimly – he lacked vividness, as the old do for the young – but she perceived his interest in her and performed for him the traditional ritual of young beauty – smiles, polite, wide-eyed attention, a profile held obligingly in this light or in that. At the ball he danced with her twice, and though she was teased about it, she was flattered that such a man of the world – he had become that instead of a mere old man – had singled her out. She accepted his invitation to the symphony the following week, with the idea that it would be uncouth to refuse.

There were several "nice invitations" like that. Sitting beside him, she dozed in the warm shadow of Brahms and thought of Randy Cambell and other romantic nebulosities who might appear tomorrow. Feeling casually mellow one afternoon, she deliberately provoked Tom to kiss her on the way home, but she wanted to laugh when he took her hands and told her fervently he was falling in love.

"But how could you?" she protested. "Really, you mustn't say such crazy things. I won't go out with you any more, and then you'll be sorry."

A few days later her mother spoke to her as Tom waited outside in his car:

"Who's that, Annie?"

"Mr Squires."

"Shut the door a minute. You're seeing him quite a bit."

"Why not?"

"Well, dear, he's fifty years old."

"But, Mother, there's hardly anybody else in town."

"But you mustn't get any silly ideas about him."

"Don't worry. Actually, he bores me to extinction most of the time." She came to a sudden decision: "I'm not going to see him any more. I just couldn't get out of going with him this afternoon."

And that night, as she stood by her door in the circle of Randy Cambell's arm, Tom and his single kiss had no existence for her.

"Oh, I do love you so," Randy whispered. "Kiss me once more."

Their cool cheeks and warm lips met in the crisp darkness, and, watching the icy moon over his shoulder, Annie knew that she was his surely and, pulling his face down, kissed him again, trembling with emotion.

"When'll you marry me then?" he whispered.

"When can you… we afford it?"

"Couldn't you announce our engagement? If you knew the misery of having you out with somebody else and then making love to you."

"Oh, Randy, you ask so much."

"It's so awful to say goodnight. Can't I come in for a minute?"

"Yes."

Sitting close together in a trance before the flickering, lessening fire, they were oblivious that their common fate was being coolly weighed by a man of fifty who lay in a hot bath some blocks away.

2

T OM SQUIRES HAD GUESSED from Annie's extremely kind and detached manner of the afternoon that he had failed to interest her. He had promised himself that in such an eventuality he would drop the matter, but now he found himself in no such humour. He did not want to marry her; he simply wanted to see her and be with her a little; and up to the moment of her sweetly casual, half-passionate yet wholly unemotional kiss, giving her up would have been easy, for he was past the romantic age; but since that kiss the thought of her made his heart move up a few inches in his chest and beat there steady and fast.

"But this is the time to get out," he said to himself. "My age – no possible right to force myself into her life."

He rubbed himself dry, brushed his hair before the mirror and, as he laid down the comb, said decisively: "That is that." And after reading for an hour he turned out the lamp with a snap and repeated aloud: "That is that."

In other words, that was not that at all, and the click of material things did not finish off Annie Lorry as a business decision might be settled by the tap of a pencil on the table.

"I'm going to carry this matter a little further," he said to himself about half-past four; on that acknowledgement he turned over and found sleep.

In the morning she had receded somewhat, but by four o'clock in the afternoon she was all around him – the phone was for calling her, a woman's footfalls passing his office were her footfalls, the snow outside the window was blowing, perhaps, against her rosy face.

"There is always the little plan I thought of last night," he said to himself. "In ten years I'll be sixty, and then no youth, no beauty for me ever any more."

In a sort of panic he took a sheet of notepaper and composed a carefully phrased letter to Annie's mother, asking permission to pay court to her daughter. He took it himself into the hall, but before the letter slide he tore it up and dropped the pieces in a cuspidor.

"I couldn't do such an underhand trick," he told himself, "at my age." But this self-congratulation was premature, for he rewrote the letter and mailed it before he left his office that night.

Next day the reply he had counted on arrived – he could have guessed its very words in advance. It was a curt and indignant refusal.

It ended:

I think it best that you and my daughter meet no more.

Very Sincerely Yours,

MABEL TOLLMAN LORRY

"And now," Tom thought coolly, "we'll see what the girl says to that."

He wrote a note to Annie. Her mother's letter had surprised him, it said, but perhaps it was best that they should meet no more, in view of her mother's attitude.

By return post came Annie's defiant answer to her mother's fiat: "This isn't the Dark Ages. I'll see you whenever I like." She named a rendezvous for the following afternoon. Her mother's short-sightedness brought about what he had failed to achieve directly; for where Annie had been on the point of dropping him, she was now determined to do nothing of the sort. And the secrecy engendered by disapproval at home simply contributed the missing excitement. As February hardened into deep, solemn, interminable winter, she met him frequently and on a new basis. Sometimes they drove over to St Paul to see a picture or to have dinner; sometimes they parked far out on a boulevard in his coupé, while the bitter sleet glazed the windshield to opacity and furred his lamps with ermine. Often he brought along something special to drink – enough to make her gay but, carefully, never more; for mingled with his other emotions about her was something paternally concerned.

Laying his cards on the table, he told her that it was her mother who had unwittingly pushed her towards him, but Annie only laughed at his duplicity.

She was having a better time with him than with anyone else she had ever known. In place of the selfish exigency of a younger man, he showed her a never-failing consideration. What if his eyes were tired, his cheeks a little leathery and veined, if his will was masculine and strong. Moreover, his experience was a window looking out upon a wider, richer world; and with Randy Cambell next day she would feel less taken care of, less valued, less rare.

It was Tom now who was vaguely discontented. He had what he wanted – her youth at his side – and he felt that anything further would be a mistake. His liberty was precious to him and he could offer her only a dozen years before he would be old, but she had become something precious to him and he perceived that drifting wasn't fair. Then one day late in February the matter was decided out of hand.

They had ridden home from St Paul and dropped into the College Club for tea, breaking together through the drifts that masked the walk and rimmed the door. It was a revolving door; a young man came around in it and, stepping into his space, they smelt onions and whisky. The door revolved again after them, and he was back within, facing them. It was Randy Cambell; his face was flushed, his eyes dull and hard.

"Hello, beautiful," he said, approaching Annie.

"Don't come so close," she protested lightly. "You smell of onions."

"You're particular all of a sudden."

"Always. I'm always particular." Annie made a slight movement back towards Tom.

"Not always," said Randy unpleasantly. Then, with increased emphasis and a fractional glance at Tom: "Not always." With his remark he seemed to join the hostile world outside. "And I'll just give you a tip," he continued: "Your mother's inside."

The jealous ill temper of another generation reached Tom only faintly, like the protest of a child, but at this impertinent warning he bristled with annoyance.

"Come on, Annie," he said brusquely. "We'll go in."

With her glance uneasily averted from Randy, Annie followed Tom into the big room.

It was sparsely populated; three middle-aged women sat near the fire. Momentarily Annie drew back, then she walked towards them.

"Hello, mother… Mrs Trumble… Aunt Caroline."

The two latter responded; Mrs Trumble even nodded faintly at Tom. But Annie's mother got to her feet without a word, her eyes frozen, her mouth drawn. For a moment she stood staring at her daughter; then she turned abruptly and left the room.

Tom and Annie found a table across the room.

"Wasn't she terrible?" said Annie, breathing aloud. He didn't answer. "For three days she hasn't spoken to me." Suddenly she broke out: "Oh, people can be so small! I was going to sing the leading part in the Junior

League show, and yesterday Cousin Mary Betts, the president, came to me and said I couldn't."

"Why not?"

"Because a representative Junior League girl mustn't defy her mother. As if I were a naughty child!"

Tom stared on at a row of cups on the mantelpiece – two or three of them bore his name. "Perhaps she was right," he said suddenly. "When I begin to do harm to you it's time to stop."

"What do you mean?"

At her shocked voice his heart poured a warm liquid forth into his body, but he answered quietly: "You remember I told you I was going South? Well, I'm going tomorrow."

There was an argument, but he had made up his mind. At the station next evening she wept and clung to him.

"Thank you for the happiest month I've had in years," he said.

"But you'll come back, Tom."

"I'll be two months in Mexico, then I'm going East for a few weeks."

He tried to sound fortunate, but the frozen city he was leaving seemed to be in blossom. Her frozen breath was a flower on the air, and his heart sank as he realized that some young man was waiting outside to take her home in a car hung with blooms.

"Goodbye, Annie. Goodbye, sweet!"

Two days later he spent the morning in Houston with Hal Meigs, a classmate at Yale.

"You're in luck for such an old fella," said Meigs at luncheon, "because I'm going to introduce you to the cutest little travelling companion you ever saw, who's going all the way to Mexico City."

The lady in question was frankly pleased to learn at the station that she was not returning alone. She and Tom dined together on the train and later played rummy for an hour; but when, at ten o'clock, standing in the door of the stateroom, she turned back to him suddenly with a certain look, frank and unmistakable, and stood there holding that look for a long moment, Tom Squires was suddenly in the grip of an emotion that was not the one in question. He wanted desperately to see Annie, call her for a second on the phone, and then fall asleep, knowing she was young and pure as a star, and safe in bed.

"Goodnight," he said, trying to keep any repulsion out of his voice.

"Oh! Goodnight."

Arriving in El Paso next day, he drove over the border to Juárez. It was bright and hot, and after leaving his bags at the station he went into a bar for an iced drink; as he sipped it a girl's voice addressed him thickly from the table behind:

"You'n American?"

He had noticed her slumped forward on her elbows as he came in; now, turning, he faced a young girl of about seventeen, obviously drunk yet with gentility in her unsteady, sprawling voice. The American bartender leant confidentially forward.

"I don't know what to do about her," he said. "She come in about three o'clock with two young fellows – one of them her sweetie. They had a fight and the men went off, and this one's been here ever since."

A spasm of distaste passed over Tom – the rules of his generation were outraged and defied. That an American girl should be drunk and deserted in a tough foreign town – that such things happened, might happen to Annie. He looked at his watch, hesitated.

"Has she got a bill?" he asked.

"She owes for five gins. But suppose her boyfriends come back?"

"Tell them she's at the Roosevelt Hotel in El Paso."

Approaching, he put his hand on her shoulder. She looked up.

"You look like Santa Claus," she said vaguely. "You couldn't possibly be Santa Claus, could you?"

"I'm going to take you to El Paso."

"Well," she considered, "you look perfectly safe to me."

She was so young – a drenched little rose. He could have wept for her wretched unconsciousness of the old facts, the old penalties of life.

Jousting at nothing in an empty tilt yard with a shaking spear. The taxi moved too slowly through the suddenly poisonous night.

Having explained things to a reluctant night clerk, he went out and found a telegraph office.

"Have given up Mexican trip," he wired. "Leaving here tonight. Please meet train in the St Paul station at three o'clock and ride with me to Minneapolis, as I can't spare you for another minute. All my love."

He could at least keep an eye on her, advise her, see what she did with her life. That silly mother of hers!

On the train, as the baked tropical lands and green fields fell away and the North swept near again with patches of snow, then fields of it, fierce winds in the vestibule and bleak, hibernating farms, he paced the corridors with intolerable restlessness. When they drew into the St Paul station he swung himself off like a young man and searched the platform eagerly, but his eyes failed to find her. He had counted on those few minutes between the cities; they had become a symbol of her fidelity to their friendship, and as the train started again he searched it desperately from smoker to observation car. But he could not find her, and now he knew that he was mad for her; at the thought that she had taken his advice and plunged into affairs with other men, he grew weak with fear.

Drawing into Minneapolis, his hands fumbled so that he must call the porter to fasten his baggage. Then there was an interminable wait in the corridor while the baggage was taken off and he was pressed up against a girl in a squirrel-trimmed coat.

"Tom!"

"Well, I'll be—"

Her arms went up around his neck. "But, Tom," she cried, "I've been right here in this car since St Paul!"

His cane fell in the corridor, he drew her very tenderly close, and their lips met like starved hearts.

3

THE NEW INTIMACY of their definite engagement brought Tom a feeling of young happiness. He awoke on winter mornings with the sense of undeserved joy hovering in the room; meeting young men, he found himself matching the vigour of his mind and body against theirs. Suddenly his life had a purpose and a background; he felt rounded and complete. On grey March afternoons when she wandered familiarly in his apartment, the warm sureties of his youth flooded back – ecstasy and poignancy, the mortal and the eternal posed in their immemorially tragic juxtaposition and, a little astounded, he found himself relishing the very terminology of young romance. But he was more thoughtful than a younger lover; and to Annie he seemed to "know everything", to stand holding open the gates for her passage into the truly golden world.

"We'll go to Europe first," he said.

"Oh, we'll go there a lot, won't we? Let's spend our winters in Italy and the spring in Paris."

"But, little Annie, there's business."

"Well, we'll stay away as much as we can anyhow. I hate Minneapolis."

"Oh, no." He was a little shocked. "Minneapolis is all right."

"When you're here it's all right."

Mrs Lorry yielded at length to the inevitable. With ill grace she acknowledged the engagement, asking only that the marriage should not take place until fall.

"Such a long time," Annie sighed.

"After all, I'm your mother. It's so little to ask."

It was a long winter, even in a land of long winters. March was full of billowy drifts, and when it seemed at last as though the cold must be defeated, there was a series of blizzards, desperate as last stands. The people waited; their first energy to resist was spent, and man, like weather, simply hung on. There was less to do now and the general restlessness was expressed by surliness in daily contacts. Then, early in

April, with a long sigh, the ice cracked, the snow ran into the ground and the green, eager spring broke up through.

One day, riding along a slushy road in a fresh, damp breeze with a little starved, smothered grass in it, Annie began to cry. Sometimes she cried for nothing, but this time Tom suddenly stopped the car and put his arm around her.

"Why do you cry like that? Are you unhappy?"

"Oh, no, no!" she protested.

"But you cried yesterday the same way. And you wouldn't tell me why. You must always tell me."

"Nothing, except the spring. It smells so good, and it always has so many sad thoughts and memories in it."

"It's our spring, my sweetheart," he said. "Annie, don't let's wait. Let's be married in June."

"I promised Mother, but if you like we can announce our engagement in June."

The spring came fast now. The sidewalks were damp, then dry, and the children roller-skated on them and boys played baseball in the soft, vacant lots. Tom got up elaborate picnics of Annie's contemporaries and encouraged her to play golf and tennis with them. Abruptly, with a final, triumphant lurch of nature, it was full summer.

On a lovely May evening Tom came up the Lorrys' walk and sat down beside Annie's mother on the porch.

"It's pleasant," he said, "I thought Annie and I would walk instead of driving this evening. I want to show her the funny old house I was born in."

"On Chambers Street, wasn't it? Annie'll be home in a few minutes. She went riding with some young people after dinner. "

"Yes, on Chambers Street."

He looked at his watch presently, hoping Annie would come while it was still light enough to see. Quarter of nine. He frowned. She had kept him waiting the night before, kept him waiting an hour yesterday afternoon.

"If I was twenty-one," he said to himself, "I'd make scenes and we'd both be miserable."

He and Mrs Lorry talked; the warmth of the night precipitated the vague evening lassitude of the fifties and softened them both, and for the first time since his attentions to Annie began, there was no unfriendliness between them. By and by long silences fell, broken only by the scratch of a match or the creak of her swinging settee. When Mr Lorry came home, Tom threw away his second cigar in surprise and looked at his watch: it was after ten.

"Annie's late," Mrs Lorry said.

"I hope there's nothing wrong," said Tom anxiously. "Who is she with?"

"There were four when they started out. Randy Cambell and another couple – I didn't notice who. They were only going for a soda."

"I hope there hasn't been any trouble. Perhaps... Do you think I ought to go and see?"

"Ten isn't late nowadays. You'll find..." Remembering that Tom Squires was marrying Annie, not adopting her, she kept herself from adding: "You'll get used to it."

Her husband excused himself and went up to bed, and the conversation became more forced and desultory. When the church clock over the way struck eleven, they both broke off and listened to the beats. Twenty minutes later, just as Tom impatiently crushed out his last cigar, an automobile drifted down the street and came to rest in front of the door.

For a minute no one moved on the porch or in the auto. Then Annie, with a hat in her hand, got out and came quickly up the walk. Defying the tranquil night, the car snorted away.

"Oh, hello!" she cried. "I'm so sorry! What time is it? Am I terribly late?"

Tom didn't answer. The street lamp threw wine colour upon her face and expressed with a shadow the heightened flush of her cheek. Her dress was crushed, her hair was in brief, expressive disarray. But it was the strange little break in her voice that made him afraid to speak, made him turn his eyes aside.

"What happened?" Mrs Lorry asked casually.

"Oh, a blowout and something wrong with the engine – and we lost our way. Is it terribly late?"

And then, as she stood before them, her hat still in her hand, her breast rising and falling a little, her eyes wide and bright, Tom realized with a shock that he and her mother were people of the same age looking at a person of another. Try as he might, he could not separate himself from Mrs Lorry. When she excused herself he suppressed a frantic tendency to say, "But why should you go now? After sitting here all evening?"

They were alone. Annie came up to him and pressed his hand. He had never been so conscious of her beauty; her damp hands were touched with dew.

"You were out with young Cambell," he said.

"Yes. Oh, don't be mad. I feel... I feel so upset tonight."

"Upset?"

She sat down, whimpering a little.

"I couldn't help it. Please don't be mad. He wanted so for me to take a ride with him and it was such a wonderful night, so I went just for an hour. And we began talking and I didn't realize the time. I felt so sorry for him."

"How do you think I felt?" He scorned himself, but it was said now.

"Don't, Tom. I told you I was terribly upset. I want to go to bed."

"I understand. Goodnight, Annie."

"Oh, please don't act that way, Tom. Can't you understand?"

But he could, and that was just the trouble. With the courteous bow of another generation, he walked down the steps and off into the obliterating moonlight. In a moment he was just a shadow passing the street lamps and then a faint footfall up the street.

4

ALL THROUGH THAT SUMMER he often walked abroad in the evenings. He liked to stand for a minute in front of the house where he was born, and then in front of another house where he had been a little boy. On his customary routes there were other sharp landmarks of the 90s, converted habitats of gaieties that no longer existed – the shell of Jansen's Livery Stables and the old Nushka Rink, where every winter his father had curled on the well-kept ice.

"And it's a darn pity," he would mutter. "A darn pity."

He had a tendency, too, to walk past the lights of a certain drugstore, because it seemed to him that it had contained the seed of another and nearer branch of the past. Once he went in, and enquiring casually about the blonde clerk, found that she had married and departed several months before. He obtained her name and on an impulse sent her a wedding present "from a dumb admirer", for he felt he owed something to her for his happiness and pain. He had lost the battle against youth and spring, and with his grief paid the penalty for age's unforgivable sin – refusing to die. But he could not have walked down wasted into the darkness without being used up a little; what he had wanted, after all, was only to break his strong old heart. Conflict itself has a value beyond victory and defeat, and those three months – he had them for ever.

The Swimmers

1

IN THE PLACE BENOÎT, a suspended mass of gasoline exhaust cooked slowly by the June sun. It was a terrible thing for, unlike pure heat, it held no promise of rural escape, but suggested only roads choked with the same foul asthma. In the offices of The Promissory Trust Company, Paris Branch, facing the square, an American man of thirty-five inhaled it, and it became the odour of the thing he must presently do. A black horror suddenly descended upon him, and he went up to the washroom, where he stood, trembling a little, just inside the door.

Through the washroom window his eyes fell upon a sign – "1000 Chemises". The shirts in question filled the shop window, piled, cravated and stuffed, or else draped with shoddy grace on the showcase floor. "1000 Chemises" – count them! To the left he read Papeterie, Pâtisserie, Solde, Réclame and Constance Talmadge in *Déjeuner de soleil*; and his eye, escaping to the right, met yet more sombre announcements: Vêtements Ecclésiastiques, Déclaration de Décès and Pompes Funèbres.* Life and Death.

Henry Marston's trembling became a shaking; it would be pleasant if this were the end and nothing more need be done, he thought, and with a certain hope he sat down on a stool. But it is seldom really the end, and after a while, as he became too exhausted to care, the shaking stopped and he was better. Going downstairs, looking as alert and self-possessed as any other officer of the bank, he spoke to two clients he knew, and set his face grimly towards noon.

"Well, Henry Clay Marston!" A handsome old man shook hands with him and took the chair beside his desk.

"Henry, I want to see you in regard to what we talked about the other night. How about lunch? In that green little place with all the trees."

"Not lunch, Judge Waterbury; I've got an engagement."

"I'll talk now, then; because I'm leaving this afternoon. What do these plutocrats give you for looking important around here?"

Henry Marston knew what was coming.

"Ten thousand and certain expense money," he answered.

"How would you like to come back to Richmond at about double that? You've been over here eight years and you don't know the opportunities you're missing. Why both my boys..."

Henry listened appreciatively, but this morning he couldn't concentrate on the matter. He spoke vaguely about being able to live more comfortably in Paris and restrained himself from stating his frank opinion upon existence at home.

Judge Waterbury beckoned to a tall, pale man who stood at the mail desk.

"This is Mr Wiese," he said. "Mr Wiese's from downstate; he's a halfway partner of mine."

"Glad to meet you, suh." Mr Wiese's voice was rather too deliberately Southern. "Understand the judge is makin' you a proposition."

"Yes," Henry answered briefly. He recognized and detested the type – the prosperous sweater, presumably evolved from a cross between carpetbagger and poor white. When Wiese moved away, the judge said almost apologetically:

"He's one of the richest men in the South, Henry." Then, after a pause: "Come home, boy."

"I'll think it over, judge." For a moment the grey and ruddy head seemed so kind; then it faded back into something one-dimensional, machine-finished, blandly and bleakly un-European. Henry Marston respected that open kindness – in the bank he touched it with daily appreciation, as a curator in a museum might touch a precious object removed in time and space; but there was no help in it for him; the questions which Henry Marston's life propounded could be answered only in France. His seven generations of Virginia ancestors were definitely behind him every day at noon when he turned home.

Home was a fine high-ceiling apartment hewn from the palace of a Renaissance cardinal in the Rue Monsieur – the sort of thing Henry could not have afforded in America. Choupette, with something more than the rigid traditionalism of a French bourgeois taste, had made it beautiful, and moved through gracefully with their children. She was a frail Latin blonde with fine large features and vividly sad French eyes that had first fascinated Henry in a Grenoble *pension* in 1918. The two boys took their looks from Henry, voted the handsomest man at the University of Virginia a few years before the war.

Climbing the two broad flights of stairs, Henry stood panting a moment in the outside hall. It was quiet and cool here, and yet it was vaguely like the terrible thing that was going to happen. He heard a clock inside his apartment strike one, and inserted his key in the door.

The maid who had been in Choupette's family for thirty years stood before him, her mouth open in the utterance of a truncated sigh.

"*Bonjour*, Louise."

"Monsieur!" He threw his hat on a chair. "But, Monsieur – but I thought Monsieur said on the phone he was going to Tours for the children!"

"I changed my mind, Louise."

He had taken a step forward, his last doubt melting away at the constricted terror in the woman's face.

"Is Madame home?"

Simultaneously he perceived a man's hat and stick on the hall table, and for the first time in his life he heard silence – a loud, singing silence, oppressive as heavy guns or thunder. Then, as the endless moment was broken by the maid's terrified little cry, he pushed through the portières into the next room.

An hour later, Doctor Derocco, *de la Faculté de Médecine*, rang the apartment bell. Choupette Marston, her face a little drawn and rigid, answered the door. For a moment they went through French forms; then:

"My husband has been feeling unwell for some weeks," she said concisely. "Nevertheless, he did not complain in a way to make me uneasy. He has suddenly collapsed; he cannot articulate or move his limbs. All this, I must say, might have been precipitated by a certain indiscretion of mine – in all events, there was a violent scene, a discussion, and sometimes when he is agitated my husband cannot comprehend well in French."

"I will see him," said the doctor, thinking: "Some things are comprehended instantly in all languages."

During the next four weeks several people listened to strange speeches about one thousand chemises, and heard how all the population of Paris was becoming etherized by cheap gasoline – there was a consulting psychiatrist, not inclined to believe in any underlying mental trouble; there was a nurse from the American Hospital; and there was Choupette, frightened, defiant and, after her fashion, deeply sorry. A month later, when Henry awoke to his familiar room, lit with a dimmed lamp, he found her sitting beside his bed and reached out for her hand.

"I still love you," he said – "that's the odd thing."

"Sleep, male cabbage."

"At all costs," he continued with a certain feeble irony, "you can count on me to adopt the Continental attitude."

"Please! You tear at my heart."

When he was sitting up in bed they were ostensibly close together again – closer than they had been for months.

"Now you're going to have another holiday," said Henry to the two boys, back from the country. "Papa has got to go to the seashore and get really well."

"Will we swim?"

"And get drowned, my darlings?" Choupette cried. "But fancy, at your age. Not at all!"

So, at Saint-Jean-de-Luz they sat on the shore instead, and watched the English and Americans and a few hardy French pioneers of *le sport* voyage between raft and diving tower, motorboat and sand. There were passing ships, and bright islands to look at, and mountains reaching into cold zones, and red-and-yellow villas, called Fleur des Bois, Mon Nid, or Sans-Souci; and farther back, tired French villages of baked cement and grey stone.

Choupette sat at Henry's side, holding a parasol to shelter her peach-bloom skin from the sun.

"Look!" she would say, at the sight of tanned American girls. "Is that lovely? Skin that will be leather at thirty – a sort of brown veil to hide all blemishes, so that everyone will look alike. And women of a hundred kilos in such bathing suits! Weren't clothes intended to hide nature's mistakes?"

Henry Clay Marston was a Virginian of the kind who are prouder of being Virginians than of being Americans. That mighty word printed across a continent was less to him than the memory of his grandfather, who freed his slaves in '58, fought from Manassas to Appomattox, knew Huxley and Spencer* as light reading, and believed in caste only when it expressed the best of race.

To Choupette all this was vague. Her more specific criticisms of his compatriots were directed against the women.

"How would you place them?" she exclaimed. "Great ladies, bourgeoises, adventuresses – they are all the same. Look! Where would I be if I tried to act like your friend, Madame de Richepin? My father was a professor in a provincial university, and I have certain things I wouldn't do because they wouldn't please my class, my family. Madame de Richepin has other things she wouldn't do because of her class, her family." Suddenly she pointed to an American girl going into the water:

"But that young lady may be a stenographer and yet be compelled to warp herself, dressing and acting as if she had all the money in the world."

"Perhaps she will have, some day."

"That's the story they are told – it happens to one, not to the ninety-nine. That's why all their faces over thirty are discontented and unhappy."

Though Henry was in general agreement, he could not help being amused at Choupette's choice of target this afternoon. The girl – she was perhaps eighteen – was obviously acting like nothing but herself – she was what his father would have called a thoroughbred. A deep, thoughtful face that was pretty only because of the irrepressible determination of the perfect features to be recognized, a face that could have done without them and not yielded up its poise and distinction.

In her grace, at once exquisite and hardy, she was that perfect type of American girl that makes one wonder if the male is not being sacrificed to it, much as, in the last century, the lower strata in England were sacrificed to produce the governing class.

The two young men, coming out of the water as she went in, had large shoulders and empty faces. She had a smile for them that was no more than they deserved – that must do until she chose one to be the father of her children and gave herself up to destiny. Until then – Henry Marston was glad about her as her arms, like flying fish, clipped the water in a crawl, as her body spread in a swan dive or doubled in a jackknife from the springboard and her head appeared from the depth, jauntily flipping the damp hair away.

The two young men passed near.

"They push water," Choupette said, "then they go elsewhere and push other water. They pass months in France and they couldn't tell you the name of the President. They are parasites such as Europe has not known in a hundred years."

But Henry had stood up abruptly, and now all the people on the beach were suddenly standing up. Something had happened out there in the fifty yards between the deserted raft and the shore. The bright head showed upon the surface; it did not flip water now, but called "*Au secours!* Help!" in a feeble and frightened voice.

"Henry!" Choupette cried. "Stop! Henry!"

The beach was almost deserted at noon, but Henry and several others were sprinting towards the sea; the two young Americans heard, turned and sprinted after them. There was a frantic little time with half a dozen bobbing heads in the water. Choupette, still clinging to her parasol, but managing to wring her hands at the same time, ran up and down the beach crying: "Henry! Henry!"

Now there were more helping hands, and then two swelling groups around prostrate figures on the shore. The young fellow who pulled in the girl brought her around in a minute or so, but they had more trouble getting the water out of Henry, who had never learnt to swim.

2

"THIS IS THE MAN who didn't know whether he could swim, because he'd never tried."

Henry got up from his sun chair, grinning. It was next morning, and the saved girl had just appeared on the beach with her brother. She smiled back at Henry, brightly casual, appreciative rather than grateful.

"At the very least, I owe it to you to teach you how," she said.

"I'd like it. I decided that in the water yesterday, just before I went down the tenth time."

"You can trust me. I'll never again eat chocolate ice cream before going in."

As she went on into the water, Choupette asked: "How long do you think we'll stay here? After all, this life wearies one."

"We'll stay till I can swim. And the boys too."

"Very well. I saw a nice bathing suit in two shades of blue for fifty francs that I will buy you this afternoon."

Feeling a little paunchy and unhealthily white, Henry, holding his sons by the hand, took his body into the water. The breakers leapt at him, staggering him, while the boys yelled with ecstasy; the returning water curled threateningly around his feet as it hurried back to sea. Farther out, he stood waist-deep with other intimidated souls, watching the people dive from the raft tower, hoping the girl would come to fulfil her promise, and somewhat embarrassed when she did.

"I'll start with your eldest. You watch and then try it by yourself."

He floundered in the water. It went into his nose and started a raw stinging; it blinded him; it lingered afterwards in his ears, rattling back and forth like pebbles for hours. The sun discovered him too, peeling long strips of parchment from his shoulders, blistering his back so that he lay in a feverish agony for several nights. After a week he swam, painfully, pantingly and not very far. The girl taught him a sort of crawl, for he saw that the breast stroke was an obsolete device that lingered on with the inept and the old. Choupette caught him regarding his tanned face in the mirror with a sort of fascination, and the youngest boy contracted some sort of mild skin infection in the sand that retired him from competition. But one day Henry battled his way desperately to the float and drew himself up on it with his last breath.

"That being settled," he told the girl, when he could speak, "I can leave Saint-Jean tomorrow."

"I'm sorry."

"What will you do now?"

"My brother and I are going to Antibes; there's swimming there all through October. Then Florida."

"And swim?" he asked with some amusement.

"Why, yes. We'll swim."

"Why do you swim?"

"To get clean," she answered surprisingly.

"Clean from what?"

She frowned. "I don't know why I said that. But it feels clean in the sea."

"Americans are too particular about that," he commented.

"How could anyone be?"

"I mean we've got too fastidious even to clean up our messes."

"I don't know."

"But tell me why you…" He stopped himself in surprise. He had been about to ask her to explain a lot of other things – to say what was clean and unclean, what was worth knowing and what was only words – to open up a new gate to life. Looking for a last time into her eyes, full of cool secrets, he realized how much he was going to miss these mornings, without knowing whether it was the girl who interested him or what she represented of his ever-new, ever-changing country.

"All right," he told Choupette that night. "We'll leave tomorrow."

"For Paris?"

"For America."

"You mean I'm to go too? And the children?"

"Yes."

"But that's absurd," she protested. "Last time it cost more than we spend in six months here. And then there were only three of us. Now that we've managed to get ahead at last—"

"That's just it. I'm tired of getting ahead on your skimping and saving and going without dresses. I've got to make more money. American men are incomplete without money."

"You mean we'll stay?"

"It's very possible."

They looked at each other and, against her will, Choupette understood. For eight years, by a process of ceaseless adaptation, he had lived her life, substituting for the moral confusion of his own country the tradition, the wisdom, the sophistication of France. After that matter in Paris, it had seemed the bigger part to understand and to forgive, to cling to the home as something apart from the vagaries of love. Only now, glowing with a good health that he had not experienced for years, did he discover his true reaction. It had released him. For all his sense of loss, he possessed again the masculine self he had handed over to the keeping of a wise little Provençal girl eight years ago.

She struggled on for a moment.

"You've got a good position and we really have plenty of money. You know we can live cheaper here."

"The boys are growing up now, and I'm not sure I want to educate them in France."

"But that's all decided," she wailed. "You admit yourself that education in America is superficial and full of silly fads. Do you want them to be like those two dummies on the beach?"

"Perhaps I was thinking more of myself, Choupette. Men just out of college who brought their letters of credit into the bank eight years ago, travel about with ten-thousand-dollar cars now. I didn't use to care. I used to tell myself that I had a better place to escape to, just because we knew that lobster *armoricaine* was really lobster *américaine*.* Perhaps I haven't that feeling any more."

She stiffened. "If that's it…"

"It's up to you. We'll make a new start."

Choupette thought for a moment. "Of course my sister can take over the apartment."

"Of course." He waxed enthusiastic. "And there are sure to be things that'll tickle you – we'll have a nice car, for instance, and one of those electric ice boxes, and all sorts of funny machines to take the place of servants. It won't be bad. You'll learn to play golf and talk about children all day. Then there are the movies."

Choupette groaned.

"It's going to be pretty awful at first," he admitted, "but there are still a few good nigger cooks, and we'll probably have two bathrooms."

"I am unable to use more than one at a time."

"You'll learn."

A month afterwards, when the beautiful white island floated towards them in the Narrows, Henry's throat grew constricted with the rest and he wanted to cry out to Choupette and all foreigners, "Now, you see!"

3

ALMOST THREE YEARS LATER, Henry Marston walked out of his office in the Calumet Tobacco Company and along the hall to Judge Waterbury's suite. His face was older, with a suspicion of grimness, and a slight irrepressible heaviness of body was not concealed by his white linen suit.

"Busy, judge?"

"Come in, Henry."

"I'm going to the shore tomorrow to swim off this weight. I wanted to talk to you before I go."

"Children going too?"

"Oh, sure."

"Choupette'll go abroad, I suppose."

"Not this year. I think she's coming with me, if she doesn't stay here in Richmond."

The judge thought: "There isn't a doubt but what he knows everything." He waited.

"I wanted to tell you, judge, that I'm resigning the end of September."

The judge's chair creaked backward as he brought his feet to the floor.

"You're quitting, Henry?"

"Not exactly. Walter Ross wants to come home; let me take his place in France."

"Boy, do you know what we pay Walter Ross?"

"Seven thousand."

"And you're getting twenty-five."

"You've probably heard I've made something in the market," said Henry deprecatingly.

"I've heard everything between a hundred thousand and half a million."

"Somewhere in between."

"Then why a seven-thousand-dollar job? Is Choupette homesick?"

"No, I think Choupette likes it over here. She's adapted herself amazingly."

"He knows," the judge thought. "He wants to get away."

After Henry had gone, he looked up at the portrait of his grandfather on the wall. In those days the matter would have been simpler. Duelling pistols in the old Wharton meadow at dawn. It would be to Henry's advantage if things were like that today.

Henry's chauffeur dropped him in front of a Georgian house in a new suburban section. Leaving his hat in the hall, he went directly out on the side veranda.

From the swaying canvas swing Choupette looked up with a polite smile. Save for a certain alertness of feature and a certain indefinable knack of putting things on, she might have passed for an American. Southernisms overlay her French accent with a quaint charm; there were still college boys who rushed her like a debutante at the Christmas dances.

Henry nodded at Mr Charles Wiese, who occupied a wicker chair, with a gin fizz at his elbow.

"I want to talk to you," he said, sitting down.

Wiese's glance and Choupette's crossed quickly before coming to rest on him.

"You're free, Wiese," Henry said. "Why don't you and Choupette get married?"

Choupette sat up, her eyes flashing.

"Now wait." Henry turned back to Wiese. "I've been letting this thing drift for about a year now, while I got my financial affairs in shape. But this last brilliant idea of yours makes me feel a little uncomfortable, a little sordid, and I don't want to feel that way."

"Just what do you mean?" Wiese enquired.

"On my last trip to New York you had me shadowed. I presume it was with the intention of getting divorce evidence against me. It wasn't a success."

"I don't know where you got such an idea in your head, Marston; you—"

"Don't lie!"

"Suh—" Wiese began, but Henry interrupted impatiently:

"Now don't 'suh' me, and don't try to whip yourself up into a temper. You're not talking to a scared picker full of hookworm. I don't want a scene; my emotions aren't sufficiently involved. I want to arrange a divorce."

"Why do you bring it up like this?" Choupette cried, breaking into French. "Couldn't we talk of it alone, if you think you have so much against me?"

"Wait a minute; this might as well be settled now," Wiese said. "Choupette does want a divorce. Her life with you is unsatisfactory, and the only reason she has kept on is because she's an idealist. You don't seem to appreciate that fact, but it's true; she couldn't bring herself to break up her home."

"Very touching." Henry looked at Choupette with bitter amusement. "But let's come down to facts. I'd like to close up this matter before I go back to France."

Again Wiese and Choupette exchanged a look.

"It ought to be simple," Wiese said. "Choupette doesn't want a cent of your money."

"I know. What she wants is the children. The answer is: you can't have the children."

"How perfectly outrageous!" Choupette cried. "Do you imagine for a minute I'm going to give up my children?"

"What's your idea, Marston?" demanded Wiese. "To take them back to France and make them expatriates like yourself?"

"Hardly that. They're entered for St Regis School and then for Yale. And I haven't any idea of not letting them see their mother whenever she so desires – judging from the past two years, it won't be often. But I intend to have their entire legal custody."

"Why?" they demanded together.

"Because of the home."

"What the devil do you mean?"

"I'd rather apprentice them to a trade than have them brought up in the sort of home yours and Choupette's is going to be."

There was a moment's silence. Suddenly Choupette picked up her glass, dashed the contents at Henry and collapsed on the settee, passionately sobbing.

Henry dabbed his face with his handkerchief and stood up.

"I was afraid of that," he said, "but I think I've made my position clear."

He went up to his room and lay down on the bed. In a thousand wakeful hours during the past year he had fought over in his mind the problem of keeping his boys without taking those legal measures against Choupette that he could not bring himself to take. He knew that she wanted the children only because without them she would be suspect, even déclassée, to her family in France; but with that quality of detachment peculiar to old stock, Henry recognized this as a perfectly legitimate motive. Furthermore, no public scandal must touch the mother of his sons – it was this that had rendered his challenge so ineffectual this afternoon.

When difficulties became insurmountable, inevitable, Henry sought surcease in exercise. For three years, swimming had been a sort of refuge, and he turned to it as one man to music or another to drink. There was a point when he would resolutely stop thinking and go to the Virginia coast for a week to wash his mind in the water. Far out past the breakers, he could survey the green-and-brown line of the Old Dominion with the pleasant impersonality of a porpoise. The burden of his wretched marriage fell away with the buoyant tumble of his body among the swells, and he would begin to move in a child's dream of space. Sometimes remembered playmates of his youth swam with him; sometimes, with his two sons beside him, he seemed to be setting off along the bright pathway to the moon. Americans, he liked to say, should be born with fins, and perhaps they were – perhaps money was a form of fin. In England property begot a strong place sense, but Americans, restless and with shallow roots, needed fins and wings. There was even a recurrent idea in America about an education that would leave out history and the past, that should be a sort of equipment for aerial adventure, weighed down by none of the stowaways of inheritance or tradition.

Thinking of this in the water the next afternoon brought Henry's mind to the children; he turned and at a slow trudgen started back towards shore. Out of condition, he rested, panting, at the raft, and glancing up, he saw familiar eyes. In a moment he was talking with the girl he had tried to rescue four years ago.

He was overjoyed. He had not realized how vividly he remembered her. She was a Virginian – he might have guessed it abroad – the laziness, the apparent casualness that masked an unfailing courtesy and attention; a good form devoid of forms was based on kindness and consideration. Hearing her name for the first time, he recognized it – an Eastern Shore name, "good" as his own.

Lying in the sun, they talked like old friends, not about races and manners and the things that Henry brooded over Choupette, but rather as if they naturally agreed about those things; they talked about what they liked themselves and about what was fun. She showed him a sitting-down, standing-up dive from the high springboard, and he emulated her inexpertly – that was fun. They talked about eating soft-shelled crabs, and she told him how, because of the curious acoustics of the water, one could lie here and be diverted by conversations on the hotel porch. They tried it and heard two ladies over their tea say:

"Now, at the Lido…"

"Now, at Asbury Park…"

"Oh, my dear, he just scratched and scratched all night; he just scratched and scratched…"

"My dear, at Deauville…"

"…scratched and scratched all night."

After a while the sea got to be that very blue colour of four o'clock, and the girl told him how, at nineteen, she had been divorced from a Spaniard who locked her in the hotel suite when he went out at night.

"It was one of those things," she said lightly. "But speaking more cheerfully, how's your beautiful wife? And the boys – did they learn to float? Why can't you all dine with me tonight?"

"I'm afraid I won't be able to," he said, after a moment's hesitation. He must do nothing, however trivial, to furnish Choupette weapons, and, with a feeling of disgust, it occurred to him that he was possibly being watched this afternoon. Nevertheless, he was glad of his caution when she unexpectedly arrived at the hotel for dinner that night.

After the boys had gone to bed, they faced each other over coffee on the hotel veranda.

"Will you kindly explain why I'm not entitled to a half-share in my own children?" Choupette began. "It is not like you to be vindictive, Henry."

It was hard for Henry to explain. He told her again that she could have the children when she wanted them, but that he must exercise entire control over them because of certain old-fashioned convictions – watching her face grow harder, minute by minute, he saw there was no use, and broke off. She made a scornful sound.

"I wanted to give you a chance to be reasonable before Charles arrives."

Henry sat up. "Is he coming here this evening?"

"Happily. And I think perhaps your selfishness is going to have a jolt, Henry. You're not dealing with a woman now."

When Wiese walked out on the porch an hour later, Henry saw that his pale lips were like chalk; there was a deep flush on his forehead and hard confidence in his eyes. He was cleared for action and he wasted no time. "We've got something to say to each other, suh, and since I've got a motorboat here, perhaps that'd be the quietest place to say it."

Henry nodded coolly; five minutes later the three of them were headed out into Hampton Roads on the wide fairway of the moonlight. It was a tranquil evening, and half a mile from shore Wiese cut down the engine to a mild throbbing, so that they seemed to drift without will or direction through the bright water. His voice broke the stillness abruptly:

"Marston, I'm going to talk to you straight from the shoulder. I love Choupette and I'm not apologizing for it. These things have happened before in this world. I guess you understand that. The only difficulty is this matter of the custody of Choupette's children. You seem determined to try and take them away from the mother that bore them and raised them" – Wiese's words became more clearly articulated, as if they came from a wider mouth – "but you left one thing out of your calculations, and that's me. Do you happen to realize that at this moment I'm one of the richest men in Virginia?"

"I've heard as much."

"Well, money is power, Marston. I repeat, suh, money is power."

"I've heard that too. In fact, you're a bore, Wiese." Even by the moon Henry could see the crimson deepen on his brow.

"You'll hear it again, suh. Yesterday you took us by surprise and I was unprepared for your brutality to Choupette. But this morning I received a letter from Paris that puts the matter in a new light. It is a statement by a specialist in mental diseases, declaring you to be of unsound mind, and unfit to have the custody of children. The specialist is the one who attended you in your nervous breakdown four years ago."

Henry laughed incredulously, and looked at Choupette, half-expecting her to laugh too, but she had turned her face away, breathing quickly through parted lips. Suddenly he realized that Wiese was telling the truth – that by some extraordinary bribe he had obtained such a document and fully intended to use it.

For a moment Henry reeled as if from a material blow. He listened to his own voice saying, "That's the most ridiculous thing I ever heard," and to Wiese's answer: "They don't always tell people when they have mental troubles."

Suddenly Henry wanted to laugh, and the terrible instant when he had wondered if there could be some shred of truth in the allegation passed. He turned to Choupette, but again she avoided his eyes.

"How could you, Choupette?"

"I want my children—" she began, but Wiese broke in quickly:

"If you'd been halfway fair, Marston, we wouldn't have resorted to this step."

"Are you trying to pretend you arranged this scurvy trick since yesterday afternoon?"

"I believe in being prepared, but if you had been reasonable – in fact, if you will be reasonable – this opinion needn't be used." His voice became suddenly almost paternal, almost kind: "Be wise, Marston. On your side there's an obstinate prejudice; on mine there are forty million dollars. Don't fool yourself. Let me repeat, Marston, that money is power. You were abroad so long that perhaps you're inclined to forget that fact. Money made this country, built its great and glorious cities, created its industries, covered it with an iron network of railroads. It's money that harnesses the forces of nature, creates the machine and makes it go when money says go, and stop when money says stop."

As though interpreting this as a command, the engine gave forth a sudden hoarse sound and came to rest.

"What is it?" demanded Choupette.

"It's nothing." Wiese pressed the self-starter with his foot. "I repeat, Marston, that money... The battery is dry. One minute while I spin the wheel."

He spun it for the best part of fifteen minutes while the boat meandered about in a placid little circle.

"Choupette, open that drawer behind you and see if there isn't a rocket."

A touch of panic had crept into her voice when she answered that there was no rocket. Wiese eyed the shore tentatively.

"There's no use in yelling; we must be half a mile out. We'll just have to wait here until someone comes along."

"We won't wait here," Henry remarked.

"Why not?"

"We're moving towards the bay. Can't you tell? We're moving out with the tide."

"That's impossible!" said Choupette sharply.

"Look at those two lights on shore – one passing the other now. Do you see?"

"Do something!" she wailed, and then, in a burst of French: "*Ah, c'est épouvantable! N'est-ce pas qu'il y a quelque chose qu'on peut faire?*"*

The tide was running fast now, and the boat was drifting down the Roads with it towards the sea. The vague blots of two ships passed them, but at a distance, and there was no answer to their hail. Against the western sky a lighthouse blinked, but it was impossible to guess how near to it they would pass.

"It looks as if all our difficulties would be solved for us," Henry said.

"What difficulties?" Choupette demanded. "Do you mean there's nothing to be done? Can you sit there and just float away like this?"

"It may be easier on the children, after all." He winced as Choupette began to sob bitterly, but he said nothing. A ghostly idea was taking shape in his mind.

"Look here, Marston. Can you swim?" demanded Wiese, frowning.

"Yes, but Choupette can't."

"I can't either – I didn't mean that. If you could swim in and get to a telephone, the coastguard people would send for us."

Henry surveyed the dark, receding shore.

"It's too far," he said.

"You can try!" said Choupette.

Henry shook his head.

"Too risky. Besides, there's an outside chance that we'll be picked up."

The lighthouse passed them, far to the left and out of earshot. Another one, the last, loomed up half a mile away.

"We might drift to France like that man Gerbault,"* Henry remarked. "But then, of course, we'd be expatriates – and Wiese wouldn't like that, would you, Wiese?"

Wiese, fussing frantically with the engine, looked up.

"See what you can do with this," he said.

"I don't know anything about mechanics," Henry answered. "Besides, this solution of our difficulties grows on me. Just suppose you were dirty dog enough to use that statement and got the children because of it – in that case I wouldn't have much impetus to go on living. We're all failures – I as head of my household, Choupette as a wife and a mother, and you, Wiese, as a human being. It's just as well that we go out of life together."

"This is no time for a speech, Marston."

"Oh, yes, it's a fine time. How about a little more house-organ oratory about money being power?"

Choupette sat rigid in the bow; Wiese stood over the engine, biting nervously at his lips.

"We're not going to pass that lighthouse very close." An idea suddenly occurred to him. "Couldn't you swim to that, Marston?"

"Of course he could!" Choupette cried.

Henry looked at it tentatively.

"I might. But I won't."

"You've got to!"

Again he flinched at Choupette's weeping; simultaneously he saw the time had come.

"Everything depends on one small point," he said rapidly. "Wiese, have you got a fountain pen?"

"Yes. What for?"

"If you'll write and sign about two hundred words at my dictation, I'll swim to the lighthouse and get help. Otherwise, so help me God, we'll drift out to sea! And you better decide in about one minute."

"Oh, anything!" Choupette broke out frantically. "Do what he says, Charles – he means it. He always means what he says. Oh, please don't wait!"

"I'll do what you want" – Wiese's voice was shaking – "only, for God's sake, go on. What is it you want – an agreement about the children? I'll give you my personal word of honour—"

"There's no time for humour," said Henry savagely. "Take this piece of paper and write."

The two pages that Wiese wrote at Henry's dictation relinquished all lien on the children thence and for ever for himself and Choupette. When they had affixed trembling signatures Wiese cried:

"Now go, for God's sake, before it's too late!"

"Just one thing more: the certificate from the doctor."

"I haven't it here."

"You lie."

Wiese took it from his pocket.

"Write across the bottom that you paid so much for it, and sign your name to that."

A minute later, stripped to his underwear, and with the papers in an oiled-silk tobacco pouch suspended from his neck, Henry dived from the side of the boat and struck out towards the light.

The waters leapt up at him for an instant, but after the first shock it was all warm and friendly, and the small murmur of the waves was an encouragement. It was the longest swim he had ever tried, and he was straight from the city, but the happiness in his heart buoyed him up. Safe now, and free. Each stroke was stronger for knowing that his two sons, sleeping back in the hotel, were safe from what he dreaded. Divorced from her own country, Choupette had picked the things out of American life that pandered best to her own self-indulgence. That, backed by a court decree, she should be permitted to hand on this preposterous moral farrago to his sons was unendurable. He would have lost them for ever.

Turning on his back, he saw that already the motorboat was far away, the blinding light was nearer. He was very tired. If one let go – and, in the relaxation from strain, he felt an alarming impulse to let go – one died very quickly and painlessly, and all these problems of hate and bitterness disappeared. But he felt the fate of his sons in the oiled-silk pouch about his neck, and with a convulsive effort he turned over again and concentrated all his energies on his goal.

Twenty minutes later he stood shivering and dripping in the signal room while it was broadcast out to the coast patrol that a launch was drifting in the bay.

"There's not much danger without a storm," the keeper said. "By now they've probably struck a cross current from the river and drifted into Peyton Harbor."

"Yes," said Henry, who had come to this coast for three summers. "I knew that too."

4

IN OCTOBER, HENRY LEFT HIS SONS in school and embarked on the *Majestic* for Europe. He had come home as to a generous mother and had been profusely given more than he asked – money, release from an intolerable situation and the fresh strength to fight for his own. Watching the fading city, the fading shore, from the deck of the *Majestic*, he had a sense of overwhelming gratitude and of gladness that America was there, that under the ugly debris of industry the rich land still pushed up, incorrigibly lavish and fertile, and that in the heart of the leaderless people the old generosities and devotions fought on, breaking out sometimes in fanaticism and excess, but indomitable and undefeated. There was a lost generation in the saddle at the moment, but it seemed to him that the men coming on, the men of the war, were better; and all his old feeling that America was a bizarre accident, a sort of historical sport, had gone for ever. The best of America was the best of the world.

Going down to the purser's office, he waited until a fellow passenger was through at the window. When she turned, they both started, and he saw it was the girl.

"Oh, hello!" she cried. "I'm glad you're going! I was just asking when the pool opened. The great thing about this ship is that you can always get a swim."

"Why do you like to swim?" he demanded.

"You always ask me that." She laughed.

"Perhaps you'd tell me if we had dinner together tonight."

But when, in a moment, he left her, he knew that she could never tell him – she or another. France was a land, England was a people, but America, having about it still that quality of the idea, was harder to utter – it was the graves at Shiloh* and the tired, drawn, nervous faces of its great men, and the country boys dying in the Argonne for a phrase that was empty before their bodies withered. It was a willingness of the heart.

Two Wrongs

1

L OOK AT THOSE SHOES," said Bill – "twenty-eight dollars."
Mr Brancusi looked. "Purty."

"Made to order."

"I knew you were a great swell. You didn't get me up here to show me those shoes, did you?"

"I am not a great swell. Who said I was a great swell?" demanded Bill. "Just because I've got more education than most people in show business."

"And then, you know, you're a handsome young fellow," said Brancusi drily.

"Sure I am – compared to you anyhow. The girls think I must be an actor, till they find out... Got a cigarette? What's more, I look like a man – which is more than most of these pretty boys round Times Square do."

"Good-looking. Gentleman. Good shoes. Shot with luck."

"You're wrong there," objected Bill. "Brains. Three years – nine shows – four big hits – only one flop. Where do you see any luck in that?"

A little bored, Brancusi just gazed. What he would have seen – had he not made his eyes opaque and taken to thinking about something else – was a fresh-faced young Irishman exuding aggressiveness and self-confidence until the air of his office was thick with it. Presently, Brancusi knew, Bill would hear the sound of his own voice and be ashamed and retire into his other humour – the quietly superior, sensitive one, the patron of the arts, modelled on the intellectuals of the Theatre Guild.

Bill McChesney had not quite decided between the two; such blends are seldom complete before thirty.

"Take Ames, take Hopkins, take Harris – take any of them," Bill insisted. "What have they got on me? What's the matter? Do you want a drink?" – seeing Brancusi's glance wander towards the cabinet on the opposite wall.

"I never drink in the morning. I just wondered who was it keeps on knocking. You ought to make it stop it. I get a nervous fidgets, kind of half crazy, with that kind of thing."

Bill went quickly to the door and threw it open.

"Nobody…" he said. "Hello! What do you want?"

"Oh, I'm so sorry," a voice answered. "I'm terribly sorry. I got so excited and I didn't realize I had this pencil in my hand."

"What is it you want?"

"I want to see you, and the clerk said you were busy. I have a letter for you from Alan Rogers, the playwright – and I wanted to give it to you personally."

"I'm busy," said Bill. "See Mr Cadorna."

"I did, but he wasn't very encouraging, and Mr Rogers said—"

Brancusi, edging over restlessly, took a quick look at her. She was very young, with beautiful red hair, and more character in her face than her chatter would indicate; it did not occur to Mr Brancusi that this was due to her origin in Delaney, South Carolina.

"What shall I do?" she enquired, quietly laying her future in Bill's hands. "I had a letter to Mr Rogers, and he just gave me this one to you."

"Well, what do you want me to do – marry you?" exploded Bill.

"I'd like to get a part in one of your plays."

"Then sit down and wait. I'm busy… Where's Miss Cohalan?" He rang a bell, looked once more, crossly, at the girl and closed the door of his office. But during the interruption his other mood had come over him, and he resumed his conversation with Brancusi in the key of one who was hand in glove with Reinhardt for the artistic future of the theatre.

By 12.30 he had forgotten everything except that he was going to be the greatest producer in the world and that he had an engagement to tell Sol Lincoln about it at lunch. Emerging from his office, he looked expectantly at Miss Cohalan.

"Mr Lincoln won't be able to meet you," she said. "He jus' 'is minute called."

"Just this minute," repeated Bill, shocked. "All right. Just cross him off that list for Thursday night."

Miss Cohalan drew a line on a sheet of paper before her.

"Mr McChesney, now you haven't forgotten me, have you?"

He turned to the red-headed girl.

"No," he said vaguely, and then to Miss Cohalan: "That's all right; ask him for Thursday anyhow. To hell with him."

He did not want to lunch alone. He did not like to do anything alone now, because contacts were too much fun when one had prominence and power.

"If you would just let me talk to you two minutes—" she began.

"Afraid I can't now." Suddenly he realized that she was the most beautiful person he had ever seen in his life.

He stared at her.

"Mr Rogers told me—"

"Come and have a spot of lunch with me," he said, and then, with an air of great hurry, he gave Miss Cohalan some quick and contradictory instructions and held open the door.

They stood on Forty-Second Street and he breathed his pre-empted air – there is only enough air there for a few people at a time. It was November and the first exhilarating rush of the season was over, but he could look east and see the electric sign of one of his plays, and west and see another. Around the corner was the one he had put on with Brancusi – the last time he would produce anything except alone.

They went to the Bedford, where there was a to-do of waiters and captains as he came in.

"This is ver' 'tractive restaurant," she said, impressed and on company behaviour.

"This is hams' paradise." He nodded to several people. "Hello, Jimmy – Bill... Hello there, Jack... That's Jack Dempsey... I don't eat here much. I usually eat up at the Harvard Club."

"Oh, did you go to Harvard? I used to know—"

"Yes." He hesitated; there were two versions about Harvard, and he decided suddenly on the true one. "Yes, and they had me down for a hick there, but not any more. About a week ago I was out on Long Island at the Gouverneer Haights – very fashionable people – and a couple of Gold Coast boys that never knew I was alive up in Cambridge began pulling this 'Hello, Bill, old boy' on me."

He hesitated and suddenly decided to leave the story there.

"What do you want – a job?" he demanded. He remembered suddenly that she had holes in her stockings. Holes in stockings always moved him, softened him.

"Yes, or else I've got to go home," she said. "I want to be a dancer – you know, Russian ballet. But the lessons cost so much, so I've got to get a job. I thought it'd give me stage presence anyhow."

"Hoofer, eh?"

"Oh, no, serious."

"Well, Pavlova's a hoofer, isn't she?"

"Oh, no." She was shocked at this profanity, but after a moment she continued: "I took with Miss Campbell – Georgia Berriman Campbell – back home – maybe you know her. She took from Ned Wayburn, and she's really wonderful. She—"

"Yeah?" he said abstractedly. "Well, it's a tough business – casting agencies bursting with people that can all do anything, till I give them a try. How old are you?"

"Eighteen."

"I'm twenty-six. Came here four years ago without a cent."

"My!"

"I could quit now and be comfortable the rest of my life."

"My!"

"Going to take a year off next year – get married... Ever hear of Irene Rikker?"

"I should say! She's about my favourite of all."

"We're engaged."

"My!"

When they went out into Times Square after a while he said carelessly, "What are you doing now?"

"Why, I'm trying to get a job."

"I mean right this minute."

"Why, nothing."

"Do you want to come up to my apartment on Forty-Sixth Street and have some coffee?"

Their eyes met, and Emmy Pinkard made up her mind she could take care of herself.

It was a great bright studio apartment with a ten-foot divan, and after she had coffee and he a highball, his arm dropped round her shoulder.

"Why should I kiss you?" she demanded. "I hardly know you, and besides, you're engaged to somebody else."

"Oh, that! She doesn't care."

"No, really!"

"You're a good girl."

"Well, I'm certainly not an idiot."

"All right, go on being a good girl."

She stood up, but lingered a minute, very fresh and cool, and not upset at all.

"I suppose this means you won't give me a job?" she asked pleasantly.

He was already thinking about something else – about an interview and a rehearsal – but now he looked at her again and saw she still had holes in her stockings. He telephoned:

"Joe, this is the Fresh Boy... You didn't think I knew you called me that, did you?... It's all right... Say, have you got those three girls for the party scene? Well, listen: save one for a Southern kid I'm sending around today."

He looked at her jauntily, conscious of being such a good fellow.

"Well, I don't know how to thank you. And Mr Rogers," she added audaciously. "Goodbye, Mr McChesney."

He disdained to answer.

2

DURING REHEARSAL he used to come around a great deal and stand watching with a wise expression, as if he knew everything in people's minds; but actually he was in a haze about his own good fortune and didn't see much and didn't for the moment care. He spent most of his weekends on Long Island with the fashionable people who had "taken him up". When Brancusi referred to him as the "big social butterfly", he would answer, "Well, what about it? Didn't I go to Harvard? You think they found me in a Grand Street apple cart, like you?" He was well liked among his new friends for his good looks and good nature, as well as his success.

His engagement to Irene Rikker was the most unsatisfactory thing in his life; they were tired of each other but unwilling to put an end to it. Just as, often, the two richest young people in a town are drawn together by the fact, so Bill McChesney and Irene Rikker, borne side by side on waves of triumph, could not spare each other's nice appreciation of what was due such success. Nevertheless, they indulged in fiercer and more frequent quarrels, and the end was approaching. It was embodied in one Frank Llewellen, a big, fine-looking actor playing opposite Irene. Seeing the situation at once, Bill became bitterly humorous about it; from the second week of rehearsals there was tension in the air.

Meanwhile Emmy Pinkard, with enough money for crackers and milk, and a friend who took her out to dinner, was being happy. Her friend, Easton Hughes from Delaney, was studying at Columbia to be a dentist. He sometimes brought along other lonesome young men studying to be dentists, and at the price, if it can be called that, of a few casual kisses in taxicabs, Emmy dined when hungry. One afternoon she introduced Easton to Bill McChesney at the stage door, and afterwards Bill made his facetious jealousy the basis of their relationship.

"I see that dental number has been slipping it over on me again. Well, don't let him give you any laughing gas is my advice."

Though their encounters were few, they always looked at each other. When Bill looked at her he stared for an instant as if he had not seen her before, and then remembered suddenly that she was to be teased. When she looked at him she saw many things – a bright day outside, with great crowds of people hurrying through the streets; a very good new limousine that waited at the kerb for two people with very good new clothes, who got in and went somewhere that was just like New York, only away, and more fun there. Many times she had wished she had kissed him, but just as many times she was glad she hadn't; since, as the weeks passed, he grew less romantic, tied up, like the rest of them, to the play's laborious evolution.

They were opening in Atlantic City. A sudden moodiness, apparent to everyone, came over Bill. He was short with the director and sarcastic with the actors. This, it was rumoured, was because Irene Rikker had come down with Frank Llewellen on a different train. Sitting beside the author on the night of the dress rehearsal, he was an almost sinister figure in the twilight of the auditorium; but he said nothing until the end of the second act, when, with Llewellen and Irene Rikker on the stage alone, he suddenly called:

"We'll go over that again – and cut out the mush!"

Llewellen came down to the footlights.

"What do you mean – cut out the mush?" he enquired. "Those are the lines, aren't they?"

"You know what I mean – stick to business."

"I don't know what you mean."

Bill stood up. "I mean all that damn whispering."

"There wasn't any whispering. I simply asked—"

"That'll do – take it over."

Llewellen turned away furiously and was about to proceed, when Bill added audibly: "Even a ham has got to do his stuff."

Llewellen whipped about. "I don't have to stand that kind of talk, Mr McChesney."

"Why not? You're a ham, aren't you? When did you get ashamed of being a ham? I'm putting on this play and I want you to stick to your stuff." Bill got up and walked down the aisle. "And when you don't do it, I'm going to call you just like anybody else."

"Well, you watch out for your tone of voice—"

"What'll you do about it?"

Llewellen jumped down into the orchestra pit.

"I'm not taking anything from you!" he shouted.

Irene Rikker called to them from the stage, "For Heaven's sake, are you two crazy?" And then Llewellen swung at him, one short, mighty blow. Bill pitched back across a row of seats, fell through one, splintering it, and lay wedged there. There was a moment's wild confusion, then people holding Llewellen, then the author, with a white face, pulling Bill up, and the stage manager crying: "Shall I kill him, chief? Shall I break his fat face?" and Llewellen panting and Irene Rikker frightened.

"Get back there!" Bill cried, holding a handkerchief to his face and teetering in the author's supporting arms. "Everybody get back! Take that scene again, and no talk! Get back, Llewellen!"

Before they realized it they were all back on the stage, Irene pulling Llewellen's arm and talking to him fast. Someone put on the auditorium lights full and then dimmed them again hurriedly. When

Emmy came out presently for her scene, she saw in a quick glance that Bill was sitting with a whole mask of handkerchiefs over his bleeding face. She hated Llewellen and was afraid that presently they would break up and go back to New York. But Bill had saved the show from his own folly, since for Llewellen to take the further initiative of quitting would hurt his professional standing. The act ended and the next one began without an interval. When it was over, Bill was gone.

Next night, during the performance, he sat on a chair in the wings in view of everyone coming on or off. His face was swollen and bruised, but he neglected to seem conscious of the fact and there were no comments. Once he went around in front, and when he returned, word leaked out that two of the New York agencies were making big buys. He had a hit – they all had a hit.

At the sight of him to whom Emmy felt they all owed so much, a great wave of gratitude swept over her. She went up and thanked him.

"I'm a good picker, redhead," he agreed grimly.

"Thank you for picking me."

And suddenly Emmy was moved to a rash remark.

"You've hurt your face so badly!" she exclaimed. "Oh, I think it was so brave of you not to let everything go to pieces last night."

He looked at her hard for a moment, and then an ironic smile tried unsuccessfully to settle on his swollen face.

"Do you admire me, baby?"

"Yes."

"Even when I fell in the seats, did you admire me?"

"You got control of everything so quick."

"That's loyalty for you. You found something to admire in that fool mess."

And her happiness bubbled up into, "Anyhow, you behaved just wonderfully." She looked so fresh and young that Bill, who had had a wretched day, wanted to rest his swollen cheek against her cheek.

He took both the bruise and the desire with him to New York next morning; the bruise faded, but the desire remained. And when they opened in the city, no sooner did he see other men begin to crowd around her beauty than she became this play for him, this success, the thing that he came to see when he came to the theatre. After a good run it closed just as he was drinking too much and needed someone on the grey days of reaction. They were married suddenly in Connecticut, early in June.

3

TWO MEN SAT IN THE SAVOY GRILL in London, waiting for the Fourth of July. It was already late in May.

"Is he a nice guy?" asked Hubbel.

"Very nice," answered Brancusi. "Very nice, very handsome, very popular." After a moment, he added: "I want to get him to come home."

"That's what I don't get about him," said Hubbel. "Show business over here is nothing compared to home. What does he want to stay here for?"

"He goes around with a lot of dukes and ladies."

"Oh?"

"Last week when I met him he was with three ladies – Lady this, Lady that, Lady the other thing."

"I thought he was married."

"Married three years," said Brancusi, "got a fine child, going to have another."

He broke off as McChesney came in, his very American face staring about boldly over the collar of a box-shouldered topcoat.

"Hello, Mac; meet my friend Mr Hubbel."

"J'doo," said Bill. He sat down, continuing to stare around the bar to see who was present. After a few minutes Hubbel left, and Bill asked:

"Who's that bird?"

"He's only been here a month. He ain't got a title yet. You been here six months, remember."

Bill grinned.

"You think I'm high hat, don't you? Well, I'm not kidding myself anyhow. I like it; it gets me. I'd like to be the Marquis of McChesney."

"Maybe you can drink yourself into it," suggested Brancusi.

"Shut your trap. Who said I was drinking? Is that what they say now? Look here: if you can tell me any American manager in the history of the theatre who's had the success that I've had in London in less than eight months, I'll go back to America with you tomorrow. If you'll just tell me—"

"It was with your old shows. You had two flops in New York."

Bill stood up, his face hardening.

"Who do you think you are?" he demanded. "Did you come over here to talk to me like that?"

"Don't get sore now, Bill. I just want you to come back. I'd say anything for that. Put over three seasons like you had in '22 and '23, and you're fixed for life."

"New York makes me sick," said Bill moodily. "One minute you're a king; then you have two flops, they go around saying you're on the toboggan."

Brancusi shook his head.

"That wasn't why they said it. It was because you had that quarrel with Aronstael, your best friend."

"Friend hell!"

"Your best friend in business anyhow. Then—"

"I don't want to talk about it." He looked at his watch. "Look here: Emmy's feeling bad so I'm afraid I can't have dinner with you tonight. Come around to the office before you sail."

Five minutes later, standing by the cigar counter, Brancusi saw Bill enter the Savoy again and descend the steps that led to the tearoom.

"Grown to be a great diplomat," thought Brancusi. "He used to just say when he had a date. Going with these dukes and ladies is polishing him up even more."

Perhaps he was a little hurt, though it was not typical of him to be hurt. At any rate he made a decision, then and there, that McChesney was on the downgrade; it was quite typical of him that at that point he erased him from his mind for ever.

There was no outward indication that Bill was on the downgrade; a hit at the New Strand, a hit at the Prince of Wales, and the weekly grosses pouring in almost as well as they had two or three years before in New York. Certainly a man of action was justified in changing his base. And the man who, an hour later, turned into his Hyde Park house for dinner had all the vitality of the late twenties. Emmy, very tired and clumsy, lay on a couch in the upstairs sitting room. He held her for a moment in his arms.

"Almost over now," he said. "You're beautiful."

"Don't be ridiculous."

"It's true. You're always beautiful. I don't know why. Perhaps because you've got character, and that's always in your face, even when you're like this."

She was pleased; she ran her hand through his hair.

"Character is the greatest thing in the world," he declared, "and you've got more than anybody I know."

"Did you see Brancusi?"

"I did, the little louse! I decided not to bring him home to dinner."

"What was the matter?"

"Oh, just snooty – talking about my row with Aronstael, as if it was my fault."

She hesitated, closed her mouth tight, and then said quietly, "You got into that fight with Aronstael because you were drinking."

He rose impatiently.

"Are you going to start—"

"No, Bill, but you're drinking too much now. You know you are."

Aware that she was right, he evaded the matter and they went in to dinner. On the glow of a bottle of claret he decided he would go on the wagon tomorrow till after the baby was born.

"I always stop when I want, don't I? I always do what I say. You never saw me quit yet."

"Never yet."

They had coffee together, and afterwards he got up.

"Come back early," said Emmy.

"Oh, sure... What's the matter, baby?"

"I'm just crying. Don't mind me. Oh, go on; don't just stand there like a big idiot."

"But I'm worried, naturally. I don't like to see you cry."

"Oh, I don't know where you go in the evenings; I don't know who you're with. And that Lady Sybil Combrinck who kept phoning. It's all right, I suppose, but I wake up in the night and I feel so alone, Bill. Because we've always been together, haven't we, until recently?"

"But we're together still... What's happened to you, Emmy?"

"I know – I'm just crazy. We'd never let each other down, would we? We never have..."

"Of course not."

"Come back early, or when you can."

He looked in for a minute at the Prince of Wales Theatre; then he went into the hotel next door and called a number. "I'd like to speak to her Ladyship. Mr McChesney calling."

It was some time before Lady Sybil answered:

"This is rather a surprise. It's been several weeks since I've been lucky enough to hear from you."

Her voice was flip as a whip and cold as automatic refrigeration, in the mode grown familiar since British ladies took to piecing themselves together out of literature. It had fascinated Bill for a while, but just for a while. He had kept his head.

"I haven't had a minute," he explained easily. "You're not sore, are you?"

"I should scarcely say 'sore'."

"I was afraid you might be: you didn't send me an invitation to your party tonight. My idea was that after we talked it all over we agreed—"

"You talked a great deal," she said. "Possibly a little too much."

Suddenly, to Bill's astonishment, she hung up.

"Going British on me," he thought. "A little skit entitled *The Daughter of a Thousand Earls*."

The snub roused him, the indifference revived his warning interest. Usually women forgave his changes of heart because of his obvious devotion to Emmy, and he was remembered by various ladies with a not unpleasant sigh. But he had detected no such sigh upon the phone.

"I'd like to clear up this mess," he thought. Had he been wearing evening clothes, he might have dropped in at the dance and talked it over with her, still he didn't want to go home. Upon consideration it seemed important that the misunderstanding should be fixed up at once, and presently he began to entertain the idea of going as he was – Americans were excused unconventionalities of dress. In any case, it was not nearly time, and, in the company of several highballs, he considered the matter for an hour.

At midnight he walked up the steps of her Mayfair house. The coatroom attendants scrutinized his tweeds disapprovingly and a footman peered in vain for his name on the list of guests. Fortunately his friend Sir Humphrey Dunn arrived at the same time and convinced the footman it must be a mistake.

Inside, Bill immediately looked about for his hostess.

She was a very tall young woman, half American and all the more intensely English. In a sense, she had discovered Bill McChesney, vouched for his savage charms; his retirement was one of her most humiliating experiences since she had begun being bad.

She stood with her husband at the head of the receiving line – Bill had never seen them together before. He decided to choose a less formal moment for presenting himself.

As the receiving went on interminably, he became increasingly uncomfortable. He saw a few people he knew, but not many, and he was conscious that his clothes were attracting a certain attention; he was aware also that Lady Sybil saw him and could have relieved his embarrassment with a wave of her hand, but she made no sign. He was sorry he had come, but to withdraw now would be absurd, and, going to a buffet table, he took a glass of champagne.

When he turned around she was alone at last, and he was about to approach her when the butler spoke to him:

"Pardon me, sir. Have you a card?"

"I'm a friend of Lady Sybil's," said Bill impatiently. He turned away, but the butler followed.

"I'm sorry, sir, but I'll have to ask you to step aside with me and straighten this up."

"There's no need. I'm just about to speak to Lady Sybil now."

"My orders are different, sir," said the butler firmly.

Then, before Bill realized what was happening, his arms were pressed quietly to his sides and he was propelled into a little anteroom back of the buffet.

There he faced a man in a pince-nez in whom he recognized the Combrincks' private secretary.

The secretary nodded to the butler, saying, "This is the man" – whereupon Bill was released.

"Mr McChesney," said the secretary, "you have seen fit to force your way here without a card, and His Lordship requests that you leave his house at once. Will you kindly give me the check for your coat?"

Then Bill understood, and the single word that he found applicable to Lady Sybil sprang to his lips; whereupon the secretary gave a sign to two footmen, and in a furious struggle Bill was carried through a pantry where busy busboys stared at the scene, down a long hall, and pushed out a door into the night. The door closed; a moment later it was opened again to let his coat billow forth and his cane clatter down the steps.

As he stood there, overwhelmed, stricken aghast, a taxicab stopped beside him and the driver called:

"Feeling ill, gov'nor?"

"What?"

"I know where you can get a good pick-me-up, gov'nor. Never too late." The door of the taxi opened on a nightmare. There was a cabaret that broke the closing hours; there was being with strangers he had picked up somewhere; then there were arguments, and trying to cash a cheque, and suddenly proclaiming over and over that he was William McChesney, the producer, and convincing no one of the fact, not even himself. It seemed important to see Lady Sybil right away and call her to account; but presently nothing was important at all. He was in a taxicab whose driver had just shaken him awake in front of his own home.

The telephone was ringing as he went in, but he walked stonily past the maid and only heard her voice when his foot was on the stair.

"Mr McChesney, it's the hospital calling again. Mrs McChesney's there and they've been phoning every hour."

Still in a daze, he held the receiver up to his ear.

"We're calling from the Midland Hospital, for your wife. She was delivered of a stillborn child at nine this morning."

"Wait a minute." His voice was dry and cracking. "I don't understand."

After a while he understood that Emmy's child was dead and she wanted him. His knees sagged groggily as he walked down the street, looking for a taxi.

The room was dark; Emmy looked up and saw him from a rumpled bed.

"It's you!" she cried. "I thought you were dead! Where did you go?"

He threw himself down on his knees beside the bed, but she turned away.

"Oh, you smell awful," she said. "It makes me sick."

But she kept her hand in his hair, and he knelt there motionless for a long time.

"I'm done with you," she muttered, "but it was awful when I thought you were dead. Everybody's dead. I wish I was dead."

A curtain parted with the wind, and as he rose to arrange it, she saw him in the full morning light, pale and terrible, with rumpled clothes and bruises on his face. This time she hated him instead of those who had hurt him. She could feel him slipping out of her heart, feel the space he left, and all at once he was gone, and she could even forgive him and be sorry for him. All this in a minute.

She had fallen down at the door of the hospital, trying to get out of the taxicab alone.

4

WHEN EMMY WAS WELL, physically and mentally, her incessant idea was to learn to dance; the old dream inculcated by Miss Georgia Berriman Campbell of South Carolina persisted as a bright avenue leading back to first youth and days of hope in New York. To her, dancing meant that elaborate blend of tortuous attitudes and formal pirouettes that evolved out of Italy several hundred years ago and reached its apogee in Russia at the beginning of this century. She wanted to use herself on something she could believe in, and it seemed to her that the dance was woman's interpretation of music; instead of strong fingers, one had limbs with which to render Tchaikovsky and Stravinsky; and feet could be as eloquent in Chopiniana as voices in The Ring. At the bottom, it was something sandwiched in between the acrobats and the trained seals; at the top it was Pavlova* and art.

Once they were settled in an apartment back in New York, she plunged into her work like a girl of sixteen – four hours a day at barre exercises, attitudes, sauts, arabesques and pirouettes. It became the realest part of her life, and her only worry was whether or not she was too old. At twenty-six she had ten years to make up, but she was a natural dancer with a fine body – and that lovely face.

Bill encouraged it; when she was ready he was going to build the first real American ballet around her. There were even times when he envied her her absorption; for affairs in his own line were more difficult since they had come home. For one thing, he had made many enemies in those early days of self-confidence; there were exaggerated stories of his drinking and of his being hard on actors and difficult to work with.

It was against him that he had always been unable to save money and must beg a backing for each play. Then, too, in a curious way, he was intelligent, as he was brave enough to prove in several uncommercial ventures, but he had no Theatre Guild behind him, and what money he lost was charged against him.

There were successes too, but he worked harder for them, or it seemed so, for he had begun to pay a price for his irregular life. He always intended to take a rest or give up his incessant cigarettes, but there was so much competition now – new men coming up, with new reputations for infallibility – and besides, he wasn't used to regularity. He liked to do his work in those great spurts, inspired by black coffee, that seem so inevitable in show business, but which took so much out of a man after thirty. He had come to lean, in a way, on Emmy's fine health and vitality. They were always together, and if he felt a vague dissatisfaction that he had grown to need her more than she needed him, there was always the hope that things would break better for him next month, next season.

Coming home from ballet school one November evening, Emmy swung her little grey bag, pulled her hat far down over her still damp hair, and gave herself up to pleasant speculation. For a month she had been aware of people who had come to the studio especially to watch her – she was ready to dance. Once she had worked just as hard for as long a time on something else – her relations with Bill – only to reach a climax of misery and despair, but here there was nothing to fail her except herself. Yet even now she felt a little rash in thinking: "Now it's come. I'm going to be happy."

She hurried, for something had come up today that she must talk over with Bill.

Finding him in the living room, she called him to come back while she dressed. She began to talk without looking around:

"Listen what happened!" Her voice was loud, to compete with the water running in the tub. "Paul Makova wants me to dance with him at the Metropolitan this season; only it's not sure, so it's a secret – even I'm not supposed to know."

"That's great."

"The only thing is whether it wouldn't be better for me to make a debut abroad? Anyhow Donilof says I'm ready to appear. What do you think?"

"I don't know."

"You don't sound very enthusiastic."

"I've got something on my mind. I'll tell you about it later. Go on."

"That's all, dear. If you still feel like going to Germany for a month, like you said, Donilof would arrange a debut for me in Berlin, but I'd rather open here and dance with Paul Makova. Just imagine..." She broke off, feeling suddenly through the thick skin of her elation how abstracted he was. "Tell me what you've got on your mind."

"I went to Doctor Kearns this afternoon."

"What did he say?" Her mind was still singing with her own happiness. Bill's intermittent attacks of hypochondria had long ceased to worry her.

"I told him about that blood this morning, and he said what he said last year – it was probably a little broken vein in my throat. But since I'd been coughing and was worried, perhaps it was safer to take an X-ray and clear the matter up. Well, we cleared it up all right. My left lung is practically gone."

"Bill!"

"Luckily there are no spots on the other."

She waited, horribly afraid.

"It's come at a bad time for me," he went on steadily, "but it's got to be faced. He thinks I ought to go to the Adirondacks or to Denver for the winter, and his idea is Denver. That way it'll probably clear up in five or six months."

"Of course we'll have to…" she stopped suddenly.

"I wouldn't expect you to go – especially if you have this opportunity."

"Of course I'll go," she said quickly. "Your health comes first. We've always gone everywhere together."

"Oh, no."

"Why, of course." She made her voice strong and decisive. "We've always been together. I couldn't stay here without you. When do you have to go?"

"As soon as possible. I went in to see Brancusi to find out if he wanted to take over the Richmond piece, but he didn't seem enthusiastic." His face hardened. "Of course there won't be anything else for the present, but I'll have enough, with what's owing—"

"Oh, if I was only making some money!" Emmy cried. "You work so hard, and here I've been spending two hundred dollars a week for just my dancing lessons alone – more than I'll be able to earn for years."

"Of course in six months I'll be as well as ever – he says."

"Sure, dearest; we'll get you well. We'll start as soon as we can."

She put an arm around him and kissed his cheek.

"I'm just an old parasite," she said. "I should have known my darling wasn't well."

He reached automatically for a cigarette, and then stopped.

"I forgot – I've got to start cutting down smoking." He rose to the occasion suddenly: "No, baby, I've decided to go alone. You'd go crazy with boredom out there, and I'd just be thinking I was keeping you away from your dancing."

"Don't think about that. The thing is to get you well."

They discussed the matter hour after hour for the next week, each of them saying everything except the truth – that he wanted her to go with him and that she wanted passionately to stay in New York. She talked it over guardedly with Donilof, her ballet master, and found that he thought any postponement would be a terrible mistake. Seeing other girls in the ballet school making plans for the winter, she wanted to die rather than go, and Bill saw all the involuntary indications of her misery. For a while they talked of compromising on the Adirondacks, whither she would commute by aeroplane for the weekends, but he was running a little fever now and he was definitely ordered West.

Bill settled it all one gloomy Sunday night, with that rough, generous justice that had first made her admire him, that made him rather tragic in his adversity, as he had always been bearable in his overweening success:

"It's just up to me, baby. I got into this mess because I didn't have any self-control – you seem to have all of that in this family – and now it's only me that can get me out. You've worked hard at your stuff for three years and you deserve your chance – and if you came out there now you'd have it on me the rest of my life." He grinned. "And I couldn't stand that. Besides, it wouldn't be good for the kid."

Eventually she gave in, ashamed of herself, miserable – and glad. For the world of her work, where she existed without Bill, was bigger to her now than the world in which they existed together. There was more room to be glad in one than to be sorry in the other.

Two days later, with his ticket bought for that afternoon at five, they passed the last hours together, talking of everything hopeful. She protested still, and sincerely; had he weakened for a moment she would have gone. But the shock had done something to him, and he showed more character under it than he had for years. Perhaps it would be good for him to work it out alone.

"In the spring!" they said.

Then in the station with little Billy, and Bill saying: "I hate these graveside partings. You leave me here. I've got to make a phone call from the train before it goes."

They had never spent more than a night apart in six years, save when Emmy was in the hospital; save for the time in England they had a good record of faithfulness and of tenderness towards each other, even though she had been alarmed and often unhappy at this insecure bravado from the first. After he went through the gate alone, Emmy was glad he had a phone call to make and tried to picture him making it.

She was a good woman; she had loved him with all her heart. When she went out into Thirty-Third Street, it was just as dead as dead for a while, and the apartment he paid for would be empty of him, and she was here, about to do something that would make her happy.

She stopped after a few blocks, thinking: "Why, this is terrible – what I'm doing! I'm letting him down like the worst person I ever heard of. I'm leaving him flat and going off to dinner with Donilof and Paul Makova, whom I like for being beautiful and for having the same colour eyes and hair. Bill's on the train alone."

She swung little Billy around suddenly as if to go back to the station. She could see him sitting in the train, with his face so pale and tired, and no Emmy.

"I can't let him down," she cried to herself as wave after wave of sentiment washed over her. But only sentiment – hadn't he let her down – hadn't he done what he wanted in London?

"Oh, poor Bill!"

She stood irresolute, realizing for one last honest moment how quickly she would forget this and find excuses for what she was doing. She had to think hard of London, and her conscience cleared. But with Bill all alone in the train it seemed terrible to think that way. Even now she could turn and go back to the station and tell him that she was coming, but still she waited, with life very strong in her, fighting for her. The sidewalk was narrow where she stood; presently a great wave of people, pouring out of the theatre, came flooding along it, and she and little Billy were swept along with the crowd.

In the train, Bill telephoned up to the last minute, postponed going back to his stateroom, because he knew it was almost certain that he would not find her there. After the train started he went back and, of course, there was nothing but his bags in the rack and some magazines on the seat.

He knew then that he had lost her. He saw the set-up without any illusions – this Paul Makova, and months of proximity, and loneliness – afterwards nothing would ever be the same. When he had thought about it all a long time, reading *Variety* and *Zit's* in between, it began to seem, each time he came back to it, as if Emmy somehow were dead.

"She was a fine girl – one of the best. She had character." He realized perfectly that he had brought all this on himself and that there was some law of compensation involved. He saw, too, that by going away he had again become as good as she was; it was all evened up at last.

He felt beyond everything, even beyond his grief, an almost comfortable sensation of being in the hands of something bigger than himself; and grown a little tired and unconfident – two qualities he could never for a moment tolerate – it did not seem so terrible if he were going West for a definite finish. He was sure that Emmy would come at the end, no matter what she was doing or how good an engagement she had.

The Bridal Party

1

THERE WAS THE USUAL INSINCERE little note saying: "I wanted you to be the first to know." It was a double shock to Michael, announcing, as it did, both the engagement and the imminent marriage; which, moreover, was to be held, not in New York, decently and far away, but here in Paris under his very nose, if that could be said to extend over the Protestant Episcopal Church of the Holy Trinity, Avenue George-V. The date was two weeks off, early in June.

At first Michael was afraid and his stomach felt hollow. When he left the hotel that morning, the *femme de chambre*,* who was in love with his fine, sharp profile and his pleasant buoyancy, scented the hard abstraction that had settled over him. He walked in a daze to his bank, he bought a detective story at Smith's on the Rue de Rivoli, he sympathetically stared for a while at a faded panorama of the battlefields in a tourist-office window and cursed a Greek tout who followed him with a half-displayed packet of innocuous postcards warranted to be very dirty indeed.

But the fear stayed with him, and after a while he recognized it as the fear that now he would never be happy. He had met Caroline Dandy when she was seventeen, possessed her young heart all through her first season in New York and then lost her, slowly, tragically, uselessly, because he had no money and could make no money; because, with all the energy and good will in the world, he could not find himself; because, loving him still, Caroline had lost faith and begun to see him as something pathetic, futile and shabby, outside the great, shining stream of life towards which she was inevitably drawn.

Since his only support was that she loved him, he leant weakly on that; the support broke, but still he held on to it and was carried out to sea and washed up on the French coast with its broken pieces still in his hands. He carried them around with him in the form of photographs and packets of correspondence and a liking for a maudlin popular song called 'Among My Souvenirs'.* He kept clear of other girls, as if Caroline would somehow know it and reciprocate with a faithful heart. Her note informed him that he had lost her for ever.

It was a fine morning. In front of the shops in the Rue de Castiglione, proprietors and patrons were on the sidewalk gazing upward, for the *Graf Zeppelin*, shining and glorious, symbol of escape and destruction – of escape, if necessary, through destruction – glided in the Paris sky. He heard a woman say in French that it would not astonish her if that commenced to let fall the bombs. Then he heard another voice, full of husky laughter, and the void in his stomach froze. Jerking about, he was face to face with Caroline Dandy and her fiancé.

"Why, Michael! Why, we were wondering where you were. I asked at the Guaranty Trust, and Morgan and Company, and finally sent a note to the National City..."

Why didn't they back away? Why didn't they back right up, walking backward down the Rue de Castiglione, across the Rue de Rivoli, through the Tuileries Gardens, still walking backward as fast as they could till they grew vague and faded out across the river?

"This is Hamilton Rutherford, my fiancé."

"We've met before."

"At Pat's, wasn't it?"

"And last spring in the Ritz Bar."

"Michael, where have you been keeping yourself?"

"Around here." This agony. Previews of Hamilton Rutherford flashed before his eyes – a quick series of pictures, sentences. He remembered hearing that he had bought a seat in 1920 for a hundred and twenty-five thousand of borrowed money, and just before the break sold it for more than half a million. Not handsome like Michael, but vitally attractive, confident, authoritative, just the right height over Caroline there – Michael had always been too short for Caroline when they danced.

Rutherford was saying: "No, I'd like it very much if you'd come to the bachelor dinner. I'm taking the Ritz Bar from nine o'clock on. Then right after the wedding there'll be a reception and breakfast at the Hotel George-V."

"And, Michael, George Packman is giving a party day after tomorrow at Chez Victor, and I want you to be sure and come. And also to tea Friday at Jebby West's; she'd want to have you if she knew where you were. What's your hotel, so we can send you an invitation? You see, the reason we decided to have it over here is because Mother has been sick in a nursing home here and the whole clan is in Paris. Then Hamilton's mother's being here too…"

The entire clan – they had always hated him, except her mother, always discouraged his courtship. What a little counter he was in this game of families and money! Under his hat his brow sweated with the humiliation of the fact that for all his misery he was worth just exactly so many invitations. Frantically he began to mumble something about going away.

Then it happened – Caroline saw deep into him, and Michael knew that she saw. She saw through to his profound woundedness, and something quivered inside her, died out along the curve of her mouth and in her eyes. He had moved her. All the unforgettable impulses of first love had surged up once more; their hearts had in some way touched across two feet of Paris sunlight. She took her fiancé's arm suddenly, as if to steady herself with the feel of it.

They parted. Michael walked quickly for a minute; then he stopped, pretending to look in a window, and saw them farther up the street, walking fast into the Place Vendôme, people with much to do.

He had things to do also – he had to get his laundry.

"Nothing will ever be the same again," he said to himself. "She will never be happy in her marriage and I will never be happy at all any more."

The two vivid years of his love for Caroline moved back around him like years in Einstein's physics. Intolerable memories arose – of rides in the Long Island moonlight; of a happy time at Lake Placid with her cheeks so cold there, but warm just underneath the surface; of a despairing afternoon in a little café on Forty-Eighth Street in the last sad months when their marriage had come to seem impossible.

"Come in," he said aloud.

The concierge with a telegram; brusque because Mr Curly's clothes were a little shabby. Mr Curly gave few tips; Mr Curly was obviously a *petit client*.

Michael read the telegram.

"An answer?" the concierge asked.

"No," said Michael, and then, on an impulse: "Look."

"Too bad… too bad," said the concierge. "Your grandfather is dead."

"Not too bad," said Michael. "It means that I come into a quarter of a million dollars."

Too late by a single month; after the first flush of the news his misery was deeper than ever. Lying awake in bed that night, he listened endlessly to the long caravan of a circus moving through the street from one Paris fair to another.

When the last van had rumbled out of hearing and the corners of the furniture were pastel blue with the dawn, he was still thinking of the look in Caroline's eyes that morning – the look that seemed to say: "Oh, why couldn't you have done something about it? Why couldn't you have been stronger, made me marry you? Don't you see how sad I am?"

Michael's fists clenched.

"Well, I won't give up till the last moment," he whispered. "I've had all the bad luck so far, and maybe it's turned at last. One takes what one can get, up to the limit of one's strength, and if I can't have her, at least she'll go into this marriage with some of me in her heart."

2

ACCORDINGLY HE WENT TO THE PARTY at Chez Victor two days later, upstairs and into the little salon off the bar where the party was to assemble for cocktails. He was early; the only other occupant was a tall lean man of fifty. They spoke.

"You waiting for George Packman's party?"

"Yes. My name's Michael Curly."

"My name's…"

Michael failed to catch the name. They ordered a drink, and Michael supposed that the bride and groom were having a gay time.

"Too much so," the other agreed, frowning. "I don't see how they stand it. We all crossed on the boat together; five days of that crazy life and then two weeks of Paris. You" – he hesitated, smiling faintly – "you'll excuse me for saying that your generation drinks too much."

"Not Caroline."

"No, not Caroline. She seems to take only a cocktail and a glass of champagne, and then she's had enough, thank God. But Hamilton drinks too much and all this crowd of young people drink too much. Do you live in Paris?"

"For the moment," said Michael.

"I don't like Paris. My wife – that is to say, my ex-wife, Hamilton's mother – lives in Paris."

"You're Hamilton Rutherford's father?"

"I have that honour. And I'm not denying that I'm proud of what he's done; it was just a general comment."

"Of course."

Michael glanced up nervously as four people came in. He felt suddenly that his dinner coat was old and shiny; he had ordered a new one that morning. The people who had come in were rich and at home in their richness with one another – a dark, lovely girl with a hysterical little laugh whom he had met before; two confident men whose jokes referred invariably to last night's scandal and tonight's potentialities, as if they had important roles in a play that extended indefinitely into the past and the future. When Caroline arrived, Michael had scarcely a moment of her, but it was enough to note that, like all the others, she was strained and tired. She was pale beneath her rouge; there were shadows under her eyes. With a mixture of relief and wounded vanity, he found himself placed far from her and at another table; he needed a moment to adjust himself to his surroundings. This was not like the immature set in which he and Caroline had moved; the men were more than thirty and had an air of sharing the best of this world's good. Next to him was Jebby West, whom he knew; and, on the other side, a jovial man who immediately began to talk to Michael about a stunt for the bachelor dinner: they were going to hire a French girl to appear with an actual baby in her arms, crying: "Hamilton, you can't desert me now!" The idea seemed stale and unamusing to Michael, but its originator shook with anticipatory laughter.

Farther up the table there was talk of the market – another drop today, the most appreciable since the crash; people were kidding Rutherford about it: "Too bad, old man. You better not get married, after all."

Michael asked the man on his left, "Has he lost a lot?"

"Nobody knows. He's heavily involved, but he's one of the smartest young men in Wall Street. Anyhow, nobody ever tells you the truth."

It was a champagne dinner from the start, and towards the end it reached a pleasant level of conviviality, but Michael saw that all these people were too weary to be exhilarated by any ordinary stimulant; for weeks they had drunk cocktails before meals like Americans, wines and brandies like Frenchmen, beer like Germans, whisky-and-soda like the English, and as they were no longer in the twenties, this preposterous *mélange*, that was like some gigantic cocktail in a nightmare, served only to make them temporarily less conscious of the mistakes of the night before. Which is to say that it was not really a gay party; what gaiety existed was displayed in the few who drank nothing at all.

But Michael was not tired, and the champagne stimulated him and made his misery less acute. He had been away from New York for more than eight months and most of the dance music was unfamiliar to him, but at the first bars of the 'Painted Doll',* to which he and Caroline had moved through so much happiness and despair the previous summer, he crossed to Caroline's table and asked her to dance.

She was lovely in a dress of thin ethereal blue, and the proximity of her crackly yellow hair, of her cool and tender grey eyes, turned his body clumsy and rigid; he stumbled with their first step on the floor. For a moment it seemed that there was nothing to say; he wanted to tell her about his inheritance, but the idea seemed abrupt, unprepared for.

"Michael, it's so nice to be dancing with you again."

He smiled grimly.

"I'm so happy you came," she continued. "I was afraid maybe you'd be silly and stay away. Now we can be just good friends and natural together. Michael, I want you and Hamilton to like each other."

The engagement was making her stupid; he had never heard her make such a series of obvious remarks before.

"I could kill him without a qualm," he said pleasantly, "but he looks like a good man. He's fine. What I want to know is, what happens to people like me who aren't able to forget?"

As he said this he could not prevent his mouth from dropping suddenly, and, glancing up, Caroline saw, and her heart quivered violently, as it had the other morning.

"Do you mind so much, Michael?"

"Yes."

For a second as he said this, in a voice that seemed to have come up from his shoes, they were not dancing: they were simply clinging together. Then she leant away from him and twisted her mouth into a lovely smile.

"I didn't know what to do at first, Michael. I told Hamilton about you – that I'd cared for you an awful lot – but it didn't worry him, and he was right. Because I'm over you now – yes, I am. And you'll wake up some sunny morning and be over me just like that."

He shook his head stubbornly.

"Oh, yes. We weren't for each other. I'm pretty flighty, and I need somebody like Hamilton to decide things. It was that more than the question of... of..."

"Of money." Again he was on the point of telling her what had happened, but again something told him it was not the time.

"Then how do you account for what happened when we met the other day?" he demanded helplessly. "What happened just now? When we just pour towards each other like we used to – as if we were one person, as if the same blood was flowing through both of us?"

"Oh, don't," she begged him. "You mustn't talk like that; everything's decided now. I love Hamilton with all my heart. It's just that I remember certain things in the past and I feel sorry for you – for us – for the way we were."

Over her shoulder, Michael saw a man come towards them to cut in. In a panic he danced her away, but inevitably the man came on.

"I've got to see you alone, if only for a minute," Michael said quickly. "When can I?"

"I'll be at Jebby West's tea tomorrow," she whispered as a hand fell politely upon Michael's shoulder.

But he did not talk to her at Jebby West's tea. Rutherford stood next to her, and each brought the other into all conversations. They left early. The next morning the wedding cards arrived in the first mail.

Then Michael, grown desperate with pacing up and down his room, determined on a bold stroke; he wrote to Hamilton Rutherford, asking him for a rendezvous the following afternoon. In a short telephone communication Rutherford agreed, but for a day later than Michael had asked. And the wedding was only six days away.

They were to meet in the bar of the Hotel Jena. Michael knew what he would say: "See here, Rutherford, do you realize the responsibility you're taking in going through with this marriage? Do you realize the harvest of trouble and regret you're sowing in persuading a girl into something contrary to the instincts of her heart?" He would explain that the barrier between Caroline and himself had been an artificial one and was now removed, and demand that the matter be put up to Caroline frankly before it was too late.

Rutherford would be angry, conceivably there would be a scene, but Michael felt that he was fighting for his life now.

He found Rutherford in conversation with an older man, whom Michael had met at several of the wedding parties.

"I saw what happened to most of my friends," Rutherford was saying, "and I decided it wasn't going to happen to me. It isn't so difficult: if you take a girl with common sense, and tell her what's what, and do your stuff damn well, and play decently square with her, it's a marriage. If you stand for any nonsense at the beginning, it's one of these arrangements – within five years the man gets out, or else the girl gobbles him up and you have the usual mess."

"Right!" agreed his companion enthusiastically. "Hamilton, boy, you're right."

Michael's blood boiled slowly.

"Doesn't it strike you," he enquired coldly, "that your attitude went out of fashion about a hundred years ago?"

"No, it didn't," said Rutherford pleasantly, but impatiently. "I'm as modern as anybody. I'd get married in an aeroplane next Saturday if it'd please my girl."

"I don't mean that way of being modern. You can't take a sensitive woman—"

"Sensitive? Women aren't so darn sensitive. It's fellows like you who are sensitive; it's fellows like you they exploit – all your devotion and kindness and all that. They read a couple of books and see a few pictures because they haven't got anything else to do, and then they say they're finer in grain than you are, and to prove it they take the bit in their teeth and tear off for a fare-you-well – just about as sensitive as a fire horse."

"Caroline happens to be sensitive," said Michael in a clipped voice.

At this point the other man got up to go; when the dispute about the check had been settled and they were alone, Rutherford leant back to Michael as if a question had been asked him.

"Caroline's more than sensitive," he said. "She's got sense."

His combative eyes, meeting Michael's, flickered with a grey light. "This all sounds pretty crude to you, Mr Curly, but it seems to me that the average man nowadays just asks to be made a monkey of by some woman who doesn't even get any fun out of reducing him to that level. There are darn few men who possess their wives any more, but I am going to be one of them."

To Michael it seemed time to bring the talk back to the actual situation: "Do you realize the responsibility you're taking?"

"I certainly do," interrupted Rutherford. "I'm not afraid of responsibility. I'll make the decisions – fairly, I hope, but anyhow they'll be final."

"What if you didn't start right?" said Michael impetuously. "What if your marriage isn't founded on mutual love?"

"I think I see what you mean," Rutherford said, still pleasant. "And since you've brought it up, let me say that if you and Caroline had married, it wouldn't have lasted three years. Do you know what your affair was founded on? On sorrow. You got sorry for each other. Sorrow's a lot of fun for most women and for some men, but it seems to me that a marriage ought to be based on hope." He looked at his watch and stood up.

"I've got to meet Caroline. Remember, you're coming to the bachelor dinner day after tomorrow."

Michael felt the moment slipping away. "Then Caroline's personal feelings don't count with you?" he demanded fiercely.

"Caroline's tired and upset. But she has what she wants, and that's the main thing."

"Are you referring to yourself?" demanded Michael incredulously.

"Yes."

"May I ask how long she's wanted you?"

"About two years." Before Michael could answer, he was gone.

During the next two days Michael floated in an abyss of helplessness. The idea haunted him that he had left something undone that would sever this knot drawn tighter under his eyes. He phoned Caroline, but she insisted that it was physically impossible for her to see him until the day before the wedding, for which day she granted him a tentative rendezvous. Then he went to the bachelor dinner, partly in fear of an evening alone at his hotel, partly from a feeling that by his presence at that function he was somehow nearer to Caroline, keeping her in sight.

The Ritz Bar had been prepared for the occasion by French and American banners and by a great canvas covering one wall, against which the guests were invited to concentrate their proclivities in breaking glasses.

At the first cocktail, taken at the bar, there were many slight spillings from many trembling hands, but later, with the champagne, there was a rising tide of laughter and occasional bursts of song.

Michael was surprised to find what a difference his new dinner coat, his new silk hat, his new, proud linen made in his estimate of himself; he felt less resentment towards all these people for being so rich and assured. For the first time since he had left college he felt rich and assured himself; he felt that he was part of all this, and even entered into the scheme of Johnson, the practical joker, for the appearance of the woman betrayed, now waiting tranquilly in the room across the hall.

"We don't want to go too heavy," Johnson said, "because I imagine Ham's had a pretty anxious day already. Did you see Fullman Oil's sixteen points off this morning?"

"Will that matter to him?" Michael asked, trying to keep the interest out of his voice.

"Naturally. He's in heavily; he's always in everything heavily. So far he's had luck – anyhow, up to a month ago."

The glasses were filled and emptied faster now, and men were shouting at one another across the narrow table. Against the bar a group of ushers was being photographed, and the flashlight surged through the room in a stifling cloud.

"Now's the time," Johnson said. "You're to stand by the door, remember, and we're both to try and keep her from coming in – just till we get everybody's attention."

He went on out into the corridor, and Michael waited obediently by the door. Several minutes passed. Then Johnson reappeared with a curious expression on his face.

"There's something funny about this."

"Isn't the girl there?"

"She's there all right, but there's another woman there too; and it's nobody we engaged either. She wants to see Hamilton Rutherford, and she looks as if she had something on her mind."

They went out into the hall. Planted firmly in a chair near the door sat an American girl a little the worse for liquor, but with a determined expression on her face. She looked up at them with a jerk of her head.

"Well, j'tell him?" she demanded. "The name is Marjorie Collins, and he'll know it. I've come a long way, and I want to see him now and quick, or there's going to be more trouble than you ever saw." She rose unsteadily to her feet.

"You go in and tell Ham," whispered Johnson to Michael. "Maybe he'd better get out. I'll keep her here."

Back at the table, Michael leant close to Rutherford's ear and, with a certain grimness, whispered:

"A girl outside named Marjorie Collins says she wants to see you. She looks as if she wanted to make trouble."

Hamilton Rutherford blinked and his mouth fell ajar; then slowly the lips came together in a straight line and he said in a crisp voice:

"Please keep her there. And send the head barman to me right away." Michael spoke to the barman, and then, without returning to the table, asked quietly for his coat and hat. Out in the hall again, he passed Johnson and the girl without speaking and went out into the Rue Cambon. Calling a cab, he gave the address of Caroline's hotel.

His place was beside her now. Not to bring bad news, but simply to be with her when her house of cards came falling around her head.

Rutherford had implied that he was soft – well, he was hard enough not to give up the girl he loved without taking advantage of every chance within the pale of honour. Should she turn away from Rutherford, she would find him there.

She was in; she was surprised when he called, but she was still dressed and would be down immediately. Presently she appeared in a dinner gown, holding two blue telegrams in her hand. They sat down in armchairs in the deserted lobby.

"But, Michael, is the dinner over?"

"I wanted to see you, so I came away."

"I'm glad." Her voice was friendly, but matter-of-fact. "Because I'd just phoned your hotel that I had fittings and rehearsals all day tomorrow. Now we can have our talk after all."

"You're tired," he guessed. "Perhaps I shouldn't have come."

"No. I was waiting up for Hamilton. Telegrams that may be important. He said he might go on somewhere, and that may mean any hour, so I'm glad I have someone to talk to."

Michael winced at the impersonality in the last phrase.

"Don't you care when he gets home?"

"Naturally," she said, laughing, "but I haven't got much say about it, have I?"

"Why not?"

"I couldn't start by telling him what he could and couldn't do."

"Why not?"

"He wouldn't stand for it."

"He seems to want merely a housekeeper," said Michael ironically.

"Tell me about your plans, Michael," she asked quickly.

"My plans? I can't see any future after the day after tomorrow. The only real plan I ever had was to love you."

Their eyes brushed past each other's, and the look he knew so well was staring out at him from hers. Words flowed quickly from his heart:

"Let me tell you just once more how well I've loved you, never wavering for a moment, never thinking of another girl. And now when I think of all the years ahead without you, without any hope, I don't want to live, Caroline darling. I used to dream about our home, our children, about holding you in my arms and touching your face and hands and hair that used to belong to me, and now I just can't wake up."

Caroline was crying softly. "Poor Michael... poor Michael." Her hand reached out and her fingers brushed the lapel of his dinner coat. "I was so sorry for you the other night. You looked so thin, and as if you needed a new suit and somebody to take care of you." She sniffled and looked more closely at his coat. "Why, you've got a new suit! And a new silk hat! Why, Michael, how swell!" She laughed, suddenly cheerful through her tears. "You must have come into money, Michael; I never saw you so well turned out."

For a moment, at her reaction, he hated his new clothes.

"I have come into money," he said. "My grandfather left me about a quarter of a million dollars."

"Why, Michael," she cried, "how perfectly swell! I can't tell you how glad I am. I've always thought you were the sort of person who ought to have money."

"Yes, just too late to make a difference."

The revolving door from the street groaned around and Hamilton Rutherford came into the lobby. His face was flushed, his eyes were restless and impatient.

"Hello, darling; hello, Mr Curly." He bent and kissed Caroline. "I broke away for a minute to find out if I had any telegrams. I see you've got them there." Taking them from her, he remarked to Curly, "That was an odd business there in the bar, wasn't it? Especially as I understand some of you had a joke fixed up in the same line." He opened one of the telegrams, closed it and turned to Caroline with the divided expression of a man carrying two things in his head at once.

"A girl I haven't seen for two years turned up," he said. "It seemed to be some clumsy form of blackmail, for I haven't and never have had any sort of obligation towards her whatever."

"What happened?"

"The head barman had a Sûreté Générale man there in ten minutes and it was settled in the hall. The French blackmail laws make ours look like a sweet wish, and I gather they threw a scare into her that she'll remember. But it seems wiser to tell you."

"Are you implying that I mentioned the matter?" said Michael stiffly.

"No," Rutherford said slowly. "No, you were just going to be on hand. And since you're here, I'll tell you some news that will interest you even more."

He handed Michael one telegram and opened the other.

"This is in code," Michael said.

"So is this. But I've got to know all the words pretty well this last week. The two of them together mean that I'm due to start life all over."

Michael saw Caroline's face grow a shade paler, but she sat quiet as a mouse.

"It was a mistake and I stuck to it too long," continued Rutherford. "So you see I don't have all the luck, Mr Curly. By the way, they tell me you've come into money."

"Yes," said Michael.

"There we are, then." Rutherford turned to Caroline. "You understand, darling, that I'm not joking or exaggerating. I've lost almost every cent I had and I'm starting life over."

Two pairs of eyes were regarding her – Rutherford's noncommittal and unrequiring, Michael's hungry, tragic, pleading. In a minute she had raised herself from the chair and with a little cry thrown herself into Hamilton Rutherford's arms.

"Oh, darling," she cried, "what does it matter! It's better; I like it better, honestly I do! I want to start that way; I want to! Oh, please don't worry or be sad even for a minute!"

"All right, baby," said Rutherford. His hand stroked her hair gently for a moment; then he took his arm from around her.

"I promised to join the party for an hour," he said. "So I'll say good night, and I want you to go to bed soon and get a good sleep. Good night, Mr Curly. I'm sorry to have let you in for all these financial matters."

But Michael had already picked up his hat and cane. "I'll go along with you," he said.

3

I T WAS SUCH A FINE MORNING. Michael's cutaway hadn't been delivered, so he felt rather uncomfortable passing before the cameras and moving-picture machines in front of the little church on the Avenue George-V.

It was such a clean, new church that it seemed unforgivable not to be dressed properly, and Michael, white and shaky after a sleepless night, decided to stand in the rear. From there he looked at the back of Hamilton Rutherford, and the lacy, filmy back of Caroline, and the fat back of George Packman, which looked unsteady, as if it wanted to lean against the bride and groom.

The ceremony went on for a long time under the gay flags and pennons overhead, under the thick beams of June sunlight slanting down through the tall windows upon the well-dressed people.

As the procession, headed by the bride and groom, started down the aisle, Michael realized with alarm he was just where everyone would dispense with their parade stiffness, become informal and speak to him.

So it turned out. Rutherford and Caroline spoke first to him; Rutherford grim with the strain of being married, and Caroline lovelier than he had ever seen her, floating all softly down through the friends and relatives of her youth, down through the past and forward to the future by the sunlit door.

Michael managed to murmur, "Beautiful, simply beautiful," and then other people passed and spoke to him – old Mrs Dandy, straight from her sickbed and looking remarkably well, or carrying it off like the very fine old lady she was; and Rutherford's father and mother, ten years divorced, but walking side by side and looking made for each other and proud. Then all Caroline's sisters and their husbands and her little nephews in Eton suits, and then a long parade, all speaking to Michael because he was still standing paralysed just at that point where the procession broke.

He wondered what would happen now. Cards had been issued for a reception at the George-V – an expensive enough place, Heaven knew. Would Rutherford try to go through with that on top of those disastrous telegrams? Evidently, for the procession outside was streaming up there through the June morning, three by three and four by four. On the corner the long dresses of girls, five abreast, fluttered many-coloured in the wind. Girls had become gossamer again, perambulatory flora; such lovely fluttering dresses in the bright noon wind.

Michael needed a drink; he couldn't face that reception line without a drink. Diving into a side doorway of the hotel, he asked for the bar, whither a *chasseur** led him through half a kilometre of new American-looking passages.

But – how did it happen? – the bar was full. There were ten-fifteen men and two-four girls, all from the wedding, all needing a drink. There were cocktails and champagne in the bar – Rutherford's cocktails and champagne, as it turned out, for he had engaged the whole bar and the ballroom and the two great reception rooms and all the stairways leading up and down, and windows looking out over the whole square block of Paris. By and by Michael went and joined the long, slow drift of the receiving line. Through a flowery mist of "Such a lovely wedding", "My dear, you were simply lovely", "You're a lucky man, Rutherford", he passed down the line. When Michael came to Caroline, she took a single step forward and kissed him on the lips, but he felt no contact in the kiss; it was unreal and he floated on away from it. Old Mrs Dandy, who had always liked him, held his hand for a minute and thanked him for the flowers he had sent when he heard she was ill.

"I'm so sorry not to have written; you know, we old ladies are grateful for..." The flowers, the fact that she had not written, the wedding – Michael saw that they all had the same relative importance to her now; she had married off five other children and seen two of the marriages go to pieces, and this scene, so poignant, so confusing to Michael, appeared to her simply a familiar charade in which she had played her part before.

A buffet luncheon with champagne was already being served at small tables, and there was an orchestra playing in the empty ballroom. Michael sat down with Jebby West; he was still a little embarrassed at not wearing a morning coat, but he perceived now that he was not alone in the omission and felt better. "Wasn't Caroline divine?" Jebby West said. "So entirely self-possessed. I asked her this morning if she wasn't a little nervous at stepping off like this. And she said, 'Why should I be? I've been after him for two years, and now I'm just happy, that's all.'"

"It must be true," said Michael gloomily.

"What?"

"What you just said."

He had been stabbed but, rather to his distress, he did not feel the wound.

He asked Jebby to dance. Out on the floor, Rutherford's father and mother were dancing together.

"It makes me a little sad, that," she said. "Those two hadn't met for years; both of them were married again and she divorced again. She went to the station to meet him when he came over for Caroline's wedding, and invited him to stay at her house in the Avenue du Bois with a whole lot of other people, perfectly proper, but he was afraid his wife would hear about it and not like it, so he went to a hotel. Don't you think that's sort of sad?"

An hour or so later Michael realized suddenly that it was afternoon. In one corner of the ballroom an arrangement of screens like a moving-picture stage had been set up and photographers were taking official pictures of the bridal party. The bridal party, still as death and pale as wax under the bright lights, appeared, to the dancers circling the modulated semidarkness of the ballroom, like those jovial or sinister groups that one comes upon in the Old Mill at an amusement park.

After the bridal party had been photographed, there was a group of the ushers; then the bridesmaids, the families, the children. Later, Caroline, active and excited, having long since abandoned the repose implicit in her flowing dress and great bouquet, came and plucked Michael off the floor.

"Now we'll have them take one of just old friends." Her voice implied that this was best, most intimate of all. "Come here, Jebby, George – not you, Hamilton; this is just my friends – Sally…"

A little after that, what remained of formality disappeared and the hours flowed easily down the profuse stream of champagne. In the modern fashion, Hamilton Rutherford sat at the table with his arm about an old girl of his and assured his guests, which included not a few bewildered but enthusiastic Europeans, that the party was not nearly at an end; it was to reassemble at Zelli's after midnight. Michael saw Mrs Dandy, not quite over her illness, rise to go and become caught in polite group after group, and he spoke of it to one of her daughters, who thereupon forcibly abducted her mother and called her car. Michael felt very considerate and proud of himself after having done this, and drank much more champagne.

"It's amazing," George Packman was telling him enthusiastically. "This show will cost Ham about five thousand dollars, and I understand they'll be just about his last. But did he countermand a bottle of champagne or a flower? Not he! He happens to have it – that young man. Do you know that T.G. Vance offered him a salary of fifty thousand dollars a year ten minutes before the wedding this morning? In another year he'll be back with the millionaires."

The conversation was interrupted by a plan to carry Rutherford out on communal shoulders – a plan which six of them put into effect, and then stood in the four-o'clock sunshine waving goodbye to the bride and groom. But there must have been a mistake somewhere, for five minutes later Michael saw both bride and groom descending the stairway to the reception, each with a glass of champagne held defiantly on high.

"This is our way of doing things," he thought. "Generous and fresh and free – a sort of Virginia-plantation hospitality, but at a different pace now, nervous as a ticker tape."

Standing unselfconsciously in the middle of the room to see which was the American ambassador, he realized with a start that he hadn't really thought of Caroline for hours. He looked about him with a sort of alarm, and then he saw her across the room, very bright and young, and radiantly happy. He saw Rutherford near her, looking at her as if he could never look long enough, and as Michael watched them they seemed to recede as he had wished them to do that day in the Rue de Castiglione – recede and fade off into joys and griefs of their own, into the years that would take the toll of Rutherford's fine pride and Caroline's young, moving beauty; fade far away, so that now he could scarcely see them, as if they were shrouded in something as misty as her white, billowing dress.

Michael was cured. The ceremonial function, with its pomp and its revelry, had stood for a sort of initiation into a life where even his regret could not follow them. All the bitterness melted out of him suddenly and the world reconstituted itself out of the youth and happiness that was all around him, profligate as the spring sunshine. He was trying to remember which one of the bridesmaids he had made a date to dine with tonight as he walked forward to bid Hamilton and Caroline Rutherford goodbye.

One Trip Abroad

1

IN THE AFTERNOON the air became black with locusts, and some of the women shrieked, sinking to the floor of the motorbus and covering their hair with travelling rugs. The locusts were coming north, eating everything in their path, which was not so much in that part of the world; they were flying silently and in straight lines, flakes of black snow. But none struck the windshield or tumbled into the car, and presently humorists began holding out their hands, trying to catch some. After ten minutes the cloud thinned out, passed, and the women emerged from the blankets, dishevelled and feeling silly. And everyone talked together.

Everyone talked; it would have been absurd not to talk after having been through a swarm of locusts on the edge of the Sahara. The Smyrna-American talked to the British widow going down to Biskra to have one last fling with an as-yet-unencountered sheik. The member of the San Francisco Stock Exchange talked shyly to the author. "Aren't you an author?" he said. The father and daughter from Wilmington talked to the cockney airman who was going to fly to Timbuktu. Even the French chauffeur turned about and explained in a loud, clear voice: "Bumblebees," which sent the trained nurse from New York into shriek after shriek of hysterical laughter.

Amongst the unsubtle rushing together of the travellers there was one interchange more carefully considered. Mr and Mrs Liddell Miles, turning as one person, smiled and spoke to the young American couple in the seat behind:

"Didn't catch any in your hair?"

The young couple smiled back politely.

"No. We survived that plague."

They were in their twenties, and there was still a pleasant touch of bride and groom upon them. A handsome couple; the man rather intense and sensitive, the girl arrestingly light of hue in eyes and hair, her face without shadows, its living freshness modulated by a lovely confident calm. Mr and Mrs Miles did not fail to notice their air of good breeding, of a specifically "swell" background, expressed both by their unsophistication and by their ingrained reticence that was not stiffness. If they held aloof, it was because they were sufficient to each other, while Mr and Mrs Miles's aloofness towards the other passengers was a conscious mask, a social attitude, quite as public an affair in its essence as the ubiquitous advances of the Smyrna-American, who was snubbed by all.

The Mileses had, in fact, decided that the young couple were "possible" and, bored with themselves, were frankly approaching them.

"Have you been to Africa before? It's been so utterly fascinating! Are you going on to Tunis?"

The Mileses, if somewhat worn away inside by fifteen years of a particular set in Paris, had undeniable style, even charm, and before the evening arrival at the little oasis town of Bou Saâda they had all four become companionable. They uncovered mutual friends in New York and, meeting for a cocktail in the bar of the Hôtel Transatlantique, decided to have dinner together.

As the young Kellys came downstairs later, Nicole was conscious of a certain regret that they had accepted, realizing that now they were probably committed to seeing a certain amount of their new acquaintances as far as Constantine, where their routes diverged.

In the eight months of their marriage she had been so very happy that it seemed like spoiling something. On the Italian liner that had brought them to Gibraltar they had not joined the groups that leant desperately on one another in the bar; instead, they seriously studied French, and Nelson worked on business contingent on his recent inheritance of half a million dollars. Also he painted a picture of a smokestack. When one member of the gay crowd in the bar disappeared permanently into the Atlantic just this side of the Azores, the young Kellys were almost glad, for it justified their aloof attitude.

But there was another reason Nicole was sorry they had committed themselves. She spoke to Nelson about it: "I passed that couple in the hall just now."

"Who – the Mileses?"

"No, that young couple – about our age – the ones that were on the other motorbus, that we thought looked so nice, in Bir Rabalou after lunch, in the camel market."

"They did look nice."

"Charming," she said emphatically – "the girl and man, both. I'm almost sure I've met the girl somewhere before."

The couple referred to were sitting across the room at dinner, and Nicole found her eyes drawn irresistibly towards them. They, too, now had companions, and again Nicole, who had not talked to a girl of her own age for two months, felt a faint regret. The Mileses, being formally sophisticated and frankly snobbish, were a different matter. They had been to an alarming number of places and seemed to know all the flashing phantoms of the newspapers.

They dined on the hotel veranda under a sky that was low and full of the presence of a strange and watchful God; around the corners of the hotel the night already stirred with the sounds of which they had so often read but that were even so hysterically unfamiliar – drums from Senegal, a native flute, the selfish, effeminate whine of a camel, the Arabs pattering past in shoes made of old automobile tyres, the wail of Magian prayer.

At the desk in the hotel, a fellow passenger was arguing monotonously with the clerk about the rate of exchange, and the inappropriateness added to the detachment which had increased steadily as they went south.

Mrs Miles was the first to break the lingering silence; with a sort of impatience she pulled them with her, in from the night and up to the table.

"We really should have dressed. Dinner's more amusing if people dress, because they feel differently in formal clothes. The English know that."

"Dress here?" her husband objected. "I'd feel like that man in the ragged dress suit we passed today, driving the flock of sheep."

"I always feel like a tourist if I'm not dressed."

"Well, we are, aren't we?" asked Nelson.

"I don't consider myself a tourist. A tourist is somebody who gets up early and goes to cathedrals and talks about scenery."

Nicole and Nelson, having seen all the official sights from Fez to Algiers, and taken reels of moving pictures and felt improved, confessed themselves, but decided that their experiences on the trip would not interest Mrs Miles.

"Every place is the same," Mrs Miles continued. "The only thing that matters is who's there. New scenery is fine for half an hour, but after that you want your own kind to see. That's why some places have a certain vogue, and then the vogue changes and the people move on somewhere else. The place itself really never matters."

"But doesn't somebody first decide that the place is nice?" objected Nelson. "The first ones go there because they like the place."

"Where were you going this spring?" Mrs Miles asked.

"We thought of San Remo, or maybe Sorrento. We've never been to Europe before."

"My children, I know both Sorrento and San Remo, and you won't stand either of them for a week. They're full of the most awful English, reading the *Daily Mail* and waiting for letters and talking about the most incredibly dull things. You might as well go to Brighton or Bournemouth and buy a white poodle and a sunshade and walk on the pier. How long are you staying in Europe?"

"We don't know – perhaps several years." Nicole hesitated. "Nelson came into a little money, and we wanted a change. When I was young, my father had asthma and I had to live in the most depressing health resorts with him for years; and Nelson was in the fur business in Alaska and he loathed it; so when we were free we came abroad. Nelson's going to paint and I'm going to study singing." She looked triumphantly at her husband. "So far, it's been absolutely gorgeous."

Mrs Miles decided, from the evidence of the younger woman's clothes, that it was quite a bit of money, and their enthusiasm was infectious.

"You really must go to Biarritz," she advised them. "Or else come to Monte Carlo."

"They tell me there's a great show here," said Miles, ordering champagne. "The Ouled Naïls. The concierge says they're some kind of tribe of girls who come down from the mountains and learn to be dancers and what not, till they've collected enough gold to go back to their mountains and marry. Well, they give a performance tonight."

Walking over to the Café of the Ouled Naïls afterwards, Nicole regretted that she and Nelson were not strolling alone through the ever-lower, ever-softer, ever-brighter night. Nelson had reciprocated the bottle of champagne at dinner, and neither of them was accustomed to so much. As they drew near the sad flute, she didn't want to go inside, but rather to climb to the top of a low hill where a white mosque shone clear as a planet through the night. Life was better than any show; closing in towards Nelson, she pressed his hand.

The little cave of a café was filled with the passengers from the two buses. The girls – light-brown, flat-nosed Berbers with fine, deep-shaded eyes – were already doing each one her solo on the platform. They wore cotton dresses, faintly reminiscent of Southern mammies; under these their bodies writhed in a slow nautch, culminating in a stomach dance, with silver belts bobbing wildly and their strings of real gold coins tinkling on their necks and arms. The flute player was also a comedian; he danced, burlesquing the girls. The drummer, swathed in goatskins like a witch doctor, was a true black from the Sudan.

Through the smoke of cigarettes each girl went in turn through the finger movement, like piano-playing in the air – outwardly facile, yet, after a few moments, so obviously exacting – and then through the very simply languid yet equally precise steps of the feet – these were but preparation to the wild sensuality of the culminated dance.

Afterwards there was a lull. Though the performance seemed not quite over, most of the audience gradually got up to go, but there was a whispering in the air.

"What is it?" Nicole asked her husband.

"Why, I believe – it appears that for a consideration the Ouled Naïls dance in more or less – ah – oriental style – in very little except jewellery."

"Oh."

"We're all staying," Mr Miles assured her jovially. "After all, we're here to see the real customs and manners of the country – a little prudishness shouldn't stand in our way."

Most of the men remained, and several of the women. Nicole stood up suddenly.

"I'll wait outside," she said.

"Why not stay, Nicole? After all, Mrs Miles is staying."

The flute player was making preliminary flourishes. Upon the raised dais two pale-brown children of perhaps fourteen were taking off their cotton dresses. For an instant Nicole hesitated, torn between repulsion and the desire not to appear to be a prig. Then she saw another young American woman get up quickly and start for the door. Recognizing the attractive young wife from the other bus, her own decision came quickly and she followed.

Nelson hurried after her. "I'm going if you go," he said, but with evident reluctance.

"Please don't bother. I'll wait with the guide outside."

"Well…" The drum was starting. He compromised: "I'll only stay a minute. I want to see what it's like."

Waiting in the fresh night, she found that the incident had hurt her – Nelson's not coming with her at once, giving as an argument the fact that Mrs Miles was staying. From being hurt, she grew angry and made signs to the guide that she wanted to return to the hotel.

Twenty minutes later, Nelson appeared, angry with the anxiety at finding her gone, as well as to hide his guilt at having left her. Incredulous with themselves, they were suddenly in a quarrel.

Much later, when there were no sounds at all in Bou Saâda and the nomads in the marketplace were only motionless bundles rolled up in their burnouses, she was asleep upon his shoulder. Life is progressive, no matter what our intentions, but something was harmed, some precedent of possible non-agreement was set. It was a love match, though, and it could stand a great deal. She and Nelson had passed lonely youths, and now they wanted the taste and smell of the living world; for the present they were finding it in each other.

A month later they were in Sorrento, where Nicole took singing lessons and Nelson tried to paint something new into the Bay of Naples. It was the existence they had planned and often read about. But they found, as so many have found, that the charm of idyllic interludes depends upon one person's "giving the party" – which is to say, furnishing the background, the experience, the patience against which the other seems to enjoy again the spells of pastoral tranquillity recollected from childhood. Nicole and Nelson were at once too old and too young, and too American, to fall into immediate soft agreement with a strange land. Their vitality made them restless, for as yet his painting had no direction and her singing no immediate prospect of becoming serious. They said they were not "getting anywhere" – the evenings were long, so they began to drink a lot of *vin de Capri* at dinner.

The English owned the hotel. They were aged, come south for good weather and tranquillity; Nelson and Nicole resented the mild tenor of their days. Could people be content to talk eternally about the weather, promenade the same walks, face the same variant of macaroni at dinner month after month? They grew bored, and Americans bored are already in sight of excitement. Things came to head all in one night.

Over a flask of wine at dinner they decided to go to Paris, settle in an apartment and work seriously. Paris promised metropolitan diversion, friends of their own age, a general intensity that Italy lacked. Eager with new hopes, they strolled into the salon after dinner, when, for the tenth time, Nelson noticed an ancient and enormous mechanical piano and was moved to try it.

Across the salon sat the only English people with whom they had had any connection – Gen. Sir Evelyne Fragelle and Lady Fragelle. The connection had been brief and unpleasant – seeing them walking out of the hotel in peignoirs to swim, she had announced, over quite a few yards of floor space, that it was disgusting and shouldn't be allowed.

But that was nothing compared with her response to the first terrific bursts of sound from the electric piano. As the dust of years trembled off the keyboard at the vibration, she shot galvanically forward with the sort of jerk associated with the electric chair. Somewhat stunned himself by the sudden din of 'Waiting for the *Robert E. Lee*',* Nelson had scarcely sat down when she projected herself across the room, her train quivering behind her, and, without glancing at the Kellys, turned off the instrument.

It was one of those gestures that are either plainly justified, or else outrageous. For a moment Nelson hesitated uncertainly; then, remembering Lady Fragelle's arrogant remark about his bathing suit, he returned to the instrument in her still-billowing wake and turned it on again.

The incident had become international. The eyes of the entire salon fell eagerly upon the protagonists, watching for the next move. Nicole hurried after Nelson, urging him to let the matter pass, but it was too late. From the outraged English table there arose, joint by joint, Gen. Sir Evelyne Fragelle, faced with perhaps his most crucial situation since the Relief of Ladysmith.*

"'T'lee outrageous! 'T'lee outrageous!"

"I beg your pardon," said Nelson.

"Here for fifteen years!" screamed Sir Evelyne to himself. "Never heard of anyone doing such a thing before!"

"I gathered that this was put here for the amusement of the guests."

Scorning to answer, Sir Evelyne knelt, reached for the catch, pushed it the wrong way, whereupon the speed and volume of the instrument tripled until they stood in a wild pandemonium of sound; Sir Evelyne livid with military emotions, Nelson on the point of maniacal laughter.

In a moment the firm hand of the hotel manager settled the matter; the instrument gulped and stopped, trembling a little from its unaccustomed outburst, leaving behind it a great silence in which Sir Evelyne turned to the manager.

"Most outrageous affair ever heard of in my life. My wife turned it off once, and he" – this was his first acknowledgement of Nelson's identity as distinct from the instrument – "he put it on again!"

"This is a public room in a hotel," Nelson protested. "The instrument is apparently here to be used."

"Don't get in an argument," Nicole whispered. "They're old."

But Nelson said, "If there's any apology, it's certainly due to me."

Sir Evelyne's eye was fixed menacingly upon the manager, waiting for him to do his duty. The latter thought of Sir Evelyne's fifteen years of residence, and cringed.

"It is not the habitude to play the instrument in the evening. The clients are each one quiet on his or her table."

"American cheek!" snapped Sir Evelyne.

"Very well," Nelson said, "we'll relieve the hotel of our presence tomorrow."

As a reaction from this incident, as a sort of protest against Sir Evelyne Fragelle, they went not to Paris but to Monte Carlo after all. They were through with being alone.

2

A LITTLE MORE THAN TWO YEARS after the Kellys' first visit to Monte Carlo, Nicole woke up one morning into what, though it bore the same name, had become to her a different place altogether.

In spite of hurried months in Paris or Biarritz, it was now home to them. They had a villa, they had a large acquaintance among the spring and summer crowd – a crowd which, naturally, did not include people on charted trips or the shore parties from Mediterranean cruises; these latter had become for them "tourists".

They loved the Riviera in full summer with many friends there and the nights open and full of music. Before the maid drew the curtains this morning to shut out the glare, Nicole saw from her window the yacht of T.F. Golding, placid among the swells of the Monacan Bay, as if constantly bound on a romantic voyage not dependent upon actual motion.

The yacht had taken the slow tempo of the coast; it had gone no farther than to Cannes and back all summer, though it might have toured the world. The Kellys were dining on board that night.

Nicole spoke excellent French; she had five new evening dresses and four others that would do; she had her husband; she had two men in love with her; and she felt sad for one of them. She had her pretty face. At 10.30 she was meeting a third man, who was just beginning to be in love with her "in a harmless way". At one she was having a dozen charming people to luncheon. All that.

"I'm happy," she brooded towards the bright blinds. "I'm young and good-looking, and my name is often in the paper as having been here and there, but really I don't care about chichi. I think it's all awfully silly, but if you do want to see people, you might as well see the chic, amusing ones; and if people call you a snob, it's envy, and they know it and everybody knows it."

She repeated the substance of this to Oscar Dane on the Mont Agel golf course two hours later, and he cursed her quietly.

"Not at all," he said. "You're just getting to be an old snob. Do you call that crowd of drunks you run with amusing people? Why, they're not even very swell. They're so hard that they've shifted down through Europe like nails in a sack of wheat, till they stick out of it a little into the Mediterranean Sea."

Annoyed, Nicole fired a name at him, but he answered: "Class C. A good solid article for beginners."

"The Colbys – anyway, her."

"Third flight."

"Marquis and Marquise de Kalb."

"If she didn't happen to take dope and he didn't have other peculiarities."

"Well, then, where are the amusing people?" she demanded impatiently.

"Off by themselves somewhere. They don't hunt in herds, except occasionally."

"How about you? You'd snap up an invitation from every person I named. I've heard stories about you wilder than any you can make up. There's not a man that's known you six months that would take your cheque for ten dollars. You're a sponge and a parasite and everything—"

"Shut up for a minute," he interrupted. "I don't want to spoil this drive... I just don't like to see you kid yourself," he continued. "What passes with you for international society is just about as hard to enter nowadays as the public rooms at the Casino; and if I can make my living by sponging off it, I'm still giving twenty times more than I get. We deadbeats are about the only people in it with any stuff, and we stay with it because we have to."

She laughed, liking him immensely, wondering how angry Nelson would be when he found that Oscar had walked off with his nail scissors and his copy of the *New York Herald* this morning.

"Anyhow," she thought afterwards, as she drove home towards luncheon, "we're getting out of it all soon, and we'll be serious and have a baby. After this last summer."

Stopping for a moment at a florist's, she saw a young woman coming out with an armful of flowers. The young woman glanced at her over the heap of colour, and Nicole perceived that she was extremely smart, and then that her face was familiar. It was someone she had known once, but only slightly; the name had escaped her, so she did not nod, and forgot the incident until that afternoon.

They were twelve for luncheon: the Goldings' party from the yacht, Liddell and Cardine Miles, Mr Dane – seven different nationalities she counted; among them an exquisite young Frenchwoman, Madame Delauney, whom Nicole referred to lightly as "Nelson's girl". Noël Delauney was perhaps her closest friend; when they made up foursomes for golf or for trips, she paired off with Nelson; but today, as Nicole introduced her to someone as "Nelson's girl", the bantering phrase filled Nicole with distaste.

She said aloud at luncheon: "Nelson and I are going to get away from it all."

Everybody agreed that they, too, were going to get away from it all.

"It's all right for the English," someone said, "because they're doing a sort of dance of death – you know, gaiety in the doomed fort, with the sepoys at the gate. You can see it by their faces when they dance – the intensity. They know it and they want it, and they don't see any future. But you Americans, you're having a rotten time. If you want to wear the green hat or the crushed hat, or whatever it is, you always have to get a little tipsy."

"We're going to get away from it all," Nicole said firmly, but something within her argued: "What a pity – this lovely blue sea, this happy time." What came afterwards? Did one just accept a lessening of tension? It was somehow Nelson's business to answer that. His growing discontent that he wasn't getting anywhere ought to explode into a new life for both of them, or rather a new hope and content with life. That secret should be his masculine contribution.

"Well, children, goodbye."

"It was a great luncheon."

"Don't forget about getting away from it all."

"See you when…"

The guests walked down the path towards their cars. Only Oscar, just faintly flushed on liqueurs, stood with Nicole on the veranda, talking on and on about the girl he had invited up to see his stamp collection. Momentarily tired of people, impatient to be alone, Nicole listened for a moment, and then, taking a glass vase of flowers from the luncheon table, went through the French windows into the dark, shadowy villa, his voice following her as he talked on and on out there.

It was when she crossed the first salon, still hearing Oscar's monologue on the veranda, that she began to hear another voice in the next room, cutting sharply across Oscar's voice.

"Ah, but kiss me again," it said, stopped; Nicole stopped, too, rigid in the silence, now broken only by the voice on the porch.

"Be careful." Nicole recognized the faint French accent of Noël Delauney.

"I'm tired of being careful. Anyhow, they're on the veranda."

"No, better the usual place."

"Darling, sweet darling."

The voice of Oscar Dane on the veranda grew weary and stopped, and, as if thereby released from her paralysis, Nicole took a step – forward or backward, she did not know which. At the sound of her heel on the floor, she heard the two people in the next room breaking swiftly apart.

Then she went in. Nelson was lighting a cigarette; Noël, with her back turned, was apparently hunting for hat or purse on a chair. With blind horror rather than anger, Nicole threw, or rather pushed away from her, the glass vase which she carried. If at anyone, it was at Nelson she threw it, but the force of her feeling had entered the inanimate thing;

it flew past him, and Noël Delauney, just turning about, was struck full on the side of her head and face.

"Say, there!" Nelson cried. Noël sank slowly into the chair before which she stood, her hand slowly rising to cover the side of her face. The jar rolled unbroken on the thick carpet, scattering its flowers.

"You look out!" Nelson was at Noël's side, trying to take the hand away to see what had happened.

"*C'est liquide*," gasped Noël in a whisper. "*Est-ce que c'est le sang?*"*

He forced her hand away, and cried breathlessly, "No, it's just water!" – and then, to Oscar, who had appeared in the doorway: "Get some cognac!" and to Nicole: "You fool, you must be crazy!"

Nicole, breathing hard, said nothing. When the brandy arrived, there was a continuing silence, like that of people watching an operation, while Nelson poured a glass down Noël's throat. Nicole signalled to Oscar for a drink and, as if afraid to break the silence without it, they all had a brandy. Then Noël and Nelson spoke at once:

"If you can find my hat—"

"This is the silliest—"

"—I shall go immediately."

"—thing I ever saw; I…"

They all looked at Nicole, who said: "Have her car drive right up to the door." Oscar departed quickly.

"Are you sure you don't want to see a doctor?" asked Nelson anxiously.

"I want to go."

A minute later, when the car had driven away, Nelson came in and poured himself another glass of brandy. A wave of subsiding tension flowed over him, showing in his face; Nicole saw it, and saw also his gathering will to make the best he could of it.

"I want to know just why you did that," he demanded. "No, don't go, Oscar." He saw the story starting out into the world.

"What possible reason—"

"Oh, shut up!" snapped Nicole.

"If I kissed Noël, there's nothing so terrible about it. It's of absolutely no significance."

She made a contemptuous sound. "I heard what you said to her."

"You're crazy."

He said it as if she were crazy, and wild rage filled her.

"You liar! All this time pretending to be so square, and so particular what I did, and all the time behind my back you've been playing around with that little…"

She used a serious word and, as if maddened with the sound of it, she sprang towards his chair. In protection against this sudden attack, he flung up his arm quickly, and the knuckles of his open hand struck across the socket of her eye. Covering her face with her hand as Noël had done ten minutes previously, she fell sobbing to the floor.

"Hasn't this gone far enough?" Oscar cried.

"Yes," admitted Nelson, "I guess it has."

"You go on out on the veranda and cool off."

He got Nicole to a couch and sat beside her, holding her hand.

"Brace up – brace up, baby," he said, over and over. "What are you – Jack Dempsey? You can't go around hitting French women; they'll sue you."

"He told her he loved her," she gasped hysterically. "She said she'd meet him at the same place… Has he gone there now?"

"He's out on the porch, walking up and down, sorry as the devil that he accidentally hit you, and sorry he ever saw Noël Delauney."

"Oh, yes!"

"You might have heard wrong, and it doesn't prove a thing, anyhow."

After twenty minutes, Nelson came in suddenly and sank down on his knees by the side of his wife. Mr Oscar Dane, reinforced in his idea that he gave much more than he got, backed discreetly and far from unwillingly to the door.

In another hour, Nelson and Nicole, arm in arm, emerged from their villa and walked slowly down to the Café de Paris. They walked instead of driving, as if trying to return to the simplicity they had once possessed, as if they were trying to unwind something that had become visibly tangled. Nicole accepted his explanations, not because they were credible, but because she wanted passionately to believe them. They were both very quiet and sorry.

The Café de Paris was pleasant at that hour, with sunset drooping through the yellow awnings and the red parasols as through stained glass. Glancing about, Nicole saw the young woman she had encountered that morning. She was with a man now, and Nelson placed them immediately as the young couple they had seen in Algeria, almost three years ago.

"They've changed," he commented. "I suppose we have too, but not so much. They're harder-looking and he looks dissipated. Dissipation always shows in light eyes rather than in dark ones. The girl is *tout ce qu'il y a de chic*,* as they say, but there's a hard look in her face too."

"I like her."

"Do you want me to go and ask them if they are that same couple?"

"No! That'd be like lonesome tourists do. They have their own friends."

At that moment people were joining them at their table.

"Nelson, how about tonight?" Nicole asked a little later. "Do you think we can appear at the Goldings' after what's happened?"

"We not only can but we've got to. If the story's around and we're not there, we'll just be handing them a nice juicy subject of conversation… Hello! What on earth…"

Something strident and violent had happened across the café; a woman screamed and the people at one table were all on their feet, surging back and forth like one person. Then the people at the other tables were standing and crowding forward; for just a moment the Kellys saw the face of the girl they had been watching, pale now, and distorted with anger. Panic-stricken, Nicole plucked at Nelson's sleeve.

"I want to get out. I can't stand any more today. Take me home. Is everybody going crazy?"

On the way home, Nelson glanced at Nicole's face and perceived with a start that they were not going to dinner on the Goldings' yacht after all. For Nicole had the beginnings of a well-defined and unmistakable black eye – an eye that by eleven o'clock would be beyond the aid of all the cosmetics in the principality. His heart sank and he decided to say nothing about it until they reached home.

3

THERE IS SOME WISE ADVICE in the catechism about avoiding the occasions of sin, and when the Kellys went up to Paris a month later they made a conscientious list of the places they wouldn't visit any more and the people they didn't want to see again. The places included several famous bars, all the nightclubs except one or two that were highly decorous, all the early-morning clubs of every description and all summer resorts that made whoopee for its own sake – whoopee triumphant and unrestrained – the main attraction of the season.

The people they were through with included three fourths of those with whom they had passed the last two years. They did this not in snobbishness, but for self-preservation, and not without a certain fear in their hearts that they were cutting themselves off from human contacts for ever.

But the world is always curious, and people become valuable merely for their inaccessibility. They found that there were others in Paris who were only interested in those who had separated from the many. The first crowd they had known was largely American, salted with Europeans; the second was largely European, peppered with Americans. This latter crowd was "society", and here and there it touched the ultimate milieu, made up of individuals of high position, of great fortune, very occasionally of genius, and always of power. Without being intimate with the great, they made new friends of a more conservative type. Moreover, Nelson began to paint again; he had a studio, and they visited the studios of Brancusi and Léger and Deschamps.* It seemed that they were more part of something than before, and when certain gaudy rendezvous were mentioned, they felt a contempt for their first two years in Europe, speaking of their former acquaintances as "that crowd" and as "people who waste your time".

So, although they kept their rules, they entertained frequently at home and they went out to the houses of others. They were young and handsome and intelligent; they came to know what did go and what did not go, and adapted themselves accordingly. Moreover, they were naturally generous and willing, within the limits of common sense, to pay.

When one went out one generally drank. This meant little to Nicole, who had a horror of losing her *soigné* air, losing a touch of bloom or a ray of admiration, but Nelson, thwarted somewhere, found himself quite as tempted to drink at these small dinners as in the more frankly rowdy world. He was not a drunk, he did nothing conspicuous or sodden, but he was no longer willing to go out socially without the stimulus of liquor. It was with the idea of bringing him to a serious and responsible attitude that Nicole decided, after a year in Paris, that the time had come to have a baby.

This was coincidental with their meeting Count Chiki Sarolai. He was an attractive relic of the Austrian court, with no fortune or pretence to any, but with solid social and financial connections in France. His sister was married to the Marquis de la Clos d'Hirondelle, who, in addition to being of the ancient noblesse, was a successful banker in Paris. Count Chiki roved here and there, frankly spongeing, rather like Oscar Dane, but in a different sphere.

His penchant was Americans; he hung on their words with a pathetic eagerness, as if they would sooner or later let slip their mysterious formula for making money. After a casual meeting, his interest gravitated to the Kellys. During Nicole's months of waiting he was in the house continually, tirelessly interested in anything that concerned American crime, slang, finance or manners. He came in for a luncheon or dinner when he had no other place to go, and with tacit gratitude he persuaded his sister to call on Nicole, who was immensely flattered.

It was arranged that when Nicole went to the hospital he would stay at the *appartement* and keep Nelson company – an arrangement of which Nicole didn't approve, since they were inclined to drink together. But the day on which it was decided, he arrived with news of one of his brother-in-law's famous canal-boat parties on the Seine, to which the Kellys were to be invited and which, conveniently enough, was to occur three weeks after the arrival of the baby. So, when Nicole moved out to the American Hospital, Count Chiki moved in.

The baby was a boy. For a while Nicole forgot all about people and their human status and their value. She even wondered at the fact that she had become such a snob, since everything seemed trivial compared with the new individual that, eight times a day, they carried to her breast.

After two weeks, she and the baby went back to the apartment, but Chiki and his valet stayed on. It was understood, with that subtlety the Kellys had only recently begun to appreciate, that he was merely staying until after his brother-in-law's party, but the apartment was crowded and Nicole wished him gone. But her old idea, that if one had to see people they might as well be the best, was carried out in being invited to the De la Clos d'Hirondelles'.

As she lay in her chaise longue the day before the event, Chiki explained the arrangements, in which he had evidently aided.

"Everyone who arrives must drink two cocktails in the American style before they can come aboard – as a ticket of admission."

"But I thought that very fashionable French – Faubourg Saint-Germain and all that – didn't drink cocktails."

"Oh, but my family is very modern. We adopt many American customs."

"Who'll be there?"

"Everyone! Everyone in Paris."

Great names swam before her eyes. Next day she could not resist dragging the affair into conversation with her doctor. But she was rather offended at the look of astonishment and incredulity that came into his eyes.

"Did I understand you aright?" he demanded. "Did I understand you to say that you were going to a ball tomorrow?"

"Why, yes," she faltered. "Why not?"

"My dear lady, you are not going to stir out of the house for two more weeks; you are not going to dance or do anything strenuous for two more after that."

"That's ridiculous!" she cried. "It's been three weeks already! Esther Sherman went to America after—"

"Never mind," he interrupted. "Every case is different. There is a complication which makes it positively necessary for you to follow my orders."

"But the idea is that I'll just go for two hours, because of course I'll have to come home to Sonny—"

"You'll not go for two minutes."

She knew, from the seriousness of his tone, that he was right, but, perversely, she did not mention the matter to Nelson. She said, instead, that she was tired, that possibly she might not go, and lay awake that night measuring her disappointment against her fear. She woke up for Sonny's first feeding, thinking to herself: "But if I just take ten steps from a limousine to a chair and just sit half an hour..."

At the last minute the pale-green evening dress from Callets, draped across a chair in her bedroom, decided her. She went.

Somewhere, during the shuffle and delay on the gangplank while the guests went aboard and were challenged and drank down their cocktails with attendant gaiety, Nicole realized that she had made a mistake. There was, at any rate, no formal receiving line and, after greeting their hosts, Nelson found her a chair on deck, where presently her faintness disappeared.

Then she was glad she had come. The boat was hung with frag-
ile lanterns, which blended with the pastels of the bridges and the
reflected stars in the dark Seine, like a child's dream out of the *Arabian
Nights*. A crowd of hungry-eyed spectators were gathered on the banks.
Champagne moved past in platoons like a drill of bottles, while the
music, instead of being loud and obtrusive, drifted down from the upper
deck like frosting dripping over a cake. She became aware presently
that they were not the only Americans there – across the deck were the
Liddell Mileses, whom she had not seen for several years.

Other people from that crowd were present, and she felt a faint
disappointment. What if this was not the marquis's best party? She
remembered her mother's second days at home. She asked Chiki, who
was at her side, to point out celebrities, but when she enquired about
several people whom she associated with that set, he replied vaguely
that they were away, or coming later, or could not be there. It seemed
to her that she saw across the room the girl who had made the scene in
the Café de Paris at Monte Carlo, but she could not be sure, for with
the faint, almost imperceptible movement of the boat, she realized that
she was growing faint again. She sent for Nelson to take her home.

"You can come right back, of course. You needn't wait for me, because
I'm going right to bed."

He left her in the hands of the nurse, who helped her upstairs and
aided her to undress quickly.

"I'm desperately tired," Nicole said. "Will you put my pearls away?"

"Where?"

"In the jewel box on the dressing table."

"I don't see it," said the nurse after a minute.

"Then it's in a drawer."

There was a thorough rummaging of the dressing table, without result.

"But of course it's there." Nicole attempted to rise, but fell back,
exhausted. "Look for it, please, again. Everything is in it – all my
mother's things and my engagement things."

"I'm sorry, Mrs Kelly. There's nothing in this room that answers to that description."

"Wake up the maid."

The maid knew nothing; then, after a persistent cross-examination, she did know something. Count Sarolai's valet had gone out, carrying his suitcase, half an hour after Madame left the house.

Writhing in sharp and sudden pain, with a hastily summoned doctor at her side, it seemed to Nicole hours before Nelson came home. When he arrived, his face was deathly pale and his eyes were wild. He came directly into her room.

"What do you think?" he said savagely. Then he saw the doctor. "Why, what's the matter?"

"Oh, Nelson, I'm sick as a dog and my jewel box is gone, and Chiki's valet has gone. I've told the police... Perhaps Chiki would know where the man—"

"Chiki will never come in this house again," he said slowly. "Do you know whose party that was? Have you got any idea whose party that was?" He burst into wild laughter. "It was our party – our party, do you understand? We gave it – we didn't know it, but we did."

"*Maintenant, monsieur, il ne faut pas exciter madame...*"* the doctor began.

"I thought it was odd when the marquis went home early, but I didn't suspect till the end. They were just guests – Chiki invited all the people. After it was over, the caterers and musicians began to come up and ask me where to send their bills. And that damn Chiki had the nerve to tell me he thought I knew all the time. He said that all he'd promised was that it would be his brother-in-law's sort of party, and that his sister would be there. He said perhaps I was drunk, or perhaps I didn't understand French – as if we'd ever talked anything but English to him."

"Don't pay!" she said. "I wouldn't think of paying."

"So I said, but they're going to sue – the boat people and the others. They want twelve thousand dollars. "

She relaxed suddenly. "Oh, go away!" she cried. "I don't care! I've lost my jewels and I'm sick, sick!"

4

T HIS IS THE STORY OF A TRIP ABROAD, and the geographical element must not be slighted. Having visited North Africa, Italy, the Riviera, Paris and points in between, it was not surprising that eventually the Kellys should go to Switzerland. Switzerland is a country where very few things begin, but many things end.

Though there was an element of choice in their other ports of call, the Kellys went to Switzerland because they had to. They had been married a little more than four years when they arrived one spring day at the lake that is the centre of Europe – a placid, smiling spot with pastoral hillsides, a backdrop of mountains and waters of postcard blue, waters that are a little sinister beneath the surface with all the misery that has dragged itself here from every corner of Europe. Weariness to recuperate and death to die. There are schools, too, and young people splashing at the sunny plages; there is Bonivard's dungeon and Calvin's city,* and the ghosts of Byron and Shelley still sail the dim shores by night; but the Lake Geneva that Nelson and Nicole came to was the dreary one of sanatoriums and rest hotels.

For, as if by some profound sympathy that had continued to exist beneath the unlucky destiny that had pursued their affairs, health had failed them both at the same time; Nicole lay on the balcony of a hotel coming slowly back to life after two successive operations, while Nelson fought for life against jaundice in a hospital two miles away. Even after the reserve force of twenty-nine years had pulled him through, there were months ahead during which he must live quietly. Often they wondered why, of all those who sought pleasure over the face of Europe, this misfortune should have come to them.

"There've been too many people in our lives," Nelson said. "We've never been able to resist people. We were so happy the first year when there weren't any people."

Nicole agreed. "If we could ever be alone – really alone – we could make up some kind of life for ourselves. We'll try, won't we, Nelson?"

But there were other days when they both wanted company desperately, concealing it from each other. Days when they eyed the obese, the wasted, the crippled and the broken of all nationalities who filled the hotel, seeking for one who might be amusing. It was a new life for them, turning on the daily visits of their two doctors, the arrival of the mail and newspapers from Paris, the little walk into the hillside village or occasionally the descent by funicular to the pale resort on the lake, with its *Kursaal*,* its grass beach, its tennis clubs and sightseeing buses. They read Tauchnitz editions and yellow-jacketed Edgar Wallaces;* at a certain hour each day they watched the baby being given its bath; three nights a week there was a tired and patient orchestra in the lounge after dinner, that was all.

And sometimes there was a booming from the vine-covered hills on the other side of the lake, which meant that cannons were shooting at hail-bearing clouds, to save the vineyard from an approaching storm; it came swiftly, first falling from the heavens and then falling again in torrents from the mountains, washing loudly down the roads and stone ditches; it came with a dark, frightening sky and savage filaments of lightning and crashing, world-splitting thunder, while ragged and destroyed clouds fled along before the wind past the hotel. The mountains and the lake disappeared completely; the hotel crouched alone amid tumult and chaos and darkness.

It was during such a storm, when the mere opening of a door admitted a tornado of rain and wind into the hall, that the Kellys for the first time in months saw someone they knew. Sitting downstairs with other victims of frayed nerves, they became aware of two new arrivals – a man and woman whom they recognized as the couple, first seen in Algiers, who had crossed their path several times since. A single unexpressed thought flashed through Nelson and Nicole. It seemed like destiny that at last here in this desolate place they should know them, and watching, they saw other couples eyeing them in the same tentative way. Yet something held the Kellys back. Had they not just been complaining that there were too many people in their lives?

Later, when the storm had dozed off into a quiet rain, Nicole found herself near the girl on the glass veranda. Under cover of reading a book, she inspected the face closely. It was an inquisitive face, she saw at once, possibly calculating; the eyes, intelligent enough, but with no peace in them, swept over people in a single quick glance as though estimating their value. "Terrible egoist," Nicole thought, with a certain distaste. For the rest, the cheeks were wan, and there were little pouches of ill health under the eyes; these combining with a certain flabbiness of arms and legs to give an impression of unwholesomeness. She was dressed expensively, but with a hint of slovenliness, as if she did not consider the people of the hotel important.

On the whole, Nicole decided she did not like her; she was glad that they had not spoken, but she was rather surprised that she had not noticed these things when the girl crossed her path before.

Telling Nelson her impression at dinner, he agreed with her.

"I ran into the man in the bar, and I noticed we both took nothing but mineral water, so I started to say something. But I got a good look at his face in the mirror and I decided not to. His face is so weak and self-indulgent that it's almost mean – the kind of face that needs half a dozen drinks really to open the eyes and stiffen the mouth up to normal."

After dinner the rain stopped and the night was fine outside. Eager for the air, the Kellys wandered down into the dark garden; on their way they passed the subjects of their late discussion, who withdrew abruptly down a side path.

"I don't think they want to know us any more than we do them," Nicole laughed.

They loitered among the wild rosebushes and the beds of damp-sweet, indistinguishable flowers. Below the hotel, where the terrace fell a thousand feet to the lake, stretched a necklace of lights that was Montreux and Vevey, and then, in a dim pendant, Lausanne; a blurred twinkling across the lake was Évian and France. From somewhere below – probably the *Kursaal* – came the sound of full-bodied dance music – American, they guessed, though now they heard American tunes months late, mere distant echoes of what was happening far away.

Over the Dent du Midi, over a black bank of clouds that was the rearguard of the receding storm, the moon lifted itself and the lake brightened; the music and the faraway lights were like hope, like the enchanted distance from which children see things. In their separate hearts Nelson and Nicole gazed backward to a time when life was all like this. Her arm went through his quietly and drew him close.

"We can have it all again," she whispered. "Can't we try, Nelson?"

She paused as two dark forms came into the shadows nearby and stood looking down at the lake below.

Nelson put his arm around Nicole and pulled her closer.

"It's just that we don't understand what's the matter," she said. "Why did we lose peace and love and health, one after the other? If we knew, if there was anybody to tell us, I believe we could try. I'd try so hard."

The last clouds were lifting themselves over the Bernese Alps. Suddenly, with a final intensity, the west flared with pale white lightning. Nelson and Nicole turned, and simultaneously the other couple turned, while for an instant the night was as bright as day. Then darkness and a last low peal of thunder, and from Nicole a sharp, terrified cry. She flung herself against Nelson; even in the darkness she saw that his face was as white and strained as her own.

"Did you see?" she cried in a whisper. "Did you see them?"

"Yes!"

"They're us! They're us! Don't you see?"

Trembling, they clung together. The clouds merged into the dark mass of mountains; looking around after a moment, Nelson and Nicole saw that they were alone together in the tranquil moonlight.

The Hotel Child

1

I T IS A PLACE WHERE ONE'S INSTINCT is to give a reason for being there – "Oh, you see, I'm here because…" Failing that, you are faintly suspect, because this corner of Europe does not draw people; rather, it accepts them without too many inconvenient questions – live and let live. Routes cross here – people bound for private *cliniques* or tuberculosis resorts in the mountains, people who are no longer *persona grata* in Italy or France. And if that were all…

Yet on a gala night at the Hôtel des Trois Mondes a new arrival would scarcely detect the current beneath the surface. Watching the dancing there would be a gallery of Englishwomen of a certain age, with neckbands, dyed hair and faces powdered pinkish grey; a gallery of American women of a certain age, with snowy-white transformations, black dresses and lips of cherry red. And most of them with their eyes swinging right or left from time to time to rest upon the ubiquitous Fifi. The entire hotel had been made aware that Fifi had reached the age of eighteen that night.

Fifi Schwartz. An exquisitely, radiantly beautiful Jewess whose fine, high forehead sloped gently up to where her hair, bordering it like an armorial shield, burst into lovelocks and waves and curlicues of soft dark red. Her eyes were bright, big, clear, wet and shining; the colour of her cheeks and lips was real, breaking close to the surface from the strong young pump of her heart. Her body was so assertively adequate that one cynic had been heard to remark that she always looked as if she had nothing on underneath her dresses; but he was probably wrong, for Fifi had been as thoroughly equipped for beauty by man as by God. Such dresses – cerise for Chanel, mauve for Molyneux, pink for Patou – dozens of them, tight at the hips, swaying, furling, folding just an eighth of an inch off the dancing floor. Tonight she was a woman of thirty in dazzling black, with long white gloves dripping from her forearms. "Such ghastly taste," the whispers said. "The stage, the shop window, the mannequins' parade. What can her mother be thinking? But, then, look at her mother."

Her mother sat apart with a friend and thought about Fifi and Fifi's brother, and about her other daughters, now married, whom she considered to have been even prettier than Fifi. Mrs Schwartz was a plain woman; she had been a Jewess a long time, and it was a matter of effortless indifference to her what was said by the groups around the room. Another large class who did not care were the young men – dozens of them. They followed Fifi about all day in and out of motorboats, nightclubs, inland lakes, automobiles, tea rooms and funiculars, and they said, "Hey, look, Fifi!" and showed off for her, or said "Kiss me, Fifi" or even "Kiss me again, Fifi", and abused her and tried to be engaged to her.

Most of them, however, were too young, since this little city, through some illogical reasoning, is supposed to have an admirable atmosphere as an educational centre.

Fifi was not critical, nor was she aware of being criticized herself. Tonight the gallery in the great crystal horseshoe room made observations upon her birthday party, being somewhat querulous about Fifi's entrance. The table had been set in the last of a string of dining rooms, each accessible from the central hall. But Fifi, her black dress shouting and helloing for notice, came in by way of the first dining room, followed by a whole platoon of young men of all possible nationalities and crosses, and at a sort of little run that swayed her lovely hips and tossed her lovely head, led them bumpily through the whole vista, while old men choked on fishbones, old women's facial muscles sagged and the protest rose to a roar in the procession's wake.

They need not have resented her so much. It was a bad party, because Fifi thought she had to entertain everybody and be a dozen people, so she talked to the entire table and broke up every conversation that started, no matter how far away from her. So no one had a good time, and the people in the hotel needn't have minded so much that she was young and terribly happy.

Afterwards, in the salon, many of the supernumerary males floated off with a temporary air to other tables. Among these was young Count Stanislas Borowki, with his handsome, shining brown eyes of a stuffed deer, and his black hair already dashed with distinguished streaks like the keyboard of a piano. He went to the table of some people of position named Taylor and sat down with just a faint sigh, which made them smile.

"Was it ghastly?" he was asked.

The blonde Miss Howard who was travelling with the Taylors was almost as pretty as Fifi and stitched up with more consideration. She had taken pains not to make Miss Schwartz's acquaintance, although she shared several of the same young men. The Taylors were career people in the diplomatic service and were now on their way to London, after the League Conference at Geneva. They were presenting Miss Howard at court this season. They were very Europeanized Americans; in fact, they had reached a position where they could hardly be said to belong to any nation at all; certainly not to any great power, but perhaps to a sort of Balkan-like state composed of people like themselves. They considered that Fifi was as much of a gratuitous outrage as a new stripe in the flag.

The tall Englishwoman with the long cigarette holder and the half-paralysed Pekingese presently got up, announcing to the Taylors that she had an engagement in the bar, and strolled away, carrying her paralysed Pekingese and causing, as she passed, a chilled lull in the seething baby talk that raged around Fifi's table.

About midnight, Mr Weicker, the assistant manager, looked into the bar, where Fifi's phonograph roared new German tangoes into the smoke and clatter. He had a small face that looked into things quickly, and lately he had taken a cursory glance into the bar every night. But he had not come to admire Fifi; he was engaged in an enquiry as to why matters were not going well at the Hôtel des Trois Mondes this summer.

There was, of course, the continually sagging American Stock Exchange. With so many hotels begging to be filled, the clients had become finicky, exigent, quick to complain, and Mr Weicker had had many fine decisions to make recently. One large family had departed because of a night-going phonograph belonging to Lady Capps-Karr. Also, there was presumably a thief operating in the hotel; there had been complaints about pocketbooks, cigarette cases, watches and rings. Guests sometimes spoke to Mr Weicker as if they would have liked to search his pockets. There were empty suites that need not have been empty this summer.

His glance fell dourly, in passing, upon Count Borowki, who was playing pool with Fifi. Count Borowki had not paid his bill for three weeks. He had told Mr Weicker that he was expecting his mother, who would arrange everything. Then there was Fifi, who attracted an undesirable crowd – young students living on pensions who often charged drinks, but never paid for them. Lady Capps-Karr, on the contrary, was a *grande cliente*; one could count three bottles of whisky a day for herself and entourage, and her father in London was good for every drop of it. Mr Weicker decided to issue an ultimatum about Borowki's bill this very night, and withdrew. His visit had lasted about ten seconds.

Count Borowki put away his cue and came close to Fifi, whispering something. She seized his hand and pulled him to a dark corner near the phonograph.

"My American dream girl," he said. "We must have you painted in Budapest the way you are tonight. You will hang with the portraits of my ancestors in my castle in Transylvania."

One would suppose that a normal American girl, who had been to an average number of moving pictures, would have detected a vague ring of familiarity in Count Borowki's persistent wooing. But the Hôtel des Trois Mondes was full of people who were actually rich and noble, people who did fine embroidery or took cocaine in closed apartments and meanwhile laid claim to European thrones and half a dozen mediatized German principalities, and Fifi did not choose to doubt the one who paid court to her beauty. Tonight she was surprised at nothing: not even his precipitate proposal that they get married this very week.

"Mamma doesn't want that I should get married for a year. I only said I'd be engaged to you."

"But my mother wants me to marry. She is hard-boiling, as you Americans say; she brings pressure to bear that I marry Princess This and Countess That."

Meanwhile Lady Capps-Karr was having a reunion across the room. A tall, stooped Englishman, dusty with travel, had just opened the door of the bar, and Lady Capps-Karr, with a caw of "Bopes!" had flung herself upon him: "Bopes, I say!"

"Capps, darling. Hi, there, Rafe" – this to her companion. "Fancy running into you, Capps."

"Bopes! Bopes!"

Their exclamations and laughter filled the room, and the bartender whispered to an inquisitive American that the new arrival was the Marquis Kinkallow.

Bopes stretched himself out in several chairs and a sofa and called for the barman. He announced that he had driven from Paris without a stop and was leaving next morning to meet the only woman he had ever loved, in Milan. He did not look in a condition to meet anyone.

"Oh, Bopes, I've been so blind," said Lady Capps-Karr pathetically. "Day after day after day. I flew here from Cannes, meaning to stay one day, and I ran into Rafe here and some other Americans I knew, and it's been two weeks, and now all my tickets to Malta are void. Stay here and save me! Oh, Bopes! Bopes! Bopes!"

The Marquis Kinkallow glanced with tired eyes about the bar.

"Ah, who is that?" he demanded. "The lovely Jewess? And who is that item with her?"

"She's an American," said the daughter of a hundred earls. "The man is a scoundrel of some sort, but apparently he's a cat of the stripe; he's a great pal of Schenzi, in Vienna. I sat up till five the other night playing two-handed *chemin de fer** with him here in the bar and he owes me a mille Swiss."

"Have to have a word with that wench," said Bopes' twenty minutes later. "You arrange it for me, Rafe, that's a good chap."

Ralph Berry had met Miss Schwartz and, as the opportunity for the introduction now presented itself, he rose obligingly. The opportunity was that a *chasseur* had just requested Count Borowki's presence in the office; he managed to beat two or three young men to her side.

"The Marquis Kinkallow is so anxious to meet you. Can't you come and join us?"

Fifi looked across the room, her fine brow wrinkling a little. Something warned her that her evening was full enough already. Lady Capps-Karr had never spoken to her; Fifi believed she was jealous of her clothes.

"Can't you bring him over here?"

A minute later Bopes sat down beside Fifi with a shadow of fine tolerance settling on his face. This was nothing he could help; in fact, he constantly struggled against it, but it was something that happened to his expression when he met Americans. "The whole thing is too much for me," it seemed to say. "Compare my confidence with your uncertainty, my sophistication with your *naïveté*, and yet the whole world has slid into your power." Of later years he found that his tone, unless carefully guarded, held a smouldering resentment.

Fifi eyed him brightly and told him about her glamorous future.

"Next I'm going to Paris," she said, announcing the fall of Rome, "to, maybe, study at the Sorbonne. Then, maybe, I'll get married; you can't tell. I'm only eighteen. I had eighteen candles on my birthday cake tonight. I wish you could have been here... I've had marvellous offers to go on the stage, but of course a girl on the stage gets talked about so."

"What are you doing tonight?" asked Bopes.

"Oh, lots more boys are coming in later. Stay around and join the party."

"I thought you and I might do something. I'm going to Milan tomorrow."

Across the room, Lady Capps-Karr was tense with displeasure at the desertion.

"After all," she protested, "a chep's a chep, and a chum's a chum, but there are certain things that one simply doesn't do. I never saw Bopes in such frightful condition."

She stared at the dialogue across the room.

"Come along to Milan with me," the marquis was saying. "Come to Tibet or Hindustan. We'll see them crown the King of Ethiopia. Anyhow, let's go for a drive right now."

"I got too many guests here. Besides, I don't go out to ride with people the first time I meet them. I'm supposed to be engaged. To a Hungarian count. He'd be furious and would probably challenge you to a duel."

Mrs Schwartz, with an apologetic expression, came across the room to Fifi.

"John's gone," she announced. "He's up there again."

Fifi gave a yelp of annoyance. "He gave me his word of honour he would not go."

"Anyhow, he went. I looked in his room and his hat's gone. It was that champagne at dinner." She turned to the marquis. "John is not a vicious boy, but vurry, vurry weak."

"I suppose I'll have to go after him," said Fifi resignedly.

"I hate to spoil your good time tonight, but I don't know what else. Maybe this gentleman would go with you. You see, Fifi is the only one that can handle him. His father is dead and it really takes a man to handle a boy."

"Quite," said Bopes.

"Can you take me?" Fifi asked. "It's just up in town to a café."

He agreed with alacrity. Out in the September night, with her fragrance seeping through an ermine cape, she explained further:

"Some Russian woman's got hold of him; she claims to be a countess, but she's only got one silver-fox fur that she wears with everything. My brother's just nineteen, so whenever he's had a couple glasses champagne he says he's going to marry her, and mother worries."

Bopes's arm dropped impatiently around her shoulder as they started up the hill to the town.

Fifteen minutes later the car stopped at a point several blocks beyond the café and Fifi stepped out. The marquis's face was now decorated by a long, irregular fingernail scratch that ran diagonally across his cheek, traversed his nose in a few sketchy lines and finished in a sort of grand terminal of tracks upon his lower jaw.

"I don't like to have anybody get so foolish," Fifi explained. "You needn't wait. We can get a taxi."

"Wait!" cried the marquis furiously. "For a common little person like you? They tell me you're the laughing stock of the hotel, and I quite understand why."

Fifi hurried along the street and into the café, pausing in the door until she saw her brother. He was a reproduction of Fifi without her high warmth; at the moment he was sitting at a table with a frail exile from the Caucasus and two Serbian consumptives. Fifi waited for her temper to rise to an executive pitch; then she crossed the dance floor, conspicuous as a thundercloud in her bright black dress.

"Mamma sent me after you, John. Get your coat."

"Oh, what's biting her?" he demanded, with a vague eye.

"Mamma says you should come along."

He got up unwillingly. The two Serbians rose also; the countess never moved; her eyes, sunk deep in Mongol cheekbones, never left Fifi's face; her head crouched in the silver-fox fur which Fifi knew represented her brother's last month's allowance. As John Schwartz stood there swaying unsteadily the orchestra launched into 'Ich bin von Kopf bis Fuß'.* Diving into the confusion of the table, Fifi emerged with her brother's arm, marched him to the coatroom and then out towards the taxi stand.

It was late, the evening was over, her birthday was over, and driving back to the hotel, with John slumped against her shoulder, Fifi felt a sudden depression. By virtue of her fine health she had never been a worrier, and certainly the Schwartz family had lived so long against similar backgrounds that Fifi felt no insufficiency in the Hôtel des Trois Mondes as cloud and community – and yet the evening was suddenly all wrong. Didn't evenings sometimes end on a high note and not fade out vaguely in bars? After ten o'clock every night she felt she was the only real being in a colony of ghosts, that she was surrounded by utterly intangible figures who retreated whenever she stretched out her hand.

The doorman assisted her brother to the elevator. Stepping in, Fifi saw, too late, that there were two other people inside. Before she could pull John out again, they had both brushed past her as if in fear of contamination. Fifi heard "Mercy!" from Mrs Taylor and "How revolting!" from Miss Howard. The elevator mounted. Fifi held her breath until it stopped at her floor.

It was, perhaps, the impact of this last encounter that caused her to stand very still just inside the door of the dark apartment. Then she had the sense that someone else was there in the blackness ahead of her, and after her brother had stumbled forward and thrown himself on a sofa, she still waited.

"Mamma," she called, but there was no answer; only a sound fainter than a rustle, like a shoe scraped along the floor.

A few minutes later, when her mother came upstairs, they called the *valet de chambre** and went through the rooms together, but there was no one. Then they stood side by side in the open door to their balcony and looked out on the lake with the bright cluster of Évian on the French shore and the white caps of snow on the mountains.

"I think we've been here long enough," said Mrs Schwartz suddenly. "I think I'll take John back to the States this fall."

Fifi was aghast. "But I thought John and I were going to the Sorbonne in Paris?"

"How can I trust him in Paris? And how could I leave you behind alone there?"

"But we're used to living in Europe now. Why did I learn to talk French? Why, Mamma, we don't even know any people back home any more."

"We can always meet people. We always have."

"But you know it's different; everybody is so bigoted there. A girl hasn't the chance to meet the same sort of men, even if there were any. Everybody just watches everything you do."

"So they do here," said her mother. "That Mr Weicker just stopped me in the hall; he saw you come in with John, and he talked to me about how you must keep out of the bar, you were so young. I told him you only took lemonade, but he said it didn't matter; scenes like tonight made people leave the hotel."

"Oh, how perfectly mean!"

"So I think we better go back home."

The empty word rang desolately in Fifi's ears. She put her arms around her mother's waist, realizing that it was she and not her mother, with her mother's clear grip on the past, who was completely lost in the universe. On the sofa her brother snored, having already entered the world of the weak, of the leaners-together, and found its fetid and mercurial warmth sufficient. But Fifi kept looking at the alien sky, knowing that she could pierce it and find her own way through envy and corruption. For the first time she seriously considered marrying Borowki immediately.

"Do you want to go downstairs and say goodnight to the boys?" suggested her mother. "There's lots of them still there asking where you are."

But the Furies were after Fifi now – after her childish complacency and her innocence, even after her beauty – out to break it all down and drag it in any convenient mud. When she shook her head and walked sullenly into her bedroom, they had already taken something from her for ever.

2

THE FOLLOWING MORNING Mrs Schwartz went to Mr Weicker's office to report the loss of two hundred dollars in American money. She had left the sum on her chiffonier upon retiring; when she awoke, it was gone. The door of the apartment had been bolted, but in the morning the bolt was found drawn, and yet neither of her children was awake. Fortunately, she had taken her jewels to bed with her in a chamois sack.

Mr Weicker decided that the situation must be handled with care. There were not a few guests in the hotel who were in straitened circumstances and inclined to desperate remedies, but he must move slowly. In America one has money or hasn't; in Europe the heir to a fortune may be unable to stand himself a haircut until the collapse of a fifth cousin, yet be a sure risk and not to be lightly offended. Opening the office copy of the *Almanach de Gotha*, Mr Weicker found Stanislas Karl Joseph Borowki hooked firmly on to the end of a line older than the crown of St Stephen. This morning, in riding clothes that were smart as a hussar's uniform, he had gone riding with the utterly correct Miss Howard. On the other hand, there was no doubt as to who had been robbed, and Mr Weicker's indignation began to concentrate on Fifi and her family, who might have saved him this trouble by taking themselves off some time ago. It was even conceivable that the dissipated son, John, had nipped the money.

In all events, the Schwartzes were going home. For three years they had lived in hotels – in Paris, Florence, Saint-Raphaël, Como, Vichy, La Baule, Lucerne, Baden-Baden and Biarritz. Everywhere there had been schools – always new schools – and both children spoke in perfect French and scrawny fragments of Italian. Fifi had grown from a large-featured child of fourteen to a beauty; John had grown into something rather dismal and lost. Both of them played bridge, and somewhere Fifi had picked up tap-dancing. Mrs Schwartz felt that it was all somehow unsatisfactory, but she did not know why. So, two days after Fifi's party, she announced that they would pack their trunks, go to Paris for some new fall clothes and then go home.

That same afternoon Fifi came to the bar to get her phonograph, left there the night of her party. She sat up on a high stool and talked to the barman while she drank a ginger ale.

"Mother wants to take me back to America, but I'm not going."

"What will you do?"

"Oh, I've got a little money of my own, and then I may get married." She sipped her ginger ale moodily.

"I hear you had some money stolen," he remarked. "How did it happen?"

"Well, Count Borowki thinks the man got into the apartment early and hid in between the two doors between us and the next apartment. Then, when we were asleep, he took the money and walked out."

"Ha!"

Fifi sighed. "Well, you probably won't see me in the bar any more."

"We'll miss you, Miss Schwartz."

Mr Weicker put his head in the door, withdrew it and then came in slowly.

"Hello," said Fifi coldly.

"A-ha, young lady." He waggled his finger at her with affected face-tiousness. "Didn't you know I spoke to your mother about your coming into the bar? It's merely for your own good."

"I'm just having a ginger ale," she said indignantly.

"But no one can tell what you're having. It might be whisky or what not. It is the other guests who complain."

She stared at him indignantly – the picture was so different from her own – of Fifi as the lively centre of the hotel, of Fifi in clothes that ravished the eye, standing splendid and unattainable amid groups of adoring men. Suddenly Mr Weicker's obsequious but hostile face infuriated her.

"We're getting out of this hotel!" she flared up. "I never saw such a narrow-minded bunch of people in my life; always criticizing everybody and making up terrible things about them, no matter what they do themselves. I think it would be a good thing if the hotel caught fire and burned down with all the nasty cats in it."

Banging down her glass, she seized the phonograph case and stalked out of the bar.

In the lobby a porter sprang to help her, but she shook her head and hurried on through the salon, where she came upon Count Borowki.

"Oh, I'm so furious!" she cried. "I never saw so many old cats! I just told Mr Weicker what I thought of them!"

"Did someone dare to speak rudely to you?"

"Oh, it doesn't matter. We're going away."

"Going away!" He started. "When?"

"Right away. I don't want to, but Mamma says we've got to."

"I must talk to you seriously about this," he said. "I just called your room. I have brought you a little engagement present."

Her spirits returned as she took the handsome gold-and-ivory cigarette case engraved with her initials.

"How lovely!"

"Now, listen: what you tell me makes it more important that I talk to you immediately. I have just received another letter from my mother. They have chosen a girl for me in Budapest – a lovely girl, rich and beautiful and of my own rank who would be very happy at the match, but I am in love with you. I would never have thought it possible, but I have lost my heart to an American."

"Well, why not?" said Fifi, indignantly. "They call girls beautiful here if they have one good feature. And then, if they've got nice eyes or hair, they're usually bow-legged or haven't got nice teeth."

"There is no flaw or fault in you."

"Oh, yes," said Fifi modestly. "I got a sort of big nose. Would you know I was Jewish?"

With a touch of impatience, Borowki came back to his argument: "So they are bringing pressure to bear for me to marry. Questions of inheritance depend on it."

"Besides, my forehead is too high," observed Fifi abstractedly. "It's so high it's got sort of wrinkles in it. I knew an awfully funny boy who used to call me 'the highbrow'."

"So the sensible thing," pursued Borowki, "is for us to marry immediately. I tell you frankly there are other American girls not far from here who wouldn't hesitate."

"Mamma would be about crazy," Fifi said.

"I've thought about that too," he answered her eagerly. "Don't tell her. If we drove over the border tonight we could be married tomorrow morning. Then we come back and you show your mother the little gilt coronets painted on your luggage. My own personal opinion is that she'll be delighted. There you are, off her hands, with social position second to none in Europe. In my opinion, your mother has probably thought of it already, and may be saying to herself: 'Why don't those two young people just take matters into their own hands and save me all the fuss and expense of a wedding?' I think she would like us for being so hard-boiled."

He broke off impatiently as Lady Capps-Karr, emerging from the dining room with her Pekingese, surprised them by stopping at their table. Count Borowki was obliged to introduce them. As he had not known of the Marquis Kinkallow's defection the other evening, nor that His Lordship had taken a wound to Milan the following morning, he had no suspicion of what was coming.

"I've noticed Miss Schwartz," said the Englishwoman in a clear, concise voice. "And of course I've noticed Miss Schwartz's clothes."

"Won't you sit down?" said Fifi.

"No, thank you." She turned to Borowki. "Miss Schwartz's clothes make us all appear somewhat drab. I always refuse to dress elaborately in hotels. It seems such rotten taste. Don't you think so?"

"I think people always ought to look nice," said Fifi, flushing.

"Naturally. I merely said that I consider it rotten taste to dress elaborately, save in the houses of one's friends."

She said "Good-by-e-e" to Borowki and moved on, emitting a mouthed cloud of smoke and a faint fragrance of whisky.

The insult had been as stinging as the crack of a whip, and as Fifi's pride of her wardrobe was swept away from her, she heard all the comments that she had not heard, in one great resurgent whisper. Then they said that she wore her clothes here because she had nowhere else to wear them. That was why the Howard girl considered her vulgar and did not care to know her.

For an instant her anger flamed up against her mother for not telling her, but she saw that her mother did not know either.

"I think she's so dowdy," she forced herself to say aloud, but inside she was quivering. "What is she, anyhow? I mean, how high is her title? Very high?"

"She's the widow of a baronet."

"Is that high?" Fifi's face was rigid. "Higher than a countess?"

"No. A countess is much higher – infinitely higher." He moved his chair closer and began to talk intently.

Half an hour later Fifi got up with indecision on her face.

"At seven you'll let me know definitely," Borowki said, "and I'll be ready with a car at ten."

Fifi nodded. He escorted her across the room and saw her vanish into a dark hall mirror in the direction of the lift.

As he turned away, Lady Capps-Karr, sitting alone over her coffee, spoke to him:

"I want a word with you. Did you, by some slip of the tongue, suggest to Weicker that in case of difficulties I would guarantee your bills?"

Borowki flushed. "I may have said something like that, but—"

"Well, I told him the truth – that I never laid eyes on you until a fortnight ago."

"I, naturally, turned to a person of equal rank—"

"Equal rank! What cheek! The only titles left are English titles. I must ask you not to make use of my name again."

He bowed. "Such inconveniences will soon be for me a thing of the past."

"Are you getting off with that vulgar little American?"

"I beg your pardon," he said stiffly.

"Don't be angry. I'll stand you a whisky-and-soda. I'm getting in shape for Bopes Kinkallow, who's just telephoned he's tottering back here."

Meanwhile, upstairs, Mrs Schwartz was saying to Fifi: "Now that I know we're going away I'm getting excited about it. It will be so nice seeing the Hirsts and Mrs Bell and Amy and Marjorie and Gladys again, and the new baby. You'll be happy too – you've forgotten how they're like. You and Gladys used to be great friends. And Marjorie—"

"Oh, Mamma, don't talk about it," cried Fifi miserably. "I can't go back."

"We needn't stay. If John was in a college like his father wanted, we could, maybe, go to California."

But for Fifi all the romance of life was rolled up into the last three impressionable years in Europe. She remembered the tall guardsmen in Rome and the old Spaniard who had first made her conscious of her beauty at the Villa d'Este at Como, and the French naval aviator at Saint-Raphaël who had dropped her a note from his plane into their garden, and the feeling that she had sometimes, when she danced with Borowki, that he was dressed in gleaming boots and a white-furred dolman.

She had seen many American moving pictures and she knew that the girls there always married the faithful boy from the old home town, and after that there was nothing.

"I won't go," she said aloud.

Her mother turned with a pile of clothes in her arms. "What talk is that from you, Fifi? You think I could leave you here alone?" As Fifi didn't answer, she continued, with an air of finality: "That talk doesn't sound nice from you. Now you stop fretting and saying such things, and get me this list of things uptown."

But Fifi had decided. It was Borowki, then, and the chance of living fully and adventurously. He could go into the diplomatic service, and then one day when they encountered Lady Capps-Karr and Miss Howard at a legation ball she could make audible the observation that for the moment seemed so necessary to her: "I hate people who always look as if they were going to or from a funeral."

"So run along," her mother continued. "And look in at that café and see if John is up there, and take him to tea."

Fifi accepted the shopping list mechanically. Then she went into her room and wrote a little note to Borowki which she would leave with the concierge on the way out.

Coming out, she saw her mother struggling with a trunk, and felt terribly sorry for her. But there were Amy and Gladys in America, and Fifi hardened herself.

She walked out and down the stairs, remembering halfway that in her distraction she had omitted an official glance in the mirror; but there was a large mirror on the wall just outside the grand salon, and she stopped in front of that instead.

She was beautiful – she learnt that once more, but now it made her sad. She wondered whether the dress she wore this afternoon was in bad taste, whether it would minister to the superiority of Miss Howard or Lady Capps-Karr. It seemed to her a lovely dress, soft and gentle in cut, but in colour a hard, bright, metallic powder blue.

Then a sudden sound broke the stillness of the gloomy hall and Fifi stood suddenly breathless and motionless.

3

A T ELEVEN O'CLOCK Mr Weicker was tired, but the bar was in one of its periodical riots and he was waiting for it to quiet down. There was nothing to do in the stale office or the empty lobby; and the salon, where all day he held long conversations with lonely English and American women, was deserted; so he went out the front door and began to make the circuit of the hotel. Whether due to his circumambient course or to his frequent glances up at the twinkling bedroom lights and into the humble, grilled windows of the kitchen floor, the promenade gave him a sense of being in control of the hotel, of being adequately responsible, as though it were a ship and he was surveying it from a quarterdeck.

He went past a flood of noise and song from the bar, past a window where two busboys sat on a bunk and played cards over a bottle of Spanish wine. There was a phonograph somewhere above, and a woman's form blocked out a window; then there was the quiet wing and, turning the corner, he arrived back at his point of departure. And in front of the hotel, under the dim porte-cochère light, he saw Count Borowki.

Something made him stop and watch – something incongruous – Borowki, who couldn't pay his bill, had a car and a chauffeur. He was giving the chauffeur some sort of detailed instructions, and then Mr Weicker perceived that there was a bag in the front seat, and came forward into the light.

"You are leaving us, Count Borowki?"

Borowki started at the voice. "For the night only," he answered. "I'm going to meet my mother."

"I see."

Borowki looked at him reproachfully. "My trunk and hatbox are in my room, you'll discover. Did you think I was running away from my bill?"

"Certainly not. I hope you will have a pleasant journey and find your mother well."

But inside he took the precaution of dispatching a *valet de chambre* to see if the baggage was indeed there, and even to give it a thoughtful heft, lest its kernel were departed.

He dozed for perhaps an hour. When he woke up, the night concierge was pulling at his arm and there was a strong smell of smoke in the lobby. It was some moments before he could get it through his head that one wing of the hotel was on fire.

Setting the concierge at the alarms, he rushed down the hall to the bar, and through the smoke that poured from the door he caught sight of the burning billiard table and the flames licking along the floor and flaring up in alcoholic ecstasy every time a bottle on the shelves cracked with the heat. As he hastily retreated he met a line of half-dressed *chasseurs* and busboys already struggling up from the lower depths with buckets of water. The concierge shouted that the fire department was on its way. He put two men at the telephones to awaken the guests, and as he ran back to form a bucket line at the danger point, he thought for the first time of Fifi.

Blind rage consumed him – with a precocious Indian-like cruelty she had carried out her threat. Ah, he would deal with that later; there was still law in the country. Meanwhile a clangour outdoors announced that the engines had arrived, and he made his way back through the lobby, filled now with men in pyjamas carrying briefcases, and women in bedclothes carrying jewel boxes and small dogs; the number swelling every minute and the talk rising from a cadence heavy with sleep to the full staccato buzz of an afternoon soirée.

A *chasseur* called Mr Weicker to the phone, but the manager shook him off impatiently.

"It's the commissionaire of police," the boy persisted. "He says you must speak to him."

With an exclamation, Mr Weicker hurried into the office. "'Allo!"

"I'm calling from the station. Is this the manager?"

"Yes, but there's a fire here."

"Have you among your guests a man calling himself Count Borowki?"

"Why, yes…"

"We're bringing him there for identification. He was picked up on the road on some information we received."

"But…"

"We picked up a girl with him. We're bringing them both down there immediately."

"I tell you…"

The receiver clicked briskly in his ear and Mr Weicker hurried back to the lobby, where the smoke was diminishing. The reassuring pumps had been at work for five minutes and the bar was a wet charred ruin. Mr Weicker began passing here and there among the guests, tranquillizing and persuading; the phone operators began calling the rooms again, advising such guests as had not appeared that it was safe to go back to bed; and then, at the continued demands for an explanation, he thought again of Fifi, and this time of his own accord he hurried to the phone.

Mrs Schwartz's anxious voice answered – Fifi wasn't there. That was what he wanted to know. He rang off brusquely. There was the story, and he could not have wished for anything more sordidly complete – an incendiary blaze and an attempted elopement with a man wanted by the police. It was time for paying, and all the money of America couldn't make any difference. If the season was ruined, at least Fifi would have no more seasons at all. She would go to a girls' institution where the prescribed uniform was rather plainer than any clothing she had ever worn.

As the last of the guests departed into the elevators, leaving only a few curious rummagers among the soaked debris, another procession came in by the front door. There was a man in civilian clothes and a little wall of policemen with two people behind. The commissionaire spoke and the screen of policemen parted.

"I want you to identify these two people. Has this man been staying here under the name of Borowki?"

Mr Weicker looked. "He has."

"He's been wanted for a year in Italy, France and Spain. And this girl?"

She was half hidden behind Borowki, her head hanging, her face in shadow. Mr Weicker craned towards her eagerly. He was looking at Miss Howard.

A wave of horror swept over Mr Weicker. Again he craned his head forward, as if by the intensity of his astonishment he could convert her into Fifi, or look through her and find Fifi. But this would have been difficult, for Fifi was far away. She was in front of the café, assisting the stumbling and reluctant John Schwartz into a taxi. "I should say you can't go back. Mother says you should come right home."

4

COUNT BOROWKI TOOK HIS INCARCERATION with a certain grace, as though, having lived so long by his own wits, there was a certain relief in having his days planned by an external agency. But he resented the lack of intercourse with the outer world, and was overjoyed when, on the fourth day of his imprisonment, he was led forth to find Lady Capps-Karr.

"After all," she said, "a chep's a chep and a chum's a chum, whatever happens. Luckily, our consul here is a friend of my father's, or they wouldn't have let me see you. I even tried to get you out on bail, because I told them you went to Oxford for a year and spoke English perfectly, but the brutes wouldn't listen."

"I'm afraid there's no use," said Count Borowki gloomily. "When they've finished trying me I'll have had a free journey all over Europe."

"But that's not the only outrageous thing," she continued. "Those idiots have thrown Bopes and me out of the Trois Mondes, and the authorities are trying to get us to leave the city."

"What for?"

"They're trying to put the full blame of that tiresome fire on us."

"Did you start it?"

"We did set some brandy on fire because we wanted to cook some potato chips in alcohol, and the bartender had gone to bed and left us there. But you'd think, from the way the swine talk, that we'd come there with the sole idea of burning everyone in their beds. The whole thing's an outrage and Bopes is furious. He says he'll never come here again. I went to the consulate and they agreed that the whole affair was perfectly disgraceful, and they've wired the Foreign Office."

Borowki considered for a moment. "If I could be born over again," he said slowly, "I think without any doubt I should choose to be born an Englishman."

"I could choose to be anything but an American! By the way, the Taylors are not presenting Miss Howard at court because of the disgraceful way the newspapers played up the matter."

"What puzzles me is what made Fifi suspicious," said Borowki.

"Then it was Miss Schwartz who blabbed?"

"Yes. I thought I had convinced her to come with me, and I knew that if she didn't, I had only to snap my fingers to the other girl... That very afternoon Fifi visited the jeweller's and discovered I'd paid for the cigarette case with a hundred-dollar American note I'd lifted from her mother's chiffonier. She went straight to the police."

"Without coming to you first! After all, a chep's a chep—"

"But what I want to know is what made her suspicious enough to investigate, what turned her against me."

Fifi, at that moment sitting on a high stool in a hotel bar in Paris and sipping a lemonade, was answering that very question to an interested bartender.

"I was standing in the hall looking in the mirror," she said, "and I heard him talking to the English lady – the one who set the hotel on fire. And I heard him say, 'After all, my one nightmare is that she'll turn out to look like her mother.'" Fifi's voice blazed with indignation. "Well, you've seen my mother, haven't you?"

"Yes, and a very fine woman she is."

"After that I knew there was something the matter with him, and I wondered how much he'd paid for the cigarette case. So I went up to see. They showed me the bill he paid with."

"And you will go to America now?" the barman asked.

Fifi finished her glass; the straw made a gurgling sound in the sugar at the bottom.

"We've got to go back and testify, and we'll stay a few months anyhow." She stood up. "Bye-bye – I've got a fitting."

They had not got her – not yet. The Furies had withdrawn a little and stood in the background with a certain gnashing of teeth. But there was plenty of time.

Yet, as Fifi tottered out through the lobby, her face gentle with new hopes, as she went out looking for completion under the impression that she was going to the *couturier*, there was a certain doubt among the eldest and most experienced of the Furies if they would get her, after all.

Note on the Texts

The texts of 'A Short Trip Home', 'The Last of the Belles', 'Majesty' and 'Two Wrongs' are based on the versions published in *Taps at Reveille* (1935). The text of 'Jacob's Ladder' is based on the version published in the *Saturday Evening Post* (20th August 1927). The text of 'The Bowl' is based on the version published in the *Saturday Evening Post* (21st January 1928). The text of 'At Your Age' is based on the version published in the *Saturday Evening Post* (17th August 1929). The text of 'The Swimmers' is based on the version published in the *Saturday Evening Post* (19th October 1929). The text of 'The Bridal Party' is based on the version published in the *Saturday Evening Post* (9th August 1930). The text of 'One Trip Abroad' is based on the version published in the *Saturday Evening Post* (11th October 1930). The text of 'The Hotel Child' is based on the version published in the *Saturday Evening Post* (31st January 1931). The spelling and punctuation have been Anglicized, standardized, modernized and made consistent throughout.

Notes

p. 8, *Norma Shearer*: Norma Shearer (1902–83) was one of the most popular Hollywood actresses of the 1920s and 1930s.

p. 9, *Constance Talmadge's*: Constance Talmadge (1898–1973) was one of the leading American actresses of the silent era.

p. 34, *one of Tad's more savage cartoons*: A reference to the popular cartoonist Thomas Aloysius Dorgan (1877–1929), more commonly known as Tad Dorgan or Tad.

p. 37, *Stuart's plume*: A reference to the Confederate general Jeb Stuart (1833–64), who famously wore an ostrich plume on his hat.

p. 37, *Hoot Gibson and Wonder Dogs and Wonder Horses... Old King Brady and The Liberty Boys of '76*: Hoot Gibson (1892–1962) was a rodeo champion and actor in cowboy films. *Old King Brady* and *The Liberty Boys of '76* were series of popular dime novels.

p. 54, *battles between Christians and wild beasts under the Antonines*: The Antonines were a dynasty of Roman emperors who reigned in the second century AD. During this period early Christians were at times subjected to persecution, including being fed to wild animals in amphitheatres.

p. 54, *George Bellows*: George Bellows (1882–1925) was an American realist painter and lithographer famous for his depictions of New York life.

p. 58, *Ralph Henry Barbour*: Ralph Henry Barbour (1870–1944) was a writer of popular sports fiction for boys.

p. 67, *Babbitt*: Derived from the name of the protagonist of the novel *Babbitt* (1922) by Harry Sinclair Lewis (1885–1951), Babbitt became a byword for a staid and conformist businessman.

p. 84, *heard Ruth Draper or read 'Marse Chan'*: Ruth Draper (1884–1956) was an acclaimed American theatre actress and 'Marse Chan' (1884) was a story by Thomas Nelson Page (1853–1922).

p. 84, *Leyendecker*: A reference to J.C. Leyendecker (1874–1951), an American illustrator famous for his magazine covers and advertising posters.

p. 86, *'After You've Gone'*: A 1918 song composed by Turner Layton (1894–1978), with lyrics by Henry Creamer (1879–1930).

p. 93, *'My Indiana Home'*: A reference to the 1917 song 'Back Home Again in Indiana', composed by James F. Hanley (1892–1942), with lyrics by Ballard MacDonald (1882–1935).

p. 106, *'At Dawning'*: A 1906 song composed by Charles Wakefield Cadman (1881–1946), with lyrics by Nelle Richmond Eberhart (1871–1944).

p. 117, *Elllis Island*: Ellis Island in the Upper New York Bay was famously the location of America's largest immigrant-inspection station.

p. 140, *Papeterie... Déclaration de Décès and Pompes Funèbres*: *Papeterie, solde, réclame, vêtements ecclésiastiques, déclaration de décès* and *pompes funèbres* mean "stationer's", "sale", "advertisement", "death certificate" and "funeral parlour" respectively. *Déjeuner de soleil* (*Breakfast at Sunrise*) was a 1927 silent film directed by Malcolm St Clair (1897–1952).

p. 144, *Manassas to Appomattox... Huxley and Spencer*: Manassas and Appomattox are towns in Virginia that were the sites of famous Civil War battles. Thomas Henry Huxley (1825–95) and Herbert Spencer (1820–1903) were British biologists and Darwinist philosophers.

p. 149, *we knew that lobster armoricaine was really lobster américaine*: The point here is that the lobster dish now known as *homard à l'armoricaine* used to be called, when it was invented in the 1860s, *à l'américaine*, but was renamed after the historical French region of Armorica by restaurateurs who disliked the association with America. This edition follows the amendment suggested by Matthew J. Bruccoli in *The Short Stories of F. Scott Fitzgerald*.

p. 158, *Ah, c'est épouvantable... qu'on peut faire* : "Ah, it's dreadful! Isn't there anything that can be done?" (French).

p. 159, *Gerbault*: A reference to Alain Gerbault (1893–1941), who single-handedly crossed the Atlantic in 1923 before circumnavigating the entire world.

p. 162, *the graves at Shiloh*: A reference to the Battle of Shiloh in Tennessee of April 1862, a major engagement in the American Civil

War, which was won by the Union forces after heavy casualties on both sides.

p. 179, *Pavlova*: Anna Pavlova (1881–1931) was the foremost ballerina of her time.

p. 186, *femme de chambre*: "Chambermaid" (French).

p. 187, *'Among My Souvenirs'*: A 1927 song composed by Lawrence Wright (1888–1964), with lyrics by Edgar Leslie (1885–1976).

p. 192, *'Painted Doll'*: A reference to 'The Wedding of the Painted Doll', a song composed by Nacio Herb Brown (1896–1964), with lyrics by Arthur Freed (1894–1973), for the 1929 musical film *The Broadway Melody*.

p. 202, *chasseur*: "Hotel messenger" (French).

p. 213, *'Waiting for the Robert E. Lee'*: A 1912 song composed by Lewis F. Muir (1884–1915), with lyrics by L. Wolfe Gilbert (1886–1970).

p. 213, *the Relief of Ladysmith*: A reference to a key event in the Boer War, when in February 1900 the Boers lifted their siege on the city of Ladysmith, which subsequently lead the British to victory.

p. 219, *C'est liquide... c'est le sang*: "It's liquid... is it blood?" (French).

p. 221, *tout ce qu'il y a de chic*: "All that is chic" (French).

p. 223, *Brancusi and Léger and Deschamps*: A reference to Constantin Brancusi (1876–1957), Fernand Léger (1881–1955) and, presumably, Marcel Duchamp (1887–1968), all major figures in abstract and conceptual art.

p. 227, *Maintenant, monsieur... exciter madame*: "Now, Monsieur, you must not get Madame excited" (French).

p. 228, *Bonivard's dungeon and Calvin's city*: François Bonivard (1493–1570) was a Protestant reformer who was famously imprisoned in the Château de Chillon on a island in Lake Geneva. The influential French Reformation leader John Calvin (1509–64) is associated with Geneva, which became the base of his activities.

p. 229, *Kursaal*: The entertainment hall of a sanatorium.

p. 229, *Tauchnitz editions and yellow-jacketed Edgar Wallaces*: Tauchnitz was a Germany-based publisher of mass-market English-language editions which were popular all across Europe. Edgar Wallace (1875–1932) was the author of highly successful thrillers.

p. 238, *chemin de fer*: Another name for baccarat.

p. 241, *Ich bin von Kopf bis Fuß*: A 1930 song by Friedrich Hollaender (1896–1976).

p. 241, *valet de chambre*: "Room attendant" (French).

Extra Material

on

F. Scott Fitzgerald's

The Last of the Belles
and
Other Stories

F. Scott Fitzgerald's Life

Francis Scott Key Fitzgerald was born on 24th September 1896 at 481 Laurel Avenue in St Paul, Minnesota. Fitzgerald, who would always be known as "Scott", was named after Francis Scott Key, the author of 'The Star-Spangled Banner' and his father's second cousin three times removed. His mother, Mary "Mollie" McQuillan, was born in 1860 in one of St Paul's wealthier streets, and would come into a modest inheritance at the death of her father in 1877. His father, Edward Fitzgerald, was born in 1853 near Rockville, Maryland. A wicker-furniture manufacturer at the time of Fitzgerald's birth, his business would collapse in 1898 and he would then take to the road as a wholesale grocery salesman for Procter & Gamble. This change of job necessitated various moves of home and the family initially shifted east to Buffalo, New York, in 1898, and then on to Syracuse, New York, in 1901. By 1903 they were back in Buffalo and in March 1908 they were in St Paul again after Edward lost his job at Procter & Gamble. The *déclassé* Fitzgeralds would initially live with the McQuillans and then moved into a series of rented houses, settling down at 599 Summit Avenue.

Early Life

This itinerancy would disrupt Fitzgerald's early schooling, isolating him and making it difficult to make many friends at his various schools in Buffalo, Syracuse and St Paul. The first one at which Fitzgerald would settle for a prolonged period was the St Paul Academy, which he entered in September 1908. It was here that Fitzgerald would achieve his first appearance in print, 'The Mystery of the Raymond Mortgage', which appeared in the St Paul Academy school magazine *Now and Then* in October 1909. 'Reade, Substitute Right Half' and 'A Debt of Honor' would follow in the February and March 1910 numbers, and 'The Room with the Green Blinds' in the June 1911 number. His reading at this time was dominated by adventure stories and the other typical literary interests of a turn-of-the-century American teen, with the novels of G.A. Henty, Walter Scott's *Ivanhoe* and Jane Porter's *The Scottish Chiefs* among his favourites; their influence was apparent in the floridly melodramatic tone of his early pieces, though themes that would recur throughout Fitzgerald's mature fiction, such as the social difficulties of the outsider, would be

Schooling and Early Writings

introduced in these stories. An interest in the theatre also surfaced at this time, with Fitzgerald writing and taking the lead role in *The Girl from Lazy J*, a play that would be performed with a local amateur-dramatic group, the Elizabethan Drama Club, in August 1911. The group would also produce *The Captured Shadow* in 1912, *The Coward* in 1913 and *Assorted Spirits* in 1914.

At the end of the summer of 1911, Fitzgerald was once again uprooted (in response to poor academic achievements) and moved to the Newman School, a private Catholic school in Hackensack, New Jersey. He was singularly unpopular with the other boys, who considered him aloof and overbearing. This period as a social pariah at Newman was a defining time for Fitzgerald, one that would be echoed repeatedly in his fiction, most straightforwardly in the "Basil" stories, the most famous of which, 'The Freshest Boy', would appear in *The Saturday Evening Post* in July 1928 and is clearly autobiographical in its depiction of a boastful schoolboy's social exclusion.

Hackensack had, however, the advantage of proximity to New York City, and Fitzgerald began to get to know Manhattan, visiting a series of shows, including *The Quaker Girl* and *Little Boy Blue*. His first publication in Newman's school magazine, *The Newman News*, was 'Football', a poem written in an attempt to appease his peers following a traumatic incident on the football field that led to widespread accusation of cowardice, compounding the young writer's isolation. In his last year at Newman he would publish three stories in *The Newman News*.

Father Fay and the Catholic Influence

Also in that last academic year Fitzgerald would encounter the prominent Catholic priest Father Cyril Sigourney Webster Fay, a lasting and formative connection that would influence the author's character, oeuvre and career. Father Fay introduced Fitzgerald to such figures as Henry Adams and encouraged the young writer towards the aesthetic and moral understanding that underpins all of his work. In spite of the licence and debauchery for which Fitzgerald's life and work are often read, a strong moral sense informs all of his fiction – a sense that can be readily traced to Fay and the author's Catholic schooling at Newman. Fay would later appear in thinly disguised form as Amory Blaine's spiritual mentor, and man of the world, Monsignor Darcy, in *This Side of Paradise*.

Princeton

Fitzgerald's academic performance was little improved at Newman, and he would fail four courses in his two years there. In spite of this, in May 1913 Fitzgerald took the entrance exams for Princeton, the preferred destination for Catholic undergraduates in New Jersey. He would go up in September 1913, his fees paid for through a legacy left by his grandmother Louisa McQuillan, who had died in August.

At Princeton Fitzgerald would begin to work in earnest on the process of turning himself into an author: in his first year he met confrères and future collaborators John Peale Bishop and Edmund Wilson. During his freshman year Fitzgerald won a competition to write the book and lyrics for the 1914–15 Triangle Club (the Princeton dramatic society) production *Fie! Fie! Fi-Fi!* He would also co-author, with Wilson, the 1915–16 production, *The Evil Eye*, and the lyrics for *Safety First*, the 1916–17 offering. He also quickly began to contribute to the Princeton humour magazine *The Princeton Tiger*, while his reading tastes had moved on to the social concerns of George Bernard Shaw, Compton Mackenzie and H.G. Wells. His social progress at Princeton also seemed assured as Fitzgerald was approached by the Cottage Club (one of Princeton's exclusive eating clubs) and prominence in the Triangle Club seemed inevitable.

September 1914 and the beginning of Fitzgerald's sopho-more year would mark the great calamity of his Princeton education, causing a trauma that Fitzgerald would approach variously in his writing (notably in *This Side of Paradise* and Gatsby's abortive "Oxford" career in *The Great Gatsby*). Poor academic performance meant that Fitzgerald was barred from extra-curricular activities; he was therefore unable to perform in *Fie! Fie! Fi-Fi!*, and took to the road with the production in an attendant capacity. Fitzgerald's progress at the Triangle and Cottage clubs stagnated (he made Secretary at Triangle nonethe-less, but did not reach the heights he had imagined for himself), and his hopes of social dominance on campus were dashed.

The second half of the 1914–15 academic year saw a brief improvement and subsequent slipping of Fitzgerald's performance in classes, perhaps in response to a budding romance with Ginevra King, a sixteen-year-old socialite from Lake Forest, Illinois. Their courtship would continue until January 1917. King would become the model for a series of Fitzgerald's characters, including Judy Jones in the 1922 short story 'Winter Dreams', Isabelle Borgé in *This Side of Paradise* and, most famously, Daisy Buchanan in *The Great Gatsby*. In November 1915 Fitzgerald's academic career was once again held up when he was diagnosed with malaria (though it is likely that this was in fact the first appearance of the tuberculosis that would sporadically disrupt his health for the rest of his life) and left Princeton for the rest of the semester to recuperate. At the same time as all of this disruption, however, Fitzgerald was building a head of steam in terms of his literary production. Publications during this period included stories, reviews and poems for Princeton's *Nassau Literary Magazine*. *Ginevra King and Ill Health*

The USA entered the Great War in May 1917 and a week later Fitzgerald joined up, at least partly motivated by the fact that his *Army Commission* uncompleted courses at Princeton would automatically receive credits as he signed up. Three weeks of intensive training and the infantry commission exam soon followed, though a commission itself did not immediately materialize. Through the summer he stayed in St Paul, undertaking important readings in William James, Henri Bergson and others, and in the autumn he returned to Princeton (though not to study) and took lodgings with John Biggs Jr, the editor of the *Tiger*. More contributions appeared in both the *Nassau Literary Magazine* and the *Tiger*, but the commission finally came and in November Fitzgerald was off to Fort Leavenworth, Kansas, where he was. to report as a second lieutenant in the infantry. Convinced that he would die in the war, Fitzgerald began intense work on his first novel, *The Romantic Egoist*, the first draft of which would be finished while on leave from Kansas in February 1918. The publishing house Charles Scribner's Sons, despite offering an encouraging appreciation of the novel, rejected successive drafts in August and October 1918.

Zelda Sayre   As his military training progressed and the army readied Fitzgerald and his men for the fighting in Europe, he was relocated, first to Camp Gordon in Georgia, and then on to Camp Sheridan, near Montgomery, Alabama. There, at a dance at the Montgomery Country Club in July, he met Zelda Sayre, a beautiful eighteen-year-old socialite and daughter of a justice of the Alabama Supreme Court. An intense courtship began and Fitzgerald soon proposed marriage, though Zelda was nervous about marrying a man with so few apparent prospects.

As the armistice that ended the Great War was signed on 11th November 1918, Fitzgerald was waiting to embark for Europe, and had already been issued with his overseas uniform. The closeness by which he avoided action in the Great War stayed with Fitzgerald, and gave him another trope for his fiction, with many of his characters, Amory Blaine from *This Side of Paradise* and Jay Gatsby among them, attributed with abortive or ambiguous military careers. Father Fay, who had been involved, and had tried to involve Fitzgerald, in a series of mysterious intelligence operations during the war, died in January 1919, leaving Fitzgerald without a moral guide just as he entered the world free from the restrictions of Princeton and the army. Fay would be the dedicatee of *This Side of Paradise*.

Literary   Fitzgerald's first move after the war was to secure gainful
Endeavours   employment at Barron Collier, an advertising agency, producing copy for trolley-car advertisements. At night he continued to work hard at his fiction, collecting 112 rejection slips over this period. Relief was close at hand, however, with *The Smart Set* printing a revised version of 'Babes in the Wood' (a short story that had previous appeared in *Nassau Literary Magazine* and

that would soon be cannibalized for *This Side of Paradise*) in their September 1919 issue. *The Smart Set*, edited by this time by H.L. Mencken and George Jean Nathan, who would both become firm supporters of Fitzgerald's talent, was a respected literary magazine, but not a high payer; Fitzgerald received $30 for this first appearance. Buoyed by this, and frustrated by his job, Fitzgerald elected to leave work and New York and return to his parents' house in St Paul, where he would make a concerted effort to finish his novel. As none of the early drafts of *The Romantic Egoist* survive, it is impossible to say with complete certainty how much of that project was preserved in the draft of *This Side of Paradise* that emerged at St Paul. It was, at any rate, more attractive to Scribner in its new form, and the editor Maxwell Perkins, who would come to act as both editor and personal banker for Fitzgerald, wrote on 16th September to say that the novel had been accepted. Soon after he would hire Harold Ober to act as his agent, an arrangement that would continue throughout the greatest years of Fitzgerald's output and that would benefit the author greatly, despite sometimes causing Ober a great deal of difficulty and anxiety. Though Fitzgerald would consider his novels the artistically important part of his work, it would be his short stories, administered by Ober, which would provide the bulk of his income. Throughout his career a regular supply of short stories appeared between his novels, a supply that became more essential and more difficult to maintain as the author grew older.

Newly confident after the acceptance of *This Side of Paradise*, *Success* Fitzgerald set about revising a series of his previous stories, securing another four publications in *The Smart Set*, one in *Scribner's Magazine* and one in *The Saturday Evening Post*, an organ that would prove to be one of the author's most dependable sources of income for many years to come. By the end of 1919 Fitzgerald had made $879 from writing: not yet a living, but a start. His receipts would quickly increase. Thanks to Ober's skilful assistance *The Saturday Evening Post* had taken another six stories by February 1920, at $400 each. In March *This Side of Paradise* was published and proved to be a surprising success, selling 3,000 in its first three days and making instant celebrities of Fitzgerald and Zelda, who would marry the author on 3rd April, her earlier concerns about her suitor's solvency apparently eased by his sudden literary success. During the whirl of 1920, the couple's *annus mirabilis*, other miraculous portents of a future of plenty included the sale of a story, 'Head and Shoulders', to Metro Films for $2,500, the sale of four stories to *Metropolitan Magazine* for $900 each and the rapid appearance of *Flappers and Philosophers*, a volume of stories, published by Scribner in September. By the end of the year Fitzgerald, still in his mid-twenties, had moved into an apartment on New York's West 59th Street and was hard at work on his second novel.

Zelda discovered she was pregnant in February 1921, and in May the couple headed to Europe where they visited various heroes and attractions, including John Galsworthy. They returned in July to St Paul, where a daughter, Scottie, was born on 26th October. Fitzgerald was working consistently and well at this time, producing a prodigious amount of high-quality material. *The Beautiful and Damned*, his second novel, was soon ready and began to appear as a serialization in *Metropolitan Magazine* from September. Its publication in book form would have to wait until March 1922, at which point it received mixed reviews, though Scribner managed to sell 40,000 copies of it in its first year of publication. Once again it would be followed within a few months by a short-story collection, *Tales of the Jazz Age*, which contained such classics of twentieth-century American literature as 'May Day', 'The Diamond as Big as the Ritz' and 'The Curious Case of Benjamin Button'.

1923 saw continued successes and a first failure. Receipts were growing rapidly: the Hearst organization bought first option in Fitzgerald's stories for $1,500, he sold the film rights for *This Side of Paradise* for $10,000 and he began selling stories to *The Saturday Evening Post* for $1,250 each. *The Vegetable*, on the other hand, a play that he had been working on for some time, opened in Atlantic City and closed almost immediately following poor reviews, losing Fitzgerald money. By the end of the year his income had shot up to $28,759.78, but he had spent more than that on the play and fast living, and found himself in debt as a result.

The Fitzgeralds' high living was coming at an even higher price. In an attempt to finish his new project Fitzgerald set out for Europe with Zelda and landed up on the French Riviera, a situation that provided the author with the space and time to make some real progress on his novel. While there, however, Zelda met Édouard Jozan, a French pilot, and began a romantic entanglement that put a heavy strain on her marriage. This scenario has been read by some as influencing the final drafting of *The Great Gatsby*, notably Gatsby's disillusionment with Daisy. It would also provide one of the central threads of *Tender Is the Night*, while Gerald and Sara Murphy, two friends they made on the Riviera, would be models for that novel's central characters. Throughout 1924 their relations became more difficult, their volatility was expressed through increasingly erratic behaviour and by the end of the year Fitzgerald's drinking was developing into alcoholism.

Some progress was made on the novel, however, and a draft was sent to Scribner in October. A period of extensive and crucial revisions followed through January and February 1925, with the novel already at the galley-proof stage. After extensive negotiations with Max Perkins, the new novel also received its final title at about this time. Previous titles had included *Trimalchio* and *Trimalchio in West Egg*, both of which Scribner found too obscure for a mass readership, despite Fitzgerald's preference for them, while *Gold-Hatted Gatsby*, *On the Road to West Egg*, *The High-Bouncing Lover* and *Among Ash Heaps and Millionaires* were also suggestions. Shortly before the novel was due to be published, Fitzgerald telegrammed Scribner with the possible title *Under the Red, White and Blue*, but it was too late, and the work was published as *The Great Gatsby* on 10th April. The reception for the new work was impressive, and it quickly garnered some of Fitzgerald's most enthusiastic reviews, but its sales did not reach the best-seller levels the author and Scribner had hoped for.

Fitzgerald was keen to get on with his work and, rather mis-guidedly, set off to Paris with Zelda to begin his next novel. Paris at the heart of the Roaring Twenties was not a locale conducive to careful concentration, and little progress was made on the new project. There was much socializing, however, and Fitzgerald invested quite a lot of his time in cementing his reputation as one of the more prominent drunks of American letters. The couple's time was spent mostly with the American expatriate community, and among those he got to know there were Edith Wharton, Gertrude Stein, Robert McAlmon and Sylvia Beach of Shakespeare & Company. Perhaps the most significant relationship with another writer from this period was with Ernest Hemingway, with whom Fitzgerald spent much time (sparking jealousy in Zelda), and for whom he would become an important early supporter, helping to encourage Scribner to publish *The Torrents of Spring* and *The Sun Also Rises*, for which he also gave extensive editorial advice. The summer of 1925 was again spent on the Riviera, but this time with a rowdier crowd (which included John Dos Passos, Archibald MacLeish and Rudolph Valentino) and little progress was made on the new book. February 1926 saw publication of the inevitable follow-up short-story collection, this time *All the Sad Young Men*, of which the most significant pieces were 'The Rich Boy', 'Winter Dreams' and 'Absolution'. All three are closely associated with *The Great Gatsby*, and can be read as alternative routes into the Gatsby story.

With the new novel still effectively stalled, Fitzgerald decamped to Hollywood at the beginning of 1927, where he was engaged by United Artists to write a flapper comedy that was never produced in the end. These false starts were not, however, adversely affecting Fitzgerald's earnings, and 1927 would represent the highest annual earnings the author had achieved so far: $29,757.87, largely from

Paris

Hollywood

short-story sales. While in California Fitzgerald began a dalliance with Lois Moran, a seventeen-year-old aspiring actress – putting further strain on his relationship with Zelda. After the couple moved back east (to Delaware) Zelda began taking ballet lessons in an attempt to carve a niche for herself that might offer her a role beyond that of the wife of a famous author. She would also make various attempts to become an author in her own right. The lessons would continue under the tutelage of Lubov Egorova when the Fitzgeralds moved to Paris in the summer of 1928, with Zelda's obsessive commitment to dance practice worrying those around her and offering the signs of the mental illness that was soon to envelop her.

Looking for a steady income stream (in spite of very high earnings expenditure was still outstripping them), Fitzgerald set to work on the "Basil" stories in 1928, earning $31,500 for nine that appeared in *The Saturday Evening Post*, forcing novel-writing into the background. The next year his *Post* fee would rise to $4,000 a story. Throughout the next few years he would move between the USA and Europe, desperate to resuscitate that project, but make little inroads.

Zelda's Mental Illness

By 1930 Zelda's behaviour was becoming more and more erratic, and on 23rd April she was checked into the Malmaison clinic near Paris for rest and assistance with her mental problems. Deeply obsessed with her dancing lessons, and infatuated with Egorova, she discharged herself from the clinic on 11th May and attempted suicide a few days later. After this she was admitted to the care of Dr Oscar Forel in Switzerland, who diagnosed her as schizophrenic. Such care was expensive and placed a new financial strain on Fitzgerald, who responded by selling another series of stories to the *Post* and earning $32,000 for the year. The most significant story of this period was 'Babylon Revisited'. Zelda improved and moved back to Montgomery, Alabama, and the care of the Sayre family in September 1931. That autumn Fitzgerald would make another abortive attempt to break into Hollywood screenwriting.

At the beginning of 1932 Zelda suffered a relapse during a trip to Florida and was admitted to the Henry Phipps Psychiatric Clinic in Baltimore. While there she would finish work on a novel, *Save Me the Waltz*, that covered some of the same material her husband was using in his novel about the Riviera. Upon completion she sent the manuscript to Perkins at Scribner, without passing it to her husband, which caused much distress. Fitzgerald helped her to edit the book nonetheless, removing much of the material he intended to use, and Scribner accepted it and published it on 7th October. It received poor reviews and did not sell. Finally accepting that she had missed her chance to become a professional dancer, Zelda now poured her energies into painting. Fitzgerald would organize a show of these in New York in 1934, and a play, *Scandalabra*, that would be performed by the Junior Vagabonds, an amateur Baltimore drama group, in the spring of 1933.

His own health now beginning to fail, Fitzgerald returned *Final Novel* to his own novel and rewrote extensively through 1933, finally submitting it in October. *Tender Is the Night* would appear in serialized form in *Scribner's Magazine* from January to April 1934 and would then be published, in amended form, on 12th April. It was generally received positively and sold well, though again not to the blockbusting extent that Fitzgerald had hoped for. This would be Fitzgerald's final completed novel. He was thirty-seven.

With the receipts for *Tender Is the Night* lower than had *Financial* been hoped for and Zelda still erratic and requiring expensive *Problems and* medical supervision, Fitzgerald's finances were tight. From this *Artistic Decline* point on he found it increasingly difficult to produce the kind of high-quality, extended pieces that could earn thousands of dollars in glossies like *The Saturday Evening Post*. From 1934 many of his stories were shorter and brought less money, while some of them were simply sub-standard. Of the outlets for this new kind of work, *Esquire* proved the most reliable, though it only paid $250 a piece, a large drop from his salad days at the *Post*.

March 1935 saw the publication of *Taps at Reveille*, another collection of short stories from Scribner. It was a patchy collection, but included the important 'Babylon Revisited', while 'Crazy Sunday' saw his first sustained attempt at writing about Hollywood, a prediction of the tendency of much of his work to come. His next significant writing came, however, with three articles that appeared in the February, March and April 1936 numbers of *Esquire*: 'The Crack-up', 'Pasting It Together' and 'Handle with Care'. These essays were brutally confessional, and irritated many of those around Fitzgerald, who felt that he was airing his dirty laundry in public. His agent Harold Ober was concerned that by publicizing his own battles with depression and alcoholism he would give the high-paying glossies the impression that he was unreliable, making future magazine work harder to come by. The pieces have, however, come to be regarded as Fitzgerald's greatest non-fiction work and are an essential document in both the construction of his own legend and in the mythologizing of the Jazz Age.

Later in 1936, on the author's fortieth birthday in September, *Suicide* he gave an interview in *The New York Post* to Michael Mok. *Attempt and* The article was a sensationalist hatchet job entitled 'Scott *Worsening* Fitzgerald, 40, Engulfed in Despair' and showed him as a *Health* depressed dipsomaniac. The publication of the article wounded Fitzgerald further and he tried to take his own life through an overdose of morphine. After this his health continued to deteriorate and various spates in institutions followed, for influenza, for tuberculosis and, repeatedly, in attempts to treat his alcoholism.

His inability to rely on his own physical and literary powers meant a significant drop in his earning capabilities; by 1937 his debts exceeded $40,000, much of which was owed to his agent Ober and his editor Perkins, while Fitzgerald still had to pay Zelda's medical fees and support his daughter and himself. A solution to this desperate situation appeared in July: MGM would hire him as a screenwriter at $1,000 a week for six months. He went west, hired an apartment and set about his work. He contributed to various films, usually in collaboration with other writers, a system that irked him. Among these were *A Yank at Oxford* and various stillborn projects, including *Infidelity*, which was to have starred Joan Crawford, and an adaptation of 'Babylon Revisited'. He only received one screen credit from this time, for an adaptation of Erich Maria Remarque's novel *Three Comrades*, produced by Joseph Mankiewicz. His work on this picture led to a renewal of his contract, but no more credits followed.

Sheila Graham   While in Hollywood Fitzgerald met Sheila Graham, a twenty-eight-year-old English gossip columnist, with whom he began an affair. Graham, who initially attracted Fitzgerald because of her physical similarity to the youthful Zelda, became Fitzgerald's partner during the last years of his life, cohabiting with the author quite openly in Los Angeles. It seems unlikely that Zelda, still in medical care, ever knew about her. Graham had risen up from a rather murky background in England and Fitzgerald set about improving her with his "College of One", aiming to introduce her to his favoured writers and thinkers. She would be the model for Kathleen Moore in *The Last Tycoon*.

Among the film projects he worked on at this time were *Madame Curie* and *Gone with the Wind*, neither of which earned him a credit. The contract with MGM was terminated in 1939 and Fitzgerald became a freelance screenwriter. While engaged on the screenplay for *Winter Carnival* for United Artists, Fitzgerald went on a drinking spree at Dartmouth College, resulting in his getting fired. A final period of alcoholic excess followed, marring a trip to Cuba with Zelda in April and worsening his financial straits. At this time Ober finally pulled the plug and refused to lend Fitzgerald any more money, though he would continue to support Scottie, Fitzgerald's daughter, whom the Obers had effectively brought up. The writer, now his own agent, began working on a Hollywood novel based on the life of the famous Hollywood producer Irving Thalberg.

Hollywood would also be the theme of the last fiction Fitzgerald would see published; the Pat Hobby stories. These appeared in *Esquire* beginning in January 1940 and continued till after the author's death, ending in July 1941 and appearing in each monthly number between those dates.

In November 1940 Fitzgerald suffered a heart attack and *Death* was told to rest, which he did at Graham's apartment. On 21st December he had another heart attack and died, aged just forty-four. Permission was refused to bury him in St Mary's Church in Rockville, Maryland, where his father had been buried, because Fitzgerald was not a practising Catholic. Instead he was buried at Rockville Union Cemetery on 27th December 1940. In 1975 Scottie Fitzgerald would successfully petition to have her mother and father moved to the family plot at St Mary's.

Following Fitzgerald's death his old college friend Edmund Wilson would edit Fitzgerald's incomplete final novel, shaping his drafts and notes into *The Last Tycoon*, which was published in 1941 by Scribner. Wilson also collected Fitzgerald's confessional *Esquire* pieces and published them with a selection of related short stories and essays as *The Crack-up and Other Pieces and Stories* in 1945.

Zelda lived on until 1948, in and out of mental hospitals. After reading *The Last Tycoon* she began work on *Caesar's Things*, a novel that was not finished when the Highland hospital caught fire and she died, locked in her room in preparation for electro-shock therapy.

F. Scott Fitzgerald's Works

Fitzgerald's first novel, *This Side of Paradise*, set the tone for his *This Side of* later classic works. The novel was published in 1920 and was a *Paradise* remarkable success, impressing critics and readers alike. Amory Blaine, the directionless and guilelessly dissolute protagonist, is an artistically semi-engaged innocent, and perilously, though charmingly unconsciously, déclassé. His long drift towards destruction (and implicit reincarnation as Fitzgerald himself) sees Blaine's various arrogances challenged one by one as he moves from a well-heeled life in the Midwest through private school and middling social successes at Princeton towards a life of vague and unrewarding artistic involvement. Beneath Fitzgerald's precise observations of American high society in the late 1910s can be witnessed the creation of a wholly new American type, and Blaine would become a somewhat seedy role model for his generation. Fast-living and nihilist tendencies would become the character traits of Fitzgerald's set and the

Lost Generation more generally. Indeed, by the novel's end, it has become clear that Blaine's experiences of lost love, a hostile society and the deaths of his mother and friends have imparted important life lessons upon him. Blaine, having returned to a Princeton that he has outgrown and poised before an unknowable future, ends the novel with his Jazz Age *cogito*: "'I know myself,' he cried, 'but that is all.'"

Flappers and Philosophers

Fitzgerald's next publication would continue this disquisition on his era and peers: *Flappers and Philosophers* (1920) is a collection of short stories, including such famous pieces as 'Bernice Bobs Her Hair' and 'The Ice Palace'. The first of these tells the tale of Bernice, who visits her cousin Marjorie only to find herself rejected for being a stop on Marjorie's social activities. Realizing that she can't rid herself of Bernice, Marjorie decides to coach her to become a young femme fatale like herself – and Bernice is quickly a hit with the town boys. Too much of a hit though, and Marjorie takes her revenge by persuading Bernice that it would be to her social advantage to bob her hair. It turns out not to be and Bernice leaves the town embarrassed, but not before cutting off Marjorie's pigtails in her sleep and taking them with her to the station.

The Beautiful and Damned

The Beautiful and Damned (1922) would follow, another novel that featured a thinly disguised portrait of Fitzgerald in the figure of the main character, Anthony Patch. He was joined by a fictionalized version of Fitzgerald's new wife Zelda, whom the author married as *This Side of Paradise* went to press. The couple are here depicted on a rapidly downward course that both mirrored and predicted the Fitzgeralds' own trajectory. Patch is the heir apparent of his reforming grandfather's sizable fortune but lives a life of dissolution in the city, promising that he'll find gainful employment. He marries Gloria Gilbert, a great but turbulent beauty, and they gradually descend into alcoholism, wasting what little capital Anthony has on high living and escapades. When his grandfather walks in on a scene of debauchery, Anthony is disinherited and the Patches' decline quickens. When the grandfather dies, Anthony embarks on a legal case to reclaim the money from the good causes to which it has been donated and wins their case, although not before Anthony has lost his mind and Gloria her beauty.

Tales of the Jazz Age

Another volume of short stories, *Tales of the Jazz Age*, was published later in the same year, in accordance with Scribner's policy of quickly following successful novels with moneymaking collections of short stories. Throughout this period Fitzgerald was gaining for himself a reputation as America's premier short-story writer, producing fiction for a selection of high-profile "glossy" magazines and earning unparalleled fees for his efforts. The opportunities and the pressures of this commercial work, coupled with Fitzgerald's continued profligacy, led to a certain unevenness in his short fiction. This unevenness is clearly present in *Tales of the Jazz Age*, with some of Fitzgerald's very best work appearing beside some fairly average pieces. Among the great works were 'The Diamond as Big as the Ritz' and the novella 'May Day'. The first of these tells the story of the Washingtons, a family that live in seclusion in the wilds of Montana on top of a mountain made of solid diamond. The necessity of keeping the source of their wealth hidden from all makes the Washingtons' lives a singular mixture of great privilege and isolation; friends that visit the children are briefly treated to luxury beyond their imagining and are then executed to secure the secrecy of the Washington diamond. When young Percy's friend John T. Unger makes a visit during the summer vacation their unusual lifestyle and their diamond are lost for ever. The novella 'May Day' is very different in style and execution, but deals with some of the same issues, in particular the exigencies of American capitalism in the aftermath of the Great War. It offers a panorama of Manhattan's post-war social order as the anti-communist May Day Riots of 1919 unfold. A group of privileged Yale alumni enjoy the May Day ball and bicker about their love interests, while ex-soldiers drift around the edges of their world.

In spite of the apparent success that Fitzgerald was experiencing by this time, his next novel came with greater difficulty than his first four volumes. *The Great Gatsby* is the story of Jay Gatsby, born poor as James Gatz, an *arriviste* of mysterious origins who sets himself up in high style on Long Island's north shore only to find disappointment and his demise there. Like Fitzgerald, and some of his other characters, including Anthony Patch, Gatsby falls in love during the war, this time with Daisy Fay. Following Gatsby's departure, however, Daisy marries the greatly wealthy Tom Buchanan, which convinces Gatsby that he lost her only because of his penuriousness. Following this, Gatsby builds himself a fortune comparable to Buchanan's through mysterious and proscribed means and, five years after Daisy broke off their relations, uses his new-found wealth to throw a series of parties from an enormous house across the water from Buchanan's Long Island pile. His intention is to impress his near neighbour Daisy with the lavishness of his entertainments, but he miscalculates and the "old money" Buchanans stay away, not attracted by Gatsby's *parvenu* antics. Instead Gatsby approaches Nick Carraway, the novel's narrator (who took that role in one of the masterstrokes of the late stages of the novel's revision), Daisy's cousin and

The Great Gatsby

Gatsby's neighbour. Daisy is initially affected by Gatsby's devotion, to the extent that she agrees to leave Buchanan, but once Buchanan reveals Gatsby's criminal source of income she has second thoughts. Daisy, shocked by this revelation, accidentally kills Buchanan's mistress Myrtle in a hit-and-run accident with Gatsby in the car and returns to Buchanan, leaving Gatsby waiting for her answer. Buchanan then lets Myrtle's husband believe that Gatsby was driving the car and the husband shoots him, leaving him floating in the unused swimming pool of his great estate.

All the Sad   Of *All the Sad Young Men* (1926) the most well-known pieces
Young Men   are 'The Rich Boy', 'Winter Dreams' and 'Absolution'. All three have much in common with *The Great Gatsby*, in terms of the themes dealt with and the characters developed. 'The Rich Boy' centres on the rich young bachelor Anson Hunter, who has romantic dalliances with women, but never marries and grows increasingly lonely. 'Winter Dreams' tells the tale of Dexter Green and Judy Jones, similar characters to Jay Gatsby and Daisy Buchanan. Much like Gatsby, Green raises himself from nothing with the intention of winning Jones's affections. And, like Gatsby, he finds the past lost. 'Absolution' is a rejected false start on *The Great Gatsby* and deals with a young boy's difficulties around the confessional and an encounter with a deranged priest.

'Babylon Revisited' is probably the greatest and most read story of the apparently fallow period between *The Great Gatsby* and *Tender Is the Night*. It deals with Charlie Wales, an American businessman who enacts some of Fitzgerald's guilt for his apparent abandonment of his daughter Scottie and wife Zelda. Wales returns to a Paris unknown to him since he gave up drinking. There he fights his dead wife's family for custody of his daughter, only to find that friends from his past undo his careful efforts.

Basil and   Between April 1928 and April 1929, Fitzgerald published eight
Josephine   stories in the *Saturday Evening Post* centring on Basil Duke Lee, an adolescent coming of age in the Midwest, loosely based on the author's own teenage years. A ninth story, 'That Kind of Party', which fits chronologically at the beginning of the Basil cycle, was rejected by the *Saturday Evening Post* because of its description of children's kissing games, and was only published posthumously in 1951. These stories were much admired by both Fitzgerald's editor and agent, who encouraged him to compile them in a book with some additional stories. Fitzgerald did not act on this advice, but between April 1930 and August 1931 he published, again in the *Saturday Evening Post*, five stories focusing on the development of Josephine Perry, a kind of female counterpart to Basil Duke Lee. In 1934 Fitzgerald then considered collecting the Basil and Josephine stories in a single volume and adding a final one in which the

two would meet and which would transform the whole into a kind of novel, but he shelved the idea, as he had doubts about the overall quality of the outcome and its possible reception. He was still favourable to having them packaged as a straightforward short-story collection, but this would only happen in 1973, when Scribner published *The Basil and Josephine Stories*.

The next, and last completed, novel came even harder, and it would not be until 1934 that *Tender Is the Night* would appear. This novel was met by mixed reviews and low, but not disastrous sales. It has remained controversial among readers of Fitzgerald and is hailed by some as his masterpiece and others as an aesthetic failure. The plotting is less finely wrought than the far leaner *The Great Gatsby*, and apparent chronological inconsistencies and longueurs have put off some readers. The unremitting detail of Dick Diver's descent, however, is unmatched in Fitzgerald's oeuvre.

Tender Is the Night

It begins with an impressive set-piece description of life on the Riviera during the summer of 1925. There Rosemary Hoyt, modelled on the real-life actress Lois Moran, meets Dick and Nicole Driver, and becomes infatuated with Dick. It is then revealed that Dick had been a successful psychiatrist and had met Nicole when she was his patient, being treated in the aftermath of being raped by her father. Now Dick is finding it difficult to maintain his research interests in the social whirl that Nicole's money has thrust him into. Dick is forced out of a Swiss clinic for his unreliability and incipient alcoholism. Later Dick consummates his relationship with Rosemary on a trip to Rome, and gets beaten by police after drunkenly involving himself in a fight. When the Divers return to the Riviera Dick drinks more and Nicole leaves him for Tommy Barban, a French-American mercenary soldier (based on Zelda's Riviera beau Édouard Jozan). Dick returns to America, where he becomes a provincial doctor and disappears.

The "Pat Hobby" stories are the most remarkable product of Fitzgerald's time in Hollywood to see publication during the author's lifetime. Seventeen stories appeared in all, in consecutive issues of *Esquire* through 1940 and 1941. Hobby is a squalid Hollywood hack fallen upon hard times and with the days of his great success, measured by on-screen credits, some years behind him. He is a generally unsympathetic character and most of the stories depict him in unflattering situations, saving his own skin at the expense of those around him. It speaks to the hardiness of Fitzgerald's talent that even at this late stage he was able to make a character as amoral as Hobby vivid and engaging on the page. The Hobby stories are all short, evidencing Fitzgerald's skill in his later career at compressing storylines that would previously have been extrapolated far further.

Pat Hobby Stories

The Last
Tycoon
Fitzgerald's final project was *The Last Tycoon*, a work which, in the partial and provisional version that was published after the author's death, has all the hallmarks of a quite remarkable work. The written portion of the novel, which it seems likely would have been rewritten extensively before publication (in accordance with Fitzgerald's previous practice), is a classic conjuring of the golden age of Hollywood through an ambiguous and suspenseful story of love and money. The notes that follow the completed portion of *The Last Tycoon* suggest that the story would have developed in a much more melodramatic direction, with Stahr embarking on transcontinental business trips, losing his edge, ordering a series of murders and dying in an aeroplane crash. If the rewrites around *Tender Is the Night* are anything to go by, it seems likely that Fitzgerald would have toned down Stahr's adventures before finishing the story: in the earlier novel stories of matricide and other violent moments had survived a number of early drafts, only to be cut before the book took its final form.

– Richard Parker

Select Bibliography

Biographies:
Bruccoli, Matthew J., *Some Sort of Epic Grandeur: The Life of F. Scott Fitzgerald*, 2nd edn. (Columbia, SC: University of South Carolina Press, 2002)
Mizener, Arthur, *The Far Side of Paradise: A Biography of F. Scott Fitzgerald*, (Boston, MS: Houghton Mifflin, 1951)
Turnbull, Andrew, *Scott Fitzgerald* (Harmondsworth: Penguin, 1970)

Additional Recommended Background Material:
Curnutt, Kirk, ed., *A Historical Guide to F. Scott Fitzgerald* (Oxford: Oxford University Press, 2004)
Prigozy, Ruth, ed., *The Cambridge Companion to F. Scott Fitzgerald* (Cambridge: Cambridge University Press, 2002)

ALMA CLASSICS

ALMA CLASSICS aims to publish mainstream and lesser-known European classics in an innovative and striking way, while employing the highest editorial and production standards. By way of a unique approach the range offers much more, both visually and textually, than readers have come to expect from contemporary classics publishing.

LATEST TITLES PUBLISHED BY ALMA CLASSICS

To order any of our titles and for up-to-date information about our current and forthcoming publications, please visit our website on:

www.almaclassics.com